The Enterprise

of

England

MORE BY THIS AUTHOR

The Anniversary
The Travellers
A Running Tide
The Testament of Mariam
Flood
The Secret World of Christoval Alvarez

Praise for Ann Swinfen's Novels

'an absorbing and intricate tapestry of family history and private
memories … warm, generous, healing and hopeful'
VICTORIA GLENDINNING

'I very much admired the pace of the story. The changes of place and
time and the echoes and repetitions – things lost and found, and
meetings and partings'
PENELOPE FITZGERALD

'I enjoyed this serious, scrupulous novel … a novel of character …
[and] a suspense story in which present and past mysteries are
gradually explained'
JESSICA MANN, *Sunday Telegraph*

'The author … has written a powerful new tale of passion and
heartbreak ... What a marvellous storyteller Ann Swinfen is – she has a
wonderful ear for dialogue and she brings her characters vividly to life.'
Publishing News

'Her writing …[paints] an amazingly detailed and vibrant picture of
flesh and blood human beings, not only the symbols many of them
have become…but real and believable and understandable.'
HELEN BROWN, *Courier and Advertiser*

'She writes with passion and the book, her fourth, is shot through with
brilliant description and scholarship...[it] is a timely reminder of the
harsh realities, and the daily humiliations, of the Roman occupation of
First Century Israel. You can almost smell the dust and blood.'
PETER RHODES, *Express and Star*

The Enterprise

of

England

Ann Swinfen

Shakenoak Press

Cover images
Robert Dudley, Earl of Leicester: Miniature by Nicholas Hilliard
Contemporary drawing of the Armada engaged by the English navy

Cover design by JD Smith www.jdsmith-design.co.uk

For

Lucas and Theo

Chapter One

'So you are determined not to work for Walsingham again?' Simon said. In this cold February weather, the theatres were closed, so Simon Hetherington was without regular employment. Occasionally James Burbage's company, Leicester's Men, would be hired during the winter months to give a performance at some nobleman's house, or even at court, but the cold weather meant hard times for them. I had invited him to sup with my father and me at our home in Duck Lane, a miserable, cramped little house which was provided with my father's hospital employment at St Bartholomew's. Simon had been looking hungry of late and he certainly wolfed down two helpings of Joan's mutton hot pot, scarcely pausing for breath.

His fair hair and delicate features meant that he continued to play women's parts, though at seventeen he was growing ever more impatient to take on men's roles. In the last year he had grown taller than I. Burbage would need to yield to his demands soon. I loved the way his face glowed when he forgot about Walsingham and began to speak of the new play his friend Thomas Kyd had written, his hands sketching in the air the music of the lines he quoted:

'My lord, though Bel Imperia seem thus coy,
Let reason hold you in your wonted joy:
In time the savage bull sustains the yoke,
In time all haggard hawks will stoop to lure,
In time small wedges cleave the hardest oak,
In time the flint is pierc'd with softest shower;

1

And she in time will fall from her disdain,
And rue the sufferance of your friendly pain.'

His voice rose and fell like birdsong. It was the flavour of honey. I wanted to close my eyes and savour it.

'Do you see, Kit, how he takes the simplest things – the taming of a bull or a hawk, the cleaving of a mighty oak by tiny wedges, the wearing away of stone by the softest of rain – and uses them to illuminate how people change? A woman may be cruel or indifferent, but with time and patience her heart may be won. He does not state this direct, like some schoolman, but suggests it, at a subtle angle, by implication. I wish I could write such poetry! I hope Burbage will let me play Bel Imperia, it's a fine, complex part, not one of your milksop maidens.'

He did not really expect me to answer. Yet I loved to hear him speak, as I loved to watch him on stage. I leaned over to poke the fire, hiding my small private smile. I was hardly Bel Imperia myself. And I certainly did not disdain him.

'So,' he said, 'remember these wise words of Kyd's, if you should ever woo a lady who is cold and distant.'

'Indeed I will.' I laughed. 'You are not yourself courting such a lady?'

He grinned back at me. 'Not yet. I have not found any who could touch my heart, or understand the beauty of such lines.'

My father was still somewhat distant with Simon, for in his view a member of one of the players' companies was not a suitable friend for the child of a distinguished professor from the university of Coimbra. For myself, I was more aware than my father seemed to be that our social position had plunged mightily since we had come as refugees to England five years earlier. It left us with little reason to stand upon our dignity. Yet his reservations also had a more serious basis, since I carried a secret which could endanger my life.

However, my father had been courteous enough to Simon this evening, and now we had all drawn our chairs close to the kitchen fire. Joan, our housekeeper and general servant, was darning my father's stockings, tilting her work to the fire for the benefit of the light. My father was reading by the dim glow of the only candle, while Simon and I talked quietly, so as not to disturb him. Firelight and candlelight played over the jars and bottles,

2

mortars and alembics of my father's profession. My profession too, for I had resumed my hospital work, turning my back on the dark and secret world contained within Sir Francis Walsingham's house in Seething Lane.

'As for Walsingham,' I said, stretching out my legs and clasping my hands behind my head. 'I told you last month that I'd not go back.'

Soon after my seventeenth birthday, on Twelfth Night, I had confronted Walsingham and said that, now the Babington conspirators were dead, I felt he no longer needed my services. He had, however, extracted a promise from me that if another crisis arose, I would return to work within his service.

'I know that was what you said.' Simon looked at me quizzically. 'But when Guy told us there was a rumour Robert Poley was to be released from the Tower, you seemed to change your mind.'

Simon was unaware of Poley's ability to blackmail me and must have been puzzled by my alarm when Guy Bingham passed on the news. Locked away in the Tower, Poley was no danger, but if he were set free, that was another matter.

'Ah, but it proved to be a rumour,' I said. 'Poley is still safely in the Tower.'

Simon opened his mouth to say something – something I might not want to hear – so I hastily went on.

'Did you see the bonfires in the streets?'

'Aye. Ever since word of the Scottish queen's execution reached London, there's been no stopping them.'

'I think it is gruesome. They've been dancing and singing in the streets throughout this part of London,' I said. 'And ringing the church bells. I know she was a party to murdering the Queen, but I don't like it. It reminds me too much of what I saw in Portugal.'

'You never talk about that.'

'I'm not going to talk about it now.'

We sat for a while in a slightly uncomfortable silence, until Simon started to tell me more about Master Burbage's plans for the company, once the playhouses opened again.

'I truly hope this year I may be given men's parts,' he said. 'I've grown too old to play the woman any longer.'

3

The old grievance had troubled him for some months, but Burbage valued his talent in playing women's roles, which none of the younger boys could match. Besides, the company needed all the varied skills of its players, for times were hard now that the Queen's Men were in the ascendant. Leicester's Men had already lost several of their best performers. Burbage was a shrewd businessman, but even he was hard put to it to turn a profit, despite having built London's first real playhouse, the Theatre, and owning shares in its neighbour, The Curtain.

'Even our costumes are growing threadbare,' Simon said. 'There's no coin to replace them. Our new plays must make shift to use what costumes we have, not require new ones.'

I thought of the hampers of brightly coloured but somewhat tawdry clothes that occupied every corner of the Theatre's tiring house. The last time I had visited the company there, at the time of their Twelve Night extravagance, I had noticed that many of the costumes were wearing thin and fragile.

'It is Sidney's funeral in two days' time,' I said to divert him, when he paused for breath. 'Shall we go, to pay our respects?'

I meant to go myself, but I would be glad of his company.

'Aye,' he said. 'I'll meet you by Paul's Cross, early.'

'Very early,' I said. 'Else there won't be an inch of ground to stand upon.'

It had been in the cold dawning of that year, on the eighth day of February, that Mary, dispossessed Queen of Scotland, sometime Queen of France, and would-be Queen of England, was finally and quietly executed. That was weeks after she had been sentenced to death for treason at her trial, and everyone wondered why she lingered on for so long.

The day after Simon supped with us, I ran into Thomas Phelippes near the Royal Exchange. After fending off his attempts to lure me back into Walsingham's service, I asked him if he knew why there had been such a long delay in carrying out the sentence on the Scots queen. Phelippes, being Walsingham's right-hand man, was likely to be privy to secrets unknown to common citizens.

4

'The Queen was reluctant to sign the death warrant,' he said. 'It was, after all, the death warrant of her own cousin, and a crowned queen. She would have preferred some other way. Some conveniently secret way of disposing of Mary. When she finally signed, so Sir Francis says, the Privy Council let no delay intervene to give her the chance to change her mind. They whipped away the warrant and rushed an executioner off to Fotheringhay at once.'

I shivered.

'I know she was a traitor and connived at the Queen's death, but . . .'

'Don't be a namby-pamby, Kit,' he said brusquely. 'The Scots queen knew what she was doing and she knew the penalty. *She* did not hesitate to conspire in the murder of *her* cousin. And don't forget: you helped to uncover the plot.'

I avoided his eyes. I would not let Phelippes see my weakness. My own part in the machinations of Walsingham's secret service still troubled me.

Now, eight days after the execution of the Scots queen, Sidney's state funeral brought London to a standstill. I met Simon near Paul's Cross soon after a freezing winter's dawn and we found a place by the west door of St Paul's to watch the sombre spectacle. The Lord Mayor and Aldermen attended, along with members of the liveried companies of the City. Children of Christ's Hospital walked in the procession, together with three hundred citizens, and thirty-two poor men given livery for the occasion, one man for each year of Sir Philip Sidney's age. It seemed that every citizen of London had abandoned his work and come to stand in the bitter cold to watch the cortège pass. And with them half the countryside from Kent to Oxfordshire.

'There's Walsingham,' I said, 'on horseback beside that carriage.'

'He looks ill,' said Simon.

'He does. He's often ill, but he drives himself mercilessly. He would never stay in his bed when it is his duty to see his son-in-law to the grave.'

I didn't attempt to hide my admiration for Walsingham. He was a man of great abilities and unstinting dedication to his country. I would just prefer not to work for him any longer.

Although I had started as a simple code-breaker and translator, I had found myself being trained as a forger and a spy.

'That's my horse he's riding,' I said.

'*Your* horse!'

I smiled. 'I rode him a lot last year. He's called Hector.'

'Not a handsome beast.'

'Don't be fooled. He can run like a champion, for which I've been grateful before now.'

'Sometimes I wonder what you were involved in, last year, working for Walsingham.'

'It is all in the past now.' I gestured towards Walsingham. 'Look, that must be Frances Walsingham, Lady Sidney, in the carriage next to him, with the blinds drawn. I wonder whether she has the child Elizabeth with her. Poor little mite, to lose her father so young.'

Simon did not answer, and I remembered, uncomfortably, that he too had lost both parents at an early age.

'Phelippes told me that Sir Philip had no money at all,' I said. 'Despite all his talents and gifts, he was poor. It seems strange, when his uncle Leicester is the Queen's favourite, but I suppose Sir Philip was one of the few honest men at court, who would not stoop to taking bribes.'

'Who is paying for all of this, then?' Simon waved a hand at the procession which was making its way slowly into the cathedral. 'The Queen?'

I laughed. 'Not she.' It was not to be spoken of, but everyone knew that Elizabeth kept a tight grip on the royal purse-strings. 'No, Walsingham has paid for it all. Phelippes says it will beggar him. That's another honest man, Walsingham. Most of the service he runs to protect Queen and country is paid for out of his own pocket.'

A stranger arriving in London that day would have thought the Queen herself had died. From where we stood, we heard them honour the soldier poet with a double volley of shot. All around us people were weeping, not only old women but young apprentices in their blue tunics, and rough sailors with their callused hands and tarred pigtails, and ragged urchins who could have dined for life on the value of just one of the rich garments in the procession. The melancholy at the loss of Sidney infected me, as it infected all England.

When the whole procession had passed inside the cathedral, some of the crowd pushed in behind, but Simon and I stayed outside. The horses had been left in the churchyard, in the care of grooms, and I noticed one of Walsingham's stable lads holding Hector. I walked over to them.

'Master Alvarez!' The boy pulled off his cap and bobbed his head in an awkward bow.

'Good day to you, Harry.'

I ran my hand down Hector's neck and he butted his head against my shoulder with an affectionate snort.

'He's not forgotten me, then,' I said.

'Not he. Hector's a grand fellow.'

Like everyone else in Walsingham's household, Harry had a special affection for the ugly, clever piebald.

'I'll come to see him soon,' I said, 'and bring him an apple.'

'You do that, Master Alvarez. We'll all be glad to see you again. We miss you about the place.'

Simon had been watching my reunion with Hector, a look of amusement on his face. 'Come,' he said. 'I'm frozen. Let's find an inn and drink a cup of hot Hippocras to Sidney's memory.'

I followed him out of the churchyard and down Cheapside to a small but clean ordinary, where we thawed out beside the fire with a flagon of Hippocras and a couple of meat pasties. Despite the warmth and the comfort, I couldn't forget the brief glimpse I had had as Frances Walsingham had stepped out of the carriage, heavily veiled, and taken her father's arm to enter the cathedral. She was just three years older than I, widowed at twenty, with one child and carrying another. Despite her pregnancy, she had travelled to the Low Countries to bring her husband's body back to England. Behind her a waiting woman led little Elizabeth by the hand. The child looked about her, wide-eyed, at the crowds of grieving strangers, her small face white against the mourning black of her tight cap.

It was barely a fortnight after Sidney's funeral when there was a knock at our door while my father and I were at home from the hospital, taking our midday meal. Joan had gone out to the pie shop round the corner to buy something for our supper, so I answered the door myself. My heart plunged into my boots when I saw who was standing there.

'Goodman Cassie,' I said, resigned. 'What can you be wanting? You'd best come in out of the cold.'

Thomas Cassie's nose was flushed scarlet with the harsh wind, which carried a gust of snow over the threshold as he stepped inside. I regarded him with a somewhat unfriendly eye. Cassie was Thomas Phelippes's most trusted servant and we had worked together in the past.

'Well?' I said.

'Don't blame me, Master Alvarez.' He cast an appealing glance at my father. 'I'm afraid Master Phelippes sent me to fetch you. There's a deal of work, he says, and you're needed.'

'I no longer serve Sir Francis,' I said firmly. 'He agreed to allow me to return to my duties at the hospital, uninterrupted by Phelippes's work.'

'Aye. But Master Phelippes was given to understand that, should there be another crisis, you were willing to come back to us.'

'What crisis?'

'Indeed, I couldn't say, sir. All I know is that they're looking worried in Seething Lane. It was bad enough, with Sir Philip dying and his lady almost out of her mind. The whole house in an uproar. Now there's been a deal of packages come in, some of them on Dr Nuñez's merchant ships.'

He shrugged. 'That's all I know.'

'You'd best go, Kit,' my father said.

Muttering crossly to myself, I scooped up the last of my stew with a chunk of bread and stuffed it in my mouth, then slung my hooded cloak around my shoulders. Through the wavy glass of the window I could see the snow coming down harder.

I reached for my satchel of medicines. 'I'll come straight back to the hospital,' I told my father.

Cassie cleared his throat nervously. 'Sir Francis has sent word to the hospital. They won't be expecting you.'

Thoroughly angry now, I stumped out of the house after him. It seemed Walsingham and Phelippes had seized control of my life once again. My mood was not improved as we made our way east, in through the City wall at Newgate, then heading to the far side of London, to Sir Francis's house in Seething Lane near the Tower. The wind was vicious, tearing at our cloaks, sometimes so strong we staggered, trying to keep on our feet. The increasingly heavy snow was mixed with pellets of ice that stung my face, so that I wished I had brought a scarf to wrap around my head. I clutched at the sides of my hood to hold it on, but the cruel fingers of the wind probed inside, till my ears were as numb as my nose and fingers.

It seemed hours before we reached the backstairs of Walsingham's house, the way all of us who worked for him came and went. Cassie left me at the foot of the stairs and I climbed them, exhausted from battling the wind and snow. My sodden boots left wet patches on the fine Turkey carpets, which looked more worn than I remembered, while the portraits along the walls looked down on me as disapprovingly as ever. I wondered whether they were Sir Francis's ancestors. No one had ever said. I tried to make out some family likeness, but the paint was dull and darkened. All that I could discern was that faint air of censure.

My reluctant tap on the familiar door was answered by 'Enter' in Phelippes's well-known voice. He was sitting at his usual desk, with its regimented piles of papers and writing materials. I saw that my desk had been commandeered to hold more papers, and had been moved away from the window to a dark corner. In the dim light of late winter no one could work there. The door to the little cubbyhole used by Arthur Gregory, the seal-forger, stood open and a band of candlelight stretched out from it to where I took my stand, frozen hands on hips, as I dripped all over Phelippes's floor.

'Well?' I said belligerently. 'Why have you called me away from my work? The hospital is overflowing with winter chest complaints. I'm needed there.'

'Good afternoon, Kit,' he said mildly, putting on his spectacles, which he had removed for close work. He gestured expressively toward the pile of papers on my old desk. 'You see my problem.'

'Your problem. Not mine. I don't work here any more.'

'No.' He bowed his head in brief acknowledgement. 'But I do not think you would refuse us your assistance in the present circumstances.'

'I am truly sorry about Sir Philip,' I said, in a milder voice. 'It is a great tragedy for his family as well as for the nation.'

'It is. And Sir Francis has made himself ill, riding to the funeral in the cold.'

'I thought he did not look well.'

'You were there? I did not see you.'

'Only in the crowd outside the cathedral. I saw you. How is the Lady Frances?'

'Distraught. She knew Sir Philip from the time she was a tiny child. Adored him.'

I nodded. I had seen it for myself when they were together.

'I am very sorry for it. And for the little girl.'

'But that is not why I sent for you, though with Sir Francis ill, more rests on my shoulders.'

'I did not suppose it was.' I walked over to the small fire burning on the hearth and held out my hands to it. They were coming back to life, and painful. My cloak continued to drip.

'Do take off your cloak, Kit,' he said irritably. 'And your wet boots. I don't mind your stockings.'

I hesitated. Removing my cloak and boots would imply I was staying. It was tantamount to capitulation.

'Oh, very well.'

I threw my cloak over a coffer near the door and prised off my boots. Set side by side in front of the fire they began to steam juicily. My stockings were wet through, but I had no intention of removing those. I wriggled my toes uncomfortably, and turned back to Phelippes.

'Are you going to tell me what you really mean by "the present circumstances"?'

He sighed.

'A sudden flood of reports coming in from our agents all over Europe – Spain, France, Rome, Portugal, the Spanish Netherlands. Something is afoot, but until we can decipher and transcribe and translate them we can't be quite sure what it is. Philip of Spain is up to his old tricks, but exactly what I cannot say. While the Scottish queen was alive and her cousin the Duke of Guise was planning an invasion last year, Philip was holding back. He has long wanted to seize England again, ever since it slipped through his fingers when Mary Tudor died.'

He snorted in disgust. 'King of England, he still calls himself! He wants to conquer the world.'

'I know,' I said. 'An arrogant and dangerous man.' I moved a stool in front of the fire and sat down. My stockings began to steam as well. 'Why do you say Philip was holding back last year?'

'If the plot by Babington and his friends had succeeded and the conspirators put the Scottish queen on our throne with the military support of France, then England would have become a protectorate of France, a powerful alliance that would have threatened Philip's possessions in northern Europe and many of his trade routes.'

'So Philip didn't want the plot to succeed?' I hadn't understood that before.

'Exactly. But – as no doubt you've heard – Scottish Mary, in laying claim to the English throne herself, named Philip as her successor to the crown of England, in the event of her death.'

I nodded. 'Philip King of Spain, rather than her own son, James King of Scotland.'

'Of course not. James is a Protestant. He doesn't bow down to the holy Catholic church and kiss the feet of the Bishop of Rome.' His tone was contemptuous. 'So she graciously bequeaths the throne of England to that good Catholic prince, who thinks he ought to be king of England anyway.'

'So?'

'So now he is beginning to move. King Philip of Spain does nothing in a hurry, but he has not forgotten the Enterprise of England. On this evidence,' he waved his hand again at the packets of reports, 'he is certainly planning something. From the few I have been able to decipher and read so far, envoys are buzzing around the Catholic nations and the Vatican like a swarm of bees. The sheer quantity of it amounts to a crisis. So this is where you come in.'

11

I sighed, but before I could respond, Arthur Gregory emerged from his tiny office with a sheaf of papers in his hands. He beamed at me. Like Phelippes he looked tired, but he seemed cheerful enough.

'Kit! I thought I heard your voice. It's good to see you again. We've missed you.'

It was just what the stable boy Harry had said. I had not thought my presence had been much felt here. I stood up and bowed to Arthur.

'I'm glad to see you too.'

He glanced at my stocking feet and smiled.

'Master Phelippes fetched you across London in this terrible weather, did he?'

'He did.' I glared at Phelippes. 'He seems to think he cannot deal with these reports himself.'

'Indeed he can't. He has even had me deciphering some of those in the easier codes, the familiar ones, and you know how slow I am. I have no head for breaking new codes, like you.'

'It isn't only reports from our own agents, then?' I turned to Phelippes.

'No. We have intercepted a number of messages passing between Madrid and Philip's agents in his various domains. Including some to Mendoza in Paris. Mendoza always means trouble. One of our sea captains came in this morning with a fresh bundle of despatches he captured on a Spanish vessel heading for the Caribbean. We haven't had a chance to decipher them yet. I thought you could start with those, given your fluent Spanish.'

'I haven't agreed yet to return,' I said, although I knew I was in retreat.

'It need not be for long.' Phelippes's voice had taken on a persuasive note I had not heard before. He must really need my help.

'Tell my patients that,' I said. 'Are they to defer all illness until Master Phelippes says I may return to the hospital?'

'It would be the same arrangement as before.' He looked relieved. He knew he was winning. 'You would still work at the hospital in the mornings, then come here in the afternoons. Sir Francis will arrange it all with the governors.'

I put my head in my hands and sighed.

'I'm sure he will. Very well,' I said. 'I will come.'

Chapter Two

*A*rthur Gregory helped me to move my table back near the window, for the benefit of the light, and we piled all the packets except the one from the Caribbean ship on to the table against the wall. All the time we were rearranging the office, Phelippes ignored us, his head down and his short-sighted eyes close to his papers. I felt a growing irritation that he could just assume I would take up my position as before in the corner of his office. During the final weeks of my service to Walsingham in the previous year I had often needed to work alone in dangerous situations. Then during the recent few months, free of them all, I had revelled in my rediscovered independence. Now, here I was, back like any junior clerk, scribbling away at my desk.

'Will this do?' I said finally, in a loud voice. 'I am not in your way?'

Phelippes looked up and peered at me across the intervening space. Then he put on his spectacles and looked vaguely around the room at what we had done.

'Aye. That will do. Have you looked at the Caribbean despatches yet?'

'Not yet,' I snapped. I looked at Arthur and raised my eyebrows in despair. He simply grinned and clapped me on the shoulder.

'Good to have you back.'

The papers he had previously been carrying he had placed on my desk while we were moving the furniture. Now he pointed toward them.

'Perhaps you should look at these as well, to be sure I have made no mistakes. I'll get back to carving some new seals. King Philip has been employing a lot of new agents and they all have their own seals. It's difficult to keep up with copying them.'

'Of course,' I said. 'I'll check them for you.'

Arthur's real talent lay in his ability to carve exquisite forged seals that even the owners of the originals would not have been able to recognise as false. Without his skills, Walsingham's activities must surely have failed long before now, for much of what we did involved intercepting enemy despatches, opening and deciphering them, then resealing them and sending them on their way. Without Arthur's immaculate seals our interference would soon have been noticed. This way England's enemies were not alerted by the disappearance of their despatches, but at the same time we kept abreast of their correspondence. I often thought it was fortunate that Arthur was an honest man. Had he turned his talents to crime, he could have become very rich indeed.

As well as intercepting foreign correspondence, Phelippes's office served as the centre point for the entire complex web of Walsingham's informers, agents and spies. At its height, the service had five hundred agents, in addition to friendly sea captains and merchants in many countries, and England's ambassadors, who kept their eyes and ears open and passed on any information they came across. Indeed, the service itself was the eyes and ears of the English state. Without it the Queen would have been assassinated long before this and the country overrun by foreign troops. I shuddered when I remembered the invasion of Portugal when I was ten. The Spanish troops had flooded across the country looting, raping and slaughtering with savage intensity. Their officers did nothing to restrain them. I had heard that some of those same officers had been shocked at the bestiality of their own soldiers, yet they had not tried to stop it. The cruelty inflicted upon the Protestant Netherlanders by the Spanish troops under the Duke of Alba, about the time I was born, had been on the same scale and it was said that in the New World the Spaniards had come near to wiping out the native people. I had no illusions about what would befall England if a Spanish army succeeded in invading.

15

I helped myself to a handful of uncut quills and a pot of ink from one of the shelves on the wall above the coffer where my wet cloak lay in a heap, and chose several different types of paper from another shelf, then I sat down at my old desk and tapped the reports and Arthur's papers into neat piles. Like Phelippes, I could work best when all the tools of my trade were in immaculate order. Taking my penknife out of the purse at my belt, I began trimming and shaping the quills to my satisfaction. Arthur had returned to his room. Apart from the scratch of Phelippes's pen and faint sounds from Arthur's miniature gouges as he carved a new seal, a comfortable silence fell over the room. Now and then the fire would spit or the coals would collapse inwards. My boots were still steaming, but my stockings were drying.

I drew Arthur's papers towards me. They dealt with activities witnessed by one of our agents in Rome. There had been much coming and going of Spanish envoys to the Vatican, who were clearly seeking papal support for whatever schemes Philip was currently plotting. The agent had managed to bribe one of the servants in the papal service to bring him news. It did not amount to much. Philip wanted gold for some great enterprise, but Pope Sixtus was as parsimonious as our own Queen and was resisting Spanish blandishments. Arthur had made a few minor mistakes in deciphering, but nothing which altered the sense of the two reports, which more or less repeated the same information.

When I had corrected them, I carried them over and placed them in the pile on Phelippes's desk where he gathered together the reports from our own agents. Back at my own desk I reached for the packet taken from the Spanish ship heading for the Caribbean. They were tied together with a bit of tarred string. This must have been done by the English sea captain, for they would never have been sent out from the Escorial like that. The smell of the tar brought back vividly my own terrible sea journey from Portugal and I held the string in my hand, my eyes closed, trying to push away the memories. I dropped it on the floor and gritted my teeth. I must concentrate on the task in hand.

Without thinking, I reached behind me to the shelf where I had always kept my own keys to the codes our agents used and those codes of our enemies which we had broken. There they all were, just as I had left them late in the previous year. I felt a little jump of pleasure in my chest as I looked at the familiar sheets. Some of them represented many hours of work and I was proud of them. Despite my reluctance, despite my annoyance with Phelippes, I began to feel the old excitement of the hunt. Opening the first of the documents, I could see that it was somewhat water-stained. Hardly surprising, for the Spanish ship had been taken, it appeared, after a fierce though brief battle. A quick glance confirmed that it was written in a new cipher. I curled my toes inside my stockings, which were now nearly dry. A new challenge. I tipped my hour-glass over. Had I lost my touch?

By the time the sand had run through the hour glass I had cracked the code and started to decipher the first despatch.

'This is from King Philip himself,' I said, breaking the silence. 'Addressed to the governor of Mexico. He is ordering the return of two thousand experienced troops by the next ships back to Spain. Also supplies of dried corn and vegetables, and salted fish.'

I rubbed the feather of my quill along the side of my nose.

'A bit different from the usual cargo of gold and silver.'

'Hmm,' said Phelippes. 'I expect his men in the New World send gold and silver anyway, as a matter of course. So. Troops. Experienced troops. He may just want them for the Duke of Parma in the Low Countries. Since the battle at Zutphen the Spanish are pressing ahead, trying to consolidate their gains in some of the areas that France claims, as well as crushing the Protestant Dutchmen.'

'But?'

'But I think it's likely he may want them for what he has been calling for many years the Enterprise of England.'

'You mean the invasion.'

'Aye. You know that we have been watching him for ten years or more, slowly building up his trained army and the great ships of his navy. One of his reasons for seizing Portugal was to secure the Portuguese navy and all her excellent ports along the Atlantic coast. They have given him a much stronger hold over the western trading routes, even if Drake and Hawkins and the others manage to pick off his ships from time to time. We know that he set his heart on conquering England long ago. Even that scoundrel Mendoza has us in his sights. When we expelled him from his embassy here three years ago he said, "Tell your mistress Bernardino de Mendoza was born not to disturb kingdoms but to conquer them." Arrogant bastard.'

'What makes you suspect Philip is planning anything other than his usual trouble-making?'

'Just a feeling in my bones. And the time is right for him. As I said before, if an invasion by the Scottish queen's Guise relations had put her on the English throne, Philip would have feared the alliance against him. Now he has been named her heir and France is riven by civil war between the Catholic League and Henri of Navarre's Huguenots, Philip has the ideal opportunity to bring his years of planning to fruition.'

'These experienced troops of his?' I pointed with my quill to the letter I was deciphering. 'The Spanish troops in the Netherlands are a trained and experienced army as well, aren't they? What troops do we have to fight them?'

'Nothing,' he said grimly. 'Save our troops raised for the campaign in the Netherlands. The Queen will not agree to a standing army. Too expensive, and possibly risky if they grew restless. We could no more resist a Spanish army if they made landfall in England than your people in Portugal did. Our only hope is our navy, and that is small enough, God knows. Philip is unscrupulous. He has been seizing every foreign ship that comes trading into any Spanish or Portuguese port, and adding them to his navy. The Venetians are furious!'

Outside the window, the dark of the winter afternoon was drawing in. Thoughtfully I fetched a candle and lit it from Phelippes's. When I had set it down on my table I looked at the packet of letters ordering supplies of food and troops to be sent to Spain.

'So – it really is a crisis, then? Or could be?'

'It could be. Or,' he conceded, 'it could be just more of Philip's obsession about seizing England, playing itself out in his endless schemes. What we need is time, time to strengthen our navy against his monstrous ambition. Do you know what his motto is?'

'I'm not sure.'

'Non sufficit orbis.'
'The world is not enough,' I said.

So it was that, despite my determination to break away from Walsingham's service, I found myself back to my old routine, spending half my time at St Bartholomew's and half at Seething Lane. The reports and intercepted messages all conveyed a similar picture: Spain was building and seizing ships, buying in supplies of food and armaments, training soldiers, hiring mercenaries, purchasing slaves for its galleys from north African corsairs, and continually pressing the Vatican for money. It was rumoured that there were English and Welsh slaves serving on the galleys which would be used to attack England, as well as Spanish and Portuguese 'volunteers', that is, men who had been unfortunate enough to be press-ganged into service in the Spanish navy. Just like the slaves, they would be shackled to their oars. If a galley was sunk, her chained oarsmen would perish with her.

Once, for two years, I had lived under the brutal regime inflicted by Spain on Portugal, until my father and I had made our escape in a merchant ship belonging to Dr Hector Nuñez to join the exiled Marranos (as we were called) in England. Our community in London at that time probably numbered between sixty and eighty souls. We were all *novos cristãos* or New Christians, having been forced to convert in our native land, but we held Jewish services of a sort on the Sabbath at the home of Dr Nuñez, though we had no rabbi. Under English law, we must also attend church services on Sundays. The penalties for failure to do so were heavy. Although we all met together at our single makeshift synagogue, the churches we attended were scattered all over London. My father and I attended St Bartholomew's beside the hospital – both church and hospital had once been part of the Priory of St Bartholomew, dissolved in the time of the Queen's father. For myself, I was unsure where my faith lay. Although I had been born Jewish, I had found much consolation in the Protestant faith of England, with its belief in reading the Bible for oneself, as Walsingham himself had once urged me to do. It was a far cry from the rigid control of the Spanish Catholic church and its reign of terror under the Inquisition.

Our Marrano community tended to fall into two distinct groups. There were the professional men like my father and Dr Nuñez and Dr Lopez. They were all doctors, bringing with them to England their advanced skill in Arabic medicine. There were also a few eminent apothecaries and one or two lawyers who had been born in England and trained here. Many of this professional class, who lived mostly near the Tower, not far from Walsingham's house, also had interests in the spice trade, some – like Dr Nuñez – owning their own ships, others – like Dr Lopez and my father – investing in the trade. My father's investments were small, for we had lost everything when we escaped from Portugal. Dr Nuñez and Dr Lopez had chosen to come to England before the Spanish invasion with its accompanying Inquisition, so they were far more prosperous than we were. Dunstan Añez, Ruy Lopez's father-in-law, had come much earlier. His grown-up children had been born here and thought of themselves as English. He was one of the leaders of our community, a wealthy man holding a distinguished position, as Purveyor of Groceries and Spices to Her Majesty the Queen, while Ruy Lopez was the queen's personal physician.

The other part of the Marrano community scraped a living as craftsmen or dealers in secondhand goods or pawnbrokers. Their homes were clustered around Bishopsgate, just outside the northeast city wall, near Bedlam and Petty France, where the Huguenot refugees had settled.

My father and I fell somewhere between these two groups. By birth and education we belonged to the professional group, but we were much poorer and our hospital cottage in Duck Lane would have fitted inside one room of Dr Añes's grand house. Still, the other men respected my father and from time to time we would be invited to dinner by one of them. Not only had Dr Nuñez provided us with passage on one of his ships when we escaped from Portugal, but Dr Lopez had secured my father's position at the hospital and his wife Sara had taken us into her home when we first arrived, destitute, in London.

Soon after I had begun work once more in Phelippes's office, we were invited to dine at the Lopez home. The weather was still very cold and I was concerned for my father. It was a long walk to Wood Street, where Ruy had bought a fine house amongst the English merchants. My father at sixty was beginning to show his age. The extra burden of work falling on his shoulders since I had gone back to working for Walsingham had started to tell on him, and now he had the first signs of a chest infection.

'Are you sure we should go today?' I asked. 'I could send a message to tell Sara that you are not well.'

'I am well enough,' he said stubbornly. 'It would be discourteous to cry off now. It is nothing but a slight cough. I have been treating it myself. Besides, it is good for us to mix in company from time to time.'

This last remark surprised me, for my father had become something of a recluse since we had come to England, unlike the old days when he had been part of a gregarious and sociable group at the university of Coimbra. Usually it was he who demurred at going anywhere. I had only once persuaded him to come with me to the festivities at the Theatre last Christmas. By 'mixing in company' I wondered whether he meant that I should strengthen my ties to our own community. Much of my time nowadays was spent amongst the English, both in Seething Lane and, whenever I had any leisure, with Simon's fellow players in Master Burbage's company. I had seen little enough of them lately, my time being so occupied between my patients and my intelligence work, though I knew from Simon that they were rehearsing new plays for when the playhouses opened again in the better weather.

As it was impossible to convince my father that he should stay at home, I persuaded him to wear gloves and wrap a thick scarf around his head and his physician's cap. We set off into the snow, which was still falling, even in March. Just inside the city gate we found a street vendor selling hot chestnuts.

'How many for a farthing?' I asked.

He scooped up a shovelful for me to see. I nodded and he gave them to me in a screwed up cone of paper. We were close to the grid where the Newgate prisoners beg passersby to give them food, so I bought another farthing's worth and pushed the chestnuts through the grid into the frantically grabbing hands.

'Now,' I said to my father, 'we don't need to eat these, for we'll be royally fed at the Lopez house.'

'I wondered why you bought them.'

'Here, put them in your pockets and keep your hands warm with them.'

Although he laughed and protested, I filled his pockets with the hot nuts, allowing myself just one to eat.

'You grow more like your mother every day,' he said.

I shook my head. 'Best not to say that aloud. Best not even to think it.'

'But I do think it, Caterina.'

I felt myself grow cold and looked about to make sure no one had heard.

'Not Caterina any longer, Father. Christoval. Kit.'

He sighed. 'I wish it did not have to be so.'

'It is better this way. How else could I earn my living? Now come, we don't want to be out in the snow any longer than we need.'

The Lopez house was well heated with generous fires in every room and heavy curtains as well as shutters over the windows to keep out any vicious serpents of cold air. There were thick carpets on the floors and the well polished furniture glowed in the light of many candles. Sara took me aside before we joined the others and gave me a quick hug. When she had taken us in five years ago, I was a terrified child of twelve. Although I had already assumed my disguise as the boy Christoval, she soon discovered that I was in fact Caterina, though she had kept her word and never revealed the truth to anyone, not even her husband, Ruy.

'So, you are back working for Walsingham again,' she said.

'Aye. Not willingly, but there is much work to be done and I could not refuse.' I grimaced. 'Secrets and plots and foreign intrigue. I've no wish to be involved, but it seems my skills are needed.'

'I am afraid Ruy is becoming ever more entangled in just such affairs. You know that he is now appointed ambassador to Dom Antonio?'

I nodded. Dom Antonio was the claimant to the throne of Portugal, the focus of the hopes of our Marrano community, for he was himself half Jewish. If he could be restored to power, and the Spanish monarch driven out of Portugal, many of my countrymen dreamed of returning home. The Queen, I knew, saw Dom Antonio as a useful counter against the King of Spain, but she was famously cautious and I wondered whether he would ever see his throne or his country again.

'Dom Antonio is living out at Eton,' Sara said, 'and Ruy is for ever back and forth, treating him and plotting with him.'

'Is he ill?'

Sara smiled a little sardonically. 'Only the illness brought on by years of self-indulgence – an excess of wine, an excess of food, and an excess of women. He is a poor leader for us to rest our hopes on.'

The dining table was much as I remembered it from our last visit, the strange foreign wood gleaming richly in the light of many candles. The two heavy candelabra which Ruy had bought from Drake's looted Spanish treasure held pure beeswax candles more than two feet high. As before, we drank from fine Venetian glass, but today our food was served on silver-gilt plates. More of the profits from Drake's privateering expeditions.

'As I see it,' Ruy said, with a smug smile, 'What Drake achieves is a better balance in the economy of the world. The Spanish steal gold and silver from the barbarians of the New World and make of them objects of great beauty. However, had they no plunder from the Americas, Spain would be the poorest country in Europe without food and wine enough to feed her own people. Therefore she uses the gold to buy provisions from the rest of us.'

'She does not so much buy, of late,' said Dr Nuñez, somewhat bitterly, 'as steal provisions from us. My ship *Fair Wind* just escaped being impounded with all her cargo in Bilbao last month.'

Ruy bowed his head in acknowledgement.

'Quite so, Hector. Spain buys or *steals* provisions from the rest of Europe. Drake then steals gold, silver and jewels from the Spaniards, to restore the balance.'

'So the only losers are the native peoples of the Americas?' I said, emboldened to speak out by Ruy's expensive wine.

'They too are recompensed,' Ruy said, raising an ironic eyebrow. 'For do the Spanish not repay them with missionary priests, who draw them into the arms of the Holy Catholic Church?'

There was a ripple of somewhat uneasy laughter at this. All those sitting around the table had a painful relationship with the church of Spain, and tales were rife of the tortures inflicted on the Indians to force them into accepting the conquistadors' idea of Christianity.

'At any rate,' said my father, 'these dishes are very fine, Ruy. You were lucky to get them.'

Ruy tapped his nose with his finger. 'I have an arrangement with Drake. Once the Queen has chosen her portion of the spoils, Drake grants me a private view of the remainder, before it goes on sale. After he has chosen his personal items, of course.'

'Of course.'

I looked down. I always found Ruy's flaunting of his wealth and his possessions uncomfortable. He would like, I was sure, to be as ostentatious as Drake himself, who loaded his new wife down with so many jewels she looked like one of those statues of the Virgin which used to be paraded through the streets in Portugal. The sheer weight of them must make it difficult for her to move.

The servants were clearing away all the dishes from the first course from the table and I let my eyes travel over the portraits on the wall opposite me. There were individual portraits of Ruy and Sara, and a large painting of the entire family, including all the children, the family dog and an exotic parrot that had lived for just a few weeks before turning up its African toes and dying in last winter's English cold. There was also a miniature of the eldest daughter Anne, who was of an age with me. It had been painted, Sara had told me, to aid in marriage negotiations Ruy was carrying out with a number of his foreign trading partners, to Anne's own dismay. She had no wish to leave England.

'It is true,' said Lopez, in answer to some question my father had asked, when I had not been attending. 'I must dance attendance on Dom Antonio with enemas of senna for his over-indulgence, and words of honey for his political demands, but we are everywhere frustrated. Drake was with me when I urged the Portuguese expedition to the Privy Council in December, and

Walsingham believes we should catch the Spaniard napping before he wakes and makes his move, but the Council is full of pusillanimous laggards. And the Queen will make no decision.'

'And the Dom himself?' my father asked.

'Impatient. Full of frustrated anger. And when he is in this mood, he drinks himself to a stupor. He was the same when we were youths, at home in Crato. He must have his will, or he will sulk. And to be sure, his money is fast running through his fingers, trying to maintain his little court. They are beginning to drift away. Or turn their coats.'

Dr Nuñez looked up sharply. 'There is a traitor amongst them?'

Lopez smiled complacently and finished his glass of wine before he spoke. Then he dismissed the servants from the room, for he was not so far cup-shotten as to lose all caution.

'You recall Mendoza, the former ambassador from Spain?'

There was a general murmur of agreement.

'Well, he is now based in Paris, as you know. One of the Dom's followers, Antonio da Vega, is in Mendoza's pay. However, his letters to Mendoza are passed across the Channel through the good offices of my cousin Jeronimo.'

Lopez stroked his beard but could not conceal a faint smirk.

'Before Jeronimo conceals the letters in his bales of goods, he is kind enough to make copies for me. I have been whispering a few nothings to da Vega, who has passed them to Mendoza, who has, no doubt, sent them on to His Majesty, King Philip.'

The men laughed, and Sara and I exchanged glances, while Beatriz Nuñez looked uncomfortable and Anne Lopez gazed down at her plate.

'I have definite word,' said Dr Nuñez slowly, 'that the Spaniards are preparing an invasion fleet. The killing of the Scots queen has only made them the more determined to attack England. My agent in Cadiz has sent reliable intelligence that the harbour there is filling up with merchantmen which have been commandeered to be converted into warships.'

He gave a bitter little laugh. 'They have even seized one of my own ships! Unlike the *Fair Wind*, the *Nightingale* could not escape in time. One of my own ships in the Spanish navy! Now there is a fine irony.'

'You have informed Walsingham?'

'Naturally.'

Lopez tapped his teeth with his fingernail and helped himself to more wine, forgetting to serve his guests. At a nod from Sara I rose and moved quietly round the table refilling glasses.

'I think we could turn this to our advantage,' said Lopez. 'It would be possible to feed da Vega with tales of England's plans – false trails, to put the Spaniard off the scent. For surely Burghley and the Queen will send Drake against Cadiz?'

'That is my belief. Sir Francis did not say so in so many words, but—'

'Yes.' Lopez interrupted. 'I can make da Vega believe that Drake is preparing for a privateering venture against Brazil or Goa, somewhere far away. Word will go from da Vega to Mendoza, and from Mendoza to King Philip, so they will believe themselves secure.'

'You must speak to Sir Francis.' There was a warning note in Dr Nuñez's voice. 'Do not embark on such a scheme without his authority, Ruy.'

'Hmm,' said Lopez, and there was a distant look in his eye that I recognised. 'It could be a pretty scheme.'

I kept my counsel while they spoke. None of them realised that I knew far more of these affairs than they did.

The following day I reported the gist of this conversation to Phelippes, for I well understood Ruy's complacent rashness. It would be characteristic of him to ignore Dr Nuñez's warning and embark on some scheme of feeding false information to Mendoza on his own, without consulting Walsingham. The result could well be the destruction of some other careful plan which Sir Francis and Phelippes were themselves carrying out.

'I see,' said Phelippes. 'Come with me. I think we need to speak to Sir Francis.

I followed him to Walsingham's own office, where he greeted me courteously.

'I am glad you are working with us again, Kit. You know that we value you.'

I mumbled something in reply. I thought he was looking a little less frail than he had done at the funeral, but he was still pale and his face was drawn with fatigue.

'Kit has been hearing something useful to us,' said Phelippes.

I repeated Ruy's talk at dinner.

'So da Vega is a traitor,' said Sir Francis, stroking his beard. 'That does not surprise me. Dom Antonio is very short of money, and what little he has he spends on himself instead of on his followers. That is not the action of a wise leader. It is to be expected that some of them will desert to a higher paymaster, like Medoza. I will speak to Dr Lopez. His scheme has some merits. And he is correct that we are considering an attack by Drake on Cadiz.'

'Why Cadiz?' I asked. 'I thought the main Spanish fleet was gathering in Lisbon, despite what Dr Nuñez said last night.'

'The port of Lisbon is very heavily defended with a battery of cannon,' Walsingham said. 'Also, it is some distance up a narrow part of the river Tejo from the coast, as I am sure you know, Kit. Therefore it is impossible to make a surprise attack. As soon as Drake started to sail up the Tejo toward the city, a galloper would be sent by land with a warning. It would soon outstrip the ships. An English fleet caught in the river would be vulnerable to ambush.'

'Oh, I see.' I had little understanding of military tactics, but I was learning. Even to my ignorant mind, this made sense. 'And Cadiz?'

'Cadiz is the centre for provisions,' said Phelippes. 'It has warehouses full of supplies to feed the men as well as weaponry and gunpowder and shot. The supply vessels are being mustered in the harbour there. And it is much more open to attack by sea. Strike at Philip's supplies and he cannot move.'

'Clever.' I said.

Walsingham gave a tight smile. 'Wars are won as much by clever tactics as by brute force, Kit, as you will learn. For although we may delay Philip's planned invasion, it will come in the end.'

His words left a chill in the air.

Walsingham took up Ruy's idea, but kept the control of it in his own hands. A very deluge of plans and schemes rained down upon Mendoza in Paris, channelled through da Vega, who believed he was passing on genuine secrets garnered from his position close to Dom Antonio. At the same time, Walsingham sent secret dispatches to the Queen's ambassador in Paris, Sir Edward Stafford, intimating that Sir Francis Drake was to make a pre-emptive strike on Spain's possessions in the New World, to cut off her supplies of money, goods and men.

I did not understand this, until Phelippes explained.

'Stafford is a rogue,' he said. 'Constantly in debt. He is an inverate gambler and falls more and more into debt with every passing week. He needs money and will sell his soul to the highest bidder. Look at this.'

He tossed a report on to my desk. It was in one of our own ciphers, one so familiar I could read it without recourse to the key.

'It is from Gilbert Gifford.'

'Aye.'

I had worked with Gifford the previous year, when we had been unravelling the plot by Babington and his fellow conspirators. Gifford had posed as a Catholic sympathiser, though he worked for Walsingham. When the conspirators were rounded up, he was so afraid for his safety that he had fled to France and had been working there ever since. To maintain his disguise, Walsingham and Phelippes continued to pretend that they believed him to be one of the conspirators. He lived a dangerous life, threatened on all sides. I ran my eye quickly over the report.

'He says he has followed Mendoza and seen him entering Stafford's house secretly by night.'

'Aye, and staying for some considerable time. Long, secret discussions by night.'

'Stafford is a traitor?'

'He is.'

'But why does the Queen not recall him?'

Phelippes shrugged. 'She has been warned. She refuses to recall him. Sir Francis is not sure why. Perhaps she does not believe Stafford is a traitor. Perhaps it is because he is the stepson of her aunt, Mary Boleyn.'

'That has never stopped the Tudors in the past,' I muttered.

'You may think such thoughts, Kit. It were better you did not voice them.'

Even so, I found it hard to believe that the Queen would allow a man known to be a traitor to continue as her ambassador in such an important posting as Paris. Sir Francis himself had been ambassador there many years before, at the time of the St Bartholomew's Day Massacre. The horrors he had witnessed then had marked him for life. After such a distinguished predecessor in the post, why was the traitor Stafford not summoned home to answer for his conduct? Yet Walsingham, knowing Stafford for what he was, could now make use of him.

Having taken Ruy Lopez's plan in hand, Walsingham controlled exactly what misleading information was leaked to da Vega, and through him to Mendoza. I am not sure how he approached Ruy or let it be known that he knew about da Vega. Certainly he cannot have mentioned my name, for Ruy never gave any indication that I had passed on the information to Sir Francis.

That flood of gossip, instructions, secret briefings and military plans which found their way to Mendoza must have had him scratching his head in confusion. Though, given his known arrogance, he may merely have assumed that it was all the result of his own cleverness. I felt no pity for him. While he was the Spanish ambassador in London he was dyed to the elbows in various plots to invade England, assassinate the Queen, and put the Scottish woman on the throne, all of which had been followed closely from Phelippes's office. Mendoza had been expelled from England, but his skin remained intact, unlike those gallant if ill-judging boys like Babington. I hoped his Spanish master would eventually roast him alive for his false intelligence.

Amid these flying rumours, on the twelfth day of April, Drake's flagship, the aptly named *Elizabeth Bonaventura*, followed by his fleet, slipped away from Plymouth.

'Sir Francis has had da Vega arrested,' Phelippes told me, as we worked on a batch of papers sent to da Vega from Mendoza, intercepted at Dover. Ever since the increased concern

29

about a Spanish invasion, I had been summoned to assist him for more hours in the day, despite my attempts to plead my hospital work.

'What will happen to him?' I asked. 'To da Vega?'

'Oh, nothing will happen to him. He was arrested before Drake sailed. And then he was questioned cunningly, as if we were not *quite* sure whether he was an honest follower of Dom Antonio or not. Sir Francis released him when he calculated that it was too late for da Vega to inform King Philip that Drake had sailed not for the New World but for Spain.'

'But won't he be a danger to us?'

'Oh, no. The spy you know is not a danger. It is the hidden spy you must fear. Sir Francis wants da Vega to think he has fooled us. That way he can be used in future to channel false information to the Spanish king.'

I nodded. The longer I worked in Walsingham's service, the better I understood how these affairs were conducted.

Sir Francis's sense of timing was accurate, but a close-run thing, for some weeks later, Dr Nuñez told me that his agent in Cadiz had sent word that the Spanish king had received da Vega's letter warning of Drake's intention to attack Spain on the last day of April, that is, on the very day when Drake began burning the ships in the confined quarters of Cadiz harbour.

'Before he set sail for home,' Dr Nuñez said, 'Drake destroyed half the Spanish fleet. He has bought us a precious year longer to prepare for invasion. Although,' he added, with a wry smile, 'he burnt my ship along with the rest.'

Chapter Three

*D*rake sailed home to a hero's triumphant welcome. Drake the hero. Drake the pirate. Drake the Dragon, *El Draque*, as the Spanish called him. He hated the Spanish as much as I did, though for different reasons. And he had the means to avenge himself on them, which I had not. Soon the story of his attack on Cadiz was being told on every street in London, growing in extravagance with every retelling. The truth itself was astonishing, and I suppose what we knew at Seething Lane was as near as anyone would ever come to an honest account of one of Drake's expeditions.

Just before sailing from Plymouth, Drake had written to Sir Francis, mentioning his fears that nervous counsellors might yet persuade the Queen to forbid the expedition – men who would 'keep their finger out of the fire', though he believed God was with him. His letter, scribbled on board ship, ended:

'The wind commands me away, our ships are under sail. God grant we may so live in His fear that the enemy may have cause to say that God fights for Her Majesty as well abroad as at home. Haste.'

Drake was right to fear the Queen's notorious ability to change her mind. A messenger was despatched post haste to Plymouth with orders to rein back the attack to a minor privateering expedition, forbidding a direct attack on the Spanish mainland, for she still clung – so Walsingham said – to a forlorn hope of peace with Spain. Burghley too was cautious, but Walsingham was convinced that the only thing that could withstand Spain was military action. The Queen's messenger arrived too late in Plymouth. Drake's fleet had already sailed.

31

The Queen's order was sent on by fast pinnace, but it was driven back by bad weather and returned to England.

'Drake may well believe that God is with him,' Phelippes said, with a grim smile. 'For the storms of Heaven meant he never received the Queen's message. Just how hard the various bearers tried to catch him we will never know, but most Englishmen are with him, heart and soul.'

Soon Drake was being praised for singeing the King of Spain's beard, a vivid picture particularly pleasing to every true-blooded Englishman. On the way home he seized a treasure ship packed with spices, silks and ivory, so the Queen herself profited from the expedition in money as well as strategy. No doubt she forgave him for not obeying her last minute order. She could always claim that she had been against it, if ever it came to peace negotiations with Spain. The attack on Cadiz had destroyed not only a large number of the ships in the harbour but most of the provisions and armaments stored in the warehouses of the port. The town itself had suffered, and not only through Drake's activities.

Two weeks after Drake returned, I was transcribing a report from one of our agents in Lisbon. As I reached the end, I could not stop myself crying out in horror.

Phelippes looked up. 'What is it, Kit? Not bad news, I hope.'

'Despicable news,' I said. 'Most of the report simply confirms what we already knew about the attack on Cadiz, but this is new. It seems that when the mayor of Cadiz realised Drake was attacking, he ordered all the women and children to take shelter in Matagorda Castle. They rushed there in great numbers, but the captain in command of the castle slammed the gates in their faces. Nearly thirty of them, mostly children, were suffocated or crushed to death.'

I could see the frightened and screaming children falling under the press of bodies, kicked, trampled and dying, the women panicking, the sound of the heavy door crashing against its frame, the terror of being trapped between the invading forces and the callous indifference of their own soldiers.

'In war it is often the innocent who suffer,' Phelippes said.

'But we aren't at war,' I objected.

'Are we not?'

The Queen and her more cautious counsellors like Burghley might attempt to keep up the pretence of peace with Spain, and many citizens must have hoped for it in their hearts, but their heads would have told them that Walsingham and Drake and Admiral Howard were right. As soon as King Philip could repair his losses, he would once again undertake his Enterprise of England. War would come eventually, despite all efforts to stave it off.

In midsummer I transcribed a despatch from our agent in Rome which contained disquieting news. We had known, since his earlier reports, that Philip's emissaries had been seeking the support of the Pope, both ecclesiastical and financial.

'Well,' I said, laying down my transcription on Phelippes's desk, 'it seems Philip has got what he wants. The Pope is to give him a million ducats and grants him the right to bestow the crown of England on whomsoever he chooses. The Infanta is mentioned.'

Phelippes grabbed the despatch and ran his eye over it.

'So, the Bishop of Rome thinks he has the disposal of our crown, does he?' He spat the words out.

'It seems so. But look at the end.' I pointed with the tip of my quill.

When he had read the last few lines, he laughed.

'Oh, very clever! His Roman Holiness is a shrewd fellow indeed. So Philip will not receive the Pope's money in advance to finance the invasion. He gets half the money only after Spanish boots are on English soil, the rest of the money to be dribbled in, bit by bit.'

'All we have to do is ensure they do not land,' I said. 'No doubt the Pope will thank us for saving his money.'

'Indeed. That is all we have to do. Well, thanks to Drake's fire party at Cadiz, we have until next summer to create a navy strong enough to withstand what Philip has been building up for years.'

'If the Spanish troops do manage to land,' I said quietly, 'we have no hope, have we?'

'None at all. They are a trained and battle-hardened professional army. We have nothing but the amateur militias and the Trained Bands, who are trained for nothing but keeping the citizens in order.'

'So we must make sure they don't land,' I said.

'That is all we have to do.'

Although despatches continued to come in from our own agents, and letters passing between Philip and his various emissaries were regularly intercepted, the volume of work in Phelippes's office diminished and I was able to spend far more of my time at the hospital, working at Seething Lane no more than once or twice a week.

For the last year I had had little opportunity to continue my studies with my mathematics tutor, Thomas Harriot, but he still called in from time to time at Duck Lane, to make music with my father and me, and we had once supped with him, when I had a chance to play his beautiful virginals. Now in midsummer, he took me for the first time to Durham House, to one of the meetings of the group that gathered about Raleigh to discuss mathematics and astronomy and navigation, and also to consider the prospects offered by the new world of Virginia, the riches in both plants and minerals to be found in that country, and the customs and beliefs of its strange people.

I had seen Raleigh in the distance, riding in procession with the Queen, but never met him or found myself in the same room before that evening. As well as Raleigh there was Henry Percy, Earl of Northumberland, him they called 'the wizard Earl'. Both Northumberland and Raleigh were patrons of my tutor and were eager to learn from him. There were others there – that strange man Dr Dee, necromancer and alchemist and the Queen's own astrologer, amongst them – all gathered in a turret room overlooking the City and the river, so that I was frozen into awkwardness, tongue-tied by the presence of so many famous gentlemen.

Northumberland did have something of the wizardly about him, his hair unkempt and his doublet buttoned awry, but he was eager and friendly. Raleigh was the quieter man, less interested in astrology and demonology, but passionate for his New World exploration. His second Roanoke venture had just departed, which was to plant a permanent colony in Virginia, but the Queen had forbidden him to accompany it. It was plain to see from his restlessness how much he longed to be on the high seas at that very moment. While Raleigh was not averse to a little privateering himself, he was not cast in the same mould as Drake. Instead of foreseeing an England living off plunder from the Spanish ships returning from the New World, he was urging the establishment of our own colonies there, so that we could benefit from such riches ourselves.

I sat on a stool somewhat withdrawn and merely listened, feeling it was not my place to join in the discussions, although Harriot had told me he was taking me to Durham House because Raleigh liked to draw clever young men into his circle and open up new ideas and new worlds to them. We had been there about half an hour when we heard footsteps leaping up the turret stairs and the door burst open, without a knock. It was a young man in his early twenties with a high forehead and hair of a gingerish brown. He wore a young man's small moustache and tiny streak of beard below the lower lip – the sort of beard and moustache which look as though the wearer has dipped his face too deep in a pot of brown beer and forgotten to wipe it afterwards. He was somewhat lavishly dressed and did not apologise either for his late arrival or his impolite entry. I thought him arrogant. His eyes swept over me and dismissed me as of no account. He was followed by another young man, and to my surprise I saw that it was Simon. He gave me one startled look, then smiled. I returned his smile reluctantly, wondering who his brash companion might be. Simon himself looked embarrassed and a little defiant.

'Ah, here at last,' said Raleigh tolerantly, motioning the two of them to chairs across the room from me. 'You know most people here, except . . .' he indicated me, 'another Kit. Kit Marlowe, this is Kit Alvarez. And your friend?'

'Simon Hetherington,' said the other Kit, ignoring me and waving a careless hand. 'Another man of the theatre. Or rather boy.'

I saw Simon flush and pitied him. His skin was so fair it always betrayed him. The debate resumed. They were discussing some of the latest discoveries in celestial navigation, and before the evening was out I had the satisfaction of being asked by Harriot to explain some of the mathematical calculations, which Marlowe was compelled to attend to. As we began to take our leave at the end of the evening, Marlowe approached me, followed by Simon. He looked me up and down.

'Quite the clever lad, isn't he, Simon?' He smiled maliciously and flicked me painfully on the cheek with a long fingernail.

'A beardless boy, and invited to lecture grown men of learning. We shall have dancing dogs next, and apes from the Indies dressed in doublets and lace.'

He looked me over again, and I was conscious of my drab physician's clothes compared with the finery he and Simon wore.

'A Portingall, are you? A Jew? We all know what should be done with the Jews, bloodsuckers and heretics.'

Bile rose in my throat and I clenched my fists, but dared not challenge him.

At that he gave a mocking laugh, flung his arm around Simon's shoulders, and propelled him out of the room and down the stairs, their feet clattering on the stone.

I found this encounter deeply unsettling. I had never before seen this fellow Marlowe amongst Burbage's company, yet he and Simon seemed to be on terms of very close friendship. Perhaps I had only myself to blame. Since we had watched Sidney's funeral procession back in February, I had hardly seen Simon, my time being so caught up in the work of Walsingham's service. Although I now had more freedom, I found myself reluctant, after meeting Marlowe, to seek out my friends amongst the players. Until that evening at Raleigh's house I had been intending to visit them again at the Theatre out beyond Bishopsgate, perhaps to make music again with Guy Bingham, their chief musician and comic actor. Over the twelve days of Christmas last winter I had seen them nearly every day and felt myself at ease amongst their motley company. Like me, many of them concealed their past, living only for the moment. The playhouse was their home, the company of players their family. They lived in a variety of lodgings, ate and dressed well when they were in funds, went hungry and pledged their costumes to Marrano pawnbrokers in Bishopsgate Without when times were hard. They were apt to give little thought for the future. Money slipped through their fingers like water. Yet they were the most easy-going company of men and boys I had ever known.

That is not to say they did not squabble, if one player was given a part that another coveted, or James Burbage tried to force them to play a part in one fashion, when they thought it should be played quite differently. But their squabbles flared up with great noise and drama, then were over in a moment.

Now, however, I was afraid to visit them. Afraid I might meet the despicable Marlowe and suffer more of his taunting. So at first I was at a loss what to say when I met Guy buying oranges at a stall in Cheapside. Since the troubles with Spain, oranges were expensive and hard to come by.

'You must be in the chinks, Guy!' I said. 'Best quality oranges.'

He grinned at me. 'I never can resist them. These are the first I've seen for months.'

He paid the stallholder, then began to juggle the oranges, to the great entertainment of the passersby. Soon quite a crowd had gathered, but he pocketed the oranges, bowed, and led me away by the elbow. We found a seat on a table tomb in Paul's churchyard, near the booksellers and not far from where Simon and I had stood on that cold February day to watch Sidney's funeral procession. Guy handed me an orange and would not listen to my protests.

'I *am* in the chinks, Kit,' he said. 'After a performance last week, a gracious lady sent for me to entertain her dinner guests by playing my lute and singing. I was well paid for it, though the lady wanted rather more of me than I was prepared to give, so I barely escaped with my virtue intact.'

He winked at me and I grinned back, through my orange. Guy had a face like a friendly monkey and I did not believe a word of it. Not the last part, at any rate.

'And where have you been hiding, Dr Alvarez?' he said. 'You are as elusive as fresh oranges.' He only called me 'Dr Alvarez' when he wanted to tease me. At first the players had not believed I was a physician, but after giving a performance at the hospital last Christmas, they knew it was true.

'Walsingham sent for me again,' I said. 'I have been working at Seething Lane as well as the hospital for weeks.'

'So why are you let out now?'

'Oh, since Drake returned, matters have been quieter.'

'Then why have you not come to see us?'

I did not answer at once, making much of wiping my face and fingers on my handkerchief and tossing my orange skin into the long grass.

'Who is this Kit Marlowe?' I burst out. 'He seems to be a great friend of Simon's.' I had not meant to say it, and once the words were out of my mouth, I could not look Guy in the eye.

'Ah, so you have met the great Kit Marlowe, have you? The golden son of Cambridge, poet extraordinary, would-be play maker. Was that at Walsingham's?'

I stared at him. 'No. Certainly not. Why should I meet him at Walsingham's?'

'He is something of a protégé of Walsingham's cousin Thomas. And I've heard it hinted that he sometimes works for Sir Francis himself.'

'I've never seen him at Seething Lane.' I felt my heart sink. Was this fellow likely to appear where I worked?

I turned to Guy and studied him. 'You don't like him,' I said.

'I do not. He is arrogant, thinks too well of himself and too poorly of others. He also has a violent temper and has been in trouble for it. How did you come to meet him?'

'It was at Sir Walter Raleigh's house. Harriot took me there for one of Raleigh's discussion evenings and Marlowe turned up there, very late, with no apologies, dragging Simon after him. He insulted me.'

'That is no surprise.'

'Is he a member of Master Burbage's company, then?'

'No, no. He's much too fine a gentleman to join a ragbag of wastrels like us. Though I have heard tell he sometimes mixes with very low company indeed, thieves and ruffians. He's only a cobbler's son, but he gives himself airs, having been a scholar at Cambridge. No, he hangs about our company, hoping to sell us a play. And he's taken lodgings with Thomas Kyd, perhaps in the hope of a recommendation.'

'So why was Simon with him? They seemed very close.' I tried to remember what I had seen. 'At least, he was making much of Simon and wanted him to join in insulting me, though Simon looked embarrassed.'

Guy grinned, and wiped his sticky fingers on his breeches.

'Well, you have to admit that Simon is a very pretty boy, and Marlowe has a liking for pretty boys.'

'Oh.'

'Oh, indeed. But do not worry, I am sure Simon does not return the feeling.'

'I do not worry. What is it to me what Simon feels?'

'What indeed? And I am sure Marlowe will not hurt your friendship with Simon. He did not join in the insults, did he?'

'He did not.'

Guy got up and brushed fragments of moss and lichen from his clothes. 'Come back with me now and see the company. We have missed you.'

Here was another surprise. It seemed that the players also missed me. I had not realised that I had made so many friends, both at Seething Lane and at the Theatre. After years of hiding away, keeping to my father's shadow, the last two years had changed my life.

'Will Marlowe be there?' I asked.

Guy drew himself up to his full height, which was slightly less than mine, and struck himself on the chest with a grand gesture.

'If he is, I will protect you with my life!'

I laughed and followed him out of the churchyard.

When we reached the Theatre, outside the north wall of the city, past the Curtain playhouse and near Finsbury Fields, we found most of the company there but, happily, no Marlowe. They were about to start a rehearsal of some new comic piece, one of those full of jokes of the moment, which would be stale in six months' time. It would please the groundlings and earn the players enough coin to live, but it was the kind of trivial thing my father looked down on. Despite my urging, he had still not come to see any of the newer, more serious plays the company performed, like those of Thomas Kyd. I wondered what sort of play Marlowe was writing. Probably as full of bombast as he was.

In the rehearsal Guy capered and tumbled, Simon simpered as a love-lorn maiden, and Christopher Haigh (who played the young lover parts) postured as a noble shepherd who was really a long-lost prince. There were a great many jeers at King Philip and his admiral Santa Cruz and some clumsy *double entendres* concerning burning ships. Burbage stopped the players from time to time in order to rearrange them on the stage or change some of the words. A young boy, who was playing one of the minor women's parts, was told off for striding about the stage like a man and looked as though he would burst into tears. Afterwards, I saw Simon take him aside and show him how to walk, taking small steps and keeping his hands clasped in front of his, so that he would not be tempted to let his arms swing loosely at his sides.

'It will be easier once you are in costume,' Simon said. 'In a farthingale and skirt you will find that your legs are so hampered you are forced to take small steps, just to avoid tripping up.'

I smiled to myself. I knew he was quite right. When I had first changed into boy's attire at the age of twelve, I had discovered how much easier it was to move than when I had worn skirts, especially those for evening or festive wear, which were heavy and stiff with embroidery and pearls. I could not imagine ever abandoning my breeches for skirts again.

'Kit!' Simon had just noticed me, sitting in the lowest tier of seats and watching the rehearsal. He climbed up and sat down next to me.

'You are a stranger here in the playhouse.'

There was a note of reproof in his voice, so I repeated my explanation to Guy of how busy I had been.

'Though it is not so long since we met,' I said. 'You will recall an evening at Sir Walter Raleigh's. You were there in company with your new friend – what was it he was called?' I spoke with all the indifference I could muster.

'Kit Marlowe,' he said, looking uncomfortable. 'He knows Raleigh. He knows many great men.'

'Indeed?'

'And he thought I would be interested to accompany him.'

'Oh? Was that it? I thought perhaps he wanted you there to witness how he vaunted himself before those same great men. To applaud his performance.'

'He was abominably rude to you. I'm sorry.' He was now looking even more shame-faced. 'And I thought your explanation of the mathematics of celestial navigation most impressive.'

'Not too much like a performing ape from the Indies? Or a blood-sucking Jew?'

'It was unforgivable, what he said.'

'You said nothing to chide him at the time. Nothing in my defence.'

'I was taken aback. And before I could think of anything to say, he had hustled me away.'

'Hmph.' I was not quite ready to forgive him, but before we could say more we were summoned to join the others for supper at Burbage's lodgings in Holywell Lane, which it seemed was his practice on the evening before the first performance of a new play. I was invited to eat with them. I did so readily, something I would never have dreamt of before last year.

It was a good evening. Burbage's wife Ellen sat down to eat with us, though she retired early. The players were in high spirits, for they were sure the comic piece would do well for the next few weeks. Full houses in the playhouse meant full bellies for players. Burbage's landlady was an excellent cook and served up a substantial meal of fish in a sauce of capers, followed by roast beef and roast mutton, dressed with leeks and carrots, then a lemon syllabub garnished with candied peel. Afterwards we cracked nuts and Guy performed a ridiculous parody of a sentimental song with new words which would have been unrepeatable in polite company.

It was growing dark as I walked home, but I was accustomed to that after my many late sessions working with Phelippes. Simon and Guy walked with me as far as their lodgings in Three Needle Street, and we parted on amiable terms. I walked the rest of the way in a happier frame of mind than I had known since that encounter with Marlowe.

Although my own life had taken a turn for the better, there was disquieting news from the Low Countries. By the beginning of August the English garrison of the port of Sluys, an important strategic foothold on the coast, had been under siege for nearly two months. The Duke of Parma, King Philip's brilliant military commander in the Spanish Netherlands, had kept them in a stranglehold, starving and worn down by constant bombardment. On the fourth of August they could hold out no longer and surrendered. News reached London a few days later. After the jubilation of Drake's raid on Cadiz, it was dismaying news indeed.

Initially Sluys had been defended by local men, but when Parma surrounded it, they had sent out an appeal to England and four companies of foot soldiers had courageously fought their way through the Spanish lines to their relief. It was clear that Parma was no longer directing his attention merely to suppressing the Dutch Protestants. He was aiming to seize ports which could be used as bases to attack England. Elizabeth sent Leicester with a large body of troops and ships to relieve Sluys but, characteristically, he failed to act. Despite enormous courage on the part of the garrison and the appeals to Leicester by their commander, Sir Roger Williams, no help came. A thousand men died. The garrison ran out of food and gunpowder, until in the end they were forced to surrender. The few remaining men were almost all wounded or maimed and Sir Roger himself left destitute.

'You see how the Spaniard's plans advance,' Phelippes said to me, after recounting the sorry fate of Sluys. 'With Sluys and Dunkerque Parma now has access to deep water harbours, eminently suitable for launching an attack on England. He will try to seize Flushing next – or Vlissingen, as the Hollanders call it.'

'I was thinking more of the men who died there,' I said sharply. 'And of the few who survived. Dr Stephens says we will see many of them in the hospital when they reach London, if they do not perish on the way.'

'Well, you must do your best to patch them up,' he said, 'for we shall need every able-bodied soldier we can scrape together to fight on board the ships of our navy.'

'I thought we had no navy. Or little enough to match the Spanish.'

Sir Francis must have overheard my last remark, for he came through the door as I was speaking.

'Our royal navy is small, Kit, but the ships of the privateers are armed and well crewed, and we are busy requisitioning every merchant ship that can be adapted for fighting.'

'I don't suppose the merchants will be glad of it,' I said, thinking of Dr Nuñez, whose ship had brought us from Portugal and who had recently lost another to Drake's festival of fire.

'No, they will not be glad of it and they will lose trade for all the time that the ships are in our hands, but a far worse future awaits them if we cannot assemble a navy of some sort. Our cannon foundries are working all day and all night, and gunsmiths, bowyers and fletchers are all at full stretch.'

I remembered the ironworks I had seen last year in the Weald, where the men, stripped to the waist, had laboured beside hellish fires directing the molten metal into the moulds for cannon. In the heat of this August I wondered they did not die of the work. Perhaps they did. My own work, sitting in Phelippes's office, quietly transcribing despatches, seemed feeble by comparison.

Dr Stephens's prediction about the wounded soldiers was soon proved right. It was said that there were around seven hundred survivors of the siege of Sluys, but some died before they could reach home. Most of the others ended up in St Bartholomew's or across the river in Southwark at the hospital of St Thomas. They had been brought back to England in some of Leicester's ships which had lingered offshore while he was too cowardly to go to their rescue during the siege. It was common knowledge that Leicester had men and weaponry enough to have lifted the siege, if he had acted. The soldiers, filthy, emaciated, bloody and in rags, were carried or limped up from the river steps to the hospital where we awaited them, shocked at their numbers and condition. There were so many that we had to put most of them on pallets on the floor until more beds could be brought in. Beds and pallets alike were crowded so close together in the wards that it was almost impossible to step between them.

Despite their injuries, many of them grave, the men were pathetically grateful to have survived not only the siege but also the ending of it. Parma – generous for once – had allowed them to depart in safety, instead of taking them prisoner. Or worse. We all knew of occasions in the past when those surrendering to Spanish troops under a promise of fair treatment were immediately and indiscriminately slaughtered. These men were lucky to reach England alive, despite wounds or severed limbs, festering sores, head injuries or blindness. Perhaps Parma thought they would not survive to fight him again.

For once, Phelippes admitted that my work at the hospital was more important than my work at Seething Lane.

When the men were first brought in, I was in a small ward where we put women who have had difficult births and have been sent to us by the midwife. They were kept here away from the other patients, partly because my father believed that soon after giving birth a woman is vulnerable to infection, and partly because the crying of the babies would disturb the other patients. Dr Stephens poured scorn on the former idea, but supported the latter, having little fondness for squalling infants.

'You will note,' my father frequently pointed out to him, in one of their many arguments about my father's advanced ideas, 'that when the mothers are kept away from other illnesses, they are much more likely to survive childbirth.'

Dr Stephens would snort in disbelief. 'If God has ordained that a woman shall die, bringing forth in the pain which is rooted in Eve's sin, nothing we can do will save her.'

My father would smile and say, 'You do not really believe that.'

That day, however, they were both occupied in seeing to the new arrivals, so I tended to the women alone. I did not even have the assistance of the young apothecary, Peter Lambert, who was busy with the others preparing salves and poultices in vast quantities. When I had made the last of the women comfortable, I walked back through to the two main wards, which were filling up fast.

It was a scene from a nightmare. I had never seen so many injured men in my life. Instead of two parallel rows of beds, well spaced, arranged along the two long walls of the ward, there were now four rows, the two outer ones infilled with straw pallets on the floor and two more rows of pallets down the centre of the room. Men were still being carried in and deposited on these. I realised that we were fortunate it was summer, for there would not have been enough blankets in the entire hospital to cover them. As it was, there were no pillows or cushions for their heads. They simply lay where they were put down, on the lumpy straw palliasses which the hospital servants had stayed up all night to make.

I walked over to my father, who was talking to the mistress of the nurses. She was a formidable woman of ample girth and iron will, but she was wringing her hands now, with tears in her eyes.

'Dr Alvarez, we cannot care for so many,' she said. 'I have not nurses enough even to wash their faces. If you expect us to change dressings or clean wounds, it cannot be done.'

'There is nowhere else for them to go, Mistress Higson,' he said. 'St Thomas's is also full. We will all do as much as we can, and we will ask in the neighbourhood whether any of the goodwives can lend assistance.'

'I cannot have strangers interfering,' she objected. 'They will do more harm than good. Of that you may be sure.'

I left them to it and walked down to the far end of the ward to begin checking the patients. It was a sickening business. I had studied under my father since childhood and had worked as his assistant in the hospital for almost four years now, so I was accustomed to the grim sights a physician encounters every day. Yet I had never seen anything like this. It was the stench of festering wounds that struck me first, so that I found myself gagging. And the whole ward was filled with a low moaning, like a storm wind, scarcely human. Occasionally there was a sharp cry of pain and away at the far end of the room one voice babbled on and on as one man raged with fever.

Peter came in with a tray, which he set down on the table just inside the door. It was loaded with fresh pots of salves and jugs of Coventry water.

We looked at each other in dismay, both overwhelmed by what lay about our feet.

'We'd best make a start,' I said. 'We'll need more bandages.'

'The sewing women have been put to cutting up all the cloth we have,' he said, 'and they've sent out for more. Ah, here we are.'

Margaret Jenkins, one of the sewing women I knew well, came into the ward with a large basket of bandage strips, which she placed next to the tray. As she turned and caught sight of the ward, she gasped and pressed her hand to her mouth.

'Oh, Dr Alvarez,' she said, 'how many are there?'

'I think we have taken in about four hundred,' I said. 'The rest have gone to St Thomas's.'

She shook her head, as though all words had deserted her, and hurried away back to the sewing room. I knelt down beside the first pallet. The soldier was a grizzled man of middle years with half his breeches torn away, his right leg bound up in a filthy bloody cloth.

He attempted a smile. 'Not a good sight, doctor.'

'Pass me the scissors, Peter,' I said, and held out my hand for them. 'What caused this?'

'Spanish bullet. Two weeks ago.' He clamped his mouth shut as I began to cut away the dirty cloth. It was stuck fast to the leg and I could not remove it without hurting him.

'Is the bullet still there?'

'No. Got. It. Out. Myself. Oh, Jesu!'

'I'm sorry, it can't be helped.' I looked down at the wound which was badly inflamed. 'How did you get it out?'

'Point of my dagger.'

He tapped the sheath attached to his belt. It was probably dirty, but at least I would not have to remove the bullet. Peter knelt on the floor beside me, holding a bowl of Coventry water. He handed me a cloth. I dipped it into the water and began to wipe away the dirt and crusted matter from the wound. The soldier bit down on his lip.

'I'm afraid this will hurt, but I need to clean it. Then I'll salve it and bind it up. There's no sign of gangrene, so you can be thankful for that.' I was thinking of Sir Philip Sidney, who died from one of Parma's bullets, followed by gangrene.

46

He nodded, but did not risk his voice in speaking. When I was satisfied that the wound was as clean as I could get it, Peter handed me the salve, which I smeared generously over the wound and the surrounding skin, then bound the leg with a clean strip of cloth.

'Now try and rest a while,' I said. 'We have to see to all of the injuries first, but later they will bring you food.'

'Thank you, Doctor.' His voice was stronger now, and he managed a weak smile. 'That salve is making it feel better already.'

'Good.' The salve was made with many cooling and antiseptic herbs, pounded in honey, which is one of the best healers God has given us. With luck, the wound would heal. I patted his shoulder and moved with Peter to the next soldier.

By now I could see my father working his way along the opposite wall, while Dr Stevens was directing four of the nursing sisters to care for some of the less serious cases. When the hospital was part of the Priory of St Bartholomew, back before King Henry's time, the daily care of the sick was carried out by nuns. Now the women who looked after our patients were secular, many of them widows, but the term 'sister' had lingered on. The mistress of the nurses, who did not normally care for the patients herself, had rolled up her sleeves and joined them. My father must have pacified her somehow.

The next soldier in the row along the near wall was a young boy, who could not have been more than thirteen or fourteen. He seemed only half conscious but it was clear that the injury was to his right hand, which was invisible inside a crude bundle of cloth. Once again I cut the bloodstained cloth away, to reveal a horribly crushed and mangled hand.

Peter looked at me and shook his head. I shrugged. It might be possible to save it, but I was doubtful. I took so long cleaning the hand and setting each finger in tiny splints that Dr Stephens came and stood over me, watching what I was doing. It made me nervous, for I knew he had a low opinion of me. Unlike him, I had not studied at the Medical School in Oxford. I had not even studied at a Portuguese university. I had learned my medicine at my father's side, like an apprentice, and I had read widely and carefully in his medical texts, but for Dr Stephens that was not a rigorous physician's training. I had not attended lectures on the great Greek physician Galen and I subscribed to the strange modern views of the infidel Arabs.

However, he was gracious enough to nod when I was finished. 'At neat job,' he said, as he turned away. From Dr Stephens, that was an accolade.

Peter grinned at me and winked.

As I finished, the boy half woke and moaned with pain. I felt a wrench at my heart, for he must have been suffering terribly for days, and he was so young. I called over one of the sisters.

'Bring me half a cup of small ale,' I said.

When she returned, I added a small amount of poppy syrup from the phial I kept in my satchel of medicines.

'Help me to lift him up,' I said to Peter.

One on either side, we eased the boy into a sitting position and I held the cup to his lips. They were cracked and blackened. Like all the soldiers he had starved during the siege and nearly died from lack of water. His eyes opened once we had him upright, but they wandered, unfocused.

'Now,' I said, 'here's is some ale for you. Drink it slowly and it will help the pain.'

Some of it dribbled down his shirt, but he managed to drink most of it. As soon as we lowered him down on to the pallet again he dropped into a deep sleep.

'That acted quickly,' Peter said.

'I think his body is so exhausted he would have slept anyway, but it will ease his pain, I hope.'

Gradually Peter and I worked our way along the row of soldiers, stopping from time to time to reassure some of our other patients who were already occupying the beds, for the sight of so many wounded men brought in amongst them was causing them distress. One aggressive fellow, who had no more wrong with him than over-indulgence in eating and drinking which had made him bilious, demanded that the soldiers should be moved out of the ward, for the noise made it impossible for him to sleep.

'Better, I think, Goodman Watkins,' I said, 'that you should go home and give up your bed to one of these wounded soldiers. Your wife can look after you now.'

I knew that his wife was a shrewish scold, who would not tolerate his malingering.

'Oh, no,' he said, rubbing his stomach and rolling his eyes, 'I am in a vast amount of pain. I have not the strength even to step out of this bed.' With that he rolled over and closed his eyes.

Peter shrugged. 'We'll send him home tomorrow. Only this morning Dr Stephens said he should go.'

We were perhaps a little more than halfway along the row when we reached a soldier with a heavily bandaged head and one arm strapped in a sling. I had noticed his eyes following me as I moved nearer to him. There was something familiar about him, but I could not put my finger on it. Kneeling down beside the pallet, I saw that, unlike so many of the men, he was fully awake and alert. Two bright eyes looked out at me from below the bandage which was wound around his head and one ear.

'Well, Kit Alvarez, I did not expect to meet you again in such a manner as this.'

I knew the face, knew the voice.

'Andrew!' I said. 'What are you doing here? These are foot soldiers. Surely you are a trooper?'

'Aye, I'm still a trooper, but a few of us were sent over to Sluys with the infantry. I have been working with the gunners this year and it was thought my experience would be of some use to those poor buggers. But there's not much use having guns when you run out of gunpowder. And there might have been need of a galloper to carry messages, but we never had the chance. The only messages sent out from the town were carried by cunning local lads who knew where to slip through the enemy lines.'

I saw that he was sweating slightly and realised that the brightness of his eyes was partly due to fever.

'Peter,' I said, 'will you fetch me some of the febrifuge tincture? And we are going to need more of the salve.'

Peter, who had been listening to this exchange with interest, nodded and got to his feet.

'Trooper Andrew Joplyn and I worked together last year.' I felt I must satisfy his curiosity. 'When I was in Sussex with Master Phelippes.'

Peter nodded. 'I remember.' He picked up his tray and headed off to the hospital still room.

49

'That was a night.' Andrew lay down with a sigh. 'Back last year. I thought those fishermen were going to catch us.'

'Because of my stupidity,' I said.

'Anyone could have had an accident in the dark,' he said. 'Still it was a fine race we had, back to Rye. Did they catch those men?'

'Aye. They were . . .' I paused, 'dealt with.'

'So you really are a physician. I'm not sure I believed you.'

'I know you didn't. Now, what is amiss with you?'

'Dislocated my shoulder. A couple of the lads pulled it straight for me. It's something we learn how to do. You can easily dislocate a shoulder, falling off a horse. The sling is just to give me some ease.'

'And your head?'

'Ah, well, that is nastier. I had a lucky escape. A bullet grazed my head just above the ear, but it didn't penetrate. Hit the poor bugger behind me and killed him. Still, it's sore.'

I began to unwind the bandage around his head. Like so many of the dressings I had already removed, this one was caked with dried blood and would not come away easily. Peter had left a bowl of Coventry water on the floor beside me, so I soaked the bandage until I could peel it away, revealing a deep gash in the side of Andrew's head, as broad as two fingers. The bullet had also torn away the tip of his ear. While I was working, Andrew said nothing, but bit down on his lower lip. Beads of sweat trickled down the side of his face.

'Aye, you were lucky,' I said, relieved that the bone of the skull was merely grazed and not shattered. 'It also looks quite clean.'

'I did my best to wash it.' His voice came out high-pitched, as if he was still struggling with the pain.

Peter came back with more salves and a bottle of the febrifuge tincture. I dressed the wound and bound it up, then gave Andrew a dose of the tincture.

'I'm not sure whether or not your hair will grow back, and you will have a nick out of the top of your ear.'

'My beauty quite spoiled, then?' He gave me a shaky smile.

'Oh, it will be quite an heroic wound.'

He smiled again and sank back on to the pallet.

'Good to see you again, Kit.'

I smiled down at him. 'And you, Andrew.'

Chapter Four

*P*eter and I continued to tend the wounded lying along the left hand wall of the ward until we reached the end. Most of the injuries were bullet wounds. In some cases the bullet had passed through the body or had been clumsily prised out, but I had to extract most of them with a scalpel and forceps. It was difficult to judge which were the more dangerous, those where a bullet had been left in the wound, preventing it from healing, or those where some dirty knife had been used to poke it out, enlarging the wound and filling it with who knew what filth.

In order to work more quickly, I showed Peter how to clean and salve the wound after I had extracted the bullet. He was quick and neat, so that by the time we reached the end of the row we were working to a steady rhythm. There were three cases where the bullet had penetrated more deeply, into chest or stomach. Those cases I left to my father and Dr Stephens, though the likelihood of the men's survival was small.

As well as bullet wounds there were burns from handling hot cannon and one man with half his face blown away when a Spanish fire arrow had caused an explosion amongst the defenders' gun powder. Mercifully he died that night, for otherwise he could only have lingered on in unbearable suffering.

When we reached the top of the room, Peter and I both stood up for a moment, to ease our backs.

'Jesu!' he said. 'My knees are on fire! And I suppose we need to start on the next row now.'

I nodded. My own knees hurt from kneeling so long on the stone-flagged floor and I was feeling dizzy, from crouching over the patients or from the horrors of the number of bullets I had extracted from raw flesh. Down by the door of the ward I saw that some of the hospital's serving women had carried in a great pot of soup and baskets of bread. They were starting to feed the men we had treated, those who were awake.

'I think we should take some food,' I said, 'before we start again. Can you ask the women to give us some soup and bread, Peter?'

He nodded and hurried away down the ward, picking his way between the men on the floor. My father came across to me.

'I'm afraid we lost the one with a bullet in his chest,' he said. 'It had punctured his lung. He died before we could do anything for him.'

I looked at him bleakly.

'Was all this suffering necessary? Sir Francis says Leicester could have saved them, saved the town of Sluys, but he is all courtly talk, a nobleman's façade – underneath it he's as cowardly as a girl. He kept his ships out at sea and did nothing.'

'A deal more cowardly than one girl I know,' my father said softly, casting his glance over my blood-stained hands and clothes. 'You have a smear of blood on your forehead.'

'Take care no one hears you,' I said. I dipped a cloth in the bowl of Coventry water and wiped my face. It felt good. 'Peter is getting us some soup, then we'll start down this next row.'

'I think you should go home,' he said. 'You're as white as a bleached sheet.'

I shook my head. 'How could I go home and leave this? I will do well enough when I have had some soup. You should eat something too. Do you know what time it is?'

'I heard the church clock strike eleven some while ago.'

'Then we might as well spend the rest of the night here. We won't be finished before morning.'

Peter came back with a tray. He had brought a cup of soup for my father too, and some rough-cut slices of the brown bread the hospital makes for our pauper patients. For myself, I think it tastes better than the fine manchet loaves served in the Lopez house. The soup had been made with beef bones and was a rich dark brown with pieces of carrots and leeks in it. I hoped it would not be too rich for men who had been near starvation before, but they were eating it eagerly. When my father had finished his, he walked along the row, warning the soldiers to take the soup slowly and to chew the vegetables carefully. I was not sure whether they heeded him.

As soon as we had eaten, Peter and I began to treat the soldiers lying on one of the rows of pallets which had been laid down the middle of the ward. There was barely space to kneel between them and some of the soldiers were gravely ill. I continued to extract bullets, but there were broken limbs to set as well. Peter fetched splints and we did the best we could, but in some cases the bone was not broken cleanly, so that I had to pick out shattered fragments before strapping the leg or arm into place. It was clear that in some cases, even if the limb mended, it would be left shorter or twisted. There was hardly a man here who would be fully whole again. And all for what? The more I saw of what had happened to these men, the more I cursed Leicester under my breath. In some ways, I held him more guilty than Parma.

We were nearly at the end of the row, and I was looking forward to resting at last, for my father and Dr Stephens had just finished all the other patients. I knelt down beside a young man with a thatch of golden curls who reminded me a little of Simon. Peter was fetching a final supply of our wound salve, while I began to unwind yet another bandage from around a blood-stained leg. The soldier watched me with a despairing look in his eyes.

'Not much use you trying to treat it, Doctor,' he said. 'It's nearly a month since a Spanish cannon ball smashed into my leg. I know what's happening.'

As I peeled off the cloth, I understood what he meant. The unmistakable stench of gangrene rose from his body. Revealed to sight, his leg was a mass of festering flesh.

'I will do what I can to ease your pain,' I said. 'But you are right.' I felt I owed him honesty.

Peter came back and together we cleaned and salved the leg, holding our breath against the stench. The lower part of the leg, from the foot to just below the knee, where the original injury was located, had turned a bluish black colour. I squeezed the toes of the soldier's foot hard.

'Can you feel that?' I asked.

He shook his head.

I tried pressing at various points up his leg. There was no feeling. Even above the knee, where the skin was not yet discoloured, he shook his head every time I pressed, until I was halfway up his thigh.

'Yes, I can feel that.' His voice was colourless with despair. I knew that he had abandoned all hope of life.

'There is only one course,' I said, hating every word. 'The leg must be amputated.'

'Is there any use in that, doctor?' His voice was so quiet I had to lean closer in order to hear him. 'Once the gangrene has taken hold, it will reach my heart, won't it? Even if it don't kill me, I'll be maimed, only half a man.'

I put my hand on his shoulder. 'Listen to me. We will save you if we can. If you live, then it is part of God's purpose that you should live. I know it will be hard, but you must make of your life the best you can.'

I felt ashamed as I spoke, sounding as righteous as a street preacher, I who had my health and strength. What did I know of the life that would lie ahead of a soldier who was left crippled? What could he do? How could he live? Yet I was all the more determined to save him.

'I will see how quickly we can fetch a surgeon,' I said. 'As physicians we are not permitted to carry out amputations, except when there is no other way, as on the battlefield, but there are surgeons we can call in.'

I patted his shoulder and rose to my feet, but he turned his head away and closed his eyes. I saw that tears were seeping from beneath his eyelids.

'Stay with him,' I murmured to Peter, and went to look for my father.

He was sitting with Dr Stephens on a bench in the corridor just outside the ward. Seeing them there together, exhausted, I was conscious how old they had both grown. Their skin was grey and slack with fatigue, their bodies somehow collapsed and sunken with the frantic effort of the last hours. The sight chilled me. I depended on these men for their wisdom and guidance, even Dr Stephens, with his old fashioned ideas.

'I have a patient who needs an urgent amputation,' I said without preamble. 'Gangrene in his leg almost up to the knee. Some nerve damage above. How soon can a surgeon be fetched?'

Faced with a practical problem they both straightened and looked at each other.

'Hawkins?' said my father.

Dr Stephens pursed his lips. 'Thompson lives nearer.'

'Aye, but Hawkins is the better surgeon.'

'You are right. Though I am not sure he will care to be roused in the middle of the night.' Dr Stephens turned to me. 'Can we wait until tomorrow?'

'No,' I said firmly. 'It must be done at once.'

'Very well.' Dr Stephens got stiffly to his feet, grunting a little. He had broken his leg badly the previous year and it still gave him trouble when he was tired. 'I'll send one of the servants for him.' He hobbled away.

'We'll prepare the patient,' I called after him. I looked at my father. 'I think we should move him out of the ward. The rest of the men are in a poor state already. No need to distress them more.'

'You are right, but where can we put him? Every corner of the hospital is full.'

'The governors' meeting room?' I said.

He made a face. 'I don't think the governors would care for that.'

'Need they know? Even the assistant superintendant is not here tonight. We can move him back after the surgery.'

He nodded. 'Very well. We can only be dismissed, after all!'

My father went to arrange the room while I returned to the ward. Peter was talking quietly to the fair haired young man, so I quickly treated the last two patients in the row of pallets, who had only minor injuries, then Peter fetched three of the men servants to help him carry the patient to the governors' meeting room. Between them they lifted him, pallet and all, and carried it out of the ward.

I walked alongside and took the soldier's hand. 'What's your name?' I asked.

'It's William, doctor,' he said in a resigned voice. 'William Baker.'

'Do you have family in London?' I had realised that he would need someone to care for him when he left the hospital. If he left it alive. On the other hand, if he did not survive the surgery – and there was every chance that he might not – we would tell his family.

'I have a sister living in Eastcheap,' he said. 'Bess Winterly. Her man is a saddler and leatherworker.'

'Good,' I said. 'I will go to see her tomorrow. Now, the surgery will be painful, I'll not lie to you, but we are fetching the best surgeon in London. And we will dose you well with poppy extract to help the pain.'

He gave a slight nod, but I could read his terror in his eyes. I felt sick myself with apprehension, although I knew I had made the right decision. If the leg was not amputated, he would be dead in days. This way, at least he had some chance of life.

Once I had seen William Baker installed on the table in the governors' room, I went back to the ward. I had given him as much poppy juice as I dared, but I did not wait to watch the butchery when the surgeon arrived. Not for nothing do soldiers call them 'saw-bones'. Peter stayed to fetch or prepare any medicines the surgeon might need. I supposed my father and Dr Stephens had also stayed. Four of the male servants would hold William down while Surgeon Hawkins sawed off the leg.

The ward was quieter now. After the pain of having their wounds dressed, and the comfort of food, most of the soldiers had fallen into the deep sleep of absolute exhaustion. During the siege, as well as suffering from starvation and thirst, they would barely have been able to sleep for weeks on end. The besiegers would have kept up a constant barrage of cannon fire, rotating their gun crews by day and by night, the purpose as much to undermine the strength and will of the defenders as to demolish the town ramparts. Well, Parma had succeeded in that. He was famed as the most skilled military commander alive, perhaps as great as Caesar or Alexander. That, I could not judge, but certainly we had no one who could match him. I knew that Walsingham thought well of Sir John Norreys, but even he could not compare to the Duke of Parma. Just because Leicester was the Queen's favourite courtier, it did not make him even a barely competent commander. Throughout the whole campaign in the Low Countries, he had displayed weakness, indecision and cowardice. In the present case, cowardice above all. Even his last minute deployment of fireships had proved a ridiculous failure, when Parma had turned them back against the English fleet.

I made my way quietly along the rows of sleeping men, stopping now and then to comfort and reassure any who were awake and in pain. Andrew was sleeping and I paused for a moment at the foot of his pallet. Asleep, he looked younger than I remembered from last year, when we had gone spying into the fishing village on the Sussex coast. Then he had seemed altogether the confident young trooper, cheerfully enjoying our escapade away from the senior men who commanded us. Now he looked no more than a sick boy, his face pale below the bandages, one hand under his head, the other curled loosely on his chest like a child's. If no infection entered the head wound, I was fairly certain he would make a good recovery. Whether he would ever regain that same carefree enjoyment of life, I was less sure.

After I had checked all the patients, including our regular patients who had already been in the hospital when the soldiers arrived, I sat down on a bench near the door of the ward. There was barely room for my feet, without kicking the patient lying nearest to me on the floor, so I tucked them under the bench and leaned my head back against the wall. I did not mean to close my eyes, but my lids felt as though some irresistible force were dragging them down. There was nothing more I could do for the moment and we were now at that graveyard watch of the night, that time when most souls flee from the body. Yet, curiously, also that time when babies fight their way into the world, as if God were holding up some celestial balance – so many souls out, so many souls in. I half smiled, feeling myself tremble on that border between waking and sleep. Had I discovered some new theological or physical truth? So many souls out, so many souls in.

I woke with a jerk and a shooting pain in my neck, as the door beside me was pushed open and four of the hospital servants carried in William Baker on his pallet, one to each corner. In the flickering light from the sconce on the wall above me, I could see that the leg was gone. William was in a dead swoon and the pallet was soaking with blood. I turned to Peter, who had followed them in. He was looking very green and his hands were shaking.

'Peter, he must have fresh bedding. He cannot lie on that. Are there any more pallets to be had?'

'I'll see what I can find.' He turned away, clearly glad of an excuse to escape.

'And blankets,' I said. 'He will be cold from the shock. The mistress of the nurses should have some.' Suddenly aware that it was not yet dawn, I added, 'If she is still awake.'

'I think I know where they are kept,' he said. 'If not, I will wake her.'

'Brave man,' I said, and he gave me a shaky smile.

'I could dare anything, after that.'

'Was it as bad as I suppose?'

'Worse. I thought the poor bugger was going to die of the pain under our eyes.'

'I gave him as much poppy as I dared.'

'I know. I don't think a barrelful would have helped. It was terrible, Kit.'

I nodded. 'Once you have found some bedding and helped me make him comfortable, you should go to bed.'

'Little point now,' he said, gesturing towards the window, which had changed from black to the first lighter tinge of grey while we had been speaking.

The servants had deposited William in the empty space where he had lain before. There was nowhere else to put him. As soon as it was light I was determined to turn Goodman Watkins out of his bed and send him home, so William could have his bed. It would be too cruel to keep an amputee lying on the floor. I stood looking down at him. Unlike Andrew, he looked older, his face ashen with pain, the skin drawn tight over his cheekbones as though it had somehow shrunk. He had bitten his lips till they bled, so while I waited for Peter, I bathed his face and spread a little honey on his ravaged mouth. He did not even stir. It was the best thing for him. While the mind is deep asleep, the body can take its chance to mend itself.

When Peter returned, we struggled to lift William on to the clean pallet. The servants had retreated as soon as they had deposited him on the floor and there was very little room to move. In the end we managed to shift the men on either side a little way, so that we could lay the fresh pallet next to him. Then I took his shoulders and Peter – with nervous hesitation – took his remaining leg. We managed to lift him across. Then Peter removed the old pallet, which was so sodden it dripped blood along the floor as he carried it away. I tucked the two blankets around the soldier, taking care to avoid the stump, which had been cauterised and bound tightly to stop any further bleeding. Peter had even managed to find a small cushion, which I eased under William's head. He moaned as I did so, and his eyelids fluttered, but did not open.

When I stood up, I saw that my father had returned with Peter and stood talking quietly to him near the door, so I went to join them.

'Dr Stephens has gone home,' my father said. 'One of us at least should get some sleep.'

'I've told Peter to do the same,' I said. I turned to him. 'You have a room in the hospital, don't you?'

Peter was an orphan, with no family that he knew of. When he had come to St Bartholomew's as a young servant, one of the licensed apothecaries, James Weatherby, had noticed his skill and intelligence, and took him on as an apprentice. I knew he had a room somewhere up in the attics.

'Aye,' he said, 'but will I not be needed here?'

My father shook his head. 'Master Weatherby is still here. He has said you may go.'

With that, Peter nodded to us and went off toward the staircase which led to the attics. Instead of his usual brisk step he plodded like an old man, hardly able to put one foot in front of another.

'You should go home as well, Kit,' my father said.

I shook my head. 'I am so tired that I'm no longer tired. I feel like a swimmer come up for air.'

Even as I said it, I had a sudden flash of memory. My sister Isabel and my brother Felipe and I, swimming in the stream that ran beside the meadow at my grandfather's *solar*, his estate in the foothills some miles above Coimbra. We used to dare each other to stay under water as long as we could, but we would pop up at last, breaking the surface like corks, gasping and laughing.

'Caterina?' My father was looking at me oddly, for I must have seemed far away.

'Ssh!' I said, glancing over my shoulder. There was no one near but the sleeping soldiers. That was twice tonight he had risked giving me away. Fatigue was making him incautious. 'Be careful, Father.'

He passed a tired hand over his face. 'I am sorry, Kit. It has been a long and weary night.'

'It has. If anyone should go home, it is you.'

'No, no. We will both stay on until Dr Stephens returns in the morning. Though I don't think we will be needed. They are mostly asleep. Thomas Derby will be back in the morning.'

Thomas was Dr Stephens's assistant, as I was my father's. He had been away for three days, fetching a shipment of supplies from Dover.

'I am going to watch over William Baker,' I said.

'Who?' My father had not caught the name before.

'The amputee. And there was that one soldier with the high fever, up at the top end of the ward. He may need more febrifuge tincture.'

'Aye, you are right. I will sit up there, in case he wakes.'

Although the first fading of the night had shown in the window, the rest of the time seemed to drag sluggishly on to dawn. I found a stool which I could fit between the rows of men beside William Baker and sat there, willing myself to stay awake. I knew if I sat where I could lean against the wall, I would fall asleep again. Even so, several times my head fell forward till my chin hit my chest and a sharp stab in my spine woke me just as I drifted into sleep. I could make out my father dimly at the far end of the ward, seated, as I had been before, with his back propped against the wall. I hoped he would be able to doze a little, for he was showing his age, and was a little frail these days, however he tried to put on a brave face.

At last the long rectangles of the windows grew a paler grey, then gradually took on a tinge of pink, about the same time as I heard some of the town roosters beginning to greet the day. I wasn't often awake as early as this. I could see, in the growing light, that my father was asleep. I was stiff with sitting so long on the hard stool, so I stood up and stretched, then slipped out of the ward and out of the hospital itself. In the courtyard the air smelled wonderfully fresh after the stench of so many sick and wounded bodies crowded together, and I drew in deep lungfuls of it. One of the hospital cats, kept to chase away any rats and mice from the storerooms, was washing himself in a pale yellow patch of morning sun, licking first one hind leg and then the other with meticulous care. Catching sight of me, he strolled over with the nonchalant benevolence of a monarch and rubbed against my leg. I tickled him behind the ears and was rewarded with a throaty rumble. When he stalked off on business of his own, I returned to the hospital, where the nursing sisters were just coming to take up their duties. Tonight we must make sure that some stayed in the wards over night, for the extra numbers we had taken in were going to need care and feeding.

When I reached the ward, I saw that my father was awake and so were some of the patients. Together, we got Goodman Watson out of his bed and dressed, and told him firmly that he was quite well enough to go home, despite his peevish protests. Then we sent for some of the men servants to lift William Baker into the vacated bed. He was still unconscious, but there was no bleeding from the stump of his leg. We could only pray that the surgeon had operated in time and that the gangrene would not spread any further.

The serving women brought porridge and small ale for the patients and we went round the ward, deciding whether any of the men were able to leave. Very few were well enough. Even those with less serious injuries were so weak from starvation that their recovery would be slow, so in the end we only sent three away, all of them with homes in London. When I came to Andrew, I saw that his fever had abated somewhat, but his skin was still dry and hot.

'How do you find yourself this morning?' I asked.

'Better,' he said. 'Last night it felt as though a blacksmith was hammering on the inside of my skull. Now it's just a tinsmith.'

He grinned at me and I smiled back. This was more like the old Andrew.

'Well, once there's only a sparrow pecking there, we'll let you go home and try to grow your hair over that groove in your skull.'

'Aye, I noticed you chopped away my locks last night.'

'You wouldn't want them sticking to the wound, I promise you. Where is your home?'

'Gloucestershire. But I won't go home, I'll go back to my barracks in Dover.'

'You won't be fit for duty yet awhile.'

'Tell my commander that.'

'If it is the same commander as last year, he seemed a sensible man.'

'No, he has been transferred to the Low Countries. We have a regular Tartar of a fellow now.'

'Then we will send a letter with you, saying that you are not fit for work for another three weeks. Three weeks *after* we release you.'

'You make the hospital sound like prison.'

'You'd not be fed so well in any prison I've heard of. It is one of the provisions of Barts, to feed the patients well. Make the most of it. Here is your breakfast coming. I'm off home myself soon, but I will see you later today.'

He looked at me seriously for the first time. 'I thank you for your care, Kit. You had a terrible night of it last night. How is that poor lad, William?'

I didn't realise he had been aware of what had happened.

'So far, he seems well enough. It's a bad shock to the body, an amputation.'

'It's a fearful thing. The army will turn him away and forget that he lost his leg serving his country. It's a cruel world out there for a one-legged man.'

'I know. I am going to find his sister today and tell her what has happened.' It was a task I was not looking forward to.

'Well, it is good he has a sister. I hope she is a loving one.' There was a touch of bitterness in his tone, but I did not probe him.

'Eat your breakfast and then rest. Sleep is the best healer.'

63

'It isn't easy on this b'yer lady floor,' he said, moving his shoulders irritably. I realised his dislocated shoulder would still be giving him pain, as well as the injury to his head.

'I know, but we weren't expecting four hundred extra patients. Now eat. I will come to see you later.'

Dr Stephens was talking to my father, who gestured to me that we should leave. I checked once more on William Baker, but he had not woken. However, his sleep seemed more natural now. I found myself yawning as if my jaw would break. Time to go home and to bed myself.

When I woke in my own bed I was momentarily confused by the broad swathe of light falling across the room. Then I remembered why I was still abed so late. I threw back the covers and rubbed my eyes. Although I had slept well, I still felt the exhaustion and horrors of the night before. I knew that when I returned to the hospital I would find that some of the soldiers had died while I was away, and others would be in a worse state than yesterday, not better.

I dressed slowly, my fingers fumbling with garters and buttons. Even in this warm summer weather I wore a doublet, for it was the best garment for concealing my shape and keeping up my pretence. I was still thin and flat-chested, though my breasts were beginning to swell. The time might come when I would need to bind them.

Down in the kitchen I found Joan on her knees, scrubbing the floor. She looked up at me, pushing a stray lock of hair out of her eyes.

'Your father has gone this half hour, but he said I was to let you sleep. And he said you had some errand in Eastcheap, so not to go to the hospital until that was done. Dr Stephens's assistant will have returned.'

'Aye, thank you, Joan. Is there anything to eat?'

'Bread and cheese and apples. Or do you want me to cook something?' She looked pointedly around at the half of the floor not yet scrubbed.

'No, no. This will suit.'

I picked my way over her bucket and brush. Putting a piece of cheese and two apples on a plate, and adding a chunk of bread which I spread with honey, I carried my breakfast outside and sat on the step to eat it, out of the way of her scrubbing. I was not looking forward to finding William Baker's sister, but I had promised, so I must go.

The city was busy. Pushing along the roads, blocking the way for carters and the occasional horseman, the crowds were making the most of the late summer sun, shopping or gossiping. Apprentice boys in their blue tunics lounged in groups at street corners, as if they had no work to do. One man led a sad looking bear on a chain and stopped from time to time, playing on a pipe to make the creature dance. The poor beast had had his claws torn out and his coat was patched with mange. There were scars of old fights on his muzzle, so I guessed he was one of the old creatures from the bear pits. If they survive but become reluctant to put on a show, the owners will sell them off cheap. A bear keeper like this man would render the bear harmless by removing his claws and most of his teeth, then make him dance for a living. This one was unwilling. He rose up on his hind legs and shuffled his feet a few steps, then sank down on his haunches and refused to move. His keeper tucked his pipe in his waistband and began lashing the bear viciously with a whip, cursing him the while.

Most people simply walked past but I stopped and caught hold of the man's whip arm. 'I will give you a shilling if you will give me your whip and buy food for yourself and your animal.'

I could see that the man himself was gaunt with hunger and had a withered leg. He looked at me as if I were mad, his mouth hanging open. I don't suppose anyone had ever given him more than a penny before. I held up two sixpenny pieces in one hand and reached out my other hand for the whip. Still gaping he grabbed the coins and bit them to be sure they were genuine.

'The whip,' I said.

He shrugged and handed it to me. I knew he would soon be able to get another, but at least they would both eat and the bear would be spared a whipping for the moment.

'Be sure and feed the bear as well,' I said.

'Aye,' he growled. 'I'm no fool. He's my livelihood.'

I left him staring at me as I walked away. The whip I snapped into four pieces and threw into the Fleet River.

There were three saddlers and leatherworking shops in Eastcheap. At the first one I was told that Jake Winterly's shop was across the street and a hundred yards further on, at the sign of the Brown Bull and Scissors. I found the sign – a remarkably placid looking bull standing next to an enormous pair of scissors, as tall as he was. The door stood open, as did most doors in the street, to let in a little air on this hot day, and the counter was folded down from the front of the shop. Over the top I could see a woman and a small boy moving about inside, setting out a row of leather beer tankards along a shelf.

'Mistress Winterly?' I said as I walked in.

She turned and smiled at me, a plump, rosy-faced woman of about forty. The boy was about seven or eight and had the same yellow curls as William.

'Aye, sir. That's me. What can I do for you?' She came forward, wiping her hands, which looked perfectly clean, on her apron.

There was no point weaving about the subject. Best to get it over with.

'I am a doctor at St Bartholomew's,' I said. 'Your brother, William Baker, was brought in yesterday.'

Her hand flew to her mouth to stifle a faint cry and she sank down on a bench.

'Was he one of those at Sluys, sir? We couldn't be sure. Last we heard, he was posted to Dover. He's a poor hand at writing letters.'

'I don't suppose many letters made their way out of Sluys,' I said, 'except official despatches slipped out by a few brave messengers. Aye, he's one of the survivors.'

'Oh, Jesu be praised!' She had gone quite white. Now her face flushed again. 'Will, go and fetch your father.'

The boy ran to a curtain which covered the door to the back shop and slipped through.

'Please, sir, take a seat. I've been that worried, not knowing whether he had been sent with those men to the Low Countries, or whether he was in that terrible siege. Is he hurt?'

I sat down on a three-legged stool facing her. 'I think all of those who survived were hurt. They made a brave stand to the very end.' I was more reluctant than ever to break the news.

'William was always determined to be a soldier. Our father was a saddler, and Jake – that's my man – was his journeyman. We wanted William to stay in the business, but there was nothing for it but he must become a soldier. He said that way he would see the world. He couldn't go for a sailor, for he'd be sick just in a wherry crossing the Thames.' She gave an indulgent sister's chuckle. 'And then, after all, he's spent most of his time guarding the Tower or down at Dover castle. I don't suppose he saw much of the world down in Kent.'

She seemed to have forgotten her question in her memories of her brother, and I was uncertain how to answer it now, but at that moment a big man pushed the curtain aside and stepped into the shop. Like his wife he was at least fifteen years older than William Baker, his hair already grizzled at the temples. I noticed that his hands were stained from the leather dyes. I stood up and made a slight bow.

'Master Winterly? I am Christoval Alvarez, a physician at St Bartholomew's. I have brought word of your brother-in-law.'

He bowed his head, then moved swiftly to his wife's side and laid his hand on her shoulder.

'He's one of the men from Sluys?' he said. 'I saw them being carried off the ship yesterday. How bad is William?'

I swallowed. 'His leg had been smashed by a Spanish cannon ball several weeks ago. I don't suppose they had much medical care in the garrison. When I saw him last night, he had developed gangrene.'

The woman pressed both hands to her mouth and tears welled up in her eyes.

'Is he dead?' The man's tone was not abrupt. I could see that he just needed to know the worst, without any more hesitation.

'We had to amputate,' I said. 'We fetched the best surgeon in London. Master Hawkins. He thinks it is clean now, and when I left the hospital early this morning, William was sleeping peacefully. But I am sure you understand. Until the leg has healed, we cannot be sure the gangrene will not return.'

The woman was weeping openly now, but silently, covering her face with her apron. I saw her husband tighten his grip on her shoulder. The child had slipped behind her and was looking first at his father and then at me.

The man cleared his throat. 'So he will be crippled. The army will throw him out.'

'Aye.' I wasn't prepared to lie to these people. I could see that they wanted the truth. 'Otherwise, he is unharmed. If he recovers, as I hope he will, he will be able to get about on crutches, but certainly he can no longer be a soldier.'

I left it hanging in the air. The woman lifted her tear stained face from her apron and looked up at her husband. Neither said anything, but he gave a small nod.

'William will come here,' he said, 'once he is able to leave the hospital. There is plenty of work that he can do. The navy is needing ale jacks and scabbards and quivers and the Saints only know what else.'

'Uncle William can share your room, Will,' the woman said, 'and he can tell you all about his adventures. Won't that be grand?'

The child nodded solemnly, then suddenly grinned. I realised that the family probably lived in the cramped quarters above the shop, but their warmth warmed me and I suddenly felt a flood of relief. This had not been quite the ordeal I had dreaded. I stood up.

'If you would like to visit William,' I said, 'I think it would do him good.' I was sure the knowledge that he would have a home and an occupation, to come to when he left the hospital, would help him recover as much as anything I could do.

'I'll come now!' The woman sprang to her feet and rubbed her face dry on her apron. 'Will, you must mind the shop for Mama – can you so that?'

The child, flushed with pride, nodded.

'Are you going back to the hospital now, Doctor? May I walk with you?'

'Certainly.'

As she took off her apron and fetched her hat from a hook at the back of the shop, I turned to her husband. 'Thank you, Master Winterly,' I said, barely above a whisper. 'That is the best medicine I can bring him. He is near despair.'

'He need not despair.' His voice was as soft as mine. 'There will always be a home for him here.'

Mistress Winterly and I crossed the city together, saying little. In her anxiety to see her brother she walked hurriedly, almost breaking into a run from time to time, then, recalling herself, slowed down again.

'Forgive me, Doctor,' she said. 'I am afraid that, if I don't hurry . . .'

'Nothing to forgive,' I said. 'But do not be afraid. There was no sign of the gangrene this morning. I am sure he will be alive when we get there.'

I hoped I was speaking the truth. Sometimes it can happen, after a very severe injury, or an amputation, that a patient may simply die of shock. It is as if the heart cannot endure any more. But William was young and, apart from his injury and the privations of the siege, he was probably strong enough. Yet sometimes, too, a mind full of despair can end a man's life, if he no longer wants to live.

The ward was not much changed from last night, though several of the regular patients had been sent home and the most badly injured of the soldiers moved into their beds. There was a little more space between the pallets on the floor. Clearly the mistress of the nursing sisters had stood firm against any women of the neighbourhood being allowed near the patients, but some of the sewing women were assisting and the women servants were just clearing away the midday meal.

I led Mistress Winterly over to William's bed. To my relief, he was still there. I had feared we might find him dead already. He lay quite still, his eyes closed, his face very pale. When I laid my hand on his brow I could find no trace of fever, which augured well. I fetched a stool and placed it beside the bed.

'Sit here,' I said. 'Take care not to lean on the bed. He will still be feeling much pain.'

Dr Stephens's assistant, Thomas Derby, came across to us.

'How is he faring, Thomas?' I asked.

'Quiet. No sign of fever yet.' He glanced at Mistress Winterly and raised his eyebrows in question.

'This is his sister, come to see him.'

'I doubt if he will wake.'

At that moment William stirred and gave a soft moan. I leaned over him. His breathing was regular, but a look of agony passed over his face like a wave and his eyes opened. He stared at me until his eyes focused.

'Doctor?'

'You are doing well, William. And see, I have brought your sister to see you. She has much to tell you.'

As we had walked, I had warned her not to weep over him, if she could forebear. I saw now with what courage she smiled cheerfully.

'Well, William, how good it is to see you at last! You are to come to us when you leave the hospital. Jake needs your help, for we are quite overwhelmed with business. So you see, you must get well, for our sake. I do not know how we can manage without you.'

I saw an incredulous look come over William's face and he reached out to take his sister's hand. I jerked my head at Thomas and we retreated.

'That is one fellow who is likely to recover,' he said. 'That's a brave woman. Does she know?'

'Aye, she knows.'

I went the rounds of my more seriously injured patients. The young boy with the crushed hand was in a high fever, but I managed to dribble some of the febrifuge tincture into his mouth, although he thrashed about and spilt much of it. The hand was still very inflamed, so I salved it again, but did not remove the splints I had fixed the night before. They were still in place and were best not disturbed. He had been moved to a bed and next to him was Andrew.

'And how do you find yourself today?' I said, perched on the edge of his bed and unwinding the dressing on his head. It was a relief not to have to kneel on the floor to do it.

'Still the tinsmiths in here,' he said, tapping the uninjured side of his head. 'Ouch, Kit, don't tear my scalp off as well!'

'Don't squall like an infant,' I said. I leaned over and sniffed the long gouge that ran above his ear. 'No nasty smells, you'll be glad to know. The ear is healing already. And the rest is beginning to dry up. It looks better than it did yesterday, even in this bright sunlight. You'll live.'

'That's good to know. So I'll soon be fit to be sent back to the Low Countries.'

I looked at him soberly as I rebandaged his head. 'Is that what will happen, do you think?'

He shrugged, and winced at the pain in his shoulder. 'Either that or fighting the Spanish at sea. Everything depends on what King Philip intends.'

'Aye. Well, Drake has bought us some time.'

'They will come some time next year,' he said with conviction. 'That is why they wanted to take Sluys. Parma is establishing his bases all along the coast of the Low Countries, facing us across the Channel. I believe they will send their army across from there, while the Spanish navy comes up from the west. Snipping us like a pair of shears.'

I nodded. 'That is what Walsingham believes as well. And he says we must defeat them at sea.'

Andrew nodded, then regretted it and put a hand to his brow. 'I forgot. I must not do that. Aye, your master is right. On land we have no hope. We trained soldiers are so few.' He cast a look around at the patients lying on the floor. 'A thousand fewer now. No, our only hope is our navy.'

'And will you be posted on shore?' I asked.

'Oh, no. We will be aboard the ships, ready to fight if we can board theirs, though I expect most of the fighting will be a cannon shot apart. We'll use our archers, of course, both to attack their crews and to shoot fire arrows. The rest of us have our muskets.'

I shivered. 'And then it will be left to us to put you all back together again.'

He gave a grim smile. 'Let us hope we both survive long enough to do just that.'

Chapter Five

It was the end of September before the hospital was back to normal. Perhaps fifty of the soldiers were sufficiently recovered to be sent home at the end of a week or two, but most needed to stay much longer. Some died and their bodies were either claimed by their families or else they went to a pauper's grave in the old churchyard where once they had buried the monks who had inhabited the priory of St Bartholomew. A few of the soldiers who seemed at first to have nothing but minor injuries proved to have more serious troubles, internal injuries or prolonged sickness brought about by the long weeks of siege and starvation. Then there were those whose injuries were known to be serious from the start.

The first soldier I had treated was one of those who proved to have hidden problems. His leg began to heal almost at once, but a week had passed before he confessed to pains in his chest. He told us that he had been hit in the side by a large piece of stone struck off the ramparts by a cannon ball. He admitted to bruises, but only later did we discover that he had broken three ribs. He had endured severe pain in silence before we found the cause, and he remained with us for several weeks.

To my relief and joy, the young boy with the crushed hand recovered well. He would bear the scars all his life, but he regained almost the full use of his fingers, although the smallest one remained twisted. He was claimed by his grandmother, a tiny woman who barely reached my shoulder, but whose energy burst from her like sparks from a bonfire. She bore him away, alternately scolding him and hugging him, while the lad blushed and hung his head as he walked past his grinning fellows.

'Did I not warn you, you great gormless lad?' she was saying as they passed through the door. 'Playing soldiers! Nothing good could come of it. You'll come home with me and tend the cows. That hand of your will soon be strong enough for milking. Playing soldiers, indeed!'

They were gone before I could hear his reply, if he dared to open his mouth at all to break in on her affectionate scolding.

Peter looked at me and grinned.

Bess Winterly came every day to visit her brother and after a few days brought her son with her. The child was subdued at first, looking around at all the wounded soldiers with round eyes, but by his third or fourth visit he was chattering to them and sharing out the cakes and sweetmeats his mother carried in every day in her basket. Our patients were well fed at St Bartholomew's, but it was plain, hearty fare. I never saw any of the men refuse Bess's treats. I was surprised that she brought the child, but one day, when he was beside Andrew's bed, learning how to weave a cat's cradle with his fingers and a length of string, she explained.

'I don't want my Will getting romantic ideas like his uncle about going for a soldier. I thought if he saw how these men have been injured, he would understand better. We want him to be apprenticed to Jake and learn a good trade.'

I nodded my understanding and thought of the small, fierce grandmother. We women are clear eyed about war while so many men seem blinded by talk of honour and glory. Yet I could hardly say so to Bess without revealing too much. So I said only, 'It is physicians and surgeons who must try to repair their bodies and give them their lives back. I hope you succeed with Will.'

She smiled at me. 'We are grateful for what you have done for William, Doctor.'

'Your visits have done him more good than I. And given him hope for the future. Tomorrow we will let him try out the crutches our carpenter has made.'

William Baker was one of the last of the soldiers to leave. The stump of his severed leg healed cleanly and there was no further sign of gangrene. I was sure that he healed the better for having laid aside his despair. It took him days to learn to manage the crutches, but he was determined, and eventually could hop across the ward unaided. When the time came for him to leave, Jake Winterly came along with his wife to take William home. He had borrowed a cart, for the distance across London was much too far for a one-legged man just learning to walk. Several of us from the hospital came to see them off from the hospital gatehouse, with young Will sitting proudly beside his father at the reins.

'You will visit us, Doctor, won't you?' William leaned down to shake my hand.

'Aye, I'll come to see how you are faring.' I decided that in a week or two I would order a leather belt from the shop, specifying that it must be made by William.

Andrew was also one of the last to leave. Although the wound in his head healed cleanly, and his ear was only slightly scarred, he still suffered persistent pains in the head and had moments of dizziness and disturbed vision. I was worried that there might have been some damage to his skull. I could find no fracture, but there might have been a crack beneath the skin, too fine to be found by probing. I consulted my father and Dr Stephens about it.

'Aye, there could be some hurt done to the skull, though it clearly has not broken through enough to harm the brain,' Dr Stephens said, after feeling all around the scar, where the new skin showed pink and fragile.

'Sometimes a blow like that can lead to bruising of the brain,' said my father, when he had asked Andrew to describe how his sight was affected – occasionally seeing objects doubled, and what looked like zigzags of lightning across his vision.

'That can often be a precursor to a severe headache, what we call a migraine,' my father explained. 'Do they occur before the onset of your headaches? And do you feel any sickness?'

'Aye,' Andrew said slowly. 'Now you ask, the flashes do come an hour or two before the headaches. And I do feel sick sometimes.'

'You have vomited at least once,' I reminded him. I looked at my father. 'Feverfew?'

'Aye. See whether Peter can find you some fresh in the stillroom or the herb garden.'

'There should be some still growing at this time of year,' I agreed. 'It is better fresh than the dried.'

I turned back to Andrew. 'You can eat it like a salad herb. Slightly bitter, but not unpleasant.'

He looked at my father. 'Will they get better? The headaches, and the other troubles to my sight?'

'Aye. It may take time, but they will get better, if you give yourself a chance to recover. No returning to army duties yet a while.'

So Andrew stayed on until we were satisfied that the headaches were no longer so severe and he had no further spells of dizziness. He left the same day as William.

'Well, Kit,' he said, as we stood under the gatehouse. 'We part again. I'll make my way back to Dover and report for duty.' He patted the front of his army tunic, washed and mended by our sewing women. 'I'm glad to have this letter from your father to give the commander, else I'd probably be in irons on bread and water for staying away so long.'

'Don't let him set you to anything too strenuous at first,' I said, without much hope.

He laughed. 'You don't know our commander. And next summer we will all be on very active service, I fear, when the Spanish dogs come.'

'Good luck to you,' I said.

'And to you, Kit.' He clapped me on the shoulder, swung his pack on to his back, and went off toward Newgate, striding out energetically and not looking back.

Twice during the time we were caring for the wounded soldiers from Sluys I had received messages from Phelippes, brought by Thomas Cassie, that he needed my help, but both times I had written back saying firmly that I could not be spared at the hospital. I reminded him of his own words, that it was essential that we patch up all our soldiers as best we could, for they would be needed when the invasion came. In November, however, a more urgent message arrived, saying that Sir Francis himself wished to see me. I no longer had the excuse of the soldiers and indeed matters were quiet at the hospital, the usual bouts of winter illness not having started yet.

75

'Very well,' I said to Cassie. 'I will come back with you.' As often before, he had come to our house at midday, knowing that it was our practice to go home for dinner on days when the work at the hospital was not too demanding.

'You will not need me this afternoon?' I looked at my father.

He shook his head. 'Best see what it is that Sir Francis wants.'

The weather had already turned colder, so I threw a cloak over my doublet, and put an apple in my pocket, hoping I might have a chance to call in to Walsingham's stables and see Hector. I tucked a pair of gloves into my belt. If Phelippes or Sir Francis kept me late, it would be even colder walking home. I was wearing the new belt made by William Baker, which he had insisted on giving me. It was made of a fine, supple leather and he had tooled it all over with Tudor roses, intertwined with ivy. Jake Winterly had not made a bad bargain, taking in his brother-in-law. And it was work William could do sitting down. He had flatly refused payment.

'I know I am alive now because you fetched a surgeon so quickly.' He gave me a pallid smile. 'I didn't think so at the time. In fact I hated you for it, putting me through all that pain, when all I wanted to do was die. But you were right and I was wrong. So I'd like you to have the belt, by way of apology.'

As Cassie and I walked along Eastcheap now, we passed the sign of the Black Bull and Scissors, where young Will waved to me from the doorway. I told Cassie the story of William Baker.

He shook his head. 'I wonder just how many more William Bakers there are, over there in the Low Countries. Those men from Sluys, they were lucky to be brought home. Most of our men fighting there have little care, only what an army surgeon can give, and I doubt that's much.'

'You are right,' I said. 'If Sir Philip Sidney had been brought home, we might have been able to save him, but perhaps he was too gravely injured to survive the journey.'

'Have you heard that the commander at Sluys, Sir Roger Williams, was himself wounded in the arm? He came home destitute, not even able to buy a horse. And because the town was surrendered, he is deemed to have failed, though the failure was Leicester's, who stayed offshore and did not come to his aid.'

'So I suppose,' I said, 'there will be no pension for Sir Roger from the Queen, or any recognition that they held out for nearly two months, waiting for reinforcements to come, until they had nothing left to eat and no gunpowder to fight with.'

He shook his head, then gave a wry smile. 'My lady Walsingham advised Sir Roger to marry a rich merchant's widow instead, and he says he may take her advice.'

I laughed ruefully. 'Well, I wish there were enough rich widows to go round all the lads we treated. Otherwise most of them have no future but to go back and fight again. Next time they may not survive.'

Going up the backstairs at Seething Lane, I met Nicholas Berden coming down. One of Walsingham's most experienced agents, he was a man I had worked with in the final days of rounding up the Babington conspirators, more than a year ago now.

'Good day to you, Kit,' he said, pausing briefly in his rapid descent. 'Busy times. Phelippes will be glad to see you.'

'Busy?' I said.

'The pace is quickening. The Spanish shipwrights are working night and day, and the king's emissaries are buying up most of Europe in provisions and weapons.' He shook his head. 'What it is, to have a bottomless purse!'

'Aye,' I said, 'not something we are familiar with in England. Is Sir Francis in his office?'

'He is. I believe he has some project for you.' With that he sketched a quick bow and hurried on down the stairs.

My heart sank. Some project? I did not care for the sound of that. If Phelippes needed me for code-breaking and translating, Berden would not have called it a project. The previous year Sir Francis had used me in a few spying missions, but I hoped he was not planning to do so again. I had heard nothing more of the Catholic Fitzgerald family, after he had placed me to spy on them. The mission with Phelippes to Sussex, however, where I had first met Andrew amongst our accompanying escort of troopers, had led to the discovery of two enemies of the Queen entering the country illegally. Afterwards, Walsingham had

77

disguised me as a messenger from one of them to Sir Anthony Babington himself. To my sorrow, I had found I liked Babington, as I had liked most of the Fitzgeralds, so I dreaded being employed as a spy again. The word project was loaded with uncomfortable possibilities.

'Enter!' Sir Francis called when I knocked on his door.

'Ah, Kit! Come in, come in.' Sir Francis rose from the chair behind his desk and came round to where two chairs were drawn near the fire.

I did not like the signs. If it had been a brief instruction, he would have stayed behind his desk. Sitting in this friendly fashion beside the fire betokened something worse.

'Hang your cloak on the peg over there,' he said. 'You'll take a glass of wine?'

'Thank you.' It was rare for me to taste anything but small ale or occasionally beer. If this was going to be a difficult interview I would at least wash it down with a glass of Sir Francis's excellent wine, which he probably obtained through the trading links of Dr Nuñez or Dunstan Añez. I took my seat and accepted the glass he handed to me. As I held it up to the firelight it glowed as rich red as one of the Queen's rubies.

'Your health, Kit!'

'And yours, sir.'

We sipped our wine as he questioned me carefully about my work with the survivors of Sluys.

'A dreadful episode,' he said, 'and not one to our credit.'

'It was to the credit of the men who held out there,' I said stiffly. 'If you could have seen, as I did, what they suffered—'

'That is not what I meant,' he said quietly. 'I do not blame them. I have had a detailed account of the siege from Sir Roger Williams. Indeed he stayed with us for a time. The disgrace lies with those who failed to go to their aid.'

I relaxed. It seemed he was not going to name Leicester, but the name hovered there in the air between us.

'We are still embroiled in the Spanish Netherlands, of course,' he said, 'fighting alongside the Protestants of the United Provinces against the Spanish tyrants. The Queen has agreed to support them, as they are amongst our few allies in Europe, along with the Huguenot faction in France, and some of the German states, and Denmark.'

He took a sip of his wine, staring into the fire, then turned to me.

'The Huguenots have remained weakened since the massacre fifteen years ago, although they have a capable leader in Henri of Navarre. The Germans are hesitant in engaging outside their own borders. Denmark used to be a strong ally, but with the death of her king, the crown has passed to his young son. Neither he nor his counsellors have any taste for resistance against the Spanish at present. Later, perhaps. But in the current crisis, we are on our own with the Hollanders. The Protestant Swiss cantons have flat refused to send us any of their very skilled troops.'

He took another sip of his wine. 'And at the same time we are threatened from the west by the Irish and from the north by those Scots who supported Mary. The Scottish king's Protestant forces may be able to hold them back, north of the border, but our own northern counties have ever been restless since the Queen's grandfather became king.'

I listened attentively to this long speech, reflecting that I had missed my involvement in state affairs in recent months. I began to feel the stirrings of interest. Nevertheless I suppressed a smile at Walsingham's tactful description of Henry VII's seizure of power from Richard of York. The Tudors had only the right of victory in battle to claim the crown of England, and everyone knew it, though no one would speak of it openly. As for the northern counties – by which Walsingham meant Yorkshire, Lancashire, Northumberland, Durham and Cumberland, a vast portion of England – they had never truly accepted the Tudors as monarchs or indeed Henry VIII's break with Rome. I was not sure where all of this was leading.

'I did not know that Denmark was no longer an ally, Sir Francis.'

'Oh, she is still nominally an ally. But we cannot count on her support in fighting the Spanish now, in the Low Countries, nor next year, when the Spanish invasion comes.'

I thought how confidently everyone talked of the invasion next year, as if it were as fixed as the cycle of the seasons. Yet the very thought of it filled me with dread. If the army landed, they would take the country, and once Spain controlled England, the Inquisition would come.

Walsingham pressed his finger tips against his lips.

'You are wondering why I have sent for you, Kit.'

'I thought Master Phelippes must need my assistance, sir, with more code-breaking.' I thought nothing of the sort, especially after that speech of Walsingham's, but I thought I would feign ignorance.

He laughed. 'Ah, Kit, you do not fool me for a minute. You know that it is more than that.'

I reddened and bowed my head, ashamed at my foolish attempt at deception.

'I am sorry, Sir Francis.'

'No, I am sorry, Kit. I will not prevaricate. Her Majesty has received a despatch from the Earl of Leicester which troubles her, and she has passed it on to me. The Earl writes that he is worried about treason and treachery. Not simply the treason and treachery we have been confronting here for years, and which you have helped to combat. He is alarmed that there may be treason and treachery in the Low Countries, either amongst the troops he commands or amongst our Dutch allies. At the moment it is no more than a suspicion. He does not cite any clear evidence.'

I had to bite back my own urge to say that the Earl himself had been guilty of treachery at Sluys, but perhaps it was not so much treachery as pure blinding cowardice. Besides, it was not my place to express such a view to Sir Francis. I waited.

'I am sending out a number of agents to different parts of our forces, to see what they can discover. Berden will go shortly, from Dover to Amsterdam. Gifford – do you remember Gilbert Gifford? – will travel to the Low Countries from Paris, but through Saxony and the Swiss cantons, to avoid notice. He will join the Earl, then move discreetly through the army. Other agents will come up from Italy and some of the German states. I need information from all parts of the army, both our own and our Dutch allies. I need to deploy as many agents as possible, and quickly.'

I continued to wait. I realised I was holding my breath. I had guessed what was coming.

He gave me a shrewd look, as if he could read what was passing through my mind. 'I want you to go as well, Kit.'

'But, sir, I have no experience!' It was the argument I had used the previous year. It had been useless then as well.

'You have some experience now. And what I want you to do is not difficult. You will go initially as a messenger from me to the Earl, carrying despatches. After all, you have played the messenger before.'

'Not in those terrible clothes!' I said. 'I burned them.'

We both laughed, breaking the tension in the room a little. The grubby clothes I had worn as Barnes's supposed messenger boy had been the subject of some mirth last year.

'No, you need not fear. You will go as an official messenger from this office, and may wear your own clothes. You will travel with Berden.'

'You said I would go initially to the Earl.' I realised that the way I phrased this implied acceptance, but I would not give way too readily.

'Aye. In the despatches, I will ask him to give you and Berden any information he may have to confirm his suspicions, though there may be nothing.'

'Perhaps there are no grounds for his suspicions,' I suggested. 'Perhaps he is imagining treason and treachery.' Perhaps, I thought, it is Leicester's way of excusing himself in advance for his next military failure.

'Perhaps,' he said, 'but we cannot be too careful. Afterwards you and Berden will separate and move amongst the troops, like Gifford and the others, keeping your eyes and ears open. When men are at leisure, drinking in ale houses or gaming with their friends, their tongues loosen. That is when secrets slip out. They'll take no notice of a young lad sitting quietly in the shadows.'

A sudden cold terror seized me. As a girl not yet eighteen, I was to consort with these drunken and possibly treacherous soldiers, listening to their secrets and passing them back to Walsingham. I would be in terrible danger. Even if they did not discover that I was Walsingham's agent, they might discover my sex. I found that my hands were shaking. I set down my empty wine glass, shook my head when Sir Francis lifted the flask toward me, then sat on my hands to steady them. At that moment I longed to throw away my disguise. What would Sir Francis say if I stood up now and declared: 'I cannot do as you ask. I am not a young man in your service. I am nothing but a girl and I dare not do what you ask.'

He was watching me carefully. I knew Sir Francis for a very shrewd judge of people and I wondered whether my face had somehow given me away. I cleared my throat.

'I...I would prefer not to go, Sir Francis. I am happy to work here for Master Phelippes. I know that my skills are useful to him. But I do not think I have the skill, the cunning, to do what you ask amongst the troops.'

'I understand that you were on very good terms with the soldiers from Sluys.'

'They were my *patients*, Sir Francis. That was a very different situation.'

'I concede that. But you have shown that you can talk to them easily, they accepted you more readily than the older physicians.'

I wonder who had told him this. Did he have an agent even inside St Bartholomew's?

'Besides,' he said, 'I need a young man to get in amongst the young soldiers, in a way Berden and Gifford and the other older men cannot. I had thought to use Kit Marlowe, who has done this work before, but he has disappeared again.'

The name hit me in the face like the slap of an icy wave.

'Kit Marlowe?' I said, my voice not altogether steady.

'Aye. I believe you met him at Sir Walter's house some months ago.'

Was there nothing this man did not know?

'I did,' I said. Then, daringly, 'I did not like him.'

He smiled grimly. 'I believe he insulted you. You have every reason not to like him. He is not always a likeable fellow. But clever. Very clever. If sometimes rash and sometimes violent.' He paused. 'Will you do this for us, Kit? Berden will be with you for part of the time, and you can always turn to him if you are in difficulty.'

In difficulty? That was a strange way to phrase it. I would be in danger of my life, if there were traitors and if they suspected me. I heaved a great sigh.

'How long would this last?'

'You would be home by Christmas,' he said, and smiled.

Christmas. I remembered last Christmas and the relief of being free of all this secrecy and plotting.

'Very well,' I said with resignation. 'I will go.'

He stood up and reached again for the flask of wine.

'I think you need another glass of this,' he said. 'It is setting in for a frost this evening. Berden had other affairs to attend to today, but he will be here again tomorrow afternoon. If you can be here about two of the clock, we will discuss together how best to proceed. Berden is a good man, very experienced. You have worked with him before.'

'Yes,' I said dully, accepting another glass of wine. 'He is a good man. I would certainly trust him. But we worked together here in England. In a strange country, I don't know . . .'

'All will be well,' he said. 'I have great belief in your talents, Kit.'

Small comfort. Walking home through the frosty night, with the hood of my cloak pulled over my head and my feet plodding slowly over the familiar cobbles, I felt nothing but dread. Yet how could I refuse a man like Sir Francis Walsingham?

By Newgate the chestnut seller stood stamping his feet against the cold. There were no other customers nearby.

'A farthing's worth,' I said, 'and another for the prisoners.'

'Right you are, master,' he said eagerly filling two twists of paper.

I pushed one through the grid to the prisoners. I could see nothing of them but a white blur of faces. Then I walked on, peeling my chestnuts and leaving a trail of shells behind me all the way to Duck Lane. Fond as I am of chestnuts, they turned to dust on my tongue.

The following morning I asked permission to leave the hospital before midday, and it was granted. It seemed that Sir Francis had made his usual arrangement with the governors, and they must have instructed the assistant superintendant, who ran the day-to-day affairs of St Bartholomew's. I also told my father that I would not come home for our usual dinner. I felt a compelling urge to see and talk to Simon. He had called a few times at the hospital while we were treating the soldiers from Sluys, but there had never been time for more than the exchange of a few words. I told myself that I wanted to draw on his experience of acting, as I had done before when undertaking a spying mission for Sir Francis. He was adept at taking on different characters and he would surely be able to give me advice once again. If I had other reasons for this urgent need to see him, I concealed them from myself.

At the Theatre, I found Guy Bingham and James Burbage backstage, seated either side of a wooden packing case, which they were using as a table. They were planning the music and the comic interludes for the next production and looked up distracted when I asked for Simon.

'He hasn't come in yet, Kit,' Guy said. 'Probably still at his lodgings in Holywell Lane.'

James Burbage grunted. 'If you see him, remind him I'll dock his wages if he isn't here in time for rehearsal. Two o'clock sharp. We must run through all the scenes of tomorrow's play before this afternoon's performance of *The Spanish Tragedy*.'

'Let us hope that is a prophetic title,' Guy said, 'for next year.'

Even here in the playhouse I could not escape the foretelling of next year's invasion.

'Where?' I said. 'Which house in Holywell Lane?'

'I thought you would know.' Guy looked surprised. 'Tall thin house, with three jetties, nearly blocking the lane. Yellow front door.'

'*Yellow*!' I felt myself colouring, that they should think I knew Simon's lodgings, but there was no reason to suppose that they meant anything by it.

'Aye. Yellow.' He laughed. 'The landlady's husband paints our scenery. He used some left-over paint from Apollo's chariot to paint his front door. You can't miss it.'

'I don't suppose I can.' I thanked them and retraced my steps to Holywell Lane, walking back a little way towards

Bishopsgate. Many of the players had lodgings here, but the house with the yellow door was unmistakeable. The building loomed over the lane, its jettied upper stories – almost certainly added illegally – made it look as if it was about to topple over on to unsuspecting passersby.

I banged at the door, but there was no answer. After I had banged twice more without success, I turned away, sure that there was no one at home. But there, coming along the lane, was Simon, carrying a basket of food.

'Kit!' He seemed genuinely delighted to see me, despite my long neglect of my friends from the playhouse.

'Come in.' He threw open the door, which was not locked. I remembered that when we had first met he had been amused that we locked the door of our poor cottage in Duck Lane, until I explained the need to keep our medicines safe.

I hesitated. 'I thought we could go to an ordinary for a meal. I must be at Seething Lane by two, and Master Burbage asked me to remind you of your rehearsal.'

'No need.' He flourished his basket. 'I have everything here that we need. Bread still warm from the oven. Cheese. Some bacon I can cook over my fire. A flask of ale. Some late pears. Come up. We are at the very top.'

I followed him through the yellow door and up the first flight of stairs, solidly built and surely as old as the lower part of the house. The next flight had clearly been added a long time ago, for although they were crudely made they were sturdy and showed years of wear. The next flight lacked a handrail, clung precariously to the plaster wall and trembled under our feet. The final floor was reached by a steep ladder, which was not even fixed to the wall. The whole upper floor was an attic, divided into three rooms by thin partitions, their doorways covered by curtains. Simon led the way into the middle room, which looked out over the lane through a half-circle window peering through the thatch of the roof. The floor sloped so steeply down towards the outer wall that it nearly propelled me through the window. The house broke every fire regulation in London, but being outside the Wall, it probably escaped the hand of the magistrates.

I looked around with interest. Simon had grown in the two years I had known him and was now a handspan taller than I. His head just cleared the beams supporting the underside of the roof, but where it dipped down to the outside wall, he would have to stoop. There were two truckle beds, with bedclothes in a tangled heap. A small table and two joint stools were piled up with discarded clothes and papers – probably the scripts of plays. On the floor were several used plates and dirty ale mugs, in one of which several flies had drowned. I wrinkled my nose.

'Pigs live better,' I said drily.

Simon looked around, as if he were seeing the room for the first time.

'I suppose we should clear up, but we're seldom here, except to sleep.'

'We?'

'I share with Christopher Haigh. It's cheaper that way.'

He began throwing the clothes from the stools on to the beds, and swept the papers on to the floor.

'It's disgusting,' I said. 'If we let the wards fall into this state, we would be driven out of the hospital.'

'Well, this isn't a hospital,' Simon said cheerfully. He crossed to the window, automatically bending his head as he neared the outside wall. He threw open the window and a blast of cold air blew in, making me huddle my cloak around my shoulders. He leaned outside, groping for something at the side of the window.

'Good,' he said, 'Christopher hasn't eaten it all.' He held up a packet wrapped in greasy paper. 'Cold beef.'

'You have a larder out there?' I was smiling.

'Aye, a big earthenware pot. Christopher fixed it on a bracket. He is not such a fine gentleman as he would like you to think. His father was a carpenter, which is useful. He knocked up the table and stools for us.'

He closed the window and laid the packet of beef on the table beside his basket. There was a small fireplace on the inner partition wall, containing an even smaller fire, but he soon poked it up and added a shovel of sea coal. While he busied himself with a frying pan and the bacon, I began to fold the clothes into tidy piles. I straightened the beds and laid the papers – they were indeed play scripts – in a neat stack on a rickety shelf nailed above one of the beds.

'Where do you clean your dishes?' I asked. I looked at the rancid grease and a creeping black mould with distaste. 'We cannot eat off these.'

'There are some clean plates over there.' He jerked his head towards a dark corner where there stood an ancient-looking cupboard I had not noticed. I found two chipped plates and carried them to the table. There were mouse dropping on the top of the cupboard, but inside it looked clean.

Simon slid half the bacon on to each of the plates and poured the dripping over it.

'Help yourself,' he said, pushing the basket towards me. He lifted out a large round loaf and sawed slices off it, directly on the table, which I noticed was scored all over where bread had been cut before.

'You must run out of clean plates eventually,' I said.

'Then we take everything down to the yard at the back and wash them with water we carry over from the conduit. You saw how many stairs there are. We don't do it every day, only when everything is dirty. Were there any clean ale mugs in the cupboard?'

I shook my head.

'Oh, well, then we'll just have to drink from the jack.'

He took the ale jack from the basket, pulled out the cork and passed it to me. I drank gingerly at first, doubtful of what it might be like, but it was excellent, so I drank thirstily, then handed it back.

We mopped up the bacon dripping with bread, then moved on to cold beef and cheese, and finished with the pears. They were the hard little pears that were still edible as late in the year as this and a welcome end to the meal.

'So,' said Simon, 'now the soldiers are all gone from the hospital, are you working with Walsingham once more?'

'He sent for me yesterday,' I said, pushing my stool back from the small table so I could stretch out my legs.

'More code-breaking?' Simon knew what I did in Phelippes's office, though I was sworn not to reveal the contents of the papers I worked on.

'I thought that was what they needed,' I said. 'But when Cassie told me it was Sir Francis who wanted to see me, I was afraid it might be . . . well, might be something more serious.'

'More serious?' Simon looked puzzled, and then concerned. 'You mean, like last year, when he sent you off, pretending to be a tutor to some gentleman's children? And then you were a scruffy messenger boy.'

'Aye, something like that.' I found I was twisting one of the buttons of my doublet round and round and released it before I pulled it off. 'He is sending me on a mission to the Low Countries, carrying despatches to the Earl of Leicester.'

Simon gave a low whistle, then stood up and piled our dirty plates on top of those on the floor. When he sat down again, he passed me the ale jack, but I shook my head.

'I need to keep my brain clear. I am to meet Sir Francis and Nicholas Berden at Seething Lane at two o'clock, to discuss the mission.'

Simon took a long pull at the ale jack, then recorked it and placed it back in the basket.

'It is more than simply carrying despatches, isn't it?'

I nodded silently.

He clasped his hands on the table in front of him and leaned toward me. 'He's asking you to spy for him, I'll be bound.'

I had never told Simon what I was doing on my various missions for Walsingham during the previous year, but he was no fool. He had guessed that I was caught up in foiling the Babington conspiracy, with its aim to kill the Queen, to use French troops under the Duke of Guise to invade England, and to put Mary Stuart on the throne. He knew without my telling him that as well as code-breaking and other activities with Thomas Phelippes, I had been used by Walsingham for spying.

I nodded. Perhaps if I did not speak the words, I had not, strictly, revealed anything.

'Come, Kit,' he said. There was a touch of impatience in his tone. 'I swear that you can trust me. I will say nothing outside this room. I will keep your secrets. You know I would not betray you.'

I did know it, and said so.

'At first, all I have to do is deliver the despatches from Sir Francis – and possibly from Burghley and the Queen as well – to the Earl of Leicester, somewhere in the Low Countries. I do not know where yet. I suppose they will tell me this afternoon. Leicester will inform me of any suspicions he has. Well, he talked of suspicions, but nothing more specific than that. I hope the whole mission is not a fool's errand.'

'And then?'

'And then I am supposed to hang about where the soldiers gather when they are not on military duty. Ale houses, mostly, I expect. And . . . just listen, I think. See whether anyone lets anything slip.'

'It sounds somewhat vague.'

'I know. And what if there *are* traitors, and they suspect that I am one of Sir Francis's agents? I'm no Berden or Gifford, with years of practice at this.'

'But you are good at playing a part.'

I looked at him in alarm, but there was nothing in his air to suggest that he had guessed the part I played every day.

'Remember last year. You had no difficulties then.'

'Well . . .' I also remembered how the Fitzgeralds' fifteen-year-old daughter had tried to seduce me and felt a bubble of slightly hysterical laughter rising in my throat. I turned it into a cough.

'I did think you might have some ideas how I should play this part.'

Simon clasped his hands behind his head and leaned back, tipping his stool on its back legs.

'The first question is: What part are you playing? You are not meant to be one of the soldiers yourself, are you?'

'I don't think so.' I was startled at the thought.

'Probably Sir Francis has something in mind for you. How do his agents usually pass themselves off?'

'I am not sure. I think sometimes they pretend to be merchants or traders of some kind, as it allows them to move around from town to town, or even from country to country. In fact, some of them really are traders. Sir Francis has links with all the great English merchant houses.' I thought of the cousins of Dr Lopez and Dr Nuñez, whose trade routes and mercantile houses in Europe and the Ottoman Empire served a second purpose for Walsingham.

'Clearly you are too young to be taken for a merchant yourself, but you could be in the service of one of the houses, carrying orders for goods, overseeing the shipping of goods. Does that sound right?'

'Aye. I think so.' I tried to imagine myself as a young clerk working for Dr Nuñez. It was not so unlikely. I would need to carry quills and a portable ink well. Perhaps empty my satchel of medicines and fill it with papers.

'Then you need to think about your costume.' Simon was staring over my head.

'Costume?'

'Your clothes. I'm thinking of this as we would stage it in the playhouse. You are a capable young servant, already a trustworthy clerk who can be sent on his master's business abroad . . .' He pondered for a few minutes.

'If this were a comedy, we would dress you one way, if a tragedy or a history, quite another.'

'I don't understand.'

'Your role is to see and hear, without being noticed, to eavesdrop but remain in the shadows. In a comedy, we want the audience to know that the eavesdropper is there. They join in the fun. Those who are being spied upon do not know what is happening, but the audience does. So we dress the spy in bright colours. He makes his presence very obvious, the audience watches his every move. But the poor lovers – it is usually lovers – simply do not see him, even when he is right under their noses.'

I nodded. I had watched this kind of scene in comedies myself.

'Now in a tragedy or a history, we want something different. The spy lurks in the darkness. Perhaps the audience does not even know he is there until everyone else has left the stage after revealing their secrets. Then he comes forward. There is the shocked realisation that the spy has heard the secrets and terrible consequences will follow. Do you see?'

I nodded again.

'So in this case we dress the spy in dull, inconspicuous clothes, so that he can blend with his surroundings, unnoticed. I think that is what you should have in mind.'

He let his stool fall forward again with a clatter.

'That cloak of yours.' He point to where I had laid it across one of the beds. 'Too pale.'

It was the soft undyed cream of natural wool. I realised what he meant. Even in the dark corner of an ale house, it would stand out, drawing attention to itself.

'You need something darker.' He got up and rummaged about amongst one of the piles of clothes, spoiling all my careful folding, then pulled out a cloak of a dull, dark brown, almost black. I did not like it as well as my own cloak, but it looked thick and warm. 'Take this. No one will notice you in this.'

'I can't take that. It's the beginning of winter. You will need it yourself.'

'Oh, I will borrow something from the playhouse.'

'If I am to borrow it, then you must take mine.'

He started to object but, perhaps seeing a determined glint in my eye, he agreed.

'Very well, we will exchange cloaks until you return from the Low Countries. When will you return?'

'Sir Francis says I will be home for Christmas.'

'Not too long then.' He sat down again. 'Your doublet and hose are sober enough. Have you a hat or cap you can pull down about your head?'

I thought for a moment. 'I threw away that dreadful woollen cap Phelippes gave me when I played the messenger boy and bought a better one in Lichfield. Would a merchant's clerk wear such a cap?'

'Why not? In the cold weather we must all keep our heads warm, and I am told it is very cold in the Low Countries. Flat as a frying pan, so the wind whistles over the polders. And damp. Nothing ever dries out. You will be scraping mould off your face, never think of my dirty plates.'

'You make it sound very inviting.'

He laughed. 'I almost wish I were coming with you. I am tired of playing sweet maidens. I should enjoy a villain's part.'

'I hope I am not a villain.'

'No, you are an innocent and trustworthy merchant's clerk. Remember what I have told you before. Think yourself into the skin of such a young man. Your own age, but of a very different profession. Inky fingers – I suppose you have those when you work with Phelippes. Busy adding up your master's accounts in your head. That should not be difficult for you, with your skill at mathematics.'

I smiled. I had known Simon would help. Already I could envisage that earnest young clerk, anxious to advance in his profession. Somewhat reserved, so he would listen to the soldiers' talk, but would not join in. I opened my mouth to say something, but at that moment we both heard the clock from a nearby church strike the half hour.

'Half past one!' Simon cried. 'We must go!'

He tossed me the dark cloak and I swung it round my shoulders as he picked up mine. Together we made our way down the ladder and the stairs, parting at the front door of the house.

'Good luck to you, Kit,' Simon said. 'Come and see us when you are back in London.'

'I will.' I started to run, for I had farther to go than he.

I reached Seething Lane in better time than I expected, for it was not yet two o'clock. Before going inside, I walked through to the stable yard. The apple I had brought yesterday for Hector was still in the pocket of my doublet, for I had been too distracted when I left to remember it. I found the ugly piebald in his stall. He greeted me with a soft whicker and rubbed his forehead against my shoulder.

'I have only a moment, my fine fellow,' I said, 'but I've an apple for you.'

I held it out on the palm of my hand and he took it delicately with his velvet soft lips.

'Good lad,' I said, rubbing him between the ears as he crunched the apple, dribbles of juice running down his muzzle and dripping on to the straw.

'Afternoon, Master Alvarez.' It was the stable boy Harry.

'Afternoon, Harry,' I said. 'I must go. Sir Francis wants to see me.'

I gave Hector's neck a final pat and crossed to the backstairs. Up there Sir Francis and Nicholas Berden would be waiting.

Chapter Six

I found not only Sir Francis and Nicholas Berden in Sir Francis's office, but also Thomas Phelippes, who nodded to me, but said nothing. I was relieved that the hands on Sir Francis's French mantel clock, bought when he was ambassador to Paris, were just reaching the hour. It chimed softly. It was a luxury my father and I could no longer aspire to, though we had once owned three striking clocks at our house in Coimbra. Now I had to judge time by the multitude of church clocks in London – not always in harmony with one another – though I had also developed a keen sense of the hour without the need for consulting a timepiece.

I hung my cloak on the same peg as yesterday. If any of them noticed that it was not my usual cloak, they said nothing. Sir Francis waved me to a chair and I sat down. Our chairs were grouped around a low table on which a map had been spread out, weighed down at the corners with inkwells, a sanding box and a small bronze Roman statue which Sir Francis normally kept on his desk. Despite this, the map threatened to roll up, so Berden took two books from a shelf on the wall to hold down the two shorter ends. While he was on his feet, he refilled the others' wine glasses and poured another for me.

Craning my neck, I could see that the hand-drawn map showed the debatable area lying between France and the Low Countries, as well as all of the Low Countries themselves as far as the German states. The border lands did not only consist of the area from which the Spanish launched attacks on the United Provinces, those Dutch lands which had declared themselves independent of Spain. Closer to France the area had also passed back and forth between the Catholic League, headed by the Duke of Guise, and the Huguenots, led by Henri of Navarre, both factions entirely beyond the control of the weak king of France, Henri III, the last of the sons of Catherine de' Medici to hold the French throne. I was unsure which French commander was in possession of which parts of the territory at present. It seemed to change from day to day.

'The Earl of Leicester is based here in Amsterdam at the moment, or at any rate according to our last report.' Sir Francis tapped the map with his forefinger. 'The army is encamped just outside Amsterdam, the Earl and the senior officers are quartered in the town. Our fleet, together with the ships belonging to our Dutch allies, lies offshore to the west. The Spanish would dearly like to seize Amsterdam, but they already hold Sluys and Dunkerque, both of which will serve them well for launching an attack on us. However, I know that they are anxious to secure Boulogne and Calais as well. Have you received any new despatches from France today, Thomas?'

Phelippes leaned forward, his hands on his knees. 'The latest word is that Navarre's forces were defeated in the most recent encounter and have retreated south and west, away from the Catholic League and the centre of its support in Paris. They will be somewhere near Orleans now.' He pointed to the edge of the map. 'Just beyond here. The forces of the Guise faction seem to be in the ascendant, as far as we can tell. At least for the moment.'

Sir Francis clicked his tongue in annoyance. 'If Guise succeeds in overthrowing the French king, which has been his object for years, he will form an alliance with Spain and allow them access to Boulogne and Calais. Perhaps Dieppe as well – that wasps' nest of Catholic traitors. That will mean a whole string of ports in enemy hands, facing us across the Channel. While the French continue to fight among themselves, they will not reinforce the Spanish forces in the Netherlands, but God knows Parma and his Spaniards are strong enough without the assistance of Guise. The most the Earl of Leicester can do is hold on to what he has in the Low Countries. There is little chance of making an advance.'

Berden set his glass down on the floor and studied the map, his chin in his hand. 'You want Kit and me to go directly to Amsterdam? Or should we spy out the area to the south and west first? Nearer to Parma's forces?'

He said it quite calmly, but my stomach lurched. It would be dangerous enough spying amongst our own troops. I had no desire to go any closer to the Spaniards. Surely it was a mad scheme? But then, I thought, this is what Berden and the other agents do all the time. I knew there was one agent called Hunter who was held in prison in Lisbon, suspected by the Spanish of spying for England. Yet even in prison he was smuggling out reports to Sir Francis about Spanish troop movements and preparations for the invasion. These men must savour the excitement, even enjoy the risk. I could not. I was more convinced than ever that I would make a poor agent.

'That is well thought on, Nicholas,' Sir Francis said, setting down his own wine glass and studying the map more closely. I felt a trickle of sweat down my backbone. He was going to agree.

'If we put you ashore somewhere here.' He pointed to the map. 'Just north of Flushing. . . Since taking Sluys, Parma has given all his attention to fortifying the area round the port of Flushing. It is clear that his orders from Philip are to concentrate on the Enterprise of England and to leave the destruction of the Protestant Netherlanders for another day.'

'By your leave, Sir Francis?' Phelippes said.

'Aye, Thomas?'

'As Nicholas and Kit will be carrying secret despatches and letters for the Earl, surely it is essential to ensure that they reach him without falling into the hands of the enemy? It were better they should go first to Amsterdam and deliver the papers. Then, if it seems wise, they may move down towards Flushing. The Earl himself, or his scouts, will be able to tell them the best route, to avoid outliers of the enemy forces. They will have fresher intelligence than we can possibly have.'

I looked at Phelippes gratefully. It would not eliminate the danger, but it would lessen it somewhat.

He did not notice my look, but went on. 'By then we may also know more about the situation in France. It would be wise if we could provide more help for Navarre. Protestant supremacy in France would be immensely to our advantage.'

He said it without much conviction and I knew what the answer would be, even before Sir Francis spoke.

'Indeed it would, but we cannot fight on too many fronts at once. Our gold is limited and our troops even more so. We cannot commit any more resources to Navarre for the present.'

'So,' Berden said, bringing them back to the matter in hand, 'we go first to Amsterdam, deliver the despatches to the Earl and seek out any information there which might bear out his suspicions of treachery amongst our own or the Dutch forces. Afterwards, we head south.'

Sir Francis nodded. 'That seems the best plan. After you have seen the Earl, you and Kit should separate and work independently, then at an agreed time meet together and travel down to near the Spanish lines.'

All this time I had said nothing. Now I ventured to speak. 'I am the novice here. What kind of information should we be listening for? Surely if there are traitors, they will not talk openly of their plans?'

Berden sat back and picked up his glass again.

'It is surprising how much men will talk when they are in their cups. But you should look out for small things as well. One man passing a note to another. A group of men huddled together in a corner, talking seriously and quietly, not wanting to be overheard. Any remark, however casual, that seems favourable to Spain or critical of the Queen. Any praise of the Pope, no matter how small, how brief. It will be a straw in the wind. Any man behaving suspiciously – concealing a weapon, going into a house in the town which is neither ale house not whore house, but perhaps a meeting place for the disaffected. Follow if possible, but keep out of sight. The Earl will instruct us as to the person we should report to. Do not attempt to challenge anyone or attack them. It is information we require, not heroics.'

'No fear!' I said, and they all laughed.

'I think you should leave as soon as possible,' said Sir Francis. 'Thomas will prepare passports for you, and orders for you to be conveyed to Amsterdam by one of the military ships crossing from Dover.'

'Do we take our own horses, or hire over there?' Berden said.

'Best take them, to save time and ensure that you have a reliable means to move about quickly from the start.'

I looked across at Phelippes and for once he smiled. 'You will be wanting that piebald, Horace, I suppose.'

'Hector,' I said. I looked at Sir Francis. 'If I may.'

'Aye. I know he served you well before. Nicholas, you have your own mount, have you not?'

'Aye, Sir Francis. He's in your stables now.'

'Let us say the day after tomorrow, then. That will give us time to prepare the papers.' He turned to me. 'I have already spoken to the governors of the hospital, Kit.'

I nodded. 'I thank you, Sir Francis.' He had probably done so before I had even agreed to go.

Before I left Seething Lane, Phelippes called me into his office, where we arranged the ciphers I should use in any reports I sent back to him.

'Anything you report to the Earl,' he said, 'you should copy to me.'

'Will the Earl not forward them to you?' I asked, not altogether innocently. Since the affair of Sluys, my opinion of Leicester was not high.

Phelippes turned and walked to the window.

'It is not that I do not trust the Earl, Kit.' He hesitated, then glanced over his shoulder at me. 'The Earl does not always realise what is important and what is not. And he is easily distracted from the matter in hand. His mind . . . it is somewhat akin to a butterfly, fitting from flower to flower, tasting now here, now there. He wrote to the Queen of his fears of treachery and treason. He may still fear them, but it may be that he will have forgotten his fears by the time you arrive and be thinking of some grand scheme to attack Parma. Or he may be seeking a way to persuade Her Majesty to allow him to come home and pass the command to that stepson of his, the Earl of Essex.'

I had never heard Phelippes criticise one of the great courtiers before, certainly not the Queen's favourite, Robert Dudley, Earl of Leicester. For a moment I was speechless, then I said, 'I have heard that where Leicester is . . . cautious' (I dared not say cowardly) ' . . . then Essex is rash, even . . . foolhardy.'

'You are correct in what you have heard, Kit, but you will not, of course, repeat it anywhere that it might cause you unpleasantness.'

'Of course not.'

'And you will be the very epitome of caution. You should be safe enough with Berden, but when you are on your own, take care. I should not like to lose my best code-breaker.'

He gave me a bleak smile and I flushed. Praise from Phelippes was rare indeed.

'I will be careful,' I promised.

Walsingham had given me permission to tell my father and anyone else near to me that I would be carrying despatches to the army in the Low Countries. There was to be no secret about that. What I was not to reveal, however, was the true purpose of the mission, to seek out any treason against Queen and country.

'The day after tomorrow!' my father said in dismay, when I told him that evening, after he returned from St Bartholomew's.

'Walsingham's orders,' I said. 'I hope there will not be a problem at the hospital. He has promised we will be home before Christmas. That is but four weeks away. And most of the chest infections and influenza strike after December.'

'We will manage, but are you prepared? Have you warm clothes enough? And where is your own cloak?'

'Oh, Simon and I have exchanged cloaks for the moment. He also warned me about the weather over there and thought his was warmer.' It was not, but I had promised not to tell my father about the spying. I had made no such promise before I had told Simon. 'Is it really so cold in the Low Countries?'

'Aye, so I have heard. They have more snow than we do in England. Their canals and polders freeze over early in the winter and stay that way until spring. You must take your warmest clothes. Joan!' He turned to her. 'You must look out Master Christoval's winter hose and shirts.'

'Aye,' she said grumpily. 'I heard you. No need to shout. I'll put them together tomorrow. I'll be bound his stockings will need mending. They always do.'

'I'll grease my heavy boots,' I said. The prospect of this bitter weather so early in the winter was depressing.

'The day after tomorrow!' my father said again suddenly, in the midst of our supper. 'We are to dine at the Lopez house that day. You cannot offend Ruy Lopez.'

'I cannot disobey Sir Francis,' I said. 'All the arrangements are being made, passports, the horses, a ship. I will go to see Sara tomorrow and beg her pardon. You may still go without me.'

He shook his head, a worried frown on his face, but he did not argue any more. Much as he valued his standing with the more eminent members of our Marrano community, he knew that the orders of the Queen's Principal Secretary and spymaster must come before all else. For all we knew, the order might have come from Her Majesty herself, though I hardly thought she would have heard of someone as insignificant as Christoval Alvarez.

The next morning early I walked to Wood Street. There were several purchases I wished to make before my journey, but I wanted to call on Sara first. She was pleased to see me, perhaps all the more so because I had scarcely visited once in recent months. I apologised for this and explained how busy we had been, caring for the soldiers from Sluys.

'Aye,' she said, leading me into her private parlour. 'That was a terrible business. I heard how badly the survivors fared.'

'Better than those who did not survive,' I said grimly.

'That is certainly true.' A maid entered carrying a tray, which she set down on a table and withdrew.

'I've sent for some Hippocras, for it seemed to me the weather was turning even colder today.' She poured us each a beaker of the steaming spiced wine and passed me a plate of small iced biscuits cut into circles and stars.

'I have come to apologise also for missing your dinner tomorrow,' I said. 'Sir Francis Walsingham is sending me over to the Low Countries on a mission tomorrow morning, so I am afraid my father must come alone.'

'A mission?' she said. 'I thought you worked in the office there, as a code-breaker and translator.'

'Oh, I do,' I said hastily, remembering that Sara knew nothing of my other activities for Walsingham last year. 'It is not exactly a mission. I am to carry a number of despatches and private letters to the Earl of Leicester. You know that he is in command of our forces there.'

She raised her eyebrows. 'Of course I know that. But why send you? Surely Sir Francis must have a regular courier service.'

'He does. But the people who work for him are spread all over Europe at present. He needed someone in a hurry.' I thought how unbelievable this sounded, but Sara was thinking of something else.

'In my view, it sounds dangerous,' she said. 'What if you were to be discovered?'

As one of the very few people who knew my true sex, I realised at once what she meant. Not discovered to be carrying secret documents, but discovered to be a girl.

'There is no need to worry,' I said, smiling at her over the rim of my beaker. 'I am so accustomed to my role as a man that I sometimes forget it myself.'

She shook her head angrily. 'Do not pretend to me, Caterina. You know how dangerous it will be.'

'I promise you I will be very careful. But do not speak that name aloud. Do not even think it.'

'No, of course not.'

'Tell me, what is happening about the arrangements for Anne's marriage?'

After that we spoke of other matters, but before I left, she was struck with a sudden thought.

'Will you be in Amsterdam, Kit?'

'Perhaps.' I was cautious, unsure how much I should reveal.

'I have a cousin there, Ettore Añez, a merchant in precious gems. He lives on Reiger Straat – that's Heron Street – at the sign of the Leaping Gazelle. He would be glad to see you and hear our news. And if you need a friend, he is there, well known in the merchant community.'

'I will remember, and if I have the chance I will take him your greetings.'

She kissed me on both cheeks and stood in the doorway as I walked away.

I made my way to Cheapside, where there are shops and street stalls selling every imaginable type of goods. There was a stationer I often frequented, where I bought a supply of quills and a neat travelling ink well so that I could carry ink without the risk of it staining my other possessions. I asked the shopkeeper to fill it with ink and he demonstrated that it did not leak. Tomorrow I would get a packet of paper from Phelippes's office. I needed all the accoutrements of a conscientious clerk to maintain the fiction of my role. I also bought two lemons. Lemon juice, like milk and urine, makes an excellent invisible ink which can hold a message fitted in between the lines of an innocent letter written in normal ink. Milk is not so easy to come by, certainly when travelling, and urine can be awkward to use in some situations.

At a stall selling cheap but sturdy clothes for workmen I bought a thick scarf and a woollen waistcoat to wear under my doublet. All this talk of the freezing weather in the Low Countries had been causing me some concern. When we had first come to England from Portugal, I had found the winters very hard to bear. I was used to them now, but dreaded anything even colder. I had left Joan mending my thick stockings by the kitchen fire this morning, but I decided to buy an extra pair.

Finally I walked down to Eastcheap, to Jake Winterly's shop. Bess greeted me excitedly and called to the men to come through from the workroom behind the shop.

'I'm here just as a customer.' I was embarrassed by all this welcome. 'I would like a smaller satchel or a wallet to fit inside this.' I held out the large satchel in which I regularly carried my physician's supplies. 'Something that would fit in the bottom. I'm afraid I can't wait for it to be made, as I'm going away from London tomorrow.'

They looked amongst their stock and found a wallet about six inches wide and the same deep, but it was about two inches too long to fit across the bottom of my satchel.

'It was made for an artist, to hold his brushes,' Jake said, 'but when it came time to pay, he had not the coin, having lost his patron to the smallpox. It has been sitting on a shelf ever since. I can soon cut it down for you.' He examined the stitching, then turned to his wife. 'Bess, fetch Dr Alvarez a beer and I'll have it done while you wait.'

He measured my satchel carefully, then carried the wallet into the workroom, while Bess ran off to the nearest ale house for a flagon of beer.

As William turned away to follow Jake, I said, 'You see that I am wearing your belt. Many have admired it and asked who made it. You are doing well, here with your sister and her husband?'

His face lit up and I noticed that it had filled out and grown rosy with health. 'Very well, Doctor. I was a fool ever to go for a soldier, but I have learned my lesson.'

Bess was soon back with a flagon of beer and insisted on taking me upstairs to sit in the family's quarters, which were cramped but ferociously clean and neat. There she pressed on me a meat pasty which I suspected was meant for their own supper, though I refused to eat more than half of it. By the time I had satisfied her that I could eat and drink no more, Jake arrived with the cut-down wallet. He had made careful work of it and fitted it into the bottom of my satchel where it effectively created a separate compartment. This time I insisted on paying for the wallet and the additional work, and went off satisfied that I now had exactly what I had pictured in my mind.

At home I removed everything from my satchel, even turning it upside down and shaking it, so that dust and crumbs scattered on the floor, to Joan's annoyance. I then packed into the wallet the most essential of my medical supplies: several small pots of wound salve, a tincture of febrifuge herbs, another to stimulate the heart in case of shock or palpitations, a phial of poppy syrup, a needle and thread for stitching wounds, a scalpel and forceps, tweezers, and a small roll of cloth for bandages. I stuffed some handfuls of uncarded wool around the breakable items, for who could tell how rough the treatment both I and my belongings might receive?

Once the wallet was fitted into the bottom of my satchel, it looked like the base of the satchel itself. I did not intend to hide it from any customs searchers – though as Walsingham's agents it was unlikely we would be searched. No, I simply did not want to draw attention to my real profession. At the same time, I would have felt uneasy to set out on a long journey without at least these few medicines.

Into the rest of the satchel I packed my clerkly supplies, together with flint and tinder in a small tin box, a change of shirt and hose, and a night shift. I would take a knapsack with a few more clothes, but if necessary I could survive with what was contained in my satchel. The neatness and compactness of my arrangements gave me a curious satisfaction, almost as if I were a warrior equipping myself for battle, a notion that had me smiling at my own absurdity.

The next morning I left at dawn to walk across the city to Seething Lane. Joan had made me up a packet of food, which I had fitted into the top of my satchel, together with my thick new scarf. As if to mock my preparations, the sun was bright behind thin clouds and the weather rather warmer than usual for November. I felt somewhat too hot in my heavy clothes, though I knew I would be glad of them on the ride to Dover.

Berden followed me up the stairs to Phelippes's office, where he was already installed behind his desk. Sometimes I wondered whether he ever slept. There was no sign of Walsingham.

Seeing me glance around, Phelippes said, 'Sir Francis is not well this morning and cannot leave his bed. He has sent a message to wish you both well.'

When we had been here two days before, I had noticed that Sir Francis's skin had that waxy tint it took on when he was ill. It was never spoken of in detail, but I knew that it was some trouble with his internal organs which had afflicted him for years. I suspected some form of kidney or urinary complaint, but was too discreet ever to mention it.

Arthur Gregory came in from his small side office and handed Berden a stick of sealing wax.

'Nicholas has his own seal for reports,' he said, 'as you know, Kit. And I have made one for you. We have had no chance to discuss a device, so I have given you a set of apothecary scales enclosed within the open arms of a set of mathematician's compasses. I hope you approve.'

He handed me an engraved seal stone of agate, set in a simple silver ring. It had been threaded on to a slim silver chain, so that I could wear it round my neck instead of on my hand, if I so chose. Safer that way, I thought, and slipped the chain over my head, allowing the ring to drop down inside my shirt.

'It is beautiful, Arthur. I never expected anything so fine!' Indeed I had not expected a seal at all. This exquisite ring was beyond anything I could have hoped for. He must have stayed up all night making it.

He smiled shyly. 'Here is some sealing wax for you as well.'

I tucked it under the flap of my satchel. It was understood without being spoken that some reports would be sent by official channels and properly sealed. Others, where greater secrecy was needed, would come anonymously, in code and unstamped by a seal. I added a sheaf of paper to my clerkly supplies and Berden picked up a small sketch based on the map we had studied before. I had no need of one, for I have a good visual memory for such things. Indeed, before I became too occupied between the hospital and Sir Francis's service, Thomas Harriot and I had been studying together the Theatre of Memory devised by Giordano Bruno, wherein one may use the imagined image of a playhouse and place in it objects, names or stages in an argument. With this fixed in one's mind, it is possible to stroll about this mental playhouse and pick up, as it were, the objects or ideas placed there. I was still a novice at the skill, but I was learning.

'Here are your passports,' Phelippes said. 'And instructions for the ship's captain at Dover. Letters of introduction to the Earl. The despatches are in two duplicate sets.'

He handed us each a bundle of letters, tied with tape.

'I'll wish you God speed and hope to receive your first reports in a week or ten days.'

We thanked him and I followed Berden down the stairs and round into the stable yard. Our horses were waiting for us, ready saddled. Hector greeted me with a whicker as I strapped my knapsack and satchel into my saddlebags, along with a horse blanket. Berden's mount was a sleek chestnut, with powerful haunches, though I thought he looked a little too slim in the leg. Once mounted we rode quickly out of the stable yard and down towards the Customs House and the legal quays, where several ships were being unloaded. Soon the rough winter seas in the Channel would reduce trade to a trickle, only the most hardy of sea captains being willing to trust their ships to the mercy of the weather. It struck me that it might not be so easy in three or four weeks' time to find a ship to bring us home.

There were the usual crowds on London Bridge, which slowed us down. I do not know why it is, but the pedestrians on the bridge always seem to creep along, unlike the bustling crowds on the streets of the city. And at this hour of the morning most of the traffic was flowing into London, opposite to the way we were riding – farmers driving carts of produce to the markets, workmen who lived south of the river coming into the city for their day's employment, women with baskets of eggs or a chicken or two, hoping for a quick sale on the street. It was too early yet for the jugglers and other mountebanks who would lay claim to a few feet of the bridge as their stage, performing for pennies thrown into a hopeful cap, until a constable chased them away.

Once over the bridge, we threaded our way through the equally crowded streets of Southwark, where there were many businesses, like tanneries, too noisesome to be allowed within the Wall. There were traders and craftsmen, too, who found it convenient not to pay city taxes, as well as certain professions mainly confined to the south bank of the river, such as the Winchester geese, who would be tucked up warmly in their beds at this hour of the morning. Most of their trade was carried out in the evening, when men had left their work, or at night, after the shows at the bear gardens and cockpits had closed.

Finally we came clear of the last of the houses and businesses of Southwark and turned on to the road which led southeast to Kent and Sussex, the route I had followed last year with Phelippes on our way to Rye. Berden was a very different companion.

'At last!' he said. 'Now we can move faster than a slug on a lettuce. Is your nag able to gallop?'

Stung, I said, 'Shall we try him?'

With that I gave Hector his head, kicked him once, and we flew away down the road, casting up a shower of mud clods in Berden's path. Behind me I heard his laugh and the thud of his horse breaking into a gallop. The chestnut was not a bad animal, but he was no match for Hector. After several miles I slowed

Hector to a steady canter, then a trot, then finally let him amble along while we waited for Berden to catch up with us. I was a little breathless myself, my nose and cheeks burning from the cold wind.

Eventually Berden reached us, still laughing.

'Pax!' he said. 'I concede the victory. I would never have thought the piebald had such speed in him.'

Hector was plodding along placidly now, like a little girl's quiet first pony.

'He is full of surprises,' I said. 'It does him good to stretch his legs from time to time. I think he grows weary when he spends too long in the stable. Your horse is not so bad, nor are you. When I have ridden with Phelippes, it has been like an old ladies' picnic, but do not tell him I said so.'

'I am sworn to secrecy,' he said. 'Shall we carry on? But perhaps not quite so fast?'

I nodded and set Hector to his beautiful smooth canter. I have never known a horse with such a lovely gait, not even my grandfather's prize stallion. He never seemed to tire, but was happy to continue at this pace for mile after mile.

Around midday we stopped to rest the horses and let them graze on the strip of sward beside the road, while we sat under a wide-spreading oak which still bore its leaves, unlike most other trees, and ate some of our food. Berden even dropped into a doze for a while. I suppose for him this was no more than another journey like a hundred others he had made. I could not relax, for my mind raced ahead to what might happen when we reached Amsterdam. And if we travelled near the Spanish army – what then? My heart jumped in panic. I hoped that part of our mission might change.

After about an hour, Berden woke neatly from his sleep, as though his body held its own internal clock. We mounted again and carried on. The further we travelled from London, the colder it grew, and as the dull November darkness drew in scarce halfway through the afternoon, we reached Maidstone and found an inn for the night. Since we were travelling on government business, we could have demanded free lodging and dinner by showing our passes, but we did not want to draw attention to ourselves, so we paid our reckoning. I had not stopped to think, until the very moment we spoke to the innkeeper, that Berden would expect us to share a room. Scarcely on our way, and already I was in danger of discovery. I was filled with panic, wondering how I could avoid it, but I need not have worried. When we retired to a chamber up under the roof, straight after eating a plain but substantial meal, Berden simply pulled off his boots and lay down on one of the truckle beds, rolling himself in the blankets and turning away from the light of our candle. I did the same. I prised off my boots, which were still stiff from the cold, for we had not been able to find a place near the fire while we ate. I laid Simon's cloak over the blankets for extra warmth and blew out the candle. The cloak, close to my face, carried a faint scent of Simon about it, which was somehow comforting, but before I could think any more about it, I was asleep.

The second day started much the same as the first, but before we stopped for a midday rest, it had begun to snow. Only a few scattered flakes at first, but Berden suggested that we should stop before it grew worse.

'We won't want to be sitting still eating in a full blown snow storm,' he said.

'No,' I agreed. 'And the horses need to graze before the grass is covered.'

Angry black clouds were building up in the northwest, heavy with threat. We turned the horses on to grass and ate quickly. Berden did not sleep this time, and I took the opportunity to unpack my thick scarf and wind it around my face and neck, over the hood of my cloak. By the time we were ready to mount, the snow was already coming down more heavily and the sky had darkened almost to night.

The previous day I had found a fallen tree to use as a mounting block, for Hector was a big horse, but today I could see nothing. Berden's horse was at least a hand and a half shorter, and he was taller than I, so he could mount easily, without a block.

Seeing me looking around, he said, 'I'll give you a leg up.'

I put my left foot in his cupped hands and he heaved me up till I could throw my right leg over Hector's back.

'Thank you,' I said.

He shrugged. 'You should not ride a horse you cannot mount without help.'

'A trooper I know told me they are trained to vault on to their horses from the rear, if need arises,' I said, 'but I am not sure Hector would like it. I could be kicked in the face for my pains.'

'I can do it,' he said. 'Once we are across the sea, I'll help you train him. You need to accustom him to being approached from behind. He seems a good-natured beast. It should not be too difficult. In this business you never know when you will need to mount in a hurry.'

We set off again without further talk and increased our pace gradually to a gallop, trying – unsuccessfully – to outrun the storm. By the time we reached Dover it was midnight black, although it cannot have been later than four of the clock. For the last hour we had been fighting our way through ever denser snow as well as the growing darkness. Our clothes and our horses were encased in a armour of frozen snow. The only relief was the fact that the wind blew from behind us and not in our faces.

Showing our passes at the city gate, we were waved through, then Berden led the way to the castle up through deserted streets already nearly a foot deep in snow. Once again our passes admitted us inside the castle wall, where flaring torches lit up a courtyard with more activity than we had seen in the whole town below.

Berden hailed a passing trooper. 'Messengers from Sir Francis Walsingham, carrying despatches for the Earl of Leicester in the Low Countries. Where can we stable our horses?'

He looked up at us, sheltering his eyes with his hand from the blowing snow.

'Follow me. It's this way.'

I slid down from the saddle. My feet were so numb I could not feel the ground and my knees gave way a little as I landed. Steadying myself against Hector's side, I flipped the reins forward over his head and followed Berden and the trooper across a slippery cobbled yard towards a run of outbuildings. Stables, storage barns, a smithy whose fire gave a welcome glow, though we could not stop to warm ourselves. The trooper struggled to draw back the bolt across the stable door and another man came to help him.

'Already icing up,' he said, through gritted teeth. His hands were blue with the cold. 'I've never known snow in November as bad as this b'yer lady storm. Not even with us stuck here on this rock with everything the sea can throw at us.'

Between them the men managed to open the door and we led the horses inside. There was an enclosed candle lantern hanging just inside the door, and another at the far end of the stables. A narrow passageway led towards it, with stalls on either side. There would be no open candles or sconces in a stable, where the slightest spark could set all that straw and hay alight in a moment.

'There's two empty stalls along here,' the trooper said. The second man had disappeared. He pulled open the half doors to two adjacent stalls. 'There's hay in the mangers. I'll fetch you a couple of buckets of water.'

'Thank you,' Berden said.

'Have you any bran mash?' I asked. 'We have ridden hard, all the way from Maidstone. Our horses need something more than hay.'

'I'll ask the head groom,' he said, and went back the way we had come.

I unbuckled my saddlebags and laid them in the passageway outside the stall, then lifted off Hector's saddle and set it on a rack beside the door. When I removed his bridle he shook his head and blew out a gusty breath of relief. It had been a hard day for him. Some life was coming back into my frozen fingers as I rubbed him down with a fistful of straw, while he inspected the hay, which was fresh and plentiful, though I hoped the trooper would find him something more sustaining. By the time I had rubbed Hector's coat dry of melting snow and checked his hooves for lumps of ice as best I could in the dim light, the trooper was back with the water. Hector had had long enough now since his wild run and had eaten something, so I let him drink, though I moved the bucket away before he had too much.

'The groom is making up some bran mash,' the trooper said. 'He'll bring it over. I need to get back to my duties.'

'We're grateful to you,' I said.

Berden looked over the partition between the stalls.

'We need to report to your commander,' he said, 'once we've seen to the horses. And we'd be glad of a meal. It was a bitterly cold ride.'

'Aye, come over to the keep when you're done. Anyone can show you to the commander's room. We eat in about an hour. You'll hear the bell. Just follow everyone else.'

With that he was gone, but I could see the groom approaching with two more buckets. He handed them to us, gave us a smile and a nod, but said nothing before he vanished into the shadows again. Hector plunged his muzzle gratefully into the bucket while I opened one of the saddlebags and pulled out the horse blanket folded on top of my knapsack. By the time I had it buckled in place, Hector had finished the mash and was nosing about hopefully in the empty bucket, until it fell over with a clatter. There was still some hay left in the manger and I put the water bucket where he could reach it. With the blanket on, he should be warm enough, for nearly every stall was occupied and the horses generated their own warmth.

'Ready?' said Berden, looking in the door of my stall.

'Aye, I'm ready.' I picked up the empty bucket that had contained the mash in one hand and closed and latched the door to the stall with the other. I gathered up the saddlebags by their central strap and followed Berden back to the door of the stables.

'Might as well leave the empty buckets here,' he said.

'Aye.' I put mine down and together we heaved the door open. It was a struggle to bolt it, but we succeeded at last. The wind had grown even fiercer, so we lowered our heads and staggered through it to the keep. Now that I was no longer occupied with Hector, I was conscious that my cloak was sodden and the wet had soaked through the shoulders of my doublet and shirt to my very skin. My feet, no longer numb, throbbed with pain. All I wanted was dry clothes and warmth, but first we must report to the commander of the garrison here at Dover Castle.

We found the commander's quarters without difficulty and a shouted 'Enter' summoned us to his presence. We went in, leaving our baggage just inside the door. The room was luxuriously furnished with thick rugs on the floor and what looked like expensive tapestries on the walls, more suited to a gentleman's country house than a military barracks. A great fire of logs blazed in the fireplace and almost at once Berden and I began to steam like a pair of cookpots coming to the boil. I tried to edge sideways nearer to the fire, but a fierce look from the man behind the desk stopped me where I stood. We were not invited to sit.

Sir Anthony Torrington was probably in his early sixties, a man sleek with good living, an assumption borne out by the choleric shade of his countenance. His beard and hair were quite white, so he might have been older. Their pure snowy colour contrasted strikingly with the red of his skin and the fine purple veins that were beginning to break through on his nose. With no other evidence to support the idea, I was convinced that this was not a man experienced in the rigours of the battlefield.

'Well?' he said, looking at us as if we were some disagreeable object he had neither time nor inclination to deal with.

I left it to Berden to reply, glad to retire behind my position as the junior here.

'Sir Anthony,' said Berden, bowing politely and summoning, despite his evident exhaustion, a small smile. 'My companion and I are travelling from Sir Francis Walsingham, carrying despatches to my lord Leicester in the Low Countries.'

He leaned over the desk and laid our passes in front of the commander.

'As you will see, we are granted quarter in all English military posts. We are also required to commandeer a ship to take us across the Channel at the earliest opportunity.'

The captain cast a cursory glance at the papers and pushed them back towards Berden.

'I daresay we can accommodate you for a brief period, but we are on high alert here and the garrison is at full strength. I will not have any of my men put to inconvenience.'

'It is my hope,' said Berden, 'that we need trouble you for one night only. We would like to take ship tomorrow.'

A grunt from the commander. 'You will need to speak to the naval commander about that, though I doubt whether any of his ships' captains will be willing to make the crossing in the present storm.'

'Thank you, sir. Let us hope it will have blown itself out by then.'

'Very well.' He waved his hand as though he were brushing away a troublesome fly, and we were dismissed, collecting our baggage and closing the door quietly behind us. I raised my eyebrows at Berden and he threw up his eyes expressively to the ceiling, but neither of us said anything.

We walked back the way we had come, to the central hall, leaving a double trail of wet footprints and drips along the stone floor. There was a fireplace here and I made for it like a bee to nectar. Berden joined me. We were both hoping that the bell to summon us to eat would ring soon.

As we stood toasting ourselves, two troopers crossed the hall and I recognised one of them.

'Andrew!' I called.

He stopped in his tracks, spun on his heel and came over to us, his companion following.

'Kit? What are you doing here? And looking like something fished out of the sea?'

He took my outstretched hand and shook it warmly.

'I wondered whether we might see you here,' I said. 'This is Nicholas Berden.'

The two men bowed and Andrew introduced the other trooper as Paul Standish.

'We are on our way to the Low Countries,' I explained, 'carrying despatches.'

He shook his head. 'You turn up everywhere, Kit. I never know where I will meet you, like the sprite in the fairy story. But why are you so wet? Have you been out in this storm? Why have you not been found quarters?

Berden shrugged. 'We saw to our horses, then reported to your commander. We were just wondering where to go.'

'Ah, the horses.' Andrew grinned at me. 'Hector, is it? I think you would care for that horse first if you were dying on your feet.'

'We are not quite dying,' I said. 'But we are very wet. And Hector is warmly housed in your stables.'

'Follow me,' he said. 'I will see you at dinner, Paul.'

113

We followed him up stairs and along a passage, until he threw open the door to a small corner room.

'There is just one man in here, and he's on duty tonight. There are two more beds.'

'How is your head, now, Andrew?' I asked. 'I see your hair has grown back.'

He lifted the hair at the side of his head, revealing a small bare patch of skin. 'Only a trace left,' he said.

'And the headaches?'

'Almost gone.'

Berden looked from one to the other of us in puzzlement.

'I was at Sluys,' Andrew explained. 'Kit tended me for a bad head injury at St Bartholomew's'

'He was shot,' I said. 'The bullet carved a groove along the side of his head your could put your finger in.'

'Bad luck,' said Berden.

'No, good luck,' Andrew replied. 'The bullet passed me by and killed the man behind me.'

'You must have been a cat in another life,' I said.

He laughed. 'Then I have another eight close escapes yet to go.'

'Where is the jakes?' Berden asked. 'I'm bursting.'

'Follow me. What about you, Kit?'

'I'm fine,' I said, turning aside. Another problem.

'When you are ready, come down to the main hall and I'll show you where we eat.'

The two of them went off and with frantic speed I changed into dry clothes, draping my wet ones over the single chair in the room. By the time Berden came back I was at the door.

'The jakes is further along on the left, if you want it.'

I nodded. 'I'll see you in the hall.'

I found the jakes and to my relief it was deserted, so I seized the chance to relieve myself before hurrying back down the stairs. Although I would be glad of the protection of Berden's company once we were abroad, travelling always in company with him would present constant difficulties.

Andrew was waiting, with a group of other troopers, standing close to the fire. He introduced them, but fatigue was beginning to catch up with me and I forgot their names as soon as

I heard them. Just as Berden joined us, also wearing dry clothes, a servant walked across the hall, clanging a large hand bell. He went to the door of the keep and pulled it open, to howls of protest from the troopers. He leaned out and rang the bell, whose sound must have been muffled by the wind for anyone more than a few feet away. One man came in, blown through the door on a blast of snow which whirled across the hall like a dancing ghost before sinking to the floor and slowly melting. The servant put his shoulder to the door, helped by the newcomer, then walked away down a corridor, still ringing his bell. The soldiers turned as one and followed him, Berden and I amongst them.

The food was such as you would expect in a military garrison. Large earthenware bowls filled with a thick mutton stew. Not elegant, but filling, and welcome after our freezing journey. Plenty of coarse bread, as much as we could eat. Good beer. To finish, an apple pie nearly two feet across for every ten soldiers. The pastry was thick enough to break teeth unless it was allowed to soak a while in the juice of the apples, but once the pastry was softened it made a satisfying end to the meal. In fact I even loosened William's leather belt a notch, to ease this unaccustomed quantity of food.

By this time I could feel sleepiness weighing me down and knew I could not stay on my feet much longer. The soldiers were getting up games of dice and cards, but they had spent their day quietly on guard duty in the castle, or drilling in the yard. They had not ridden near forty miles, most of it through a blizzard. Not that it seemed to worry Berden, who went off to join a game of cards. I understood why. Berden was known to have some skill in that quarter. Before he retired he would almost certainly have increased the weight of his purse.

I dragged myself up from the bench, where I had been sitting, almost comatose, and turned to Andrew.

'It's no good. If I do not go to my bed I will fall asleep on the table.' I looked around as the soldiers made for the double doors at the end of the room. At the other end the officers had been eating at a table on a dais raised about a foot above the floor.

'Is the officer in charge of the naval squadron up there?' I inclined my head towards the officers, who were also preparing to leave.

'Second from the right,' Andrew said. 'Sir Edward Walgrave. A different man altogether from our esteemed commander. Do you want me to introduce you?'

I shook my head. 'Not tonight. But tomorrow we will have to ask him for a ship.'

'He's a reasonable man and a fine commander, but if the storm continues, he may not want to let one of his ships set sail.'

I shuddered. 'I don't want to go to sea in this, but we may have to.'

'We will pray it has abated by tomorrow.'

'Thank you, Andrew,' I said. 'I really must go to bed.'

'Good night, Kit.'

I found my way back to the hall easily enough, for most of the soldiers were heading that way and gathering in groups, laughing and pulling out packs of cards and boxes of dice. A servant was walking about, filling tankards with ale. It looked as though Berden would be occupied for a long time yet.

The stairs were not far way. I plodded up them as if I were asleep already and walking in a dream. As I passed a window, firmly closed with shutters, I could hear the howling of the wind, which sounded louder than ever. I put my eye to the crack between the shutters, where a little light shone through from the flaring torches down below in the open courtyard. I could see very little except a dense cloud of whirling snow that spun in the air as if reluctant to settle. Yet it certainly would settle and the lying snow would probably be knee deep by tomorrow. What would we do if a ship could not be found to take us to the Low Countries? We could not linger here. Once in our room I pulled off my spare boots, collapsed on to the cot in the furthest corner and rolled myself up in the blankets. Before I had even straightened the pillow under my head I fell into a sleep of pure exhaustion.

Chapter Seven

When I woke the following morning Berden had already been and gone, at least so it seemed from the knapsack ready packed and set on top of his bed with his cloak laid over it. The third bed was now occupied, the bedclothes merely an anonymous hummock, the other soldier returned from night duty. There was a small window in the room, but I did not open the shutters for fear of waking him.

I pulled on my lightweight boots and laced them, then checked the clothes I had worn the previous day. They were mostly dry, except for the cloak, which I left spread out across the chair, so I folded them and packed them into my knapsack. Thanks to my having greased my heavy boots before setting out from London, they had let in only the cold and not the wet. My satchel had not been opened since our meal during the previous day's ride. There was still a heel of a stale loaf, a piece of hard cheese and two apples, large new season's ones. I left the food untouched, in case I should need it later. Before going down in search of something to break my fast, I risked a quick visit to the jakes. I met one soldier coming out and we nodded to each other, but there was no one else about.

I found Berden in the room where we had eaten the night before, talking – or rather listening – to a group of men who had also come off night guard.

'Nearly froze our balls off,' one them was saying, and he spat on the floor before burying his nose in a tankard of beer.

'Aye,' another grumbled. 'Don't see much point in having us patrolling the ramparts during a blizzard. Nothing to be seen through the snow, and nobody – friend or enemy – fool enough to go out in it anyway.'

'That's Torrington for you,' the first man said. 'It isn't him standing up there dead of the cold. Oh, no! Sir Anthony is tucked up in his warm bed, thank you very much.'

I noticed that the servants had laid out food and drink on a table against the wall, so it seemed that as the men came off or went on duty they could help themselves. I filled a plate with cold meats and bread, and poured myself a modest beaker of small ale. I would have been glad of some of Joan's lumpy porridge on this cold morning, but I carried my food over to the table and sat down next to Berden. He grinned at me but said nothing, jerking his head to indicate the soldiers, who were still complaining.

On my way downstairs I had passed the window where I had tried to look out the previous evening. The shutters were still closed but they rattled in the wind.

When I had taken the edge off my hunger, I said to Berden, 'Have you looked outside this morning?'

He nodded. 'Still snowing, and still that foul wind, though perhaps not quite as bad as last night. When we've eaten, we'll ask about a ship.'

'I've seen the naval commander,' I said. 'Andrew pointed him out last night after you left. Did you do well at cards?'

He smiled blandly. 'Not bad. Came away the richer by five shillings.'

I didn't ask whether he cheated. Perhaps he was just skilful.

'He is called Sir Edward Walgrave,' I said. 'The commander in charge of the Dover squadron. Andrew says he is a different type from Torrington.'

'It is men like Torrington who will lose us the war against Spain,' Berden said bitterly. 'Gentlemen put in command of soldiers who have no army experience themselves.'

'That's not so unusual,' I said, tearing a chunk off my bread and eating it. Freshly made this morning. The army cooks had been up betimes. I thought of Leicester, in charge of the army in the Low Countries. He did have some experience in war, and all of it disastrous.

'At least our sea captains are the best in the world,' I said.

'Aye, aye, they are, even though most of them are pirates half the time.'

'Don't you mean privateers?' I asked with a laugh. When a captain was licensed by the Queen to seize Spanish ships, he was transformed by royal magic from a pirate to a privateer, and so – nominally, at least – much more respectable.

When I had finished eating, I brushed the crumbs off my doublet and we went in search of Sir Edward Walgrave. He received us courteously, but shook his head when Berden explained that we had urgent despatches for the Earl of Leicester and needed a ship to take us to the Low Countries.

'You can see what the weather is like,' he said, gesturing towards his window, where the shutters had been folded back. There was glass in the window and it admitted some light, but it also revealed a prospect of driving snow, which had piled up on the outer sill and rose halfway up the window. 'I cannot risk one of my ships in this. It would be madness to attempt it.'

'Sir Francis Walsingham has commanded us to leave England immediately,' Berden said. He sounded remorseless, but I hoped Sir Edward would prevail. The thought of setting out on a sea voyage in that blizzard was enough to frighten a seasoned sailor, and I myself had only once travelled by sea. I had no wish to drown for the sake of a short delay.

While they argued, I walked over to the window, which looked out over the courtyard where, I was sure, the men would normally be drilling. It was deserted. I saw the head groom come out of the stables, struggle to bolt the door, and then run across to the shelter of the keep, slithering and sliding in snow up to his knees.

'Nicholas,' I said, without turning round, 'you can see for yourself that we cannot sail in this blizzard. Sir Francis himself would not expect it.'

I walked back to the desk where Walgrave sat, fiddling anxiously with a quill, Walsingham's orders lying in front of him.

Berden shrugged. He had tried, but of course he knew that it was impossible. At least he could honestly report to Sir Francis that we had done our best to leave Dover immediately. He picked up the papers from Walgrave's desk. The commander sat back with a look of relief on his face.

'I promise you, Master Berden,' he said, 'the moment I feel it is safe for you to sail, I will have one of my fast pinnaces made ready. They are much smaller than our warships, but less apt to be top heavy in rough seas, and they are newly built, sleek and fast. A pinnace will take you across to the coast swiftly and will also be able to sail up the canal to Amsterdam, which a larger ship could not do.'

'Will it be large enough to take our two horses?' I asked.

'Certainly. And it would have been madness to take horses to sea in this storm. They would have panicked and kicked the sides out of the ship.'

I thought this might be an exaggeration, but I let it go. This man understood far more of the sea than I could ever hope to know.

'Sir Edward,' I said, 'I have been told that the Dutch canals freeze over in winter. When we need to return to England, is the canal running up to Amsterdam likely to have frozen?'

'They do their best to keep the waterway open, breaking up the ice as it forms. But in a really bad winter, it will freeze, do what they will. In that case you will need to ride to the coast and take ship there.' He looked at Berden. 'Does Sir Francis wish my ship to wait until you are ready to return?'

'No. Come back for us in three weeks. All the way through to Amsterdam if you can. If you cannot, we will meet you on the coast.'

When we had made what arrangements we could, we left Walgrave's office. He told us to come back the next morning and we would take stock of the weather then.

'Well, I suppose we must kick our heels for another day,' Berden said, as we walked back to the great hall. 'I realise it would not have been safe to have made the journey today.'

'No doubt you can find another card game or two,' I said with a grin.

'No doubt I can. Perhaps not with the same soldiers. What will you do with yourself?'

'I will see if Andrew is about. Perhaps he will show me more of the castle. There is little else to do. I've no skill with cards or dice, so I won't bother you.'

In the hall we parted company and I did not see him for the rest of the day. After some time I found Andrew and he readily agreed to show me around the castle. It was a strange rambling place, but clearly located here for its strategic importance.

'It was the Romans who built here first,' Andrew said. 'The lighthouse near the church is part of their original fortress.'

'I can understand why they would want this vantage point,' I said. After our tour of the castle we had donned our cloaks and boots and stepped out on to the ramparts overlooking the sea. Snow was still drifting down, but not as heavily as yesterday, though the wind whipped our cloaks so that they cracked like ship's canvas.

'The Romans would have been able to keep watch over all the sea traffic moving up and down the Channel, wouldn't they?' I said. 'Particularly when the Saxons started to come sniffing round the shores of Kent.'

'Aye,' Andrew said, 'and it would have been important in the later days of the Empire, when everything was falling apart. Whoever was in command in Britain would be able to guard against rivals preparing an attack from over there.' He waved a hand out in the direction of the sea. 'On a clear day you can see France from here.'

It was hard to believe. The sea and the sky merged together in a blurring of snow and grey cloud, which seemed no more than a few miles away.

'I think it is snowing even harder over in France,' I said.

'It could be. I hope you will not have too hard a time of it over in the Low Countries.'

'I have been well forewarned. We should be back in England before Christmas.'

'Do you . . .' he hesitated, looking embarrassed, 'do you celebrate Christmas, Kit?'

'You mean, because I am a Marrano? I am a baptised Christian, Andrew.'

'I'm sorry. I do not altogether understand these matters.'

'I am not certain I even understand myself who and what I am. My family is part Jewish by descent, but also part Christian. My grandfather is one of the ancient Christian Portuguese nobility. And although my family attended the synagogue in

Coimbra, we also attended church, as my father and I do here in England. I take communion.'

'I did not mean to pry into your private affairs.'

'It does not matter. But it is confusing, when you are a child, and even now . . . But after all, it must have been the same, for people here. Your parents and grandparents. Thirty years ago, everyone in England was supposed to be Catholic. Before that, Protestant. Again before that Catholic. And now Protestant again.'

'You are right. Too complicated for a simple soldier like me!' He laughed. 'I am happy to be a Protestant and a loyal subject of the Queen.'

'As I am,' I said, not specifying which I meant. 'And I will indeed be celebrating Christmas. Last year I had a high time with the players in James Burbage's company.'

I might have said more, but it was growing very cold. Before we turned back to the warmth of the keep, Andrew pointed down to the port which lay almost at our feet, sheltered by a massive harbour wall.

'There you can see our Dover squadron of ships assembling,' he said, 'ready for the invasion. You will be crossing in one of the pinnaces. Over there, do you see?'

Through the thin curtain of snow I saw half a dozen small ships at anchor on one side of the harbour. They were slim and elegant, but they looked overly fragile to me, to confront the dark grey and angry waters of the Channel which lay beyond the harbour wall.

We made our way back to the keep, for it was growing dark as well as cold by now. Coming in to the hall I was momentarily dazzled by the light, for the sconces on the walls had already been lit and a fire was blazing in the enormous fireplace. There were even candles in standing candelabra placed here and there about the floor. Someone (not Torrington, I was sure) had decided that the barracks needed to fend off the winter dark. Andrew and I shook the snow from our cloaks and stamped our boots, as the men gathered near the fire looked up in astonishment at anyone so mad as to venture outside unnecessarily.

That evening we dined as before with the soldiers and before retiring for the night I opened one of the shutters of the window in the corridor outside our room. The snow had almost stopped falling and although a strong wind rushed in through the opening, I thought it was perhaps a little less than it had been at the height of the storm. I hastened to close the shutter before the cold air brought protests from anyone. I was glad to wrap myself up in my blankets and have one more night of rest.

The next morning a silvery winter sun lay slantwise across the mounded snow. During the night all the outdoor surfaces had been sprinkled with frost, as if a prodigal hand had broadcast diamonds like barley seed across the face of the world. So intense was the sparkle reflected off the snow that I had to screw up my eyes and look away.

When we had eaten, Berden and I made our way once again to Sir Edward Walgrave's office. It was clear that he was not only expecting us but knew what Berden would say as soon as he was through the door.

'Aye,' Walgrave said, before Berden could open his mouth. 'The storm is much slackened. I have sent word for one of the pinnaces to be prepared, the *Silver Swan*. It will be ready for you in an hour, and you can leave on the ebb tide.'

'I thank you, sir,' Berden said. 'We will make ready, then take the horses down to the port.'

Walgrave nodded. 'If you need blinkers, one of the grooms can provide them. I will arrange for the ship to return for you in exactly three weeks' time. It will come to Amsterdam, as we agreed, unless the canal is frozen, in which case it will anchor near the mouth of the canal. If your plans change, try to send a message to me, though I fear few ships will be carrying letters if the weather continues bad.'

We thanked him again and made our way back to our chamber to collect our belongings. The other soldier was there, asleep. I never saw him awake. So we prepared in silence. I changed into my heavy boots and donned my woollen waistcoat under my doublet. Berden also had a knitted garment, a sort of sleeveless tunic, which he added under his doublet. Neither of us had any illusions about how cold it would be at sea.

123

As we descended the stairs, I said, 'I will see whether the cooks will give us some food to carry with us. I expect there will be something to eat on board ship, but once we are put ashore, it may not be so easy to get a meal.'

'Sound thinking, Kit,' he said. 'Though Sir Francis did provide a purse of Dutch guilders, in case our English coin will not buy us food and shelter. I'd best give you some of them, in case we should be separated.'

At a turn in the stair he stopped and reached into his purse. Counting out a handful of the unfamiliar coins, guilders, schellings and Dutch pennies, he passed them to me and I slipped them into my own purse. I had no idea how much any one of them would buy and resolved to ask Berden to instruct me in Dutch money and prices while we were at sea. This was yet another way in which I felt unprepared for this mission. To Berden, who had spent many years travelling all over the nations of Europe, it had probably never occurred that it might be a problem for me.

'While you plead with the cooks,' he said, 'I'll report to Sir Anthony Torrington and tell him we are leaving.'

I nodded, glad to avoid the pompous garrison commander. 'I will meet you in the stables,' I said.

It seemed the army cooks were accustomed to requests for food to be carried on journeys, for the man I spoke to, once I had found the kitchens, made me up a bundle without demur, firmly tied in a large pudding cloth. There were two meat pasties and two raised pies, a loaf almost as long as my forearm, a couple of handfuls of dried raisins in a screw of paper, and half a dozen small apples. To this he added a leather jack of ale. To my thanks he responded with a cuff to my shoulder.

'Can't have you young lads starving!' he said. From the girth of him, he would have made three of me, always a sure sign of a good cook.

At the last minute he cut an enormous chunk off a great wheel of cheese and had to untie the cloth to add it. We were not likely to starve for a day or two at least.

The courtyard had begun to be marked with passing feet, crossing between the keep and the various outbuildings. Even so, the snow was still deep enough to soak my hose above my boots as far as my knees. Already I began to shiver. Berden was in the stable when I arrived, clearly his meeting with Torrington had been brief. He was saddling his horse and looked over the partition as I went into Hector's stall.

I held up the bundle of food for him to see.

'Excellent,' he said. 'Do you want blinkers for your horse, in case he mislikes boarding a ship?'

'No, I think not. Hector is generally calm as long as he can see about him. I expect blinkers would frighten him more than the ship.'

'Very well. I shall take some for Redknoll. He's travelled by ship before, but he doesn't care for it.'

I soon had my saddlebags packed and Hector saddled. I made sure I had one of the cook's small apples in my pocket in case he needed tempting to board the ship, for I knew his weakness for apples. When I was ready I led him out into the courtyard, followed by Berden. Just outside the stable door the snow was churned up with hoof prints, so a scouting party must already have ridden out. The mounting block which stood to one side had been cleared of snow, and I was able to mount easily, but I was conscious of Berden's earlier criticism, that I should not ride a horse I could not mount without assistance.

We rode out of the castle gatehouse and headed downhill towards the port, picking our way carefully, for the road was icy. A few times the horses slipped on the cobbles. The harbour was worse. All the surfaces were glassed over with a sheen of ice, forcing us to dismount and lead the horses slowly and carefully to where we could see that one of the larger pinnaces had been moored close in to the harbour wall. Her name, *Silver Swan*, was carved on her stern, amid a riot of leaves and roses. A ramp led from the quay to the ship and mercifully someone had had the foresight to strew it with straw.

Berden stopped by the near end of the ramp and fixed the leather blinkers to his horse's head. Redknoll threw up his head at first, but quickly accepted them. I did not know whether Hector had ever worn blinkers, but here, on an icy harbour quay, with a ramp that rippled up and down with the movement of the ship, did not seem the place to experiment. Berden stepped on to the ramp and clicked his tongue for his horse to follow. The horse

125

planted his feet firmly and leaned back against the reins. For several moments there was a battle of wills between man and horse, but at last Redknoll placed a hesitant hoof on the ramp, then another, until at last Berden had managed to lead him on to the deck of the ship. The horse stood there trembling, as much from fear, I guessed, as from the cold.

Now it was my turn. Praying that I would not make a fool of myself, I took the apple out of my pocket and held it up so Hector could see it. He snorted and reached forward. I backed away a few steps to the edge of the ramp, until the reins tightened between us.

'Come on then, my lad,' I said, in as quiet and normal a voice as I could manage, for I was afraid myself. Afraid of boarding that ship for the rough crossing, afraid of what lay ahead. Afraid, even, that if Hector should panic, he might knock me into the sea. With its fringe of ice around the edges, the harbour would not allow anyone who fell in to live for long. I must not let Hector sense my fear, for any horse can tell when you are afraid and Hector and I were closer than many a rider and horse.

Hector eyed me, eyed the apple, and rolled a nervous eye towards Berden's horse, standing shivering on the ship's deck. If anything, the movement of the water in the harbour had increased. It was well sheltered from the open sea, but even within the stony embrace of the harbour wall the insidious surge of the open Channel could be felt. Not only that but the strength of the wind was increasing, whipping up waves which chopped back and forth between the ships. The pinnace heaved and the ramp slid fractionally to one side.

I dared not hesitate any longer. I turned my back on Hector and stepped on to the ramp with as nonchalant an air as I could muster. For a moment I was caught between the rippling of the planks beneath my feet and the taut resistance of the reins in my hands. Then I felt the tension on the reins grow slack. I heard the dull thud as Hector stepped on to the ramp behind me, setting it wavering still more. A few steps. A few more. Hector and I stumbled off the end of the ramp and on to the deck together.

It felt as though I had held my breath all the way across, but now I turned and palmed the apple to Hector, who took it neatly from my hand.

'That's a grand fellow,' I said, patting his neck and leaning for a moment against his shoulder as I felt my knees growing weak beneath me.

Berden smiled at me as he lifted the blinkers off his horse.

'Well, he did it without blinkers, then.'

'Aye,' I said. 'I think a horse, like a man, is happiest when he knows what lies before and around him.' I did not have to say where I stood on such matters.

'True enough,' Berden said soberly, 'but some men, like my horse here, must needs have the truth partially hidden from them, or they have not the courage to go steadily forward.'

We began to lead the horses into a rough canvas shelter the sailors had erected toward the front of the deck before the mast, to serve as a temporary stable.

'And which would you rather be, Nicholas?' I asked. 'The man who sees clearly both ahead and to the sides? Or one who prefers only to see so much and no more?'

'Oh, I find that in our profession, the wisest course is to see both ahead and to both sides, if you wish to survive.'

'And perhaps also behind as well?'

'Aye.' He looked at me gravely. 'That as well.'

Now that we were aboard, the ship's crew began to make ready to leave. While we tethered the horses as best we could to keep them steady when the ship began to toss, and removed their tack, we could hear the sound of running bare feet slapping on the deck and occasional shouted orders, though it was clear these men knew their tasks with few directions from their officers. There were some bales of straw in the makeshift stable that we arranged around the horses to give them some protection, should they be thrown about once we were on the open sea. By the time we were finished and ducked out under the flap of canvas that closed the end of the stable, the ramp had been pulled aboard, the mooring ropes cast off, and the pinnace was being rowed out of the harbour.

The *Silver Swan* could be propelled either by a single bank of oars or by sails, but here in the harbour it was easier to manoeuvre while rowing. Our pinnace was neither one of the very small ones which are used as tenders for the great warships and for carrying messages between them within a fleet, nor was it one of the largest which are in truth small warships themselves, armed with anything up to a dozen cannon. It carried six small cannon and must be deemed large enough to cross the Channel unaccompanied. Recalling the fishing boat which had smuggled the two conspirators ashore last year near Rye, I realised that this ship was almost twice as long.

Once we were clear of the harbour, the ship's captain gave the order to hoist sail. The mainmast carried a quadrangular spritsail, with a triangular staysail before it. There was rigging from the bowsprit to the mast for a foresail, but the crew did not at first hoist this. Although the wind had abated somewhat from its fiercest at the height of the storm, it was still blowing hard enough to whip the hood of my cloak from my head. I reckoned the captain would not risk full canvas while the wind was this high.

'Master Berden and Master Alvarez?' The captain had come over to where we stood on the rear deck, trying to stay out of the way of the sailors as they went about their business.

'Aye,' said Berden, extending his hand.

'Captain Thoms,' he said, shaking our hands in turn. He looked at me curiously. 'You are Spanish?'

'Certainly not,' I replied, somewhat curtly. It was not the first time I had been taken for Spanish. 'I am Portuguese and no friend of Spain.'

'Ah.' He nodded in comprehension. 'Well, I am instructed by Sir Edward to take you all the way up to Amsterdam. I am afraid it will be a rough crossing.'

Even as he spoke we reached the open Channel, out of the lea of the land, and the ship kicked like a wayward horse. I grabbed hold of one of the shrouds to steady myself, and so did Berden, though Thoms rode the tossing deck as though it were flat calm.

'As long as we have this following wind,' he went on, as if he had not noticed the movement of the ship, 'we should reach the coast of the Low Countries before dark, but I will not sail up the canal at night. Too risky, both for the sake of the ship and in case the Spanish forces have moved closer.'

'Are they that close?' I asked. 'I thought they were back near Sluys.'

He shrugged. 'Who knows what Parma will do? But it is wise to be cautious.'

He called an order to the steersman to head further out to sea and turned back to us. 'Dangerous sandbanks off the coast of Kent, the Goodwin Sands. Many a ship has been lost there.'

I shivered. The thought of going aground in this bitter weather, out of sight of any help by land or sea, was the very stuff of nightmares. The captain took my shiver for cold.

'Come,' he said, 'there is no need for you to stand on deck in this wind. Come into my cabin.'

The stern of the ship held the captain's cabin and two other smaller ones for his officers, while the men slept below decks. Not that there would be much sleep for anyone, I imagined, on this journey. Thoms led us into a comfortable room which – had it not leapt up and down and side to side – could have been any gentleman's study on land. It was panelled in polished wood and had a wide window at the far end, looking out over the stern of the ship. On the right a bunk was neatly made up with colourful blankets, in the centre a table was screwed down to the floor, as were the four chairs around it. The rolled up papers stored in racks on the wall were probably charts.

'Will you take a glass of wine?' Thoms said, and without waiting for an answer took a flagon and three glasses from a cupboard.

We sat round the table like any civilised company on shore, except that both the flagon and the glasses had heavy bases for stability, and when I raised the glass to my lips, the motion of the ship knocked it against my teeth. Mercifully I felt no seasickness. On my only other journey by sea, from Portugal to England, I had also been spared that pernicious affliction. Berden looked a little queasy. I was glad that in this, at least, I would not be the weaker of the two of us.

'Do you make this crossing often?' Berden asked. 'Over to the Low Countries?'

'Aye,' said Thoms. 'Ever since we have been helping the Dutchmen against the Spanish we have been back and forth, carrying supplies and men. And bringing the casualties home. I was second officer on the warship that brought Sidney's body home.' He shook his head. 'Less than a year ago now, though it seems like a lifetime. Poor Lady Sidney, she was wild with grief, and her not much more than a girl herself.'

'And carrying a child,' I said. 'I saw her at her father's house not long afterwards.'

'They say the child was born delicate,' Berden said.

'It is not to be wondered at,' I said. 'And the other little girl fatherless now.' I had a sudden vivid picture in my head of the child being led into St Paul's for the funeral.

'Were you on one of the ships that evacuated the survivors of Sluys in the summer?' I looked at Thoms, whose calm demeanour was reassuring on this storm-driven ship. I could imagine Andrew and the others in his care.

'I was. By then I was in command of the *Silver Swan* and we carried thirty of them back from Sluys and up the Thames to London.'

'Thirty!' Berden looked about him, as if he could see the prostrate forms of the injured soldiers heaped up.

'Aye. We pressed into service every ship we had nearby, to fetch the men away before Parma changed his mind. We had to lay them out in rows on the deck, like cargo, and run them home. Fortunately the weather was good, else I don't think we could have brought them home alive in rain.'

'Kit here is a physician.' Berden inclined his head towards me, 'as well as working for Walsingham. He tended some of them at St Bartholomew's.'

'Four hundred, there were,' I said. 'We also had to lay them out in rows.'

'I never want to carry out such an evacuation again,' Thoms said, refilling our glasses. 'It might never have been needed, if we had gone in sooner and broken the siege, saved Sluys and driven Parma away. He wouldn't now be in possession of the good harbour there at Sluys.'

I realised what he had said. 'You mean you were sent to Sluys with Leicester's fleet?'

'I was.' He smiled grimly. 'It was not a pleasant experience, sitting idle just offshore, watching until the guns inside Sluys fell silent. We knew they were running short of gunpowder. And we made a pathetic little sortie with fireships, that was turned against us, so we had to retreat with our tails between our legs. Drake would have gone straight in, as soon as he reached the Low Countries.' He gave an impatient sigh. 'Well, 'tis all over and done now. After I carried the wounded back from Sluys I was ordered to join the squadron at Dover. We are building up the naval defences for when the Spanish come in the new year.'

He rose to his feet. 'Please feel free to use my cabin as your own. I must go back on deck. We will dine later.'

When he had left and closed the door of the cabin behind him, I studied Berden, sitting across from me. He had not touched his second glass of wine.

'Best if you don't drink that.' I nodded toward his glass. 'If you are feeling nausea, you had better lie down.'

'Ha, coming the physician, are you, Kit?'

I shrugged. 'Take my advice or not, as you please, but you will feel it less if you lie down and close your eyes.'

'On the captain's bunk?'

'Why not? He is not using it.'

He shook his head, then clearly regretted it. 'Perhaps you are right.' He stood up, staggering a little, and made his way carefully over to the bunk, where he pulled off his boots and lay down. I unfolded one of the blankets and spread it over him.

'Close you eyes and try to sleep,' I said. 'It will help.'

He did close them and muttered, 'Never have been able to endure the sea, and this is worse than usual.'

I did not answer, but left him quiet and went back out on deck.

Although no snow was falling, the heavy clouds sagged overhead as though they would sink down and smother us with the weight of their unshed burden. The captain had still not given the order to hoist the foresail, but even without it we were speeding along. There was no land to be seen in this murk of night darkness in the daytime, so it was impossible to judge how quickly we were moving relative to land, but the bow wave rolled and creamed along the sides of the ship, then streamed out behind in a double ribbon of foam as far as the eye could see, which was not far before it vanished into the gloom. How fast we were really going would depend on the movement of the tides, which I had no way of judging.

I went into the canvas stable to see how the horses were faring. They were stirring uneasily but both turned their heads as though grateful that they were not alone on this fearful ship. We had left them some hay, which was nearly finished, and their water bucket had fallen over, spilling what was left of its contents and rolling away into a corner. I decided against fetching more water, which would certainly spill again as the ship rolled. Instead I felt in my saddlebag for the apples and gave each horse one, then sat on the upturned bucket and ate a piece of the cheese. Anxiety had robbed me of my appetite in the morning, but now fighting my way across the deck against the wind had made me hungry. Besides, two glasses of wine on an almost empty stomach was beginning to go to my head.

The apples and my companionship seemed to calm the horses, so I stayed where I was for a long time, leaning my back against Hector's forequarters and even dozing a little. One of the sailors found me there, come to summon me to the captain's cabin to dine.

I followed him along the deck and saw that the foresail had now been raised, which explained the busy sounds I had heard outside the stable as I was drifting in and out of sleep.

'Has the wind dropped?' I asked the sailor. 'I see you have put up the foresail.' It did not feel to me as though the wind was any less.

He shook his head. 'Nay, there's no slackening of the wind, but t'captain wants our best speed till we're near land. We'll furl it soon as land comes in sight.'

I peered around. The ship seemed to move inside a dark bubble, with nothing to be seen beyond a hundred yards or so all around. 'How can we see the land? It's almost as dark as night.'

'Captain knows this coast. He can feel it, like a cat with its whiskers.' He grinned and lowered his voice. 'Thom Cat, we call him. He'll feel the land before we see it. Cunning as a cat too. Best sort of captain to serve under.'

I was prepared to take him at his word, and stepped into the captain's cabin when he opened the door for me. Berden was up, sitting in one of the bolted chairs. He had lost some of his earlier pallor. The captain was studying a chart he had laid open on the table.

'We thought you must have gone overboard,' Berden said, but not as if he meant it.

'I was with the horses. They seem to be taking it better than we might have expected. How are you feeling?'

'Much better. I've apologised to Captain Thoms for lying on his bed.'

The captain looked up. 'No need for apology. I used to get sick myself when I first joined the navy, but I soon found my sea legs.'

I sat down on one of the other chairs.

'How old were you when you joined?'

'Ten. I was a boy on one of Drake's ships, the year he and Hawkins made their first voyage to the Americas. Rose up from that to this.' He waved his hand, indicating the comfort that surrounded us. I had heard of the small boys who fetched and carried below decks, bringing gunpowder and cannon balls and wadding to the gunners. They led a grim life.

'Where did you go with Drake? Berden asked.

'The Isles of the Spanish Main, mostly. Chasing treasure ships and sometimes overpowering them. I was with him in San Juan when the Spanish broke the agreed truce and attacked our fleet of ships, trapping us in the harbour, where we had gone in for water and repairs. Only two ships escaped and dozens of our men were taken prisoner, then tortured and murdered most cruelly by the Spanish. Luckily I was on Drake's ship which managed to break out and sail home. He has hated and mistrusted the Spanish ever since.'

'He's right to do so,' I muttered. I knew of this episode in Drake's past. Probably everyone in England did, for there had been broadsheets and ballads a-plenty about it, which had helped to fire up the general English hatred of Spain.

Before we could question the captain further about his adventures in the New World, a sailor came in carrying a tray. He wore a dirty apron wrapped around him and tied in front, bringing with him a kind of radiated warmth from the ship's kitchen and the rich smell of mutton pottage. I realised that I had become very cold sitting with the horses. When he handed me an elegantly fluted pewter bowl filled to the brim, I cupped my hands around it at first for the benefit of the heat. The bread was fresh, perhaps brought from Dover. But perhaps not. There is no end to the ingenuity of sailors. Perhaps they had baked it on board. I refused more of the captain's excellent – but very strong – French wine and confined myself to small ale. I noticed that Berden did the same, though he managed to eat both some bread and some pottage, with no visible ill effects. Maybe he too was finding his sea legs.

Berden and the captain talked of the many countries they had visited while we ate. I kept silent. Partly because I was familiar with only Portugal and England, countries they both knew well, but partly because I was growing sleepy. I had slept somewhat fitfully the previous night, anxious about our mission, and now that I had no responsibilities but to sit still and be conveyed in this ship on to the next stage in our journey, fatigue was beginning to creep over me.

By the time we had finished our pottage and sampled the bowls of fruit and nuts the sailor brought us, there were sounds of running footsteps out on deck and the captain was sent for. I could feel the change in the ship's motion when the foresail was lowered, so I decided to go out on to the deck to see whether I could gain any sight of land and to try to chase away sleep, for despite the early November dark it could not be later than perhaps five of the clock. We had finished our meal by candlelight, so when I went outside I could see nothing at first but a surrounding snow-filled darkness, which seemed to have thickened while I was in the cabin. Gradually my eyes adjusted themselves to the lesser light.

The foresail had indeed been lowered and the two remaining sails were trimmed to a different angle. I sensed that the wind was now striking my right cheek instead of coming from the stern of the ship, so either the wind had changed direction or the ship had. The sailor I had spoken to before came past and I put out a hand to stop him.

'I can see nothing, but you said the captain would take in the foresail when he spied land?'

'Aye, it's over there.' He gestured ahead and to starboard.

'I still cannot see anything.'

'Look. Follow my arm. There, where the darkness thickens. That's land. The Low Countries. And that's what they are. Low. They don't rise up like our white cliffs at Dover. Hardly more than a hillock of mud a few feet above the sea.'

I squinted along his arm. Now that he had pointed out where to look, I could just make out a slightly thicker, darker smudge amidst the surrounding grey of the day. And perhaps, just faintly, a light.

'Is that a light I can see? To the left of where you are pointing?'

'You've found it now? Aye, there's a church there where the minister puts a lantern in the tower every night to guide the fishermen in to shore. We'll anchor near there and carry on up to Amsterdam in the morning.'

He hurried on toward the main mast, where several of the sailors were adjusting ropes. A young boy had been sent up the mast as a lookout. He scrambled up as if he were climbing a small tree in his father's garden, but I had to look away, dizzy at the very thought of it.

I fixed my eyes on that tiny glint of light which marked the shore. I no longer felt sleepy. The closer we drew to land, the closer I came to my uneasy mission. It was the ship that had changed direction, I realised, not the wind, and the result was that waves were striking it crossways, causing it to pitch and twist, so that I had to seize hold of the railing that ran along the ship's side to avoid being thrown across the deck.

Gradually the light in the church tower grew larger and clearer, the loom of the land more substantial, though, as the sailor had said, the land was so low it barely rose above the level of the sea. As the ship dipped and rose, fighting against the sideways slap of the waves, it seemed as though we would be driven away from land, out into the trackless sea again. But Captain Thoms knew his ship and knew the ways of wind and sea. After what seemed like hours, as my fingers stiffened with cold on the railing, our ship slipped at last into the lea of a curved harbour wall and stopped bucking, like a horse suddenly tamed. Even the voice of the wind, which I realised had been booming in the sails all day, was suddenly quiet. There was a flurry of activity as the sailors lowered the sails and bundled them together. The anchor rattled out on its chain. The boy slid down from the mast. We had arrived.

Chapter Eight

*B*y the time the *Silver Swan* was anchored within the quieter waters of the harbour it had grown so dark that nothing could be seen of the land save an even denser darkness, apart from the lantern which still shone out from the church tower. We were aware of other ships or fishing boats nearby from the faint sound of voices carried over water, and the aroma of cooking which drifted past in snatches. The ship's crew went below for a well-deserved meal, while we took a light supper with the captain and three other officers, a fish pottage with more of the fresh bread, followed by four different kinds of cheese and washed down with more of the captain's fine red wine.

I allowed myself two glasses of the wine, for there was no need for me to stay alert now we were in harbour and I was looking ahead to how I might discreetly spend the night. The captain offered us his cabin, saying he would share with the officers.

'I plan to sleep with the horses,' I said, in as offhand a manner as I could manage. 'It will help to settle them in their strange surroundings, and it will be warm enough, with the heat of their bodies.' I was by far the youngest of the company, so perhaps it did not seem out of place that I should take this upon myself.

'Are you sure, Master Alvarez?' Captain Thoms said. 'I cannot think you will be very comfortable.' He did not sound, however, as though he would be particularly difficult to persuade.

'And I will leave your cabin to you,' Berden said, 'since there is a spare bunk in one of the officers' cabins.'

137

I saw that he was prepared to accept the arrangement, to my relief.

'Kit thinks more of the comfort and safety of those horses than of his own.' Berden turned to Thoms with an indulgent smile. 'He will be happiest if he can keep an eye on them.'

I gave them all a cheerful look. Let them think what they would, even that, as long as it meant I had somewhere private to bed down for the night.

When I came out of the captain's cabin, carrying a candle lantern to light my way along the deck, I found that it was snowing again. The wind had dropped, but the snow fell relentlessly, as though the clouds had just been waiting for this lull in the wind to empty their burden on the land. Already it was beginning to settle on the deck and when I had felt my way forward over the slippery boards to the temporary stable, I saw that the dips in its canvas were filling up with snow. Once inside I spoke quietly to Hector and Redknoll, then knocked the sagging areas of canvas from below, to send the loose snow cascading down the side of the tent. It was a fruitless task. They would soon fill up again, for the snow was coming down ever harder.

I hung the lantern from a nail in one of the uprights supporting the canvas, then set about making myself a bed. There was a space of about six or eight feet between the two horses, partly filled by the bales of straw Berden and I had piled up to protect them from knocks. I dragged these to form two sides of a sort of bed space for myself, and filled the centre with loose straw, placing my knapsack at one end to serve as a pillow. The captain had given me two blankets, which I spread over the straw. Sitting back on my heels, I decided that I would have as comfortable a night as anyone on board, and probably as warm. The horses had watched my preparations with interest, lowering their heads and blowing encouragingly at me as I worked. When I had arranged everything to my satisfaction, I took off my boots, blew out the lantern and wriggled down under the blankets.

As anyone will tell you, who has ever slept on straw, it provides a springy, sweet-smelling bed, but there are always a few sharp ends which prick and tease you until you have sought them out and banished them. It was probably half an hour before I had rid myself of these irritants, and then I found that my knapsack was lumpy and uncomfortable. Poking around inside it in the dark, I realised that it was my spare boots that were pressing against my ear, so I pulled them out and laid them beside my bed.

After that I was comfortable enough, but had thoroughly woken myself up. Even the effects of the heavy wine had worn off, so that I found myself lying and staring open-eyed into the dark, until shapes emerged – the two horses who stamped and snorted from time to time, a glimmer of light from the far end of the ship, where a lantern hung beside the sailor on watch. Through a gap in the canvas flaps I could see the snow falling, driven slantwise like silver rods against the lantern light. The ship rocked gently with the movement of the confined waves here within the harbour, barely noticeable after our wild tossing out in mid Channel.

I had hoped to fall asleep quickly, but now thoughts of the mission ahead chased themselves around in my unwilling brain. The first part, I told myself, would be easy. We would sail up the canal to Amsterdam tomorrow. I was not sure how long that would take. Either tomorrow evening or the next morning we would seek out the Earl of Leicester and deliver the despatches and personal letters. We each carried a set, the duplicates given us by Phelippes, as a precaution in case something befell one of us before we reached Leicester. Then what would happen? Leicester might wish to write replies to some of the documents, but he could not send them back by us. Not immediately, at any rate. Either he would have to wait until we returned to England, or he would have to send a courier of his own. I hadn't thought of this before and hoped Walsingham had made it clear to him that we had other work to do.

One thing was puzzling about this mission. Walsingham had never quite made clear to us whether we were to inform Leicester of our real purpose in coming to the Low Countries, to spy out any of the traitors he suspected. I found this strange and somewhat worrying. Did Walsingham assume we would discuss it with the Earl? He had said something about asking the Earl to tell us of his suspicions. Or were we to proceed, as so often in Walsingham's affairs, in secrecy? If we did not tell the Earl, he might find our own activities suspicious and have us arrested. I turned over restlessly, with a great rustling of straw. Hector stooped his head and blew in my face. Rather wetly. I rubbed my face on my sleeve and turned back again.

Perhaps Walsingham had instructed Berden what we were to do and he had forgotten to tell me. Or chosen not to. In the morning I would ask him outright, when I could have speech with him alone, not easy on board ship. I turned over again, more quietly this time and Hector did not stir. Perhaps he was asleep. I closed my eyes. And after we had seen the Earl? What then?

At some point I must have slept at last, for the next thing I knew was the sound of feet passing the stable. It was filled with a bright reflected light, which meant that the snow had stopped falling but was lying thickly enough to create the magical brilliance of a world under a blanket of white.

I pulled on my boots and laced them tightly, stowed my spare boots back in my knapsack, and folded my blankets to return them to the captain. My bed of straw had been comfortably warm, so that I hesitated to venture out into the snow, but I could not laze here any longer.

As I made my way back to the stern of the ship, with the blankets over my arm, I saw the sailor who had served us yesterday coming out of the captain's cabin. He raised his hand to his woollen cap and held the door open for me.

'Good morning to you, Doctor Alvarez,' Captain Thoms said. 'Come and eat. I regret I did not give you your proper title yesterday. Master Berden told me, after you left, how you work as a physician at St Bartholomew's. I should have realised when we spoke of the survivors of Sluys, but . . . that is a painful memory. Forgive me.'

Embarrassed by this apologetic speech, I smiled, with a wave of my hand, indicating that it did not matter. My title of 'Doctor' was purely an honorary one, for without university training I could not become a member of the Royal College of Physicians. Thoms clearly understood my unspoken acceptance of his apology and invited me to sit down.

'They have provided us with porridge this morning, I see,' he said. 'I hope you have no objection to such humble food.'

'It is excellent on such a cold day.' I said with a smile. 'Just what I was thinking in the middle of the blizzard at Dover.'

As he was serving me a large bowl of porridge, Berden and the other officers came in and soon the cabin was filled with the steam from our bowls and from our breath. The captain brought out a large pot of honey from one of his cupboards and passed it round for us to stir into the porridge.

'My sister and her husband have a farm in Kent,' he explained. 'Orchards, mostly, and some cows and sheep. They also keep bees, so whenever I am in Dover harbour, they send me over several pots of honey.'

'It is excellent for your health,' I said, 'and also a sovereign treatment for wounds, should one of your men be injured.'

'I will remember that,' he said with a smile, 'when we come to fight the Spanish. Good for you inside and outside, then?'

'Aye.' I ate several spoonfuls of the porridge, which was smoother than Joan's and all the better for the addition of the honey. 'Do you carry *cochlearia officinalis* for your men?'

He gave me a puzzled look. '*Cochlearia officinalis*?'

'Aye, scurvy grass. If you regularly give your men scurvy grass infused in ale, it will prevent all the unpleasant effects of scurvy, which so often afflict sailors. Bleeding gums. Loosened teeth. Swollen and painful joints. All unnecessary. Or you may eat the leaves like a salad.'

'I thought lemons were the preventative.'

'Oh they are, but expensive and not always easy to obtain. Scurvy grass is plentiful and grows abundantly in coastal areas. You would find it everywhere around the shore in Kent.'

'I will take note of that then, and see that we obtain a supply when we return to England. As you say, scurvy is a foul affliction. In my young days with Drake I remember many men suffering from it on our long voyages to the New World.'

'Many illnesses can be avoided by a careful diet,' I said ruefully, 'but sadly, as physicians we mostly see the results of a poor one.'

Our discussion was interrupted by one of the sailors coming in to say that the tide had turned and was set fair for heading up the canal to Amsterdam. We all went out on deck, where the captain and officers were soon occupied in directing the preparation of the ship for the next stage of the journey. The anchor was raised and the oars run out to manoeuvre the ship from the harbour into the mouth of the canal.

'Do you think they intend to row all the way?' I asked Berden in a low voice. 'It would be quicker to ride.'

'I suppose it must depend on the direction of the wind.'

There was not much wind at the moment, but what there was blew from behind us as we entered the canal. The question was settled when we saw the mainsail hoisted, then the staysail, and finally the foresail. Captain Thoms was taking advantage of every scrap of wind that would help us on our way. Once the sails filled and the ship stirred with that innate life that sails engender, the oars were shipped. Much to the relief of the sailors, I imagined.

The darkness of the previous day had prevented our understanding of the true manoeuvrability of the pinnace, but today was clear and bright, the winter sun sparkling on the snow-covered fields on either side of the canal, and it was soon obvious how well the small ship handled. She slipped up the canal as gracefully as a swan, her sails held in taut curves like the wings of a soaring bird. The waters creamed under her forefoot, spreading out to the banks of the canal and marking our path into the low, marshy country which stretched ahead of us, dotted with pumping mills to drain water from the fields and here and there a neat village of a few houses encircled by pastures. Once he was satisfied with the ship's trim, the captain came to stand beside us in the bows.

'I thought the Dutch canals were straight,' I said, 'but this one winds like a river.'

'That is because it is a river,' he said, 'or at least it was. It connects the German Ocean with the Zuiderzee, and the Hollanders have widened it and straightened it in places, but it silts up constantly as new sand banks form. And that causes it to freeze all the more readily in winter. When it's navigable, it provides a much shorter access to the town, instead of sailing a good way north, then turning east round the islands and coming in to Amsterdam that way. You will see that when we reach the Zuiderzee. It looks as calm as a giant's duck pond on a quiet day, but it's a treacherous stretch of water.'

'Why is that?' I asked.

'Again, shifting sand banks, which are the greatest danger to ships, but also it is notorious for terrible floods which rush in and break down the banks the Hollanders have built to try to hold it back. Thousands of people have died in the floods, but the farmland round about is so rich and profitable that they keep moving back. It is a strange country. Water and land constantly changing every year, sometimes every month.'

I soon realised that what both Captain Thoms and Sir Edward Walgrave had called a canal was far from what I understood by the term. It was in fact a series of interconnected waterways, some of them natural rivers which had been widened in places or reinforced by raised banks, others short lengths of straight canal dug through spits of land to connect the rivers. At times we seemed to wander aimlessly through a flat landscape where reed beds towered as high as the ship's deck. How the captain found his way through this maze, I could not imagine. A larger ship than our pinnace could never have followed this route. Three or four times we encountered bridges, which forced the crew to furl the sails and lower the mast on to a kind of wooden crutch, so that we could pass under them, using our oars. In some places the canal wound so sharply that it was impossible to use our sails.

We were not the only vessel on the water, though by far the largest. We met barges moving both inland and down to the sea, loaded with boxes and barrels. Some had a single sail on a stumpy mast, some were rowed. There were others, flat as punts, which the captain said were called 'trekschuiten' and were pulled by men or horses walking along the path which followed the line of the waterway.

'They call that the "jaagpad",' he said, pointing to the path, where a man and woman were plodding along, heads down, towing a flat barge loaded with piles of huge round cheeses. It had a tiny cabin in the stern, while perched on the very tip of the bow, in front of the cheeses, a small terrier barked encouragement to the labouring couple.

'Hard work,' I said.

'Aye. But they are a strong and independent people, the Hollanders. They will not easily allow themselves to be crushed by Spain, however many victories Parma may win on the battlefield.'

At length we passed a small town, which Captain Thoms said was called Leiden, and after that the waterway opened out. Our sails were hoisted and we moved ahead with the water foaming under our bows. Ahead lay an area even flatter than the countryside we had already traversed, a wide area of inland lakes interspersed with marshes, half water, half tussocky muddy land.

'Is this the Zuiderzee?' I asked.

Captain Thoms laughed. 'Not this. No, this is the Haarlemmermeer, one of the most treacherous areas in the Low Countries.'

'Treacherous!'

'More treacherous to the people who dwell round its margins than to us. It is a victim of what they call the "wolfwater", the water which rises in these low-lying inland lakes – fast, unpredictable – and devours whole villages.'

I shivered. 'But not treacherous for us?'

'Treacherous enough. We must pick our way through it, where the water is deep enough. Shifting mudbanks here, not sandbanks. Easy enough for us to become stranded.'

He walked away to supervise the lowering of the sails. We would have to make our way again under oars. The wide marshland seemed almost deserted, except by birds, for there were flocks of ducks and moorhens, solitary herons standing in the shallows like sentinels, a flight of gulls screaming raucously overhead. The very smell of the place was different, a reek of mud and rotting vegetation. Over on the eastern edge of the deceptively quiet waters I saw a few small fishing boats, and beyond them smoke rising from a cluster of cottages. Otherwise, desolation.

At length we came to the end of the Haarlemmermeer, passing through a short canal into what the captain said was the Oude Meer. The sails were hoisted again and the ship picked up more speed, heading northeast.

'We are nearly at the Zuiderzee now,' Captain Thoms said.

Even as he was speaking I could see the wider waters ahead and soon we had sailed out on to what seemed to be a vast inland lake, though Thoms assured us it was salt. The ship came about

144

and veered to starboard. The foresail was lowered, and then the mainsail, so that we made our way more slowly under staysail alone. Captain Thoms climbed out on to the base of the bowsprit, holding on to the rigging with one hand and leaning far out over the water, swinging the lead himself. As he checked the lead line, he signalled to the steersman to guide the ship first to port and then to starboard, to avoid the sandbanks.

I was so absorbed in watching him that it was only when Berden tapped my arm that I looked up and saw the buildings of Amsterdam drawing near. There were ships everywhere, some clearly warships, some merchant vessels, while dodging in amongst them were round-bellied fishing boats, small pinnaces, and open rowing boats. Satisfied that he had found the main channel into the town, Captain Thoms climbed back on to the deck, nodded to us as he passed, then gave the order to lower the staysail and run out the oars.

As the *Silver Swan* was brought neatly in, between the anchored and moored vessels, I could appreciate the captain's skill. He had found a space beside the quay and himself took over the steering to lay the ship alongside without a bump. While the sailors were busy mooring the ship and running out the ramp, Berden and I saddled the horses and strapped on our luggage. This time I led the way across the ramp on to the quay, Hector following me with blithe unconcern. Berden had not put the blinkers on Redknoll and when the chestnut saw how calmly Hector crossed the ramp, he followed us, after only a slight hesitation. The captain stepped ashore behind us.

'Our thanks to you, Captain Thoms,' Berden said, shaking his hand. 'We will hope to see you here in three weeks' time.'

'Aye, unless the canal ices over. If it does, I will meet you where we moored last night.'

'Thank you, Captain.' I shook his hand in my turn. 'It was a rough crossing, as you predicted, but you brought us here safely.'

'I hope it will not be worse on our return,' he said with a smile. 'In three weeks, then.'

He turned to go back on board ship, where the sailors were already dismantling the stable. Then he glanced back over his shoulder.

'I will see about the scurvy grass while I am back in England, Doctor.'

I raised a hand in acknowledgement, then we led our horses off the quay and into the busy crowds of the port. There was a Babel of voices around us, in which I could pick out French, Spanish and Italian as well as English, though the majority were speaking an unknown language which I supposed must be Dutch. Although it was unknown to me, somehow I almost felt I could understand it, for its rise and fall closely resembled English and even scattered words sounded like English.

Berden appeared to know where to go, for once we had mounted our horses he headed off confidently along a narrow cobbled street beside a waterway which might have been a river or a canal. I could not be sure. I knew that the town, like Venice, was built on a cluster of small islets of slightly higher ground rising up in the middle of a bog, but thanks to the skill of the Dutch engineers, more and more land was being reclaimed. At the moment the plan of the city was confusing and already dusk was falling.

'How can you find your way in this place?' I said.

'I've spent some time here,' Berden answered, speaking over his shoulder, for it was too narrow for us to ride abreast. 'There is talk that someday they will rebuild the town, or at least straighten out some of the meandering waterways.' This as we rode over yet another hump-backed bridge. 'But the town will need to become a good deal richer, and the Hollanders free of the Spanish, before they can undertake so large a building project.'

We crossed an open square with a public well in the middle and turned into a wider street, so that I was able to bring Hector up beside him.

'Nicholas, before we see the Earl – is he to be told what our real mission is, here in the Low Countries, besides carrying despatches?'

'No,' he said, 'Sir Francis has decided we should behave as if we were nothing more than messengers. It is not that he does not trust the Earl, for they have been close friends for many years, but sometimes the Earl is a little careless in his talk. And the loyalty of some of those about him on these foreign shores may be doubtful. Remember, there have been English traitors who have deserted to Spain. And recently things have become strained between the Earl and the Dutch leaders. Although he is no longer called Governor General, they find many of his actions high-handed. He is a poor diplomat and does not consult them as he should. If there is a traitor close to the Earl's own person, such a man might catch a whisper of our mission, or even guess from the way the Earl conducts himself towards us. Our wisest course is discretion.'

'Good,' I said. 'That seems best to me too. Though knowing that we work for Walsingham, and knowing what he wrote to the Queen in his recent letter, the Earl may himself guess why we have come.'

'That is a risk, of course,' Berden conceded, 'that we must take. Here, this is the house where the Earl and his immediate entourage are lodging.'

I looked where he pointed. The house was built in what I was coming to recognise as a typical Dutch style as we rode through Amsterdam. It was tall. Four regular storeys with an attic storey above, behind the characteristic fluted gable high above the street. Most of the houses had an opening here, much like the hatch in an English hay barn, through which the hay can pitched down, except that here there was usually a hoist extending out over the street. The houses, I assumed, must also serve as places of business for the merchants of Amsterdam. The house Berden pointed out had the opening in the high gable end, but there was no hoist and the opening was shuttered. Three shallow steps led up to the front door and there was an archway to the left which appeared to lead through to outbuildings or a garden to the rear of the building.

We dismounted and secured our horses to tethering rings set into the front wall of the house. By the time I had slung my satchel over my shoulder and Berden had removed his wallet of papers from his pack, the door was opened by a serving man in the Earl's livery. Someone must have been watching from a window.

'Messengers from the Queen's Principal Secretary,' Berden said, 'with private despatches for his Lordship.' He held out his official pass and jerked his head at me to do the same.

147

The servant studied them, then nodded and held the door wider. We entered a central hallway with doors leading off on either side and at the far end a graceful curved staircase, up which the servant led us, still without a word. On the first floor he stopped in front of a door and knocked.

'Enter,' a voice called from within. The servant opened the door, stood back to allow us to pass, then withdrew, closing the door quietly behind him.

The Earl of Leicester was sitting in a large cushioned chair beside the window, with his legs sprawled out and a flagon of wine at his elbow. Two younger men were sitting with him, one in military uniform, one not. A table in the centre of the room showed where they had recently dined. It still held plates and goblets of silver gilt, an epergne heaped high with exotic fruits, and a solid gold salt the size of a small bucket, shaped like a clam shell held aloft by a Triton. The walls were hung with rich tapestries depicting scenes from classical myth, and a fire burned within a carved marble fireplace. The curtains at the window were of eastern damask. Everything spoke of comfort, the kind of comfort provided by an ample fortune.

I studied the Earl, while trying to appear not to do so. Perhaps two years before this I had seen him ride in procession with the Queen at the celebrations to mark the anniversary of her succession. I had not been very close to him on that occasion, but even so I was sure he had since been marked by age in the intervening years. His hair and beard were grown quite grey, whereas they had been dark brown before. He must be in his middle fifties, but it seemed a rapid change in so short a period, so that I wondered if what I had heard was true, that the courtiers had their hair dyed in order that they might still appear young. It was said that the Queen liked to have young men about her. As her favourite, perhaps the Earl strove to maintain the look of perpetual youth, to please her or to satisfy his own vanity. Here on campaign in the Low Countries it might be that he had given up the practice.

His skin was dry and faded with age and his face was lined. Above all, I noticed his eyes. They looked both anxious and exhausted. Here was a man who knew himself to be out of his depth, risen to a position beyond his abilities, whatever might be the boast to his peers at court. Suddenly I felt a stab of pity for him. For a year I had been despising him, blaming him for Sidney's death and most certainly for the disaster at Sluys. Yet I realised with unexpected clarity that this was a man who was expected by the Queen to be a hero, a military champion in the mould of Alexander, though he was in truth a man more suited to the frivolous chatter of the palace or the undemanding exercise of the tennis court or the bowling green than to the rigours of warfare.

These thoughts flashed through my head in the time it took us to cross the room and bow deeply before the Earl.

'So, Nicholas,' he said, affably enough, 'have you brought papers from Sir Francis?'

I had not realised that Leicester would know Berden by sight, but presumably he had come on similar errands before.

'We have, my lord. May I present Christoval Alvarez, who is a physician as well as serving Sir Francis?'

I bowed again.

'Ah, the code-breaker,' the Earl said, 'we have heard of your talents, and of the good service you did Her Majesty last year.'

My bow nearly ended in a tumble to the floor. Leicester had heard of me?

'My lord,' I said, straightened up and seeing those tired eyes scrutinising me carefully. Perhaps I should not pity him after all.

Berden stepped forward and handed Leicester his wallet of despatches. Leicester took them, but did not open the wallet. He laid it on the table next to the wine flagon.

'Mine are but duplicates, my lord,' I said, placing them on the table. 'Sir Francis sent them in case of accidents on the way.'

'You must have had a rough crossing of it,' Leicester said. 'Yesterday, was it?'

'It was, my lord.' Berden looked slightly queasy at the memory. 'After the worst of the blizzard, but still it was . . . rough.'

Leicester threw back his head and laughed. 'I can see that you are not a good sailor, Nicholas. And what of you, Dr Alvarez?'

'I am not troubled by seasickness, my lord. Happily.' I risked a smile and the Earl smiled back.

'Come,' he said, 'you must eat. We have dined, but I will send for more.'

He merely clapped his hands and the servant who had shown us upstairs appeared in the doorway. He must have been standing just outside. I opened my mouth to make a polite refusal but Berden gave a tiny shake of his head. It seemed we must accept, though I would much have preferred to have found an inn and settled in there.

Servants swiftly cleared the remains of the meal from the table and laid fresh dishes, then carried in grilled fish and roasted meats and a salad composed of out-of-season greens, which must have been grown in a hot house, like the fruits on the epergne. Apart from these, and the ostentatious golden salt, the meal and the dishes were not very different from dinners at our home in Coimbra, though no doubt both Berden and Leicester expected me to be overawed by it all.

While we ate, the Earl plied Berden with questions about the current state of affairs in London, particularly the progress in building up the navy. I merely listened quietly as I ate. Berden himself put a few questions about matters here in the Low Countries, which the Earl answered readily enough. There was little to report. Parma was strengthening defences around his coastal positions and had not made any recent advances against the Dutch. We were already well aware of the English Catholic traitors in the army – Sir William Stanley and Rowland York. Earlier in the year, when Leicester was in England, he had left them in command of the city of Deventer and the Sconce of Zutphen. In the Earl's absence they had both defected to the Spanish and handed over their commands and their armies to Parma in return for bribes. This treason on the part of English officers had aggravated the tension between the Earl and the Hollanders, though his responsibility for their defection could probably be set down to incompetence, rather than treachery.

During all this discussion, and indeed ever since we had come in, the two younger men had sat in silence, though I noticed that they listened intently. As though finally recalling their presence, Leicester introduced them.

'Sir John Worthington, one of my cavalry captains, and Mijnheer van Leyden, who acts as liaison between our forces and those of the United Provinces.'

Both men rose and bowed; Berden and I did the same. Worthington was a very sleek, elegant officer, whose immaculate uniform had clearly never seen a battlefield. His glance passed over me indolently. I noticed he paid closer attention to Berden, although I did not gain the impression they had ever met. I could not quite make out van Leyden. A little older than Worthington, even in civilian clothes he carried much more distinctly the air of an army officer, or perhaps simply of a man accustomed to commanding others. It was something in the way he held himself. By contrast, he studied me more closely than Berden. From the corner of my eye I had caught something pass between Berden and van Leyden – a glance, a tiny movement of the head – which I read as a sign that they knew each other, but would not acknowledge it openly.

At last it seemed we were free to leave. Berden bowed again to Leicester.

'We must find ourselves an inn, your Lordship. We thank you for an excellent dinner.'

I murmured agreement.

'You may stay here, if you wish,' Leicester said. 'I am sure there are rooms enough.'

'That is most kind,' Berden said, 'but we would not wish to trouble you or your staff further. We may not stay in Amsterdam after this night. Dr Alvarez and I have some further errands to undertake for Sir Francis,' he said, 'before we return to England. Our ship will fetch us home in three weeks. If there should be any letters you wish to send with us, shall we call before we leave?'

'Aye. There is sure to be something. I wish you good fortune in your "errands" for Sir Francis.' He smiled somewhat wolfishly, so that I wondered how much he had guessed of our real purpose in coming here.

With more bows and courtesies we left the room, to find the same liveried servant waiting to show us out. Our horses were stamping impatiently in the cold outside. I was concerned that they had been left so long unprotected, for the wind was rising again and an aura of damp rose from the canal which ran along the street. I shivered. It had been warm in the Earl's room, with that large fire blazing, and we had not been invited to shed our cloaks, so the cold damp air struck us now all the more forcibly.

We set off back towards the square with the public well, where Berden said there was a comfortable inn called the Prins Willem.

'They do not forget their William of Orange,' he said, 'so wickedly assassinated.'

'I think it was that assassination which has made Sir Francis all the more vigilant over the Queen's safety,' I said. 'Phelippes told me that she took it very badly, saw her danger as all the greater.'

'Well, if the Spanish can succeed in murdering one prince, it will convince them that they have a good chance of succeeding again.'

'Nicholas,' I said, 'did you know either of those men? The ones with Leicester?'

'Worthington – I have heard his name but know nothing more about him. As for van Leyden, yes. We have met in the past, when he was acting as an interpreter.'

'He is to be trusted?'

'As much as any of the Hollanders, I suppose. They are beginning to lose their trust in us.'

'They have some cause.'

'There are arguments on both sides, Kit. This war against Spain here in the Low Countries seems like to go on for ever and Sir Francis has told me that the Queen has become very impatient with all it has cost us in money and men's lives. She thinks the Dutch leaders do not show sufficient gratitude for our aid. On the other hand, they are our loyal allies. If we abandon them and Spain overruns this country, it will be child's play for Spain to attack England, and almost certainly conquer us. Spain's troops – their battle-hardened troops – will no longer be tied down here. They can easily be carried across the Channel, where there is no hope that we can resist them.'

'I understood from Phelippes that the Hollanders once welcomed Leicester and nominated him Governor General.'

Berden grinned. 'Her Majesty did not care for that. It gave the Earl too much power. She forced him to resign the position.

And now they have fallen out of love with him. We would have far greater success here with Sir John Norreys in command, but Leicester hates him.'

'Because he is a gifted soldier?'

'Aye, almost certainly. Amongst other reasons. And when it comes to appointing a commander for the army in England, next year, when the Spaniards attack, who do you think the Queen will choose?'

'Not Norreys?'

'Not Norreys.'

'But Leicester's history in command of armies is but one disaster after another!'

Berden smiled and shook his head. 'Who are we, to question the judgement of monarchs?'

The Prins Willem had a room for us and stabling for our horses. I was glad to see Hector safely into a warm stall that did not toss under his feet like the ship and was protected against the rising winter wind by brick walls rather than thin canvas. When the horses were fed and watered, and buckled into their blankets, we made our way back to the inn.

'Nicholas,' I said, remembering, 'you have not taught me how to vault on to a horse from the rear, as you promised.'

'There has been no opportunity,' he protested, 'and here in the middle of the town is not the place. When we travel south and are out in the countryside, then there will be a chance.'

'We are going down to the Spanish lines, then?' I hoped my fear did not show in my voice.

'That is what Sir Francis wants, so that is what we must do, if we can. Before that, however, we must part company for a while. I have business in Den Haag. I think you should stay here in Amsterdam and, as Sir Francis said, keep your eyes and ears open amongst the troops. Stay inconspicuous, but find out what you can. I'll return here when I have finished in Den Haag.'

'How long will that be?' I asked, as we opened the door into the warmth and light of the inn.

'At least a week. Perhaps ten days. That will leave us a week to head down towards Parma's army, then three or four days to come back to Amsterdam or make for the coast if the canal is frozen.'

As we had already dined at the Earl's residence, we told the inn keeper, who spoke good English, that we did not need food, but made our way to our room. It was comfortable and very clean, much cleaner than most of the English inns I had encountered in my rather limited experience. Berden dropped his pack on one of the beds.

'I'm going down for a drink and to listen to the men drinking here. I noticed that most of them were English soldiers.'

I nodded. I too had noticed. 'I shall go to bed. I am tired.'

He laughed. 'Somewhat uncomfortable with the horses last night, was it?'

'Not really.' I did not tell him that I had been kept awake by fear of what the next stage of our mission entailed.

When he had gone, I seized my chance to use the pisspot in privacy, then shed my boots and lay down on my bed. The straw mattress was topped with one stuffed with goose feathers, and there was another goose feather mattress for a cover. For the first time in several days I was truly warm. Within minutes I was asleep.

The next morning as we broke our fast in the inn parlour with cold meats and cheeses, Berden told me he had paid for the room for the next week.

'I have told the inn keeper that you will be remaining in Amsterdam, while I will be travelling about. It is unlikely that I will return in less than a week, but no need to tell him that.'

'You said you know the town well,' I said. 'Do you know Reiger Straat?'

'It's not far from here. Go back to the Earl's house, then follow the canal until it flows into another one. Reiger Straat runs off to the left, along that canal. Why do you ask?'

'A friend of mine told me her cousin lives there. If I had the chance, she asked me to take him news of her family.'

He considered this for a moment, frowning. 'You had best tell me the name of your friend and her cousin.'

This annoyed me somewhat, for I felt it was no concern of his, but I was in some sense under his direction, so I said, 'It is Sara Lopez, the wife of Ruy Lopez, the Queen's personal physician. Her cousin is Ettore Añez, a merchant dealing in precious stones, the nephew of Dunstan Añez, the Queen's Purveyor of Spices.' I laid a good deal of emphasis on these links to the Queen.

His face cleared. 'Ah, that is quite permissible. Dr Lopez has been of service to Sir Francis, and so has Senhor Añez.'

I wasn't sure which Senhor Añez he meant, but I let that pass. 'So you will have no objection if I call on Senhor Añez?' I said, with an edge of false humility in my tone.

He looked at me sharply. 'These are dangerous times, Kit. You should realise that. And in a foreign country one must be particularly careful to watch every step. Take care that you do so while you are alone in the town. I know that you are new to this . . . business. Caution and discretion are often the only shield for an intelligencer from arrest or even death, and don't forget it.'

I felt my cheeks burning as I said, 'I'll not forget.'

'Good.' He dismissed the subject and instead explained the route he would be following and said again that he was unlikely to return in less than a week.

I saw him out to the stables and waited while he saddled Redknoll. Then he was on his way.

When he had disappeared around a corner of the narrow street, I felt, suddenly, curiously, alone. Berden was not exactly a friend, but he was a steady companion, totally to be trusted, and much more experienced than I. I realised now how much I had depended on him ever since we had left Seething Lane. Now that I was on my own, I was uncertain what I should do. It was all very well for both Sir Francis and Berden to tell me to keep my eyes and ears open, but I could not sit all day in an inn, hoping that I would be fortunate enough to overhear some careless talk. What should I do with all the rest of my time? The soldiers were certain to have military duties during the day and were most likely to frequent the inns in the evenings. It was still early morning and a whole day stretched ahead of me.

I decided that the best way to occupy this first day was to start finding my way about the town. Such knowledge might be useful later. It seemed a confusing maze of twisting streets and unexpected waterways, but Berden had learned to find his way about it and so could I.

For the rest of the day I made forays out from the square in which the Prins Willem stood, building up a map of the town in my head. I went on foot, not on horseback, partly because I found that an easier way to memorise the streets and partly because, mingling in with those on foot, I was less likely to draw attention to myself. Indeed I found that there were fewer horsemen than in London. Even most of the carts were either pushed by men or hauled by large dogs, something I had not seen either in Portugal or England. A few coaches and heavier carts were drawn by horses, and the occasional nobleman or official rode past, but few ordinary men went mounted. As I did when in London, I walked everywhere, though I decided that in a day or two, when Hector had rested from the journey, I would ride out into the countryside, perhaps to the English camp, where most of the troops were billeted.

Amsterdam seemed a clean and tidy small town. The people were well though not richly clothed and I saw only one beggar, a man who had lost both legs, so I took him for a former soldier. He sat on a little wheeled platform beside the steps up to one of the severely plain Dutch churches, with one of those large dogs at his side, occasionally playing simple melodies on a pipe. Berden had explained the Dutch coins to me before he left, so I picked out a small one from my purse and dropped it into the man's upturned cap, where there were few others. He nodded his thanks, still playing.

'You shouldn't encourage him.'

The voice, an English voice, came from behind me and I spun quickly on my heel.

It was a fat man, in rude good health, who shook his head disparagingly.

'We don't like beggars in Amsterdam.'

'But you are English.'

'English father, Dutch mother. I bestride the Channel, and have lived in both countries.' He laughed heartily at his own image, spreading his arms wide. Then his face darkened. 'And as I say, we do not like beggars in Amsterdam.'

'And how is that poor fellow to live, having lost both legs?' I was furious, thinking of William Baker and his great good fortune in having a family and an occupation. 'I assume he lost them fighting the Spanish.'

'Aye, I did that.' The beggar spoke in English, though with a noticeable accent. 'Blown off by a cannon ball at Zutphen.'

'A year ago?' I said. 'Where Sir Philip Sidney died?'

'Aye. He was a good man.'

'You see.' I turned back to the fat man who had accosted me. 'An old soldier. We should be grateful to him and his kind.'

The fat man shrugged, which brought his chest up to meet his cascading chins. 'You have no proof. He may be lying.'

The beggar's dog gave a low growl and the hairs stood up on his neck, but the beggar smoothed them down and whispered some words in Dutch.

'I think not. I am a physician and I have seen such injuries before, some from Sluys.'

Why should he assume the beggar was lying? There must be many maimed soldiers in the Low Countries after the long years of fighting. Something stirred in my memory. I was sure I had seen the fat man before. Then I remembered. The previous evening in the Prins Willem, he had been at the far side of the parlour when Berden and I had been arranging our room with the inn keeper. He had been with a group of similar men, all large and well fed, drinking heartily and, I was sure, speaking Dutch. I had not noticed him this morning, when Berden and I had been breaking our fast in that same parlour, but it had been early and not many people were about.

As if he caught some sign of recognition in my eyes, the fat man held out his hand.

'Cornelius Parker, at your service.' He bowed.

I shook his hand and returned the bow.

'You are here with the army?' he said. 'One of our young officers?'

'No, no. Merely a messenger, and here in Amsterdam for a short time only, before I return to England.'

'Well, if I can be of any service to you while you are here, Master . . .?'

'Alvarez,' I said, trapped by the habit of courtesy into giving my name.

His eyes widened. 'Spanish?'

157

'No.' I would not elaborate to this importunate stranger.

'I am a merchant here in Amsterdam. Fine fabrics, many imported from the east, Constantinople, Ragusa, even silk from China. I would be happy to oblige you in any way I can. I have the entrée to many fine houses, and amusements of every sort.' He leered and winked at this, which distorted his superficially amiable features and made it plain exactly what kind of entertainments he had in mind.

I simply bowed, and since it was clear I would say no more, he bowed yet again and walked off, surprisingly briskly for a man of his bulk. I realised that the maimed soldier had been listening to every word of this exchange. Exasperated, I looked down at him, smiled and shrugged.

'He will not get any custom from me.' I dropped another coin into the hat, a larger one.

The soldier did not return my smile but looked at me seriously, then reached up and laid a hand on my arm.

'Be careful,' he said. 'That is a bad man.'

Chapter Nine

I was oddly disturbed by this encounter. What did the maimed soldier mean, that Cornelius Parker was a bad man? I had caught a flash of something between them. In view of Parker's condemnation of beggars and his imputation that the man might be lying about being an ex soldier, it would be understandable if it was an indication of anger and resentment on the beggar's part, yet it had seemed like something else. As if the two men knew each other and an old hostility existed between them. Clearly the soldier spoke only limited English, so his warning had contained just those few simple words, yet as I continued my exploration of Amsterdam, I could not forget them.

I retraced my steps to the square with the public well, where a group of women were now drawing water, and turned along the street we had taken yesterday to the Earl's house. Berden had told me to follow the street along the canal until it met another, and then turn left on Reiger Straat. It proved to be further than I expected, but I found it at last. The houses overlooking this canal, like those near the Earl's lodging, were large and prosperous, though there was much more activity here. The cranes jutting out from the top storeys were in use at several of the houses, lowering goods on to barges on the canal or lifting other goods from the boats into the houses. This must be the heart of the merchants' quarter of the town. I found the sign of the Leaping Gazelle, where Sara's cousin Ettore Añez lived, but there were many men coming and going through the front door, so I hesitated to intrude. I would return when the business of the day was over, or the following morning.

Unable to shake off the memory of the beggar's warning, I decided to return to the church and ask him to explain just what he had meant, but by the time I had found my way back – and I managed to lose myself twice – there was no sign of him or his dog. A woman was selling hot sweet pastries from a tray hanging from her neck and I bought one. As I ate it, I asked her if she knew where I could find the beggar I had seen there that morning.

Giving me an odd look, she said, 'I do not know, Me'heer. Sometimes he is there, sometimes not. I do not know where he lives.'

It was clear she thought it strange that I should ask. Not wanting to draw attention to myself, I gave a quick nod, as if it was of no importance, and made my way back to the inn.

That evening I decided to sit in a corner of the inn parlour, nursing a tankard of Dutch beer and doing as I had been instructed, keeping my eyes and ears open. Like the previous evening, it soon filled up with soldiers, mostly English, but a few Dutch, who came to eat and drink and play cards. They talked loudly of nothing in particular, complaints about the delays in their pay, an officer who bullied the younger men, the lack of decent boots. Nothing unusual. Very much the same kind of talk as I had heard at Dover Castle. A sudden angry argument erupted between one group of English soldiers and the Dutchmen, with accusations of slacking and cowardice being thrown about. It was starting to turn nasty when Niels Penders, the innkeeper, came through from the back room and broke up the impending fight. He was a big man, but his tactic was cheerfulness and jokes, not force, followed by free beer all round, which seemed to settle the dispute, for the moment at least.

There was nothing suspicious or even interesting in the soldiers' talk. This evening there were few civilians in the inn, and no sign of Cornelius Parker. I wondered why he had been here the previous evening, when it did not seem to be an inn much frequented by the local Hollanders. I also wondered whether my encounter with him had been entirely a chance one. Could he have followed me? It seemed unlikely, and the idea probably sprang from the nervousness I felt at being alone in this foreign town, with no particular business to pursue. Yet I could not quite shake it off. Could Parker have discovered that I was here on errands for Walsingham, or had he seen us visiting the Earl yesterday? But why should that be of interest to a draper, a merchant dealing in expensive imported fabrics? All the Dutch merchants, I knew, suffered as a result of Spanish blockades of many of their ports. Their merchant vessels were forced to run the gauntlet of the Spanish ships which prowled the Channel, and were only able to sail down past the English coast under escort from Dutch or English warships before they could reach the Atlantic and make their way west to the New World or south to the Mediterranean and Africa. So it was in the interests of all the merchants for the war with Spain to be brought to an end by an English and Dutch victory.

Why had the beggar warned me against Parker?

Tired from my hours of walking over the snow-covered cobbles of Amsterdam and seeing little purpose in eavesdropping any longer on the soldiers' talk, I decided to go to bed. On the way, I asked Niels Penders to send some hot water to my room. It arrived soon after I did, carried in by a girl of about my own age, the innkeeper's daughter Anneke. She smiled and curtseyed, and set the bucket of steaming water down beside the table that held a jug and basin. When she was gone, I dragged the clothes coffer against the door to block it, poured the water into the basin, and stripped to the skin.

For days, ever since we had left London, I had slept in the same clothes I wore all day, and I felt tired and grubby. It was a luxurious pleasure to wash all over with the scrap of soap I had brought with me. I had no towel, but a fire had been laid in the small fireplace and after rubbing myself with my cloak I soon dried by toasting myself in front of it. I then washed out my stockings, my shirt and my undershift, wringing them out as best I could and draping them over a chair in front of the fire, which I made up with logs from a basket provided by the inn. I slipped my night shift over my head with a sigh of pure pleasure. Tonight, at least, I could sleep in comfort.

The coffer I left in place behind the door, but I laid my clean shirt, breeches and spare hose ready, in case I should need to dress in a hurry, and with that slid beneath the feather bed and blew out my candle. Within minutes I was asleep.

The next morning I woke slowly, vaguely aware of a cock crowing somewhere not far off, and the clatter of hooves beneath my window. The clothes I had washed, being of thin fabric, had dried in the night, so I folded them and packed them into my knapsack. I dressed in the clean clothes I had laid out and drew the coffer away from the door, hoping that no one would hear the noise I made. Before eating the previous night I had checked that the ostler had fed Hector, but I thought I would visit the stables before breaking my fast. It was still quite early, so it might be possible to call on Ettore Añez before he was too much caught up in the business of the day.

Hector seemed comfortable and well fed, so as soon as I had eaten I set off again on foot for Reiger Straat. There had been no further snow during the night, so what had already fallen was churned up and dirty with the passage of feet and stained with horse droppings. Perhaps because I knew the way, the house seemed nearer this time. The hoists and the barges were not yet as busy as they had been the day before, and only one man emerged from the door of the house at the sign of the Leaping Gazelle, so I decided to make my way up the shallow steps and knock.

The door was opened immediately by a smartly dressed servant who asked me something in Dutch. I replied in English.

'Is this the home of Mijnheer Ettore Añez?'

'Certainly, sir,' he replied in faultless English, with no trace of accent. 'Who shall I say is calling?'

'Dr Christoval Alvarez,' I said, 'a friend of his cousin Sara Lopez from London.'

'If you will wait here a moment, sir.' He bowed and climbed the stairs to the next floor, where I heard the knock on a door and the murmur of voices. I might have been in a gentleman's house in London, received by one of his upper servants.

The man came quickly downstairs again.

'If you would follow me, Dr Alvarez?'

On the first floor he knocked at a door, then opened it without waiting for an answer, and I stepped inside. A large window faced the canal, filling the room with reflected light dancing off the water. As I entered, a tall man, thin and elegantly dressed, came towards me with both hands outstretched, beaming at me with genuine pleasure.

'Dr Alvarez! My cousin has told me much about you and your father in her letters. I am delighted to meet you and to welcome you to Amsterdam.' He turned to the servant who was just closing the door. 'Alfred, bring us some refreshments.'

He indicated two comfortable chairs pulled close to the fire. 'Please, please, sit down. You will take a little wine? You must tell me all the news of Sara and the children.'

It was not much more than an hour since I had eaten at the inn, but in courtesy I could not refuse. As I gave Ettore the latest news of Sara's family, including the prospects for Anne's marriage, the servant returned bearing a tray which he unloaded on to a table conveniently placed between the two chairs. A crystal and silver flagon of pale gold wine, two Venetian goblets, two fine linen table napkins, two silver gilt plates and another one loaded with a selection of sweetmeats, tiny sugared pastries, and marchpane shapes. It appeared that Ettore Añez lived every bit as well as the Earl of Leicester.

'And are you in Amsterdam for long, Dr Alvarez?' he asked. He was far too discreet to ask what my business here was.

'Perhaps another week or ten days,' I said. 'I am awaiting the return of a colleague who had business elsewhere in the United Provinces.' I had decided that Ettore Añez seemed a trustworthy man. He was, after all, the cousin of my oldest friend. I would not tell him everything, but I could see no harm in telling him what was common knowledge.

'We have come from Sir Francis Walsingham, carrying despatches and letters for the Earl of Leicester.'

'You have seen the Earl?'

'Aye, the evening we arrived. The day before yesterday.' I paused, then thought I would venture a question. 'When we saw the Earl, there were two men dining with him: Sir John Worthington, one of his cavalry captains, and a Dutchman, Mijnheer van Leyden. I wondered whether you knew anything about them.'

Ettore poured us each more wine while he considered.

'I know very little about Worthington. Little more than his name, in fact. He may be a cavalry captain, but I doubt whether he has ever led a cavalry charge in battle. I understand that he is one of the Earl's favourites, kept well away from any real fighting.' He paused, sipping his wine, then ate a few of the tiny pastries.

'Van Leyden, now, I do know. He is a merchant here in Amsterdam, dealing in spices from the islands of the east. Or at least he was. Last year he lost his two largest ships, one to storms in the Indian Ocean, one to the Spanish. He was ruined, forced to sell his two remaining ships and look about for other employment. That was when he took up a position with the English.'

I understood from the way he said 'the English' that he did not regard himself as belonging to that nation, although we had spoken entirely in English, not Portuguese and certainly not Dutch. Perhaps, like my father and me, he felt himself still a stranger in northern Europe, even though, like his cousin Sara, he had been born here and never lived in Portugal. The sense of being an outsider is not easily overcome, even after one or two generations.

'What do you think of him?' I asked bluntly. 'Van Leyden?'

He gave me a thoughtful look in which I caught a sudden resemblance to Sara. 'He is not generally liked. There was no great mourning when he went out of business last year. There had been talk of false weights, of spices adulterated with cheaper produce, or tainted with mould. I would say that he is not altogether trustworthy. Moreover he has been humiliated by his losses, and I believe that he is not a man to take that well. Such humiliation can make a man dangerous.'

'Hmm,' I said, digesting this. 'So do you think van Leyden himself might be dangerous?'

'Dangerous to whom?'

'Well, I suppose to the Earl, as he seems to be on intimate terms with him, dining in his house. And also perhaps to the alliance between England and the United Provinces.'

'That alliance is already on quaking ground,' Añez said. 'Each side blames the other for failure on the battlefield. Zutphen was a disaster. Sluys a tragedy. It has reached a point where the commanders on both sides distrust each other, while the common

164

soldiers come to blows in the streets. This is no way to withstand the Spanish, especially with a general of Parma's skill in command of them.'

I had not realised things were so bad. Were the fears Leicester had expressed about treason and treachery merely this general falling out between the two nations? Or was there something more particular?

'I believe the Earl has asked the Queen repeatedly if he might return home,' I ventured.

'Very likely.' He nodded. 'One can hardly blame the man. He is not a soldier. I am no soldier myself, but even I can understand that he has no grasp of military matters. But who would replace him?'

'Perhaps his stepson, the Earl of Essex.' I gave a wry smile, reflecting my view of Essex. 'Sir John Norreys would be the wiser choice.'

'I agree. When you saw the Earl, did you gain any idea of his plans?'

'No, we were not made privy to anything of such importance.'

Añez held up the wine flagon again, but I shook my head and put my hand over my glass.

'There was something else,' I said, 'that I wanted to ask you.'

'Certainly.'

'It may be nothing, yet I found it disturbing.'

I gave him a brief account of my meeting with Cornelius Parker and the cryptic warning from the beggar, and explained that I had seen Parker at our inn the previous night.

'You say he accosted you in the street, uninvited?'

'Aye. Came up behind me and remonstrated with me for giving a small coin to the maimed soldier. I was taken aback. And even more so when he offered me "entertainments", unspecified.'

'And the beggar warned you that he is a bad man.'

I nodded.

He sat back in his chair, studying the fire. 'Cornelius Parker is as slippery as an eel. I doubt you could pin any crime to him, yet, like van Leyden, rumours cluster about him. Many of his goods are what he says they are, fine fabrics imported generally through Constantinople. Yet it is whispered that his ships sometimes carry other goods – arms which he trades with the Spanish and the Musselmen – slipped in amongst the bales of cloth. He has other business interests as well, brothels here in Amsterdam, in Den Haag and even in Antwerp.'

'I thought Spain controlled Antwerp now.'

'It does.'

I took off my cap and ran my fingers through my hair. 'Do you mean that Parker is in the pay of the Spanish?'

He shrugged. 'That I cannot say. It is as certain as can be that he has dealings with them.'

Something else struck me. 'Is he a Catholic?'

Añez shook his head. 'That I do not know. It is not safe to admit to being a Catholic these days, here in the United Provinces. I am sure he attends the free Dutch Protestant Church, but may nevertheless be a secret Catholic.'

I thought of the Fitzgerald family, where Walsingham had sent me last year. They had taken me with them to an English Protestant service like any respectable family, yet they celebrated the Catholic mass in secret.

'I would have supposed,' I said slowly, 'that for a man like Parker, his best interests are served by continuing to trade legitimately, rather than engaging in dangerous activities.'

'That would seem to be true. But men can be swayed by many things – passion for a cause, revenge, or, for men like van Leyden or Parker, money. I think that Parker, like van Leyden, could be a dangerous man.'

'Aye. Well, I thank you for your information, Senhor Añez.'

'To such a friend of my cousin Sara, I am Ettore.'

I smiled. 'My friends call me Kit.'

We shook hands on it as I stood up to leave. So absorbed had I been in our conversation that it was only now that I noticed how dark it had grown. The glint from the canal had disappeared and the very room was full of shadows.

'There will be more snow soon, I think,' he said.

'Aye, I'd best be back at my inn before it starts. I am staying at the Prins Willem.'

'The best inn here in Amsterdam, though not the most expensive. The soldiers can become noisy in the evening.'

I laughed. 'So I have noticed.'

He walked with me down the stairs to the front door.

'If you should need any more information, or any help,' he said, 'do not hesitate to come to me.'

'I thank you.'

We bowed our farewells and parted at the top of the steps. As I headed back along Reiger Straat, which had become busy again while we talked, I pulled on my cap and flipped the hood of my cloak over it. Already it had begun to snow, just a few idle flakes drifting down to be lost in what was already lying on the ground, but the clouds were big-bellied with the weight of the unshed masses that would fall before evening. I thought there was just time to try to find the beggar once more before I sought the shelter of the inn. The way to the church where I had seen him was easier for me to find now, but there was no sign of him, nor of the woman selling pastries. Indeed the streets were emptying fast as everyone made for shelter.

I walked back to the Prins Willem, hastening my pace as the snow began to fall in earnest. By the time I reached the inn my shoulders were coated with a layer of snow and the dirty snow in the streets had been covered with a fresh blanket of white. It was so dark that some of the shop keepers had already lit the torches outside their premises at midday. Although I had not been carrying out Walsingham's original instructions, sitting in corners listening to the gossip of soldiers, I felt that I had gained far more valuable information from my visit to Ettore Añez. Clearly both van Leyden and Cornelius Parker were men who needed watching.

For the next two days it snowed without ceasing, a steady, relentless fall. At first there was little wind, but toward the end of the second day a stormy gale blew up, driving the snow into drifts against the sides of buildings until in some places they reached nearly to the height of the windows. Few people stirred outside. Some of the soldiers still came to the inn during the evening, but Niels Penders told me that they were men billeted in the town. Those quartered in the camp outside Amsterdam were

167

confined to their tents, and a wretched time they must have been having out there in the bitter cold. Inside the inn we were kept warm by roaring fires in every room, the food was plentiful, and clearly the inn had a cellar abundantly stocked with beer and wine and even a form of aqua vitae.

I visited Hector several times a day, but the stable was solidly built of brick and the grooms had a fire in their room at one end, whose warmth filtered through to the horses. Confined to the inn, with no one to talk to except the innkeeper and his family and nothing to occupy me, I grew irritable with boredom, but there was nothing for it but sit out the storm. I wondered where Berden was – still in Den Haag, or perhaps caught by the storm on his way back to Amsterdam. In the afternoon of the second day, a carter who had struggled to the inn with a load of logs told us that the canals were freezing. News I did not welcome. It seemed we would have a bitter ride toward Parma's troops, then a journey to the coast before we could meet our ship for the return journey. That was, if Berden ever returned and we could manage to ride anywhere at all. So thick was the snow by now that I feared being trapped in Amsterdam for weeks, until the thaw came.

The night of the second day of blizzard, I lay in bed listening to the wind howling round the corners of the building with a viciousness that seemed almost animate. Every so often there came a crash as a tile was ripped off the roof of the inn or one of the nearby buildings. There had already been a leak in the roof, Marta Penders told me, requiring buckets up under the eaves. It was close to a chimney, so the heat of the fire melted the adjacent snow, sending it dripping through the hole where two tiles had been torn away. All day and all night the bucket had to be emptied at regular intervals, for there would be no chance of mending the roof in this storm.

At last I slept and when I woke the world seemed strangely silent. The wind had dropped and light was filtering in around the shutters of my window. I crossed the floor, wincing at its icy touch on my feet, and opened them. A low red sun cast its light over a glittering snow-covered town, The wind had vanished. The snow was no longer falling. Down below I saw a workman, bundled up in a thick cloak, a scarf wound round his head and hat, making his way slowly across the square and leaving the first footprints to mark it, except for the feathery patterns of birds' feet which were lightly etched on the surface. Away to the right I could see the canal, no longer a body of water shifting and stirring, but a solid road of ice. Even as I watched, I saw a group of young men sit down on the bank and strap skates to the soles of their boots, then laughing and shouting they launched themselves out on to the frozen canal, dipping and swooping across the ice. My heart lifted at seeing them and I longed to be able to glide like that, as swift and free as a bird in the air.

A few minutes later another group arrived, families with young children, carrying large round trays like the ones used to bring in huge joints of meat to the inn dining parlour. To my amazement, I saw parents setting the trays down on the ice and lifting children – quite small children, some as young as three or four – on to the trays. All the children were carrying pairs of stout sticks and once on the ice they began to propel themselves along by thrusting the sticks against the ice, almost as if they were rowing a boat. The youngest children did little but spin round and round on the spot, but the older ones, more skilled, were soon skimming along the ice at extraordinary speed, darting in amongst the skaters. At any moment I expected to see a collision, but it seemed both the skaters and the children were used to this extraordinary form of sport. I laughed at the spectacle, the boredom of the last few days quite banished as I dressed warmly and went downstairs. I thought that if I could not join in, at least I could go and watch the fun on the canal.

Everyone seemed cheered by the change in the weather. It was still bitterly cold, but the sight of the sun after the darkness of the blizzard was itself enough to raise one's spirits. I spent the morning watching the sport on the canal, then after dinner decided to try once again to find the beggar and discover whether he could tell me more. Ettore Añez had given me his view of Cornelius Parker, but I wondered whether the beggar knew something else, something perhaps from the back streets of the town which would have been hidden from a merchant, a dealer in precious stones.

As I crossed the square I saw women turning away from the public well. Although I could not understand their speech, from their gestures it was clear that the well was frozen. Underfoot the top layer of the snow had also frozen into a hard crust which crunched and shattered under my feet, so that they sank into the softer snow below. It reached to my knees. Soon my boots and stockings were soaking and my legs felt as icy as the canals, but I ploughed on until I reached the church where I had first seen the beggar. He was not there.

A small crowd of local people was emerging from the church, shaking the hand of the minister and calling out brief greetings to each other before hurrying away to the warmth of their homes. As the minister went back into the church, I followed him.

Most of the people of Amsterdam I had met knew some English, so I spoke to him in English, hoping that he would understand.

'Dominee, may I ask you about one of your parishioners?' There was no evidence that the soldier was one of his parishioners, but it seemed a reasonable guess.

He turned and smiled politely. 'What do you wish to know?' His English was almost without any accent.

'A few days ago I spoke to a former soldier, who was playing a pipe and begging outside your church. We spoke about Sluys. I am a physician from England who cared for many of the survivors. I thought I would speak to him again, but he is not there now. Perhaps it is too cold.'

I knew that I was being deliberately misleading in mentioning Sluys, but felt I needed to give some reason for my interest in the man.

'I know the man you mean, Mijnheer. He does indeed live in this parish, though he rarely attends church. His sufferings, I am afraid, have turned him from God. His name is Hans Viederman.'

'And you say he lives nearby?'

'He does. If you turn right outside the door of the church and follow the narrow passage that runs along our outside wall, there are a few small houses on the other side. Hans's house is the last of these.'

'Does he have family?'

The minister shook his head sadly. 'When he came home from the fighting, with . . . his legs like that . . . crippled, his wife left him and took their little boy with her. She has gone to live with her parents in a village about five miles from Amsterdam.

I felt a flash of anger on the soldier's behalf. 'She abandoned him, when he had most need of her?'

He hesitated, then said, 'He had moments of terrible rage, after what happened. His wife was perhaps afraid. Or could not live with him any longer. We should not judge, who do not know everything that lies between man and wife. He is better now. He survives, though perhaps he may never be able to forget his bitterness.' He gave me a smile of great sweetness. 'Go and see him. Any hand reaching out in friendship will do him good. I expect he had decided to stay within doors in this cruel weather.'

'I will,' I said, 'and I thank you, Dominee.'

Following the minister's directions, I ploughed my way through the snow in the alleyway. It must be a shortcut through from one main street or square to another, for the snow was churned up by many feet. As I reached the end, I realised it led to yet another canal. At the last house, a wretched hovel of one storey with a roof of tattered reed thatch, I knocked loudly on the door. There was no answer, so I knocked again, calling out, 'Hans? Hans Viederman? I am the Englishman who spoke to you a few days ago. Beside the church. May we speak?'

This time there was a noise from inside, a scrabbling of claws and an anxious barking. So the dog was there at least. Where the dog was, the man was likely to be. Tentatively I tried the door, which was neither locked nor bolted. Reasoning that the man, crippled as he was, might be in difficulty, I opened the door and stepped inside. A furry shape hurled itself at me out of the dark interior and I staggered back, but the dog was not attacking me. He licked my hand and whined and wagged his tail all at once. The house felt curiously empty. It was also bitterly cold, while the damp seemed to seep in through the walls and roof, as though they were sucking it up from the surrounding snow and ice.

'Hans!' I called again. 'It is Dr Alvarez. Do you need help?'

He would not know my name, but perhaps my profession would provide reassurance. I was growing more and more uneasy. The dog ran from me toward the back of the house, then ran forward to me again. I followed him, groping my way in the small amount of light thrown by the open door. There appeared to be just one room, though it was difficult to judge until my eyes had adjusted to the dark interior.

He was lying on the bare boards at the far end of the single room, below the closed shutters of the only window. One stool. A rough table on which stood an empty plate, scattered with breadcrumbs, and an overturned ale mug made of stained horn. The stumps of his legs protruded from under the table, but the rest of his body was hidden from view, so I crouched down beside him. His wrist when I lifted it was as cold and clammy as the ice on the streets, but I did not need the absence of any pulse to tell me he was dead. His throat had been cut almost from ear to ear. There was a great deal of blood, but so cold was it in the house that it had frozen. The dog sat down beside me and whined softly in his throat.

Because of the bitter cold in the house it was difficult to judge how long the soldier had been dead, but the frozen blood indicated that it was many hours. I sat back on my heels, my heart pounding, unsure what I should do. I was a stranger here, and I was supposed to keep in the shadows, yet I could not leave this death unreported. Unsure of what legal system operated here – did they have coroners? – I realised that the best thing to do was to go back to the church and tell the minister what I had found. As I stood up, a frightening thought struck me. Could this death have any connection with Cornelius Parker, who had seen me speak to the soldier? Cornelius Parker whom the soldier called a 'bad man' and whom Ettore Añez considered untrustworthy and possibly dangerous? For although I might call it a death, it was in truth a murder.

I found the minister in the church, to my relief, for I did not know where he lived or who else had authority here.

'Dead?' he cried in a shocked voice. 'This bitter weather. There are always some of the poor who are taken.'

'It was not the cold,' I said grimly. 'His throat was cut.'

172

He pressed the knuckles of his right hand against his mouth, but even so could not suppress the cry that broke from him.

'Killed? Murdered?'

I nodded. 'I am a stranger here, a messenger come with despatches for the Earl of Leicester. I do not know how you manage such things here in Amsterdam.' I looked at him appealingly. 'I will be leaving in a day or two. Can you take charge? I would not know what to do.'

'Of course, of course.' He patted my shoulder absentmindedly. 'You are not much more than a boy yourself. I will see that everything is taken care of.'

'I touched nothing,' I said, 'except to take his pulse, though that was futile. It was his dog led me to him.'

'His dog, of course. Something will have to be done about his dog.' His passed a worried hand over his face.

'I am staying at the Prins Willem, Dominee,' I said, 'if you need me, but really there is no way I can help. I simply saw him once by the church steps and gave him a few small coins.'

He nodded. 'Someone would have found him, sooner or later. I do not think you will be needed.' He took my hand and shook it. 'Thank you for coming to me. Many would simply have fled.'

I felt like fleeing myself, but managed to walk quietly out of the church and down the steps. The dog was sitting on the bottom step, and I stopped to caress his head.

'Poor fellow,' I said. 'I wonder what will become of you now?'

It was nearly dark as I hurried back to the inn, my heart beating fast as I thought of Cornelius Parker and that terrible wound. Several times I looked over my shoulder, but no one appeared to be following me, so I reproved myself for wild imaginings. What had this murder to do with me, a stranger passing through the town?

The inn was a haven of warmth and food and comfort. The usual crowds of soldiers were sitting around their usual tables, at the moment merely cheerful with beer and the improvement in the weather. I ordered a tankard of strong beer and when Marta had poured it, asked for a chop and greens. I carried my beer to a table tucked into a dark corner but near enough to the fire to feel some warmth, for I found I was shaking, now that I was safely off the street and within the embrace of four walls.

As I ate my food and drank a second beer, the soldiers eating and drinking at the central tables became more rowdy and noisier, but for once I welcomed their racket for its contrast with that cold empty house and the defenceless man lying alone and dead. I had finished eating and was growing sleepy with the warmth and the beer, when the door opened and a group of newcomers entered. One of them was Cornelius Parker, a man unmistakable from his girth and his domineering voice. I drew back from my table into the shadows. I was trapped now, for I could not go to my room without passing them.

There were three other men with him, clearly from their clothes and speech also Hollanders. They had their backs to me as they shed cloaks and scarves, hanging them on pegs inside the door and listening while Parker held forth in Dutch. For the first time I was frustrated that Dutch was a language I had never thought to learn. The men sat down round a table at the far side of the room from me, waving to Niels to bring them beer. Then as one of the men turned to address Parker I realised it was van Leyden.

All that Ettore Añez had told me about the failed merchant flashed through my mind and I recalled how I had last seen him, very much at ease, having dined with the Earl of Leicester and then enjoying his company in his private rooms. The back of my neck began to prick and I felt a trickle of sweat run down my spine. Cornelius Parker and van Leyden together. It seemed an ominous combination. I tried to convince myself that, as they were both members of the merchant community here in Amsterdam, they were bound to be acquainted, for this was a much smaller town than London, and even in London the merchants know one another, just as the members of the medical community do. All four men looked relaxed and unconcerned as they ordered food and more drink, looking fair set to spend the rest of the evening at the inn.

Time stretched out with maddening slowness. I longed for my bed but was somehow sure that I should not draw attention to myself by getting up and crossing the room to the door. At the same time, there seemed nothing sinister in the men's behaviour. If Cornelius Parker had any connection with the death of Hans Viederman, he gave no indication of it. At last there was a stirring amongst the men and I sighed with relief. They were standing up, shaking hands, bowing, taking leave of one another. Two of the men donned their cloaks, waved a final farewell, and left. The other two sat down again, heads together. Parker and van Leyden.

Now that initial sense that something was afoot overcame me again. The men were talking in lowered voices, quite unlike their earlier loud bonhomie. They looked furtive. Parker glanced over his shoulder in my direction, but I was sure he could not see me, half hidden by one of the great oak posts supporting the ceiling. It was merely an instinctive gesture, checking to see whether they were observed. The soldiers by now were thoroughly absorbed in their card game, those who were not already asleep and snoring on some of the benches.

Parker's obvious nervousness drew my attention even more sharply towards them. I saw him take out a purse of coin and pass it over the table to van Leyden. Then he glanced around again. Reassured that no one was watching, he drew something out of his pocket and set it on the table. It was a small glass phial. Van Leyden was saying something urgent. Parker shook his head and put out his hand to the phial. His nervousness showed itself in the way his hand shook and he knocked the phial over, although he righted it at once and pushed it toward van Leyden. The other man wrapped a handkerchief around the phial and slipped it into his own pocket. The purse had already disappeared. With very little further talk, the two men stood up and Parker poured a handful of coins into the innkeeper's hand. Then they were gone. I heard the outer door of the inn slam shut and at once I was on my feet.

As casually as I could, I made my way past the table where the men had been sitting. There was a small puddle of some liquid lying on the surface, which must have leaked from the phial when Parker knocked it over. Blocking the view of the table with my body, I dropped my handkerchief over it, wiped it up and pocketed my handkerchief again, then calling a goodnight to Niels and Marta I made my way to the stairs and my chamber.

Half frightened and half excited, I ran up the stairs, all tiredness forgotten. Once inside my chamber, I lit my candle, using a spill from the fire which, as usual, one of the maids had laid for me. Not knowing quite what to expect, I sat down on the edge of my bed and drew out my handkerchief. The liquid had made a stain, faintly grey in colour. Raising it to my nose, I smelled the damp patch. Then to be quite certain, I touched it lightly with the tip of my tongue. It had a bite like a bee sting, tempered by a cloying sweetness.

Now I knew what was in the phial. Belladonna. Deadly poison.

Chapter Ten

I realised that my hand, holding the stained handkerchief, was shaking. I got to my feet and walked over to the fire. Even as I raised my hand to throw the handkerchief on to the flames, I stopped. Cornelius Parker had given van Leyden money. Then he had given him a phial of belladonna. Van Leyden had seemed to be arguing with him. I closed my eyes and tried to picture them again, tried to read their intentions from their gestures and expressions. The more I concentrated on it, the more it seemed that van Leyden was not refusing the task, he was asking for more money.

So Parker, or someone he worked for, was paying van Leyden to poison someone. Van Leyden was willing, but wanted to be paid more. Parker had dealings with the Spanish. Van Leyden had the ear of the Earl of Leicester. My father had often told me that, when diagnosing illness, the simplest explanation of the symptoms was often the right one. The simplest explanation of these symptoms was that the Spanish wanted Leicester poisoned and van Leyden would be the instrument.

The poison could be meant for someone else. I was ignorant of all the by-ways and subtleties of the factions and enmities in Amsterdam, but I did know, from my own observations and general rumour – but above all from what Ettore Añez had told me – that there were divisions between the Dutch and the English over the war with Spain. I knew from what I had heard from Phelippes before leaving London that the Queen considered that she had already spent enough money and sacrificed enough English lives on behalf of the Dutch. Phelippes also believed that at the slightest excuse, Elizabeth would try to treat with Philip of Spain if she thought it would avert the threatened invasion.

What would poisoning Leicester achieve? It would remove the present commander of the English forces in the Low Countries. Leicester might be a poor commander, but if he were suddenly murdered chaos was bound to ensue. Parma could take advantage of that and sweep over the ill defended Low Countries. Or alternatively, if England believed the Dutch had poisoned the Earl as a result of their mistrust of him, English troops could, or would, be sent to attack the Dutch, which, in the end, would achieve Parma's purpose without his having to risk the life of a single Spanish soldier.

Whichever way one looked at it, the consequences would be terrible.

As physicians we sometimes use belladonna to physic a weak heart or relieve pain or relax knotted muscles. It is then employed in tiny quantities and only in the hands of a skilled practitioner. Beyond that, even in quite small doses, it is fatal. I looked down at the handkerchief in my hand. No, I must not burn it. I must keep it safe as proof, if proof were needed, of what had passed between Cornelius Parker and van Leyden. I folded the handkerchief carefully, with the stained portion on the inside, and tucked it into the pocket of my shirt, inside my doublet.

The easiest way to administer belladonna would be in some very strong-tasting food or wine. I believed that a man of the Earl's sophistication would detect it at once in his wine. That left food. When Berden and I had dined at the Earl's house, the food had been brought up, ready prepared, from the kitchen. We had eaten roast beef with a very rich accompanying sauce. It would be possible to conceal the taste of belladonna in such a sauce, at least until it was too late and the victim had already consumed a fatal dose.

I suddenly remembered a recent case when it was discovered that a man sent by the treacherous English exiles in France was found to be working in the royal kitchens, planted there as an assassin. Fortunately he had been discovered before he could act, but the case had caused repercussions and fear, leading to increased vigilance around the Queen. If there was a cook or a scullion working in Leicester's kitchen who was part of a conspiracy, it would be a simple matter for him to stir the contents of that phial into some thick, rich sauce. The result might be to poison others as well as the Earl, but I had no illusions that traitors cared about such things.

The poison might not be intended for the Earl, but for some personal enemy of Parker or van Leyden, but I could not take that risk. I must warn Leicester of the possibility. Conscious that I had heard a church clock strike midnight some time ago, I realised I could not call on the Earl tonight, but I must go as early as possible in the morning, to forestall any action by van Leyden. He would probably not wait long once the poison was in his possession.

I went back downstairs and found Marta Penders clearing away dirty beer mugs and plates in the parlour, which was now empty of any customers.

'Mevrouw,' I said, when she looked up, startled, to see me come in the door, 'will you have me called early tomorrow? Before dawn? I have some early business I must attend to.'

'Certainly, Me'heer,' she said with a smile. 'I will call you myself.'

'I thank you.' I managed a smile for her, and took myself off to my chamber.

For the first time since I had bathed, I went to bed in my day clothes, only removing my boots and doublet, since I wanted to leave quickly in the morning. Try as I might, I could not sleep. My body ached for rest, but my mind teemed with speculation. And over and over I saw Hans Viederman lying cold on the beaten earth of his floor in a pool of frozen blood, with his dog whining beside him. Could his death, his murder, be connected to the two men who had whispered together over a purse of coin and a tiny bottle of poison? Perhaps Hans knew something, or had seen something. Perhaps he had overheard the two men speaking together. An impotent beggar, seated on his wheeled platform far below their line of sight, a nobody, an unregarded object familiar in the street – he might, unobserved, have discovered something. No one would ever know now. And probably his murderer would never be caught.

I must have slept at last, for I was woken by Marta Penders knocking on my door while it was still dark. I called out my thanks and crawled reluctantly from beneath the warmth of my feather bed. Once I had donned my boots and doublet I caught up my cloak and ran downstairs. The Penders family, who never seemed to rest, were breaking their own fast in the parlour.

'Come, Dr Alvarez,' Niels said, 'will you join us? There is plenty.'

I hesitated. I realised that it was still far too early to call on the Earl, so I thanked him and sat down to the usual Dutch breakfast of cold meats and several kinds of cheese, washed down, today, with hot spiced ale.

'To keep out the cold,' Marta explained, as she poured a generous measure for me. 'The frost is harder than ever this morning. What will it be like in January?'

'What indeed,' I said. 'Master Berden and I should be returning to England soon, but I fear we will have a cold journey of it.'

'Indeed you will. I am glad I do not have to travel.'

I looked round at their friendly, uncomplicated faces. Things might go badly for them if serious hostilities were to break out between the two nations. I wanted to ask them what they knew of Parker and van Leyden, but such questions would be indiscreet, perhaps even dangerous.

Once outside I could see the first faint glimmer of light in the sky away to the east, and the darkness of night had thinned enough for me to find my way to the Earl's house. The surface of the snow had frozen hard again, so that I had to watch my step. Several times I slipped and only saved myself from falling by catching hold of a tree or a wall. Once I did fall, sprawling full length in the snow and striking my shoulder hard against the projecting step of a house. It took a moment or two for me to get to my feet, for all the breath had been knocked out of me. My shoulder hurt and was probably bruised.

I reached the Earl's house at last, feeling somewhat battered from my fall. As I had hoped, his servants were already astir. A maid was sweeping the front steps free of snow and through the archway at the side of the house I could hear activity in the stables. I perched on a bollard, used for mooring the canal boats, about twenty yards from the house, glad of the chance to sit down. From here I could see who came and went, and could judge, from the activity about the house, how soon it might be possible to call on the Earl. If I saw van Leyden arrive, I would go in at once, otherwise I would wait.

Time crawled by. There was no sign of van Leyden. Perhaps I had misunderstood what I had witnessed last night. Perhaps van Leyden was intending to poison someone, but not the Earl. When I saw that all the shutters of the house had been opened and a boy in military dress had been admitted, clearly carrying a satchel of despatches, I decided to approach and ask if I might see the Earl. By now the sun was up and the people of Amsterdam were busy about their affairs in the streets.

The same liveried servant admitted me and, recognising me, agreed at once to ask if the Earl would see me. He led me up the stairs as before and asked me to wait outside the door to the Earl's private parlour while he went in. After a few moments he bowed me through. The Earl was seated at the dining table, facing me, while another man sat opposite him, his back toward me.

The Earl smiled politely. 'Dr Alvarez, come in. Are you returning to England so soon? I thought it was to be at least another ten days before you leave us.'

I remembered that we had promised to call and see whether the Earl had any papers he wished us to carry. He must think that was why I was here.

'My lord,' I said, bowing, 'Master Berden has not yet returned to Amsterdam, for I expect he has been delayed by the bad weather. We are not yet ready to leave. I wished to see you about another matter.'

I advanced further into the room and as I did so, the other man turned to look at me. It was van Leyden.

I was so shocked that I froze where I was. How could van Leyden be here? I had watched the house from before dawn. He had certainly not entered the house while I had been watching. Then the truth hit me with the physical force of a blow. Van Leyden must be living here. I knew that he acted as a go-between for the English and Dutch armies. What more natural than that he should be quartered in the Earl's accommodation in Amsterdam? He must have come straight back here last night after he left the Prins Willem.

As I stood there, speechless, I felt the blood drain from my face, then flood back again. From my own medical knowledge I recognised it as a sign of shock. But I must not lose my nerve. I bowed to van Leyden, who returned my bow. There was nothing in his manner to suggest that he suspected me of any knowledge of his affairs.

'My lord,' I said again, 'I would beg the opportunity to speak to you about a private matter.' I tried not to catch van Leyden's eye as I said it.

Leicester looked annoyed. It was clear that I had interrupted their meal and he had little time for importunate visitors at this early hour of the morning.

'Can it not wait?' He gestured brusquely at the table with its half consumed dishes. I wondered whether I was already too late.

'I will take up only a few moments of your time, my lord.' I bowed again, hoping my respectful and humble tone would assuage his annoyance.

He sighed deeply, wiped his mouth on his napkin and threw it down. 'Very well. Van Leyden, you can fetch those papers you translated for me and we will discuss them when I have finished with Dr Alvarez.'

Van Leyden rose and bowed to Leicester. With his back to the Earl he gave me a venomous look, which I hoped sprang only from his interrupted meal and not the realisation of why I was here. As soon as he had left the room and I heard his footsteps ascending the stairs to the next floor, I stepped hurriedly nearer to Leicester and lowered my voice.

'My lord, I believe I have stumbled upon a plot to poison you.'

At that Leicester sat up sharply, no longer looking irritated and bored. I recalled that there had been several attempts on his life before, so he was probably not surprised.

The words tumbled out in my haste to explain before van Leyden returned.

'I have been warned about two men in Amsterdam who might be dangerous, then yesterday evening they were sitting in the inn where I am staying, the Prins Willem. They had their heads close together, not wanting to be overheard.'

182

'Did you hear them?' He snapped the words out.

'They were speaking Dutch, my lord.'

'Go on.'

'One man passed a purse of coin to the other, then a small phial of liquid. In his haste he knocked it over and a little spilled on the table. They left soon after, but I wiped up the spill with my handkerchief.' I took out my handkerchief and handed it to him. 'It is belladonna. Deadly poison.'

'What made you think it was intended for me?' He took the handkerchief and looked at the stain, but did not smell or touch it.

'The first man was Cornelius Parker, who has dealings with the Spanish and is not trusted by the merchant community here.' I paused. 'My lord, you may have realised that Master Berden and I were sent here because of your suspicions of treachery. I believe this is what I have discovered.'

'You have not said why you think I was to be the victim.'

I looked at the half eaten dishes. 'You do not feel any ill effects this morning?'

'Of course not.' He was becoming angry.

'My lord, the second man, the man who took the money and the poison, was the man who was here just now, van Leyden.'

His reaction was quite unexpected. He threw back his head and roared with laughter. 'You are much mistaken, Dr Alvarez. Van Leyden is a loyal friend and servant. I would trust him with my life. I do trust him with my life. Here, take your handkerchief and your tale of poisoning. I think you have been misled by the enthusiasm of youth and your master Walsingham's belief in traitors hiding behind every wall hanging. Young men must have their adventures to make themselves important.'

He thrust the handkerchief back at me and waved me away. 'Off with you. I shall finish my meal. And van Leyden will enjoy the joke when he returns.'

I was growing angry myself. 'I beseech you, my lord, do not speak of it to him.'

'Away with you,' he said, turning back to the table.

There was nothing more I could do. I bowed and left the room. Embarrassed and humiliated, I closed the door softly behind me and stood for a moment leaning against it with my eyes shut, trying to control my anger. Leicester had treated me like a stupid child. What difference did my youth make? I had not asked to be sent on this mission by Walsingham and had been reluctant and wary about coming. The increasingly bitter weather was warning enough that I would be needed at the hospital, yet here I was, kicking my heels in an alien town. When I did discover treachery at work, I was laughed at. The shock of finding Hans Viederman's body rushed over me again and I felt sick. I had seen injuries enough even in my short life, and dead men too, but I had never before seen a murdered man, nor one in such pitiful circumstances. I was sure that Hans's murder and the whispered conspiracy between Cornelius Parker and van Leyden were somehow connected and boded ill for Leicester, yet he would not listen to my warning.

I opened my eyes to see the Earl's servant looking at me in concern. I had forgotten that he remained just outside the door, waiting for any summons.

'Dr Alvarez,' he said, 'are you ill?'

I shook my head. 'No, I thank you.' I studied his face. He gave every impression of being a loyal servant to his master. I would have to take a chance. 'But your master may be ill soon.'

'What do you mean?' He spoke sharply and took a step nearer to me.

At that moment I became aware of voices coming from above our heads, at the top of the next flight of stairs. One of them was van Leyden's.

'I need to speak to you,' I said urgently. I looked around. 'Somewhere that we will not be overheard.'

He gave a single brisk nod, then jerked his head toward a door opposite. 'This way.'

It was a small service room, lined with cupboards and windowless. I wasted no time.

'What is your name?'

'Robert Hurst, Doctor.'

'Well, Robert, I believe your master to be in danger. Last night I saw a man called Cornelius Parker pass a bottle of poison to that man.' I jerked my chin up. 'To van Leyden. He also paid him a purse of coin. I also know from an eminent merchant here in the city that Parker has dealings with the Spanish and both men are untrustworthy. Both would do anything for money. Moreover, I believe Parker may be involved in the murder of a former soldier called Hans Viederman.'

I saw that the name meant something to Hurst.

'Because of Parker's Spanish connections and van Leyden's presence in this household, I believe that the poison is intended for the Earl. The Earl himself was suspicious of treachery, that was why Master Berden and I were sent here by Sir Francis Walsingham.'

The most surprising thing about our hasty, whispered conference was that Hurst did not look surprised.

'I too have worked for Sir Francis in the past,' he said, causing me to be the one surprised. 'I have been in the Earl's employ for five years now, and he trusts me.'

'He does not trust me,' I said bitterly. 'Or at any rate he does not believe me. He laughed at my warning and sent me away like a chastened cur.'

'His manners,' Hurst said, 'tend to be arrogant. All the more so when he suspects he may be in danger. What do you want me to do?'

'Find the poison if you can, and destroy it. Is it possible for you to search van Leyden's room? It is in a small phial of green glass, about this big.' I held my finger and thumb four inches apart. 'It is stoppered with an ill-fitting cork. That is how I managed to get a sample. It is belladonna.'

'And if I cannot find it?'

'Try to persuade the Earl to listen, perhaps he will heed you, even if he turns me away. And watch everything that is prepared for him to eat, especially if van Leyden goes near it. He may have a confederate in the kitchen.'

I handed him my handkerchief.

'This stain, here, this is what leaked from the bottle. Any apothecary can tell you what it is.'

He nodded. 'If I fail, and the Earl takes the poison, is there any remedy?'

'The antidote derives from the calabar bean. If he shows signs of paralysis, staggering, blurred vision, fetch his own physician immediately and warn him that it is belladonna. If the poison is administered, it will be in something with a strong flavour, to disguise the taste. A rich sauce or a thick soup, perhaps.'

'I will do everything I can.'

We both froze as we heard footsteps cross the floor outside and then the sound of the Earl's door opening and closing.

'Van Leyden is back,' I said.

'I must go back to my duties,' Hurst said. 'But as soon as I have the chance, I will search van Leyden's room. Where are you lodged in the town?'

'The Prins Willem.'

'I know it.'

'I must go,' I said. 'If you can, send me word. When we leave the Low Countries we will be returning to England on a ship called the *Silver Swan*.'

He nodded and clasped my hand briefly. In that short time he had been transformed from a discreet servant standing in the shadows to a fellow agent of Walsingham's. I felt a wave of relief that my instincts had proved right. We let ourselves quietly out of the room and went down the stairs as softly as possible. Without further words he saw me out of the front door and closed it behind me.

I walked swiftly away, hoping that neither the Earl nor van Leyden was looking out of the window, wondering why I had taken so long to leave the house. The sun was well up now, but there was no warmth in the air. The snow was as hard frozen as it had been before dawn. My mind churned with possibilities. If Hurst managed to find the poison before van Leyden could use it, he could take it to the Earl and, I hoped, persuade him that what I told him was true. Leicester might still make light of it, assuming the poison was intended for someone other than himself. But even in that case, would he keep van Leyden in his household? A known poisoner?

On the other hand, if Hurst did not find the phial and van Leyden added it to the Earl's food, could he be stopped from eating it? And if he did eat it, could he be treated in time? So many possibilities. Well, I had done my best to prevent a possible murder. What of the other murder? I found my feet, which had taken me unconsciously back to the square with the well, now driving me on in the direction of the church where I had spoken

186

to the minister. I would go and ask him what had happened in the matter of Hans Viederman. I wondered why Hurst seemed to know the name. I cursed myself for not asking, but I had been in too much haste to warn him of the danger to the Earl.

The snow was heaped up on either side of the church steps, but someone had cleared the steps themselves. On the lowest one, Hans's dog was lying, a picture of shivering misery, his head on his paws, but his eyes open. When he saw me he leapt down the step and ran toward me, wagging his tail and whining. I stooped to rub him behind his ears. He greeted me joyfully, weaving about my legs and licking my hand. I wondered whether he associated me with finding his master and somehow believed I could bring him back again.

'I'm sorry, old fellow,' I said. 'I wish I could help.'

He followed me up the steps and into the church, though I was not sure whether he was allowed inside. The minister, who was himself sweeping lumps of frozen snow from the floor, smiled and shook his head.

'I have been trying to bring him inside, but he insists on staying out there in the cold. I think he is waiting for his master. Come, Mijnheer. There is a stove in my vestry. It is a little warmer than here.'

When we were seated by the tiny stove, which the minister fed with logs, he offered me a glass of ale and some of the hard, tasteless bread the Dutch eat with their wine. Aware that I had never told him my name, I introduced myself.

He bowed. 'I am Dirck de Veen. Minister of the church of Sint Nikolaas.'

I bowed my acknowledgement. 'What will become of him, the dog?'

He shook his head. 'I don't know. He was never truly a working dog. He was Hans's family dog, but went to war with him. When Hans returned, with both legs gone, he trained the dog to pull that wheeled platform he used, though he could also push it along himself, the way the children move their sleds on the ice.'

'I've seen them.'

'Perhaps someone will take him on as a working dog. One of Hans's neighbours has already tried, but he ran away at once and came back here.'

'Could you keep him yourself?' I was not sure why I was so concerned with the dog. It was as though by caring what became of him I could somehow make amends to Hans for what had been done to him. I had the uneasy feeling that Cornelius Parker had overheard him warning me and that had somehow led to his death.

Dirck shook his head, and smiled sadly. 'Nee. I am afraid my stipend is very small. I have not the means to feed a large dog like that.'

'How did Hans manage?'

'I think he often fed the dog before himself. And some of the shopkeepers, especially the butchers, who have known Hans all their lives, took pity on them and gave them both the scraps and off-cuts of their meat.'

I looked down at the dog. 'He has come inside the church now.'

'Aye. It is the first time. He has taken to you.'

'May I?' I held up one of the pieces of dry bread.

'Of course.'

The dog ate it swiftly and sat down beside me, his eyes fixed on my face, clearly hoping for more. I fed him another piece.

'I really came to ask what has happened about Hans.'

Dirck sighed. 'I reported his death to the town authorities, saying I had found him, to avoid mentioning you, which would merely have confused them. His body has been taken away to the town charnel house until the ground thaws enough for burial. It will have to be a pauper's grave, but I have asked that he be buried here, at his own parish church.'

I nodded. 'But what of his killer?'

'I do not know.' He shook his head. 'I fear there is little chance that he will ever be found. No one knows of anyone who would want to do this terrible thing. Hans possessed nothing worth stealing, he interfered with no man's business. He seemed to have no enemies, though he had few friends in recent years.'

'I think . . .' I paused. 'It is possible that a man called Cornelius Parker might be involved.'

I saw the name meant something to the minister, who looked alarmed.

'Not long before he was killed,' I said, 'Hans warned me against Parker, who may have overheard. I am here on business from the Queen's Principal Secretary, Sir Francis Walsingham, to the Earl of Leicester. I suspect that Parker means him harm. The Earl.'

He looked even more alarmed and half rose from his seat before sinking back again.

'Best that we keep out of it, then,' he said. 'Parker is a powerful man.'

'I do not want to cause you danger,' I said, 'but should I tell the town authorities?'

He shook his head firmly. 'No. That would be unwise. Parker has friends there. Best if you go back to England and forget this. Pray for Hans's soul, as I will do.'

I was reluctant to follow his advice, which seemed the action of a coward, but there was little I could do, alone, in this foreign town. I believed him to be an honest man, and probably not a coward, though cautious. I bowed my head in acceptance, and left soon after, followed out of the church by the dog.

It had begun to snow again and the wind blew it into my face as I started back to the inn, so I did not notice at first that the dog was still following me. Only when I reached the inn and stopped to stamp my boots free of snow on the steps did I see the dog a few feet away, watching me expectantly. I should never have fed him, however poor the fare. Though I would have expected him to go in preference to one of the butchers who had fed him in the past.

'It is no use, poor lad,' I said. 'I cannot give you a home. I do not even live here. You must find some other master.'

He sat down patiently in the snow and merely watched me. Already his coat was covered with a thin layer of the fresh snow. I hardened my heart and went into the inn, closing the door behind me.

When I reached my chamber, I was astonished to find Berden there, sitting on a chair in front of the fire, his boots off, toasting his steaming stockings in front of the flames.

'Nicholas!' I said. 'When did you arrive? Is all well?'

'About an hour ago. The innkeeper told me you went out before dawn. I've been waiting for you and trying to thaw out the ice in my blood.'

'It has just started snowing again,' I said, as I pulled off my boots and set them beside Berden's to dry out. 'When can we leave this god-forsaken place?'

'Do you not care for Amsterdam? I'll wager you have had a better time of it than I have, riding about the countryside in this b'yer lady filthy weather.'

'Do not be so sure.' I put my head out of the door and managed to catch the eye of one of the maids. 'Can you bring us some hippocras?'

She returned quite soon with a steaming jug and two pottery mugs. I waited until I had poured it out before I settled down to tell Berden everything that had happened to me while he had been gone: my encounter with the beggar and Cornelius Parker, my visit to Ettore Añez and his information, my finding of Hans Viederman's body, and the meeting between Parker and van Leyden.

At this last he leaned forward and opened his mouth to speak, but I held up my hand to silence him and told him what had happened earlier that day – my visit to the Earl and my attempt to warn him, his scornful dismissal of me and my warning, my discussion with Robert Hurst, and finally my visit to the church and what I had learned from the minister about Hans and Parker.

When at last I was silent, Berden rubbed his cheeks with both hands, then leaned his elbows on his knees.

'I see that I was wrong about your quiet time here in Amsterdam.' He gave a rueful grin. 'I am sorry I was not here to support you. Between the two of us we might have managed to persuade the Earl of the seriousness of the danger. I wonder why he treated you so. Was it merely bravado? Perhaps he did believe you, but for some reason wished not to show it. And my visit to

Den Haag was wasted time anyway. The man I sought was not there, he had gone into Italy.'

'Do you think we should go back to the Earl?' I said. 'Or trust to Robert Hurst to protect him?'

'I have never met Hurst, in the way of Walsingham's business,' he said slowly, 'so I did not recognise him when we called on the Earl before. I have heard that he was one of Sir Francis's more trustworthy agents. I think he was sorry to lose him. But perhaps that was merely pretence. Perhaps Sir Francis placed him deliberately in Leicester's service. It would not be the first time he appeared to be doing one thing while really doing another.'

I was relieved to hear this. 'So you think we should leave matters in Hurst's hands?' I was glad at last to have Berden here to share the responsibility.

'I think we must. We still have to travel down to Parma's lines.'

I shivered. 'In this weather?' I would not admit to anything other than dismay at such a winter journey.

'It is part of our mission here in the Low Countries. I think we should leave tomorrow. Given the state of the roads it will probably take us the best part of three days to get there, and the same to ride back to the coast, where our ship will anchor. No use hoping the canal will be clear enough for Captain Thoms to sail up to Amsterdam.'

'That will only give us about a day down near Parma. What can we do in the time? It seems a great waste of effort in the expectation of very little return.' I found myself suddenly longing to mount Hector and ride straight for the coast, to wait there until our ship arrived.

Berden shrugged. 'We must follow our orders. Like you, I expect very little profit from it. The weather has put a stop to most travel, so two Englishmen riding about the country are more likely to draw attention than escape it. I doubt that we will be able to make any clandestine observations.'

'More likely risk capture and imprisonment by the Spanish,' I said gloomily.

'At least we both have fast horses,' he said, 'so we can probably outrun them.'

191

'Hector hasn't been ridden since we arrived,' I said. 'He will be stiff and out of condition.'

'Perhaps you should exercise him a little today. My Redknoll has had more than enough exercise and will be glad of a brief rest in the stable here.'

'A sensible idea,' I said. 'Once we have dined, I will ride him round to Ettore Añez's house to bid him farewell. That will give Hector a chance to stretch his legs.'

That is what I did. When I went out to the stable, I found that Hans's dog was still lurking about. He followed me into the stable, where Hector lowered his head to sniff the dog's head, while the dog stood quite still. The horse seemed glad to see me, as he always did, even though I had no apple for him this time. I removed his blanket and saddled him, politely refusing the offer of one of the grooms to help. I folded the blanket and laid it across Hector's withers, in front of the saddle, so that I could leave him some warmth while I spoke to Ettore Añez. As I used the mounting block in the stable yard, I recalled that Berden had promised to teach me to vault on to Hector's back from the rear, but he still had not done so. At the moment he was dozing in front of the parlour fire and I doubted there would be much opportunity on our ride south.

I rode Hector across the square to the street that led to the Earl's house, the dog trotting along behind. I held Hector down to a very slow walk, remembering how slippery the streets had been that morning. I could not risk the horse falling and possibly breaking a leg. As we passed the Earl's house I slowed further and looked it up and down, but nothing seemed amiss. All was quiet.

In Reiger Straat, business was being carried on as usual, but rather less energetically than it had been the first time I came here. I tied Hector up outside Ettore's house and strapped the blanket over him, saddle and all. It would give him some protection. Although the earlier snow had ceased, the heavy sky threatened more. The dog settled down next to him, as if it was his rightful place.

Ettore greeted me as courteously as before. When I told him that we would be leaving the next morning, he said, 'Ah, that is unfortunate. I had hoped that when your companion returned I might invite you both to dine.'

'I'm afraid he is quite set on leaving tomorrow, and he is the senior man.'

'Of course, I quite understand.'

When refreshments had been brought in as before, I gave Ettore a complete account of what I had observed of Parker and van Leyden, how the Earl had rejected my warning, and how Hurst would try to prevent any harm coming to him.

'This is a bad state of affairs indeed,' he said. 'If the Earl were to be poisoned here in Amsterdam, not only would he suffer. The whole town and the whole country would be held responsible for his death.'

'One man has died already,' I said, and told him about Hans Viederman.

He did not seem surprised. 'I think your assumption that this is somehow connected with Cornelius Parker is probably correct. If he did not do the deed himself he almost certainly paid someone to do it. So, Hans Viederman is dead.' He sighed.

'You knew him?' I was surprised. Where could their paths have crossed, the wealthy merchant and the beggar?

'He was a musician, a composer, before he was pressed into the army. That should never have been allowed, but by the time it was known, he was gone. He was a fine musician, very gifted.'

I thought of the squalor of that leaky cottage with its earth floor and hardly any furniture.

'I do not understand,' I said, 'when he returned to Amsterdam, even though he had lost his legs, could he not have continued with his music? How could the loss of his legs have affected that?'

Ettore gave me a compassionate look. 'Hans lost more than his legs in the fighting, Kit. He lost his spirit. His soul, if you like. When he first returned, he took to drink, hit his wife and child, could not work. There was no music left in him. Then his wife abandoned him and he lost his house. When there was nothing left, he took to begging on the streets. Some of us tried to help him, but he was a difficult man. He threw our offers of help back in our teeth. He said he had lost his legs, his music and his family; he would not lose his independence as well.'

I looked down at my clasped hands and felt tears pricked my eyes. 'He was playing a pipe when I saw him.'

'Perhaps he was beginning to find his way back to his music at last. Now we will never know.'

'Poor man.'

'Aye, poor man. One of thousands in this war.'

When I left Ettore's house I thanked him for his kindness and asked him to send me word if he heard anything more about Parker and van Leyden, or whether an attempt was indeed made on Leicester's life, although I expected I would hear news of this last through Walsingham's office.

Hector and the dog were waiting patiently for me in the street and I rode slowly back to the inn.

The next morning Berden and I rode south out of Amsterdam. No word had come from Hurst. I hoped van Leyden had not harmed him. I took a warm farewell of the Niels Penders and his family, who had made my stay at the inn remarkably comfortable. I did not think I had ever been lodged so well. As the dog seemed determined to follow me, I persuaded one of the grooms to shut him in the stable until we left. In truth I was glad to see the back of Amsterdam. The memories of the dead Hans, the two conspirators, and Leicester's arrogant dismissal of me all overshadowed the comfort of the inn and the pleasure of meeting Ettore Añez. On the other hand, I was dreading the ride ahead.

As we had feared, the road was in a terrible state, with high drifts blown up into banks on either side and stretches of the road either churned and filthy or else almost impassable. At the end of three days' riding, and two nights spent in the worse kind of roadside inns, Berden reckoned that we were nearing the outlying posts of the Spanish army. The local people we questioned were evasive, constantly glancing over their shoulders as if they feared a hidden Spaniard behind every bush. It was understandable. If they were this close to the Spanish army, they could be attacked at any time. Had they been noticed speaking to Englishmen, their fate might be worse. We found an inn for our third night, a miserable hovel little more than the poorest kind of peasant house which provided ale for the villagers to drink and had one room to accommodate travellers. That night we did not even remove our boots when we retired to our chamber.

There had been whispered conversation between the local men drinking in the dirty ale room while we were trying to chew our way through a pottage of gristle nestled in an unnameable grey liquid. Berden spoke some Dutch, but even he could not understand the broad local dialect. The men kept glancing at us furtively, then whispering again, which caused my scalp to prickle in apprehension.

As we were sitting on our beds, deciding whether to risk the bedbugs and fleas or to sit up all night, I turned to Berden. 'I have a bad feeling about those men,' I said. 'I don't think the horses are safe.'

He grunted. 'You may be right.'

I picked up my satchel and knapsack. 'I think I will sleep in the stable. It cannot be any dirtier than this.'

I watched him debate with himself. He had seemed very tired when he returned to Amsterdam and one night's decent sleep there had not restored him much. The days and nights on our journey had been exhausting.

'No need for you to come,' I said. 'I doubt they will try to steal the horses if one of us is there.'

'Very well, but be careful, Kit.'

'I will.' We had been given only one candle here, but Niels Penders had pressed on me a candle lantern and a supply of candles when we left the Prins Willem, assuring me that I would find the inns of the south very primitive, lacking the most basic of essentials. I was glad of it now, lighting a candle from the stump we had (reluctantly) been given here, and fixing it in the lantern. There was no fire in the room, the only fire in the whole house being a central hearth in the ale room downstairs, the smoke escaping through a hole in the roof. I left one of the candles with Berden, for the stump would not last much longer, and made my way downstairs. I had to walk through the room where some of the men were still drinking. They watched me with hostile eyes as I headed outside to the stable. I wondered why they were so hostile. After all, England was here to support the Dutch against the Spanish. They should have seen us as friends. Perhaps it was because we were better dressed than they and seemed more prosperous. Although our clothes were very workaday and plain, some of them were dressed in little better than much mended rags. Such men, I thought, will do anything for money. Even steal horses or betray their country's friends. It was not a comfortable thought.

It was very cold in the stable. Even though we had put on the horses' blankets, they still shivered from time to time, and so did I. For a while I sat on a dirty up-turned bucket, but I grew colder and colder, until my feet were numb. To gain some ease, I walked about until they thawed a little. The more I thought about those men, the more apprehensive I became, until I decided to saddle the horses, in case we needed to leave in a hurry. I could throw their blankets over their saddles and they could hardly be any colder than they were already. I had finished Redknoll and was just buckling Hector's bridle when I heard a noise at the door. I stiffened, but slipped the leather through the buckle, my fingers clumsy. The noise came again, a scratching noise. It was probably rats. I relaxed and loaded my gear into my saddle bags. When they were strapped in place, I went to the door, carrying the lantern. Opening the door a crack, I looked down, expecting to see the two evil eyes of a rat. Instead, a furry shape flung itself through the door, nearly knocking the lantern out of my hand. It was Hans's dog.

Steadying the lantern and saving the lit candle from falling out into the straw, I leaned on the door to close it again. The dog was frantic in his eagerness to leap up on me, trying to lick my face. I set the lantern down on a beam and sat down rather suddenly on the bucket, allowing the dog to express his joy at having found us. He must have followed us for miles. His coat was sodden and matted and he was desperately thin. I had nothing to give him but an end of the dry bread we had been given with the pottage and which I had been unable to break with my teeth. I gave it to him and he chewed it up at once.

'Well,' I said, 'what am I to do with you? Why didn't you stay at the inn? I'm sure they would have fed you. It would have been a good home. I don't think I can take you back to England.'

While I was still pondering this, feeling a warmth towards the dog who had cared enough to follow me so far, I heard more noises outside the stable. Stealthy footsteps and a whisper, quickly cut off. The only weapon I carried was a Spanish dagger given to me by my father last year when I had to cross the dangerous streets of London at night. I drew it now and laid my hand on the dog's head to calm him. He seemed to understand, for he quietened at once, though I could feel the tension in his body.

Suddenly the stable door was thrown open and I could see the shapes of three men silhouetted against the light of a half moon. They were startled at the sight of me standing there beside the lantern, with a drawn dagger in my hand, and hesitated, then they moved forward. The dog began to growl. Two of them stopped and one said something in Dutch. The third man shook his head and came closer. I saw the glint as he drew his sword. Then everything was a confusion of noise. The dog leapt at the nearest man, one of the others ran off shouting, the third stood uncertain whether to run or stay. I went for him with my dagger and slashed him across his right arm before he could draw his own dagger. The man who had been attacked by the dog was yelling with pain and kicked out, but failed to hit the dog and instead lost his balance on the slippery ground and fell. The man I had injured had his dagger out now and was coming for me.

Lights began to go on in the inn and I saw another man running toward the stable. I was about to lose heart, for I could not fight off three men, but then I saw it was Berden, with his sword in his hand. As the man with the dagger lunged at me, Berden struck his dagger from behind, sending it sailing up into the air to land somewhere out in the dark. The man gave a yell of pain and clutched his wrist with his left hand. In the poor light I could just make out blood beginning to flow down his arm from where I has slashed him. He looked round wildly, then took to his heels.

'Just some greedy peasants,' Berden said contemptuously, planting his foot on the chest of the man still lying on the ground, 'hoping to steal our horses. But I heard that first one who ran off shouting that he would fetch the soldiers. There's only one kind of soldier around here, so I think we should be off. Can you fetch my pack, Kit, while I see to this fellow and saddle the horses?'

'They are saddled already,' I said, sheathing my dagger. 'I thought we might need them. I'll get your pack.'

'Where did this dog come from?' The dog was still standing over the prostrate man, growling whenever he showed any signs of moving.

'That's the dog I told you about, Hans Viederman's dog, that I shut in the stable back in Amsterdam. He must have escaped and followed us all the way here.'

'It seems as well that he did.'

'Aye,' I said fervently. 'I couldn't have held that man off with nothing but my dagger.' I picked up the sword he had dropped and threw it as far as I could into the bushes behind the stable.

When I got back with Berden's pack, he had found a length of dirty rope in the stable and tied up the man who continued to curse, steadily and fluently, until Berden stuffed a rag in his mouth. I had seen no one in the ale house but the slatternly inn wife. I suspected that it had been her husband who had run off first and gone in search of Spanish soldiers.

'It's time we left,' Berden said, strapping on his saddlebags and stuffing Redknoll's blanket in one. He had already removed Hector's blanket. 'What are you going to do with the dog?'

As if he knew we were speaking of him, the dog came over and sat at my feet, looking up at me trustingly.

'I can't leave him here,' I said. 'They'll kill him, after what he did to that fellow.'

'He won't be able to keep up with the horses,' Berden said. 'Not at the pace we'll be going at.'

'I'll have to carry him,' I said. 'Is there any more rope?'

'A length here.' He handed it to me.

I led Hector over to a large stone and used that to mount, for there was no mounting block. 'Pass the dog up to me,' I said.

'He'll bite me.'

'I don't think so.'

Nervously, Berden lifted the dog, who accepted it docilely, and laid him in front of me, across Hector's withers. I wound the rope around my waist, then several times around the dog and knotted it firmly. It was a very makeshift harness, but there was no time for anything else. Berden was mounted and turning his horse impatiently back towards the road we had followed earlier that day.

198

'Hurry, Kit!'

'I am ready now.'

Berden had the candle lantern in his hand, which gave little enough light, but with that, together with the poor illumination that came from the moon whenever it peered out from behind the clouds, we found the road.

'We'll have to risk a canter at least,' he said, 'but we dare not gallop, not on this road, not until there is more light.'

'Aye.' I was having difficulty, needing to reach my arms round the large dog to hold the reins, but I could not leave him behind. 'Back to Amsterdam? Or do you want to stay longer near the Spanish lines?'

'No. I think we have discovered enough for Walsingham's purposes. Clearly the peasants in this area are of doubtful loyalty, ready to go over to the Spanish. We'll ride back until we reach the ship canal, pick up any despatches from the Earl, then make for the coast.'

With that he turned and kicked Redknoll into a canter. Hector and I, and the dog, were close on his heels.

Chapter Eleven

*W*e rode as fast as we dared, and in silence, until we were well clear of the village, then Berden reined in Redknoll and I stopped beside him. The dog was slipping sideways off Hector, so I heaved him back into place. Despite his large frame, he was much lighter than he should have been and I could feel his ribs and the knobs of his spine. I tightened the rope that held us together and tried to make him more comfortable. He licked my hand, but seemed very feeble. His attack on the man with the sword had taken the last of his strength.

'I hope we have done enough to satisfy Sir Francis,' I said, still somewhat breathless after what had happened. 'I am not trained to fight. Wounding that man in the arm was pure chance.'

'You did well,' Berden said. 'Unfortunately I did less well. While you were inside, the man on the ground managed to reach his knife and slashed me before I could disarm him.'

'What!' I cried. 'You are wounded? Why have you said nothing?'

'It was more urgent to get away before they returned with soldiers. It's not deep, I think.'

'You must let me see to it,' I said.

He shook his head. 'Not yet. We cannot afford the time to delay. It is my left arm. It will keep until we are further on our way.'

'Then let us hurry.'

We set off again. Although we had made a good start, I found myself straining my ears for any sound of pursuit. Nothing to be heard yet, but for how long? There was no other road north from the village. Any pursuers had no need even to follow our tracks, they had only to keep to the same road. After a short while, Berden halted again.

'This candle is nearly burnt out. Have you more?'

'Aye.' I twisted round and dug my hand into my saddlebag to unbuckle my satchel. When I passed a fresh candle to Berden he was able to light it just before the stump went out. He fixed the new candle in the lantern and we rode on.

The next time we eased to a walk, to give the horses some rest, I asked, 'What shall we do? Will it not be dangerous to sleep at the inns where we stayed before?'

He thought for a moment before replying.

'You are right. It might be. We do not know how far this disaffection, this treason, extends.'

'We cannot ride for three days without a break,' I said. 'The horses hardly had time to rest tonight.'

'Aye. We may need to rough it.'

'Sleep in the open? We will freeze.'

'Or a barn or a sheep fold.' I could just make out his wry grin in the lantern light. 'The life of one of Walsingham's agents is not always a comfortable inn and a private chamber with its own fire.'

I grinned back. 'So I am learning.'

We rode on at a steady pace as the moon disappeared, first behind clouds and then below the horizon. The loss of moonlight made it feel colder and I was glad of the small warmth of the dog against my stomach and chest. The faint glimmer of the candle lantern in Berden's hand was the only means of lighting our way, though by now our eyes had adjusted to the dark.

After what seemed an interminable night, the sky began to lighten. Dawn could not be far off. We crossed a bridge that I remembered from our southward journey.

'The last inn we stayed at was not far from here,' I said. It was strange to hear my own voice, for neither of us had spoken for several hours.

'Aye, it was.'

'I think we should stop there for a meal,' I said, 'and feed the horses, before we carry on. If we are pursued this far, it will be no mystery for them to know that we have passed this way, for there is no other. We need not stay long, but the horses must rest and eat.' I also intended to see to the wound in his arm, but I did not say so.

'You are right,' he conceded. 'We will eat and rest the horses.'

It must have been more than an hour before we reached the inn, further than I remembered, but by then the sun was up and there was a chance we would be able to have a meal.

It was a humble place, but compared with the squalor of last night, it was a palace. Berden went in to order us a meal, while I saw to the horses. By bribing the stable boy with a few coins, I got oats for the horses as well as hay. After rubbing them both down and putting on their blankets, I left them to rest and went into the inn through the stable yard door, carrying our saddle bags. The dog had lain exhausted in the straw, but now he dragged himself to his feet and followed me.

Berden was in the small parlour, where a fire had been lit and was beginning to burn through. There were two mugs of beer on the table, and a bowl of water for the dog, which he drank thirstily.

'I have bespoke a stewed lamb's shank for us and some scraps for the dog,' Berden said. 'And the inn wife was already baking fresh bread.'

'We should ask for food to carry with us as well,' I said, 'to see us through the rest of the day.'

He nodded agreement. I unbuckled my satchel and probed about in it until I could get my fingers around the wallet of medicines in the bottom and draw it out. It had lain there undisturbed since we had left London.

'What is that?' Berden asked.

'Medical supplies. I never travel without them. I want to look at your arm.'

'Oh, very well.'

He sighed, but removed his doublet and rolled up his left sleeve. Now that there was plenty of light, I saw that both were torn and blood stained. I went to fetch water from the kitchen, which I told them to boil, then carried it carefully back to the parlour.

'The smells in the kitchen promise well,' I said, as I began to clean the wound.

He ventured a smile, but then gritted his teeth. Despite his dismissal of the wound as minor, I could see that it was giving him a good deal of pain. Like any knife wound, it was quite narrow, but it was also deep, running from his elbow to just above his wrist, and the skin around the wound was already enflamed. The knife had driven grit and dirt into the broken flesh and it took me some while to clean it all out. Neither of us spoke while I worked. When I was satisfied that it was clean, I spread it with a salve of honey, beeswax and comfrey.

'I am afraid I must stitch this,' I said. 'It will hurt, but the healing will be much quicker and it will leave less of a scar.'

Berden drank deeply of his beer.

'Do it,' he said in a tight voice.

It needed eight stitches to bring the torn edges together, but it was done at last. I spread on more salve, then bandaged the whole lower arm. He rolled down the sleeve of his shirt and gave me a weak smile, not his usual broad grin.

'I thank you, Kit. I shall recommend to Sir Francis that every mission by his agents should include a physician.'

I laughed and threw the rag I had used to clean the wound into the fire. The dog was now stretched out in front of the warmth and I crouched down to stroke him. It was then that I realised that he too had been wounded.

'It seems you are not the only one that fellow hurt,' I said, getting up and carrying my satchel over to the fire. 'The dog has a sword slash in his side.'

'Poor lad,' Berden said, 'he's a brave animal.'

'He is.' I set about treating this wound much as I had Berden's, though it was made more difficult because the dog's hair was matted with blood, which had dried and hardened over the wound. I was afraid the pain would drive him to bite me, but he lay still and resigned. Because of the caked hair, which I had to snip away, it took all the longer to clean and the inn wife had brought in the lamb shank and bread before I had finished.

'You start,' I told Berden. 'I will finish here first.'

I used the same salve, but I did not attempt to stitch the dog's wound. It was not quite as deep as Berden's and I did not think the dog would remain still long enough for me to put in the stitches. By the time I was able to sit at table, the inn wife had brought in a large bowl of meat scraps and porridge for the dog, and we all set to with the same eager hunger.

'Who knows when he last had anything to eat,' I said, inclining my head toward the dog.

'Not for days, by the look of him. What will you do with him?'

'I don't know. He saved my life back there. His master is dead. It seems cruel to abandon him.'

'I suppose we could take him back on the ship with us, but what then? Is there room for a dog in your life?'

I shrugged. 'I have never thought about it. I shall need to talk to my father. Perhaps I can find a friend to take him in.' There was Sara, I thought, or Simon, or one of the other players. James Burbage would want to train him to act in comedies. I smiled. 'I am sure I can find him a home.'

We stayed at the inn at least two hours, but by then Berden was becoming restive and I was uneasy myself. We could not be sure whether the Spanish soldiers, made aware of Englishmen prowling near to their army, would pursue us this far, but we still felt too close to be easy in our minds. We bought a supply of food from the inn, saddled the horses and went on our way. I was able to contrive a better harness to hold the dog in place in front of my saddle, without chafing his wound, which must have suffered on the first part of our journey.

That night we found a half derelict sheepfold to sleep in, or rather to shelter in, for neither of us was able to sleep much, because of the cold. We scraped away an area of snow within the enclosure so that the horses could graze. I removed Berden's bandage and checked his wound, which still looked enflamed, but no worse. The dog had licked away most of the salve, so I spread more on and this time wrapped a bandage around his body. Either it was his natural instinct to lick the wound, or he enjoyed the taste of the salve.

By the next day we were less anxious. We had put a good deal of distance between ourselves and the village where we were attacked. Also, we had reached a more populated part of the country, with villages every few miles and other roads leading off in different directions. It would not now be so easy to follow us. And here we found the local people friendly and welcoming.

That night we risked stopping at an inn, though I decided to sleep with the horses and Berden told me the next morning that he had slept in his boots, in case he heard an outcry from the stable yard again.

I laughed. 'I think we were safe enough here. I was just being cautious.'

That afternoon we reached the canal, or rather the maze of waterways, that linked Amsterdam to the German sea. By now we had both quite lost track of the date, but we thought it must be near the time when Captain Thoms's ship would return for us. It was a short ride from here into the outskirts of the town, not far from Leicester's quarters. While Berden went to collect any despatches he might wish us to carry back to England, I walked the horses up and down the street to keep them warm. I had no wish to be humiliated again by the Earl's scorn. As soon as Berden returned, we rode back to the waterway, turning along it by the frozen path that led to the sea. It was too late to reach the coast that day, so we spent one more night in an inn and about noon the next day we reached the small port.

I saw the *Silver Swan* almost at once, easy to pick out from amongst the others at anchor because the sailors had once again erected the canvas stable on the foredeck. The ship was anchored some way out in the harbour, so it took us time to attract their attention, but when we did, they raised the anchor and began to row toward the quay. The sight of that familiar ship flooded me with relief. Soon we would be away from here and headed home.

We dismounted and I lifted the dog down to the ground and unwound the rope. He had neither collar nor lead, but I trusted he would stay close beside me. As soon as the ship was moored alongside and the ramp run out, Captain Thoms came ashore and shook our hands.

'Excellent,' he said. 'We arrived last night, so no time was wasted on either side. You have done what you came to do?'

'Aye,' said Berden. 'Shall we get the horses aboard?'

Redknoll had decided he had no more fear of ships and crossed the ramp calmly, followed with rather showy nonchalance by Hector, who immediately turned to the stable as one who comes home.

'How soon can we leave?' Berden asked, as we unsaddled the horses and built the straw bales around them for protection from knocks.

'The tide turns in about an hour,' the captain said. 'The ebb tide will give us a good start. We can leave then.'

He went to see to his ship while we finished settling the horses. He had made no comment about the extra passenger in the form of the dog, who had already scratched himself out a nest in some of the loose straw.

They were an efficient crew. It seemed less than an hour later that Berden and I were sitting in the captain's cabin as the sailors rowed the ship out of the harbour into clear water and hoisted the sails. There was not much wind, so all three sails went up. I hoped that there would be no storm on the homeward journey, so there was only the cold to contend with. While on deck I had noticed that many of the ropes were sheathed in tubes of glassy ice that cracked and shattered as the sails were hoisted and the ropes ran through pulleys. As usual, most of the sailors went barefoot, for a better grip on deck or when they climbed the rigging. Their feet were blue with cold. Even in the cabin I was grateful for the small enclosed brazier that gave off a little heat. I held out my hands to it and the chilblains that had begun to develop during our ride from Amsterdam began to sting. Of course one should not expose chilblains to the heat of a fire, but the temptation was too great, until I was forced to draw my hands back and rub them. I cursed myself silently for my folly. The dog had left his straw bed and followed us into the cabin, so when the captain joined us, having set the ship on its course, I apologised for the dog.

'No need to apologise,' he said, 'I like dogs and have two myself at home. How did you come by him, and why is he bandaged?'

I recounted a brief version of the dog's history, saying only that his master was dead – not that he had been murdered – and that he had defended me when I was attacked.

The captain stroked the dog, running his ears through his fingers. 'It seems he is worth keeping then. Ah, that reminds me.' He got up and went to one of the cupboards set into the wall, which I saw was filled with papers and writing materials.

'This came for you by messenger this morning from Amsterdam.'

I was surprised. Few people would have known that I would be taking ship here. It was a letter, merely inscribed 'Dr Alvarez', and closed by red wax which bore no imprint of a seal. Unconsciously I felt for the seal ring that I still wore around my neck but had had no occasion to use. Because of the blizzard and our trip to the south, there had been no opportunity to send word to Phelippes. I slid my thumbnail under the wax to lift it and unfolded the letter.

It was an unfamiliar hand. I looked down at the signature. 'Hurst'.

The gentleman we both serve is in good health, thanks to the measures you recommended. He wishes me to convey his thanks and gratitude. The other person you know of has departed without leave, we know not where. The gentleman returns home shortly. I wish you a safe journey.
Hurst.

I beamed at Berden. 'Hurst has been successful. And it seems the Earl no longer thinks me a fool.' I decided to say no more for the present.

The captain was still on his feet, bringing out a flagon of his good wine and three heavy-bottomed glasses.

'Good news, then?'

'Aye, good news.' I folded the letter up again and slipped it inside my doublet. I was surprised at the pleasure it gave me. I was vindicated, and my actions had almost certainly saved the Earl from poison. He might not have died, but his health had not looked good to me, so even prompt medical attention might not have saved him if he had taken the belladonna.

We moved to our seats round the captain's table and he poured out the wine. 'We should reach Dover sometime tomorrow, depending on the weather.'

'Good,' I said. 'I have had enough of the Low Countries.'

They both laughed.

'And what is the dog called?' the captain asked.

In all this time the dog had remained nameless. The only person who might have known his name, the minister Dirck de Veen, had never mentioned it.

'I will have to find him a name,' I said. 'I think it should be a Dutch name. Pieter?'

'Jan?' said Berden. 'Lars?'

The dog ignored us.

'I knew a captain called Rikki,' said Thoms. 'It's usually a child's nickname, but he was a big man, very brave.'

'Rikki?' I said. The dog looked up and thumped his tail. 'He seems happy with that.'

'It is short for Richard,' said Thoms, 'and that means "valiant". From what you tell me, it is appropriate.'

I leaned down and caressed the dog's head. 'Rikki it shall be.'

Our return journey, compared with our outward one, was uneventful. Although it remained bitterly cold, there was no further snow but a steady following wind that carried us down the coast of the Low Countries until we came too near the Spanish-controlled ports and Thoms turned the ship toward England. The only concern was when we drew near the shifting shoals of the Goodwin Sands just as the early winter dark began to close down on the following day. In order to avoid any danger, Thoms steered the ship in a wide westward arc and the lookout perched at the top of the main mast sang out that he could see a Spanish ship in the distance, perhaps off Dunkerque. For a while there was an atmosphere of tension aboard, but by the time we had cleared the shoals the ship was lost to sight and we headed in toward Dover.

It was too late to start for London, so we would stay one night in the castle, relieved to be back on English soil and among friends. Before we left the ship, Captain Thoms had presented us each with a pot of his sister's honey. In return, I drew out the two lemons I had carried with me all the way and never used, for I had sent back no despatches, secret or otherwise. Despite their rough journeys, the lemons were unharmed, and I gave them to Thoms.

'Two lemons for you,' I said, 'against the scurvy.'

He smiled. 'I am grateful to you, Doctor. And see, I have also laid in a supply of dried scurvy grass.' He opened the cupboard where he kept his wine and showed me a bundle of the dried herb.

'Excellent,' I said. 'That will serve your men well in the winter, steeped in hot ale. In the summer you will be able to buy fresh.'

We bade him and his men farewell and led the horses over the ramp on to Dover quay. Whether they knew they were back in England, I could not tell, but they seemed pleased to leave the ship. Rikki trotted at my heels, already beginning to look stronger after a few days of good food.

Up at the castle we left the horses and the dog in the stable and reported to Sir Anthony Torrington, who told us, rather ungraciously, that we could be accommodated for one night. He was one of those men who like to give the impression that they are busier than they really are, so spent his time moving papers about on his desk and barely glancing up at us. One of the soldiers showed us to a room, where we would be obliged to share with two others this time, but both were on night guard duty, so after exchanging a few words of greeting we did not see them again.

I saw nothing of Andrew until we joined the soldiers for a meal and then we had little time to talk, for he too was about to go on duty.

'It was successful, your time in the Low Countries?' he asked.

'Successful, aye,' I said. 'And also eventful. I have come back with a dog and Berden with a knife injury, but we achieved what we were sent to do.'

'Good. I may not see you again before you leave, but if I am in London, I will visit you at St Bartholomew's.'

'I did not think you would want to cross that threshold again,' I said with a smile, 'for it must hold bad memories.'

'No, you are wrong. What I remember is being made well again.'

With that, he was off.

Before retiring for the night I called in at the stables and asked one of the grooms whether Rikki could stay with them until the morning.

'I think he might not be welcomed in the soldiers' quarters,' I said.

'He'll do fine with us, Doctor. I fetched him a bone from the kitchen.'

Rikki looked up from the bone and scrambled to his feet, ready to follow me, but I shook my head and pointed down to the floor. 'Wait there,' I said. The dog could not be expected to understand the command or even my English words, but he seemed to understand the gesture. He returned to his bone and did not try to follow me when I left.

The next morning we set out for London. The snow was as heavy here as it had been in the Low Countries, so it was not until early afternoon on the third day that we reached Seething Lane. I hoped that Sir Francis would be here and not at his home in Barn Elms, for I had no wish to cross the river again and go riding about the Surrey countryside.

We went first to Phelippes's office, which held a welcome warmth after our long cold ride from Dover. I unwound the scarf from my head and hung my cloak on the back of my chair. Phelippes looked up from his papers.

'Ah, there you are,' he said, quite as if we had merely stepped out of the room and not been away for nearly a month.

'Is Sir Francis in?' Berden asked, easing off his cloak. His left arm was still somewhat stiff, though the injury was beginning to heal cleanly.

'He is. I will take you to him.'

Arthur Gregory put his head round the door of his room and smiled at us, but said nothing. Then Phelippes led us along the hallway to Sir Francis's office.

We spent the rest of the afternoon with Sir Francis, delivering Leicester's despatches and going over in detail exactly what we had done every day we had been away. He even questioned us about the situation at Dover Castle, the strength and morale of the garrison, what ships had been in the harbour, our general impression of military preparations. Berden was much better at answering his questions than I was, and I realised just how observant he had been.

When it came to Amsterdam, however, everyone's attention was focused on me. Sir Francis took me through my account twice, obliging me to recall every detail about Cornelius Parker, van Leyden, and the murder of Hans Viederman. He was also very attentive to the information given me by Ettore Añez.

'We know of Parker, of course,' he said, almost to himself.

I explained how I had gone to Leicester with my fears about a poison plot, and how he had laughed at me and thrown me out.

'Luckily,' I said, 'Robert Hurst was in service with him there.'

Sir Francis nodded. As I had suspected, he already knew this. Had probably placed Hurst there himself. I told him how I had alerted Hurst and given him the evidence of the handkerchief.

'When we reached our ship,' I said, 'a letter had just been sent to me there.'

I took out Hurst's letter and handed it to Sir Francis, who read it quickly, then beamed at me.

'Excellent, Kit. You have done just as you should. It seems His Lordship has now realised that what you suspected was true. He will be grateful to you.'

'But van Leyden seems to have escaped, sir.' To me this seemed more urgent.

'For the moment, perhaps.'

'And the murderer of Hans Viederman, will he ever be brought to justice?'

'I doubt it, Kit. What is most important is that you have averted a plot to kill England's foremost Earl.'

I thought Hans's death was important too, but realised I should not say so.

'And this other man, Cornelius Parker?' I said. 'He is implicated. He deals with the Spanish.'

'I will have him watched. If he proves dangerous, we will take measures against him.'

When at last Walsingham dismissed us, I bade Berden farewell, unsure whether I would see him again, which seemed strange after being in his company for most of the last month. I went down the backstairs and round to the stable yard, to collect Rikki and my belongings and to say my other farewells, to Hector. Many would think me foolish, but I always felt Hector

211

could read my thoughts and knew that we were parting again. I closed my eyes and pressed my forehead against his neck, my hand buried in the thick hair of his mane. Stupid tears filled my eyes and I blotted them against his silky, ugly coat. I had come to love this horse, but I could not allow any of the grooms to see me crying over him. Neither Walsingham nor Phelippes had said anything to me about further code-breaking work, so I would have no excuse to see Hector again, though I would try to slip in here from time to time and give him an apple. With a final pat, I turned my back on him and fetched my satchel and knapsack from the tack room, where Rikki had stayed with the grooms.

'It is good to see you again. Dr Alvarez,' the head groom said as he handed me my belongings. 'Was the snow as bad as this in the Low Countries?'

It was no surprise to me that my destination was known to him. The last people Walsingham would be able to keep secrets from were his own servants.

'Aye, it was,' I said. 'Worse, even. The canals were frozen, with people skating on them.'

'I've heard of that. We used to skate on the pools in the Kent marshes when I was a lad. Made our own skates out of mutton bones. Then when I first come to London – the winter of '64 it was – the Thames froze and we sported on the river. Skating, dancing, tumblers, bear baiting. Even the Queen came and joined the fun. I wonder whether the river will ever freeze again.'

'I'm in no hurry,' I said. 'This is cold enough for me.'

He laughed and patted the dog. 'Been in the wars, has he?'

'Aye. Took a sword slash meant for me.'

'Did he!' He raised his eyebrows. 'That's a good dog to have by you.'

'He is that. Come, Rikki.'

The dog scrambled to his feet at once. One thing I had learned in Amsterdam was that their word for 'come' sounded just like ours, so Rikki had no difficulty understanding me.

We set off across London, which was as snowbound as Amsterdam, but here the snow was dirtier. London is a busier city and the horse traffic is heavier, so the snow, which must have last fallen some days ago, was badly stained. Somehow you do not notice the horse dung in the normal way of things, but when it lies on the pure white of snow it seems more offensive. As we walked across London, Rikki was distracted from time to time by irresistible smells, and also stopped several times to make the acquaintance of other dogs. I had never noticed before quite how many dogs roamed the streets, with or without owners.

When I reached Eastcheap I decided to stop at Jake Winterly's leather shop. Bess greeted me with her usual delight and urged me to come upstairs for a meal, it being nearly supper time.

I shook my head. 'I must go home to my father, Bess. I am just back from abroad, but you can see that I have acquired a dog.'

We both looked at Rikki, who sat alert, watching us.

'I need a collar for him.'

'We have plenty.' She cast an expert eye, then reached into a cupboard behind her. 'This should fit.' It was a supple length of cow hide with a plain buckle and no ornamentation. 'Unless you would like something prettier.'

'No, this is good.' I clasped it round Rikki's neck. Bess had judged right. The collar fitted well, with just enough slack for comfort. 'I should have a lead as well, I suppose, though he is obedient enough even without one.'

I paid for both items, rolled up the lead to fit in my pocket, and left my good wishes for the rest of the family.

Rikki shook his head a few times as we continued on our way, and once sat down and scratched at the collar. Clearly he had never worn one before, but I felt it was wise to fit him with one. The city dog catchers of London never hesitate to kill stray dogs, for they are believed to carry the plague. They would at least hesitate briefly before drowning a dog wearing a collar.

At we neared Duck Lane I noticed that Rikki had scented the smell of the Shambles and all the butchers' shops around Smithfield. I had given little thought to how I was to feed him, but at least we were well placed for butchers' scraps. I had told Berden I would find a home for the dog when I reached London, but it was becoming more and more difficult to think of parting with him.

It was almost dark when I reached home and saw a shaft of candlelight falling from the kitchen window, not yet shuttered. Our ground floor windows were glazed, but it was cheap glass, full of swirls and lumps. Through it I could see movement, but nothing clearly. Upstairs we had only shutters, which were closed against the cold. I opened the door and stepped inside, enveloped at once in warmth and steam. Joan was bending over and stirring a pot hanging from a hook over the fire; my father was sitting in his carved chair at the table, a book open in front of him, his chin resting on his hand and his eyes closed.

At the rush of cold air and the sound of the door, Joan swung round and my father opened his eyes. He looked confused for a moment, then stood up and came to me, holding out his arms. We hugged each other.

'Kit! Home at last! We did not know when you would be here.'

'I reached London this afternoon, but had to report to Sir Francis.' I put down my baggage on the coffer and closed the door. Rikki had followed me in and stood looking about him with interest.

'Wisht!' Joan rushed over, flapping her apron and aiming a kick at him. 'There's a dirty stray followed you in off the street.' She made a grab for the door and pulled it open. 'Be off with you!'

'No!' I caught hold of Rikki's collar as he shrank away from her and began to retreat. 'He's mine. At least, he's with me. Leave him be, Joan.' I closed the door again.

'A dirty cur like that? Get him out of my kitchen, Master Alvarez.'

I was tempted to say that it was not her kitchen but my father's. However, that was not the way to deal with Joan.'

'If he is dirty, that is no more than I am, after weeks of travelling. Besides, he is injured. He took a sword thrust meant for me and saved my life. I will wash him tomorrow.'

Joan turned to my father, her hands on her hips. 'Dr Alvarez, we cannot have a filthy cur in the kitchen. He is probably carrying the plague.'

Rikki was listening to this conversation, looking from one to the other of us.

'If he carried the plague, I would have it by now,' I said. 'I have ridden for days with him in front of my saddle, his body up against mine. I've no symptoms – not as yet, anyway.'

Joan looked at me sceptically, her mouth pursed up with disapproval, but my father laughed. 'Leave them be, Joan. We are just happy to see Kit safely home. You say the dog is with you, Kit. Do you mean to keep him?'

'Yes,' I said, finally making up my mind and all the more stubbornly in the face of Joan's objections. 'His master is dead and he came to me. The least I can do is give him a home.'

'Dead, is he?' Joan muttered, turning back to her cooking. 'Dead of the plague, most like.'

'No,' I said sharply. 'He was murdered.'

I should not have said that, but I was suddenly exhausted and cold and could not tolerate her complaints any longer. I sank down on to a bench and Rikki pressed himself against my leg. I heard my father draw a sharp breath.

'Murdered! You say he saved your life, the dog?' he said.

'Aye, but that was later. I will tell you about it tomorrow. Tonight I am too tired.'

The next morning I did tell my father what had happened in the Low Countries, when we were on our way to the hospital and out of earshot of Joan. The first problem in owning a dog had already presented itself. I did not feel Rikki would be safe left with Joan, who would probably drive him out, whatever my father or I said. Yet I could not take him into the wards of the hospital. I had him on the lead, which he did not like, and hoped I could leave him with the doorkeeper in his lodge.

My father's reaction to the account of my journey was silence at first. Then he said, 'I do not like the way Sir Francis is using you, as if you were one of his agents. When you went to work there first, it was as a code-breaker and translator, in the office of Master Phelippes.'

And as a forger, I thought, but did not say aloud.

'It seems to me,' he went on, 'that he is sending you into unnecessary danger. I know he does not realise that you are but a girl. Yet what he asks is too much even for a boy as young as you. You are not yet eighteen.'

'Nearly,' I said, a little stung by those words: 'but a girl'.

'I believe he often uses students,' I said, 'for it's common for them to travel about in Europe. No one finds that suspicious. And they would be of an age with me.' I recalled that Simon had told me that Marlowe had worked for Walsingham while still a student at Cambridge.

'In any case,' I added, 'I see no reason for him to use me again. This time he had no one else available to go with Nicholas Berden. And Berden is very experienced.'

'Hmph. Was it not he who led you into danger, near the Spanish army?'

'Only following instructions from Walsingham. Besides, thanks to Rikki here, I came to no harm.'

Wanting to divert him from these thoughts, I drew a heavy purse out of my doublet and handed it to him. 'I did not want to give you this in front of Joan, in case she asked for more wages!'

He looked at the purse in surprise, feeling the weight of it in his hand. 'What is this?'

'Payment from Sir Francis. He did not expect me to work for a month unpaid. Buy yourself some warm clothes for this cold weather.'

'Books!' he said, his eyes gleaming.

As I knew he would.

My life fell back into its old pattern, working every day at the hospital with my father and Dr Stevens where, as I had expected, the wards were already filled with patients suffering from the usual winter complaints, ranging from coughs and sore throats through to chest infections and pneumonia. And, as in every winter, we did our best, but we lost some, mainly those who were already weakened by poverty and a poor diet. When I asked Peter Lambert to prepare scurvy water for pauper children with rickets, I thought of Captain Thoms and his sailors and wondered how their preparations for the invasion were faring.

Christmas came and I spent it again with the players. My time away and my experiences in the Low Countries had somehow created a distance between us, so that things were not as easy as they had been. Marlowe spent some of the time with us, and I noticed that he and Simon were on very good terms, something I did not like. Yet, what could I say? They were part of the same world, this world of the playhouse, despite the fact that Marlowe had come there from Cambridge. It seemed that he had great ambitions as a playwright, though Burbage had not yet agreed to mount one of his plays, which he said were too elaborate and too expensive.

Marlowe had other irons in the fire. He was carefully cultivating Sir Francis's younger cousin, Thomas Walsingham, as his patron, and travelled down to Kent to spend part of the Christmas festivities at his estate. As far as Thomas Walsingham was concerned, Marlowe was not part of the disreputable world of the playhouse, but a gentleman poet, a university man. Certainly Marlowe dressed the part and I often wondered how he came by the money for such finery. His own family was humble, his stepfather nothing more than a bricklayer, so whence the riches? Some may have come from Thomas Walsingham, some from work for Sir Francis, but perhaps some came from a more disreputable source.

When I raised this with Simon, during the time Marlowe was down in Kent, it led to our first real quarrel.

'How dare you suggest such a thing!' Simon shouted at me, his face flushed and furious. 'Marlowe is an honourable man.'

The angrier Simon became, the colder I grew. 'I find it strange that he has so much coin to throw about,' I said, in a hard, level voice. 'He has neither family nor occupation. If it were anyone but your beloved Marlowe, you too would be suspicious.'

'He is not my beloved Marlowe,' he said through gritted teeth. 'I just do not like to see an honest man accused.'

'I did not accuse him,' I said. 'I merely raised the question. And I wonder why that makes you so angry.'

'He probably won it at cards,' Simon blustered, 'or by betting on horses. That is what gentlemen do.'

'Ha!' I said, stung. 'What do you know of what gentlemen do?' I thought briefly of my own life in the highest ranks of Coimbra society before I came to England, but I could not speak of it.

'Why do you not ask,' Simon jeered, 'when he comes back to London? "I am curious, Kit Marlowe, about your riches. Will

217

you settle an argument between Simon and me?" That way we will know.'

'Perhaps I will,' I said, and stormed off.

I did not go back to the playhouse for two days, but then it was Twelfth Night and James Burbage had pressed me to join the players. I did not want to insult him, so I went with them for a meal at their favourite inn. Simon seemed to have forgotten our quarrel and Marlowe had not returned, but I kept my distance, until Burbage reminded everyone that it was my birthday, and they all drank a toast to me. A new year for me and a new year for the country, with the threatened invasion looming ever nearer. 1588.

My resentment of Marlowe (and I confess it was touched with considerable jealousy) did not prevent my occasional visits with Harriot to Raleigh's circle during these months. Sometimes Marlowe was there, sometimes not. Although our discussions were mostly concerned with scientific matters, affairs of the nation could not be shut outside the turret door. Ever since Drake's daring assault on the Spanish navy at Cadiz, we had known that Spain would rebuild and retaliate. The only question was: When? In the spring – as I had feared – I was summoned to Walsingham again, to my desk in the little back room, and my work with Phelippes. Once again I spent the mornings at St Bartholomew's and the afternoons at Seething Lane. Berden was away somewhere on another mission. From hints dropped, I suspected he had gone to meet Gilbert Gifford in Paris and perhaps provide money or other support for Henri of Navarre's Huguenot rebels.

Rikki's wound had healed well and once I had given him a bath and combed the tangles out of his fur, he was revealed as a light sandy brown instead of the much darker shade he had first appeared. I was able to buy scraps for him from the local butchers, using some of Walsingham's money, which my father insisted I take.

'If the dog saved your life,' he said, 'the very least we can do is feed him well.'

Rikki filled out and became the large, sturdy animal he was meant to be, and his loyalty to me was absolute and unquestioning. When I was working at the hospital, he stayed with the doorkeeper, who grew fond of the dog and often shared his own meals with him. When I worked at Seething Lane, he went with me and soon insinuated himself into Phelippes's office. At night he slept in my chamber and – I must admit it – on the end of my bed. Joan learned to tolerate him, though not to like him, so that the dog likewise learned to keep his distance from her.

As spring drew on, and passed, the burden of deciphering and copying grew ever heavier. We knew that Spain was rebuilding her fleet, and she would not be taken by surprise again. When summer came, she would invade.

One day, Walsingham called me into his office.

'Ah, Kit.' He beamed at me. 'I have received a letter from the Earl of Leicester.'

He laid his hand upon a packet lying on his desk. It looked too thick to be a letter.

'Sir?' I said, unable to think of anything else to say.

'It refers to the service you did him in Amsterdam.'

I had a sharp memory of Leicester's scornful laughter and his dismissal of me which was hardly better than a kicking.

'Hurst persuaded him, I assume, that what I said was true.'

'Indeed. Hurst found the bottle of poison amongst van Leyden's possessions and took it to the Earl. They sent for an apothecary, who confirmed that it was belladonna. When van Leyden was summoned and questioned, he made some blustering reply, and offered to fetch papers to show that the belladonna was intended for medical use. They waited for him to return. By the time they realised he was not going to return, he had vanished.'

I nodded. I had guessed that something like this must have happened. The Earl had trusted van Leyden and would have given him every chance to vindicate himself. I did not think the Earl was a good judge of men.

'As you know,' Sir Francis continued, 'the Earl returned to England in December.'

'Aye, sir, I had heard. And Baron Willoughby appointed in command of the English army there, in his stead.' I paused. 'Not Sir John Norreys.'

I knew, as Walsingham knew, that Sir John Norreys was England's best and most experienced soldier. In his youth he was notorious for the slaughter of Irish women and children, carried out under the orders of the Earl of Essex, father of the present Earl. Nowadays he was most famous for his military strategy. If anyone could match Parma, it was Norreys.

'Why was Norreys not given command?' I asked.

Walsingham shook his head. 'Do not play the innocent with me, Kit. Norreys is but a commoner, knighted for his services.'

He let that hang in the air. He too was a commoner, knighted for his services.

'Peregrine Bertie, Lord Willoughby, outranks him.'

'I had heard,' I said cautiously, 'that Lord Willoughby said that if he himself was sufficient for the task, then Norreys was superfluous.'

Walsingham laughed aloud, something he did not often do. 'Best keep that to yourself. Now, the reason I called you here is this.'

He patted the packet again and I assumed a look of polite enquiry. I could not imagine what this was about.

'The Earl arranged for a medal to be struck, when he left the Low Countries, to commemorate his service there, and his departure. His reluctant departure.'

I recalled all I had heard about the Hollanders' increasing distrust and contempt for Leicester, but said nothing.

'He has sent one of these medals to me, to be presented to you in recognition of your service to him.' Walsingham unfolded a stiff sheet of paper and held out to me something wrapped in a piece of red silk. I got up from my chair and he handed it to me.

Inside the silk was a heavy medal of solid silver, about the size of a crown piece. On one side was a bust portrait of the Earl, like a Roman emperor, but adorned with a beard and a fashionable modern hat. On the other, somewhat puzzlingly, a flock of sheep to the left and one solitary sheep to the right. Sheep?

Around the Earl's head were the words: ROBE. CO. LEIC. ET IN BELG. GVBER. 1587. In other words: 'Robert Earl of Leicester and Governor of the Low Countries 1587'. I turned it over again. The sheep on the right wasn't a sheep. It was meant to be a dog, presumably a shepherd's dog, looking over its shoulder at the indifferent sheep. This side bore the legend: NON GREGEM SED INGRATOS INVITUS DESERO.

I looked up at Walsingham and gave him a wry look. 'Unwillingly I leave not the flock but the ungrateful ones.'

'Aye.'

'The dog is meant to be the Earl?'

'Aye.'

Neither of us made any further comment on the medal. We both knew that Leicester had been appealing to the Queen for months to be allowed to leave the Low Countries. I wrapped the medal again in its piece of silk and stowed it carefully in my doublet.

'I am most grateful to His Lordship,' I said gravely, 'and will write at once to thank him for his gift.'

'Good,' Walsingham said. 'I have heard that the United Provinces have struck a counter medal.' He allowed himself a small smile.

'That would be interesting,' I said.

He nodded and I returned to Phelippes's office. It would also be an interesting letter to write, if challenging.

Chapter Twelve

For months most people in England had clung stubbornly to the belief that Drake's raid on Cadiz had crippled Spain's navy permanently. This was the gossip on the streets, in the ale houses, among our patients. Anything else was too terrifying to confront. But at last this collective wilful blindness was swept away as rumours spread and were accepted as the truth. The tangible reality of the ships being built in Spain became common knowledge and forced the whole country – not just those at the centre of power and those of us who worked for them – to understand that the prospect of a Spanish invasion was not simply some nightmare. It was real, and it was going to happen. England was a tiny country, ruled by a woman, however much we revered her. The Queen's navy was pitifully small, the ships themselves small, though our great captains were amongst the finest in the world. Spain possessed the largest empire on the face of the earth. Her ships were huge, their fire-power vaster than anything we could muster. The man-power she could draw upon, to sail her ships and form her army, was many times what we could assemble. In the Low Countries, Parma's army waited – a large, disciplined and experienced force.

To augment our sea power, every private ship, merchantman or privateer, was commandeered into the navy. All the fishermen in England were bidden to join our navy, even the trinkermen who fished the Thames. Many did not wait to be summoned, but volunteered as a patriotic fervour swept the country. So many wherrymen pledged their service to the Queen that it was a problem to find a boat to transport you across the Thames.

It was more difficult to create an army out of nothing. Apart from the local militia bands, which were made up of citizen volunteers who enjoyed parading and ordering their fellow townsmen about, the only soldiers we possessed in England were the garrison at Berwick, to keep out the Scots, the garrison at the Tower, to protect London and the Queen, and the garrison at Dover, to guard the coast from attack across the Channel. For any of these soldiers to be deployed against the Spanish would be to risk attack elsewhere. The soldiers stationed at Dover would at least be in position to face an invasion. Our soldiers in the Low Countries were a poor match for the Spaniards when it came to battles – poorly commanded, underpaid and disaffected – they could hardly be relied on even if they could be returned to England, leaving our flank to the northeast exposed.

There was little I could do to show my loyalty to my adopted country, other than sit at my desk in that cramped back room and rack my brains over the coded despatches and intercepted letters, but I was happier now than I had been nearly two years before, when I had taken an unwilling part in the entrapment of Babington and the Scottish queen. I had no scruples about the Spaniards, my people's ancient enemies.

I sat back on my stool one day, flexing my cramped fingers.

'I wish I could take a more active part against the Spaniards,' I said to Phelippes. 'They raped and burned my country. I would I could join the fleet when we sail out to meet them. Thrust my sword into one of those misbegotten scoundrels.'

It was bravado, but I was restless. I am not quite sure how serious I was in this masculine, bellicose talk. Perhaps I had become infected by the general mood on the streets. I had not, after all, enjoyed our skirmish with the traitorous Dutch peasants near the Spanish army a few months earlier.

Phelippes looked up from his work, then set aside his quill and polished his spectacles on a silk handkerchief.

'Do not underrate the work you are doing, Kit. Perhaps you might kill a Spaniard or two, should it come to hand-to-hand fighting. But one day's work of yours here will save more English lives and end more Spanish ones than you could ever hope to do as a simple soldier on board ship.'

'Do you truly believe so?' I had always felt there was something of a barrier between Phelippes and myself, but now that our mutual enemy was drawing so near, I needed reassurance, even if it meant revealing a glimpse of weakness in myself.

He put on his spectacles again and directed a sharp glance at me across the room. 'I do. And you should believe it too.' He gave me one of his rare brief smiles. 'You are of value to England, Kit.'

I would never love this work as I loved my physician's calling, but in that moment I did feel a burst of pride. So that he might not read it in my face, I leaned down and made much of scratching Rikki behind his ears. Of course I could never wield a sword on one of England's ships – I had no skill in swordsmanship in any case. I would have been cut down at once. It merely seemed that, after my journey into the Low Countries with Berden, my life now was very dull, especially when I knew that Walsingham's agents were spread out all over Europe, from Spain and Portugal to the Holy Roman Empire, from the bleak Russian steppes to the mysterious streets of Constantinople, and from Cairo to Jerusalem. I had never thought I would envy them, and my experiences in the Low Countries had given me an understanding of the danger and discomfort their missions involved, but I was tired of my work of code-breaking, however important Phelippes might claim that it was.

Then one evening in early summer, when I had spent the day in Phelippes's work, a servant arrived from Dr Nuñez asking if I might be released to dine with him, as he was awaiting a packet of letters on one of his ships, due on the evening tide, and he expected some of them to be in code. I knew by now just how closely both he and Dr Lopez worked with Walsingham, supplying him with intelligence and arranging the carrying of letters and the transport of couriers and intelligencers all over Europe, even as far as the Sultan's empire.

Phelippes agreed that I might go, so I ran down the backstairs and out into the soft spring sunshine, taking Rikki with me and glad to be free of the close air in the small office. I walked along Seething Lane and around the corner to Mark Lane. Dr Nuñez greeted me kindly, as he always did, and we sat down alone to dine, for his wife was visiting an aged aunt, who was ailing.

'You think important matters will arrive on this ship?' I asked.

'Word from Spain,' he said.

I shivered. I could not help it.

'The Spanish . . . they're so powerful,' I said in a small voice. 'I remember how they marched into Portugal and we made no resistance. I was a child and did not understand how it could happen, how our Portuguese soldiers could vanish into the mist and leave us to face the Spanish. We stood in the street and watched the ranks of Spanish soldiers marching by, their faces full of contempt, their banners so arrogant, and we so humiliated. How can England withstand them? It will all begin again: the occupying army, the persecutions, the Inquisition.'

I could hear the panic in my voice. There are some memories that never leave you.

'They will find us out and destroy us,' I said.

Dr Nuñez ran his hand down his beard, which was turning white.

'I know your family suffered, Kit. And my wife and I had come here to England before Spain invaded Portugal. But we too saw what the Inquisition could do, although my own family managed to escape it.'

He patted my hand, then poured me another glass of wine, and I drank it down without tasting it.

'As for England withstanding the Spanish fleet . . . do you remember your Greek history? The battle of Salamis?'

'Yes,' I said. 'The Persians had bigger and stronger ships, but the Greeks out-manoeuvred them in their smaller, faster vessels.'

'Exactly. I think you will find that Drake and Howard have also read their Greek history.'

There was a knock on the door and one of the servants came in, carrying a packet of papers secured with thin ribbon. Rikki sat up from his place beside the small summer fire and looked at me expectantly. Dr Nuñez untied the ribbon and began to sort through the papers.

'Many of these are of no interest to us tonight. Dockets for cargo, personal letters we carry for friends and fellow merchants.'

He stiffened suddenly and laid his hand on one thin folded sheet of paper. I saw that his hand shook as he lifted the seal with a knife.

'This will be the one. Bring the candle closer.'

I moved the candlestick between us and took the sheet from him. It held a bland, meaningless message about supplies of Rhenish wine, but the lines of ink were widely spaced. Another message would be contained in those spaces, written in lemon juice or milk or urine. I held it close to the candle to warm and the letters emerged, browned by the heat, hastily written. The code was the one used normally by Dr Nuñez's agents. He could have deciphered it himself, but he was slow and his eyesight was failing.

A few minutes later we were back in Seething Lane, which I had left barely an hour before. I had to slow my impatient steps, for the old man's knees were arthritic and he could not keep up my pace, while Rikki followed us soberly, as if he sensed that something was afoot. This time we went to the front door and were shown at once into the dining parlour where Walsingham was at meat. He started up from the table and looked from one to the other of us. Dr Nuñez pushed me forward and I held out the sheet of paper with my transcription at the bottom of it.

'Well?' said Sir Francis.

I looked at him, and my own hand holding the paper was shaking.

'The Armada has set sail.'

The fleet had left Lisbon on the twenty-eighth of May. It was now the fifth of June.

For the next few days, I went very early to the hospital each morning, when the pre-dawn light was filtering through the river mist. Since that first message from Dr Nuñez's agent, Walsingham had told me that I was to report to Phelippes every day, but I could not abandon my patients altogether, nor could I allow them to become a burden to my father. On that particular summer morning, less than a week later, I had given permission for two women to be sent home, applied fresh dressings to half a dozen injuries, fixed a new splint to a broken arm and given Peter Lambert instructions about medicines to be dispensed, all before I hurried away to Dr Nuñez's house to collect any despatches which might have arrived on the previous evening's high tide.

In Phelippes's office I began to sort through them before I even sat down on my stool. 'There is one here from Bordeaux,' I called to Phelippes, 'I'd best transcribe that first.'

He came across the room while I warmed the paper at my candle. As it was written in Dr Nuñez's familiar code I could read it straight off, as easily as if it had been written in English:

The fleet is seven miles across from end to end, like a gigantic crescent of huge ships bearing down towards England.

I stared blindly at him, trying to envisage a fleet seven miles across – the distance from London to . . . where? I could not even begin to imagine it. And already the fleet had been sighted off Bordeaux. A sick panic seized my stomach. The Spanish, the loathsome Spanish! They had robbed me of home and family, imprisoned me, driven me into this life of lies and deception, and now they were pursuing me inexorably again.

No! I shook myself. Ashamed. What was I? Some insignificant creature, a mere beetle beneath the Spanish boot. England was their prey. England and our Queen.

Phelippes said nothing, but even he, usually so severe and contained, turned pale.

'Seven miles across,' he said softly. 'Is there anything else of note?'

I sorted through the remaining four despatches Dr Nuñez's manservant had given me.

'There's one here from Antwerp.'

Walsingham had informers even in Spanish-controlled Antwerp, but only rarely were they able to slip a message through enemy lines. It appeared, from several superscripts on the outside of the paper, that it had travelled via Paris, and then also on from Bordeaux.

I trembled as I read it out, deciphering as I went:

Here in the Spanish Netherlands, the Duke of Parma is preparing a second fleet, a fleet of barges, which will carry a trained army of thirty thousand men across the Channel to invade England, under escort of the warships now sailing up from Spain.

'That perfidious scoundrel!' I cried, forgetting for once to hold my tongue and hide my feelings. 'All these last months he has been pretending to treat for peace with the Queen! How could she be so deceived?'

Despite the fact that Burghley himself, diplomat and peacemaker, had warned her that this time there was no escaping war with Spain, we had known in Walsingham's office since early spring that the Queen had been negotiating for peace, offering in secret (as we discovered through our intelligencers in the Duke of Parma's camp) to sacrifice the Protestant Netherlanders who were our allies, and even to surrender to Parma England's own holdings in the Low Countries. I remembered the Penders family at the Prins Willem, the minister Dirck de Veen, and Sara's cousin Ettore Añez. What would become of them if we deserted them? It was shameful. Shameful of the Queen, who had ignored both Burghley and Walsingham. I knew my words and my thoughts were disrespectful, but more than Parma were prepared to act treacherously in this affair. I had no doubt that Parma had never intended to make peace in the Low Countries, but merely used the Queen's overtures to gain time for the Spanish invasion.

Phelippes did not answer me, but went at once to fetch Walsingham so that he might read the despatches for himself.

'At last,' Sir Francis announced grimly as he cast his eye over my hastily written transcriptions, 'at *last*, our preparations against invasion have begun, but it will be a mighty scramble if we are to be ready in time for this.' He tapped the papers with his finger.

He picked up the Antwerp despatch and held it at arm's length, the better to read it.

'Thirty thousand trained soldiers.' There was a look of near despair on his face. 'Thirty thousand in addition to those aboard the Spanish fleet. We cannot possibly withstand such an army.'

'The string of warning beacons is being set up?' said Phelippes.

'Aye. All along the south coast from Cornwall to Kent, and on up here to London.' Walsingham shrugged and sighed.

228

'I heard,' I was hesitant, for I did not usually put myself forward in Sir Francis's presence, 'that the citizen militias have been ordered to ready themselves. But have they the arms to defend us?'

Walsingham gave a snort of disgust.

'Armed with their pitchforks and flails, their 'prentice clubs and tailors' yards, and their stout English hearts, they stand ready to repel a professional Spanish army equipped with muskets, cross-bows and cannon! Nay, Kit, if our navy cannot prevent the Spaniards from landing, you will soon be able to speak Spanish to our new masters.'

He paced back and forth across our small room, then paused, looking out of the window over the neighbouring roof tops toward the docks and gripping the sill with his long, fine hands.

'At any rate Drake and Howard and Hawkins are ready with our small but skilful navy, waiting at Plymouth and the other ports along the south coast. If they cannot repel the Spanish fleet, I hold out little hope for us.'

He turned to face us. 'What concerns me most at present is that we have had no word from Amsterdam for several weeks. We need to know what is afoot in the Low Countries. Who do you have out there at present, Thomas?'

'I have been concerned as well,' Phelippes said. 'Mark Weber went out soon after Berden and Kit returned and he was sending regular reports until about three weeks ago. He was reporting on the morale of our soldiers, which is not good. He had also traced van Leyden to a village outside Amsterdam, apparently lying low. In addition, he said that Cornelius Parker had disappeared for a time, apparently on a buying mission to Constantinople, but had returned on one of his ships to Amsterdam. That was in his last despatch. There has been nothing since.'

'We must send someone else to discover what is happening with our army there, and to find Weber, if possible. He is part Dutch, is he not?'

'Aye, his father was Dutch and he speaks the language.'

'Is Lord Willoughby not reporting regularly?' I asked.

'Lord Willoughby tells us what he thinks we want to hear,' Walsingham said. 'What I need to know is the mood amongst the men themselves. How prepared they are. Whether many are likely to desert. Whether we are now on better terms with the Hollanders, as Willoughby claims, or whether he is asserting this merely in order to claim greater success than the Earl. Most importantly, whether we are in a position to harry the Spanish army so that they cannot spare thirty thousand men to be sent across the Channel. Whether, if we recall our men, the Hollanders can hold out against Parma, or even attack him, so that he will be unable to fight on two fronts.'

We were all silent for some minutes.

'Sir John Norreys is there,' I said at last. 'Can he not keep Parma's army occupied, so that it cannot be sent to join the forces sailing up from Spain?'

Walsingham shook his head. 'The Earl of Leicester is to command the land forces here in England to resist the Spanish attack. As soon as I send him this latest information, which I will do today, he will want to summon Norreys back from the Low Countries. He will not confess to it, but he knows he cannot command a military campaign as Norreys can.'

Once again, there was silence. The two men looked at me, then exchanged looks.

'Kit,' said Phelippes, 'I think we must send you.'

I felt as though I had been prodded with a red hot poker. I gaped at him. 'Me? But I haven't the skills. I speak no Dutch.'

And I thought of my father's words. I am but a girl.

'You conducted yourself very successfully before in Amsterdam,' Walsingham said.

Phelippes nodded. 'Your lack of Dutch is no impediment. Most of the Hollanders speak some English. And you have your connection with Ettore Añez, who is eminent in the Amsterdam merchant community, as well as being the nephew of the Queen's Purveyor of Spices.'

'But before, I went with Nicholas Berden,' I said. 'One of your most senior agents. He understood what you wished us to do. He speaks some Dutch.'

'We do not normally send out our agents in pairs, Kit,' Phelippes said. 'And were you not saying, only the other day, that you wished you could do something more active in the Queen's cause? Now is your chance.'

Caught in my own trap, I thought. In future, I should watch my tongue.

'What would I have to do?' I asked reluctantly.

'Find out all the things Sir Francis has just mentioned,' Phelippes said. 'And above all, discover what has happened to Mark Weber. That is most important, for he will possess the information we need. It may simply be that his reports have gone astray, or it may be that something has happened to him.'

'He told you he had located Cornelius Parker,' I said. 'The last person I know of who crossed Cornelius Parker had his throat cut.'

'Aye, but he was a man who had lost his legs. He would not have stood much chance against an assassin. Mark is a competent swordsman.'

'I am not,' I said flatly. 'I have never even held a sword. My training has all been directed to saving life, not taking it.'

They looked at each other again.

'You will need to leave as soon as possible.' Phelippes said. 'We cannot tell how many days' grace we have before the Spanish fleet arrives, that will depend on the weather and the state of the winds. At the moment, they would seem to be holding the fleet back, loading supplies, perhaps. Or practising naval manoeuvres. You will need to bring word to us before Parma can embark his forces. Their plan must be to take the fleet into one of the Spanish controlled ports, or more than one of them, once it reaches the Channel. Then the soldiers will be embarked on these barges the message speaks of, to be escorted across the Channel by the war fleet. They will not attempt to move the army from the Low Countries until they have the protection of the Spanish warships. To move sooner would be suicide, for our ships would pick them off in the barges.'

'Perhaps Kit needs some weapons training before leaving,' Walsingham said. 'I can summon a weapons master from the Tower tomorrow.'

He looked at me critically. I am tall for a girl, but slender, a fact which has made it easier for me to maintain my disguise as a boy, but no one would judge me muscular, with a soldier's build.

As if he read my thoughts, Walsingham said, 'Skill and speed are more important in the use of a sword than great strength. That and a good eye for judging your opponent's next move. As a physician you must spend much of your time judging men's characters. That will stand you in good stead.'

He turned to Phelippes. 'Make sure Kit is provided with a sword. Something light and lethal. I will arrange for training tomorrow. Best to go to the Tower, not fetch a master here. You can have one day to learn the basic skills, Kit. You must leave the next day.'

One day to learn to use a sword? It was madness!

'Should I ride Hector this time?' I asked, hoping he would agree.

He shook his head. 'I need you to travel fast. Thomas can prepare permits for you to use post horses. And a ship from Dover will be able to take you right into Amsterdam at this time of year. The crossing should be quick too. Be sure you ask for their fastest pinnace, Thomas.'

With that he left us. I looked at Phelippes and shrugged, spreading out my arms in a helpless gesture.

'You wanted an active role,' he said with a grim smile. 'Now you have it.'

The following day I reported to Seething Lane early and was told to go at once to the Tower and enquire for Master Scannard. I had never been inside those grim walls before, though I knew some Londoners came for entertainment to see the wild beasts kept there, many of them gifts to the Queen from foreign rulers. A guard in the gatehouse directed me to Master Scannard's quarters, located amongst the many buildings surrounding one of the Tower's courtyards.

He was a small, wiry man, not the powerful soldier I had expected, but I remembered Sir Francis's words, that skill and speed were more important in a swordsman than great strength. When I had introduced myself, he merely nodded and without warning threw a sword at me.

I managed to catch it by the hilt, more by luck than anything else.

He nodded. 'Good.'

From then on it was clear he was a man of few words. All morning he demonstrated moves, then made me repeat them again and again. And when he crossed swords with me, again and again he sent my sword flying. As it drew near midday, I was beginning to hold my own for a little longer, but by the time we stopped briefly for bread and ale, my whole body was drenched in sweat and my right wrist felt as though it was on fire. When I tried to pick up my mug of ale, my hand was shaking so much that the rim of the mug clattered against my teeth.

'You'll need strapping on that,' was all he said.

He bound my wrist tightly, which gave me some ease during our afternoon training, but I knew that when I reached home that night I would need to rub my wrist and my whole arm with a muscle embrocation. By the time he released me in the late afternoon I was more physically exhausted than I had ever been in my life and dreaded the thought that the next morning I must set out at once for the Low Countries again.

Master Stannard handed me a scabbard and sword belt. 'Master Phelippes has provided these for you, and the sword you have been using today. You are beginning to show some aptitude, but I have little hope for you against a skilled swordsman.'

With that he turned away and marched back to his quarters. It was the longest speech he had made all day. I was not sure whether I should be pleased or mortified by his assessment. Before returning home I called in at Seething Lane for Phelippes's final instructions.

'There is little more to say than what we discussed yesterday,' he said, handing me a bundle of papers for Lord Willoughby. 'I suggest you stay at the same inn as before. They are known as honest people and Mark Weber stayed there for a time, though he may have moved on. Find out if they know anything. You should also call on Master Añez. See what facts he can give you. Get what honest information about the army that you can from Lord Willoughby, but make your own enquiries – discreetly – amongst the soldiers.'

'If things have not changed much since I was last there,' I said, 'the soldiers will be very angry at not being paid. Do you know whether funds for the army have been sent?'

'Some funds, certainly. Possibly not sufficient. And possibly the money has not found its way down to the common soldiers.'

'You mean corruption? The army command has been skimming it off?'

He shrugged. 'It is the way of the world, Kit. Do not tell me you are too innocent to realise that.'

When I reached home, Rikki greeted me rapturously. I had been forced to leave him with my father, for I was sure he would not be welcomed at the Tower. I would have to leave him again while I went on this new mission, though I hoped it would soon be over. My father was resigned to my leaving again, though I knew very well that he did not like it.

During the evening I washed thoroughly, feeling dirty after my day of sword practice, then I packed my satchel, replenishing the medical supplies in the wallet, including some embrocation for my aching muscles which were now causing me some pain. I left behind my clerk's equipment, all but a sheet or two of paper, the sealing wax, one quill and the ink pot. I had not needed them before, but I might on this journey. This left room in the top of my satchel for a spare shirt, stockings and shift. I planned to carry only my satchel and travel light. I added the passes Phelippes had provided and the purse of Dutch coins that Sir Francis had given me, and my preparations were complete.

Although I was tired, I found it difficult to sleep. My whole body ached and my mind was troubled by thoughts of what I would find in Amsterdam. Making general enquiries would not be difficult, but tracking down the missing agent Mark Weber could well lead me into danger. I did not like the knowledge that his last despatch had reported the return of Cornelius Parker.

I left early the following morning, entrusting Rikki to my father, and setting off to collect the first post horse at the stable near the north end of the Bridge. I felt awkward wearing the sword belt, the sword swinging against my side. How anyone could move normally so encumbered, I could not imagine. My small dagger lay easily against my right hip, but with every step I took the sword seemed ready to tangle itself in my legs, making me feel foolish.

Phelippes's pass procured me one of the best government post horses, a long rangy beast who had a good turn of speed but who seemed indifferent to me. It must be an unpleasant life for a horse, constantly changing riders, valued for nothing but the speed at which they can gallop from post to post. I changed horses about every fifteen miles and reached Dover that evening, exhausted and very saddle sore.

I chose not to report to the commander of the garrison, Sir Anthony Torrington, who had been singularly unwelcoming before, but found one of the more junior officers. Flourishing Phelippes's warrant giving me priority in all government premises I demanded – and got – a small room to myself. Although I dined with the soldiers as before, I saw no sign of Andrew, but this hardly surprised me, for the whole garrison buzzed like a wasps' nest struck with a stick. By now everyone was well aware that the Spanish Armada, a fleet more vast than any could imagine, was sailing at its best speed for our shores.

The following morning I was down on the quay at first light, in search of the fast pinnace, the *Good Venture*, that Phelippes had ordered for me. And on the quay I met Andrew.

'Kit, good morrow,' he said. 'I was this minute coming in search of you. Are you ready to leave? We can catch the turn of the tide.'

'Are you crossing to the Low Countries as well?' I asked. 'On the *Good Venture*?'

'Aye. And I was told you were to be on board.'

Together we made our way along the quay to a slender ship, longer and narrower than Captain Thoms's vessel, so gleaming and new it looked as though she had just been launched, which I soon learned was the case.

'Just arrived from the Chatham shipyards,' Andrew said. 'Apart from sailing round from the Medway, this will be her first voyage. She is one of the newest ships, built above all for speed.'

We boarded by means of a plank no more than a foot wide, unlike the solid ramp which had been provided for the horses, and I saw that though the ship was young, most of the crew had the weatherbeaten look of experienced sailors. There was very little superstructure, just a low cabin in the stern, and six cannon were ranged along her gundeck, three to a side.

Hardly had our feet touched the deck and our presence been acknowledged by a black-bearded man I took to be the captain, than the plank was drawn in, the mooring ropes cast off, and we were on our way.

In all this haste Andrew and I had hardly exchanged a word. Now we ducked out of the sailors' way and found a sheltered corner on the foredeck, in the lee of the foresail.

'But why are you going to Amsterdam, Andrew?' I said.

'I have orders to bring back a squadron of foot soldiers from our army based there,' he said. 'I am made a captain now.'

'Congratulations,' I said. 'But are you not a trooper?'

'Aye, my orders are to seek out men who can ride, even though they may be enrolled as foot soldiers as the moment. We need more cavalry. They cannot be fully trained, not in time, but if I can find enough who at the very least know one end of a horse from the other, then we can teach them some simple manoeuvres. The advantage of cavalry over infantry is that we can move about the country more quickly.'

'Of course.'

'So if we are needed somewhere in a hurry we can ride there, even dismount to fight on foot if we cannot train them to fight as cavalry.'

It sounded like a desperate measure to me, but I held my peace.

The ship had been moving fast while we spoke. Already Dover was disappearing behind us. The ship heeled over, slicing through the waves faster than I had ever seen a ship move.

'A fair speed,' I said, bracing myself to keep on my feet as we heeled further.

'A fine ship,' a voice said behind us. It was the black-bearded man. 'I am Captain Faulconer. Captain Joplyn I have already met and I understand that you are Dr Alvarez.'

'I am.' I shook his hand and bowed.

'If we had a fleet of ships as fine as the *Good Venture*, we could round up the sluggish Spaniards as a dog rounds up sheep,' he said. 'Even our merchant ships and privateers have a fair turn of speed. We will show them what English sailors are made of.'

I remembered what Dr Nuñez had said about the battle of Salamis and nodded, although I did wonder whether Captain

Faulconer was partly moved by an inclination to boast of the navy before a captain of the army.

The journey up the Channel and along the Dutch coast showed just how fine a ship this was, and the whole crew conducted themselves as though they were already rehearsing for war. There was to be no sitting in the captain's cabin, drinking wine on this voyage. Instead we dined, like the crew, on deck, standing and snatching mouthfuls of ship's biscuit, dried meat, and ale when we could. We might be important passengers, carrying orders from high officers of state, but the times were such that no concessions could be made to our comfort.

So fast was our journey that we reached the waterway leading to Amsterdam before dark, though of course we were now at the height of summer's longest days, whereas my previous journey here had been in the short, dark days of winter. In seemed Captain Faulconer was familiar with the route to Amsterdam, for he did not stop in the harbour but headed at once for the canal. There was still light enough to see our way, but with the approaching evening the wind had dropped, so the sails were lowered, the oars run out, and the sailors set to. By now they were stripped to the waist, for it had been warm work manning the ship under the summer sun. Now came the sweaty, demanding labour of rowing many miles up the canal. Once we were fairly under way, the captain joined us again. Andrew and I had found seats on two of the water barrels.

'We are making a fair speed, even under oars,' Andrew said.

'Aye, she's a very light ship,' the captain said. 'Light to sail and light to row. Not so hard on the men.'

By the time we had berthed in Amsterdam it was dark. Andrew and I walked to the centre of the town together, where we parted, I to stay at the Prins Willem, Andrew to seek out the officers' quarters in the town before riding out the next day to the army camp to recruit his men. I wondered how willing they would be, whether they would prefer to remain here in the Low Countries, where the campaign had temporarily reached a stalemate, or would prefer to return home to face an invading Spanish army. On the whole, I suspected they would rather come home to England and their families, even if they then deserted.

'How soon can you finish your business in Amsterdam?' Andrew asked before we parted. 'I am to get these men back to England as quickly as possible, but the ship was commandeered for your use, so it will only leave when you are ready.'

'I do not know.' I shook my head. 'Come to the inn in three days' time and I may know my plans better then.'

At the Prins Willem I was greeted like a member of the family, plied with an enormous meal I could not finish, and showed into my old room. The inn keeper's daughter even brought me a bucket of hot water without my asking for it.

The next morning I sought Niels Penders when his early morning duties were over and asked if I might speak to him. We sat down together in the small parlour in the back premises used by the family.

'I am searching for a man, half English and half Dutch,' I began, 'who stayed here a few weeks ago. His name is Mark Weber. He was in regular touch with his friends in England until about three weeks ago. Since then there has been no word and his friends are worried. I wondered whether you could tell me when he left here and whether you know where I can find him now.'

'Mark Weber?' He nodded. 'Aye, there was a man of that name who stayed with us. He arrived soon after you left, Dokter. About Christmas time. He was here in Amsterdam for several months, then he went away until . . .' He scratched his head. 'It would be . . .' He went to the door and called out, 'Marta! Me'heer Weber, when was it that he came back?'

I could not hear her answer, but he returned and sat down again. 'Marta says it was six weeks ago. She has a better memory for such things than I have. Ja, it would have been about six weeks ago.'

'And then?' I prompted.

'One evening I saw him talking with Me'heer Parker, the cloth merchant. You spoke of him when you were here. Did he have business with Me'heer Parker?'

'He might have had,' I said cautiously.

'They went out together, quite late. The next morning Me'heer Weber returned, collected his belongings, paid his bill and left.'

'How long ago was that?'

He ran his fingers through his hair, which was growing thin on top. 'That would have been about three-four weeks ago.' He looked at me anxiously. 'And your friends have not heard from him since?'

I shook my head. 'They have not. He did not tell you where he was going?'

'Nee. He was very polite, thanked us, and wished us farewell. That was all.'

Ever since my first visit I had liked and trusted this family, so I said, 'Mijnheer Penders, what do you know about Cornelius Parker?'

At my question, he looked uncomfortable and for several minutes he did not speak, but filled the time getting up and opening a hanging cupboard, from which he drew out two small glasses and a bottle of the curious thick yellowish liqueur they drink in these parts. When he had set the glasses down on the table between us and resumed his seat, he raised his glass to me, and sipped the liqueur thoughtfully. I took a small sip. I had not liked the stuff when I had tasted it before, but did not wish to offend him.

'Me'heer Cornelius Parker has a bad reputation,' he began slowly. 'I tell you this in confidence, Dokter?'

'Of course.' I nodded, and took another sip.

'Much of it is probably rumour, idle gossip. I cannot vouch for the truth of it, but he is said to smuggle arms to the Spanish. A traitor to the States General, Dokter. Yet nothing has been proved against him, nothing has been done to stop him.' He put down his glass and began to drum on the table with his fingers. 'When such a thing happens, as you know, money has probably changed hands.'

'A bribe?' I said. 'Corruption? More treachery?'

He shrugged. 'It may not even be treachery. Perhaps simple greed, a lust for money. We live in dangerous and treacherous times, Dokter. Even the leaders of the various provinces do not agree on what path to take to the future. Some are so weary of war they would make peace with Spain and Parma at any cost. Too many lives lost, you understand. They think it would be better to live under the heel of Spain than in a state of perpetual war.'

'Spain will bring the Inquisition,' I said. 'Believe me, I have seen it in Portugal. You Dutch Protestants will be seen as heretics and suffer at the hands of the Inquisition.'

'I know that very well. But there are others who persuade themselves that it will not happen here. Such men, if they also have a greed for gold, might wink their eyes at illegal trading by Cornelius Parker.'

'Do you think Mark Weber went with Parker? He would see Parker as the enemy, and report back to England. I cannot understand what has happened.'

'Nor I.'

He held up the bottle, but I shook my head. I had not managed to finish the first glass. There was little else he could tell me, but he promised to make discreet enquiries, to try to discover whether Parker was still in Amsterdam and whether anyone knew the whereabouts of Mark Weber.

When he was called to the inn parlour by a group of farmers demanding beer, I looked around for somewhere to dispose of the remains of my drink. There was a blue and white glazed pot containing some sort of fern standing on a corner cabinet. Glancing guiltily toward the door, I tipped the viscous liquid on to the earth as the base of the plant, where it lay like some noxious slime, reluctant to soak away. Marta was sure to notice it as soon as she came into the room. Feeling not a little foolish, I drew my dagger and scraped up the soil until the stain was covered, then patted it down with my hand. Leaving my empty glass on the table, I slipped out, nodding to Niels and heading for the street door.

I had learned that Lord Willoughby was now living in the house where I had attended Leicester half a year before, so I made my way there quickly with the packet of despatches from Sir Francis. Amsterdam in early summer looked very different from the frost-bound town of last winter. The Hollanders have a great love of flowers and there were tubs and pots everywhere, on windowsills, beside front doors, even on the barges lined up along the canals. Many of the houses fronted directly on the street, with a double V of steps leading to their front doors, while small windows at street level let light into basement kitchens. By many of these front doors overflowing pots of cranesbills and heartsease and love-in-a-mist adorned every step. Some houses even had cunning shelves fitted outside their windows holding more flowers. I saw several singing birds in cages hung from hooks beside upper windows.

Yet all this cheerful abundance was not reflected in the faces of the people I passed in the street. They wore the same haunted look as the people of London. The spectre of war was even closer here than in England, though the Hollanders might reflect that if Philip's mind was bent on the conquest of England, they might be spared for a while yet.

At Willoughby's quarters I was shown into a cupboard-like room and told to wait, while a condescending liveried servant carried away my packet of despatches to His Lordship. I was reluctant to hand them over to any but Willoughby himself, but I was given no choice. After I had kicked my heels for over an hour by the ornate mantel clock I had seen in the hallway, whose chimes reached even through the door, the servant returned.

'You are to call here in one week's time to carry my lord's report back to Sir Francis,' he said, looking down his long nose which seemed to quiver with contempt at any person under the rank of lord.

Once, I might have given him a sharp answer, that I was commanded by Sir Francis and not his master, but two years in Walsingham's service had taught me discretion in holding my tongue – most of the time, at least. I merely nodded and left, cursing my loss of time.

Out in the street, I turned in the direction of Ettore Añez's house. It was well past dinnertime and my stomach ached, but I was anxious to learn whether he could help me in the matter of finding Mark Weber. He was as welcoming as before, and if he was surprised at seeing me again only six months after my previous visit to Amsterdam, he did not show it. Moreover, he must have detected something in my looks that told him I had not dined, for he summoned cold meats and bread to be brought, and himself carried a bowl of early apricots over to the table placed between us.

'Apricots?' I said, surprised.

He smiled. 'I had a shipment coming in from Italy, and my agent there always sends some fruits. They come to ripeness earlier in the south. Now,' he looked at me shrewdly, 'I think this is more than a visit of courtesy.'

Before leaving London I had discussed Ettore with Phelippes. It seemed he had, from time to time, acted for Sir Francis in small matters and was to be trusted. As I took the edge off my hunger, I laid before him the matter of Mark Weber – his disappearance and what I had learned from Niels Penders about his having departed in company with Cornelius Parker.

Ettore shook his head.

'That is not good news,' he said. 'There is a growing conviction amongst us – I speak of the Amsterdam merchants – that Parker has definitely been supplying arms to the Spaniards. Oh, certainly, they have their own sources from home, but to reach the Low Countries they must either come overland through France – and as you know, Philip of Spain is not on good terms with the French – or else they must come by sea up the Channel, and run the gauntlet of English ships. The Spanish captains are wary of El Draque and his fellow pirates, or privateers, as I think you English call them.'

He grinned.

'Parker trades in silk fabrics with the Turks, who are also excellent gunsmiths. And he is known to have connections with Prague, where they have been developing further uses of gunpowder. Because his ships fly the flag of the United Provinces, they sail up the Channel unmolested by English ships and, since they are known to the Spaniards, also unmolested by them.'

He paused, tapping his teeth with his fingernail.

'He would not be so incautious as to put in boldly to one of the ports held by the Spanish, Sluys or Gravelines or Dunkerque. That would quite give his game away. No, he lands his goods quite openly in Amsterdam.'

'Are there no customs officers here?' I asked. 'No port officials who inspect the cargoes coming in?'

'Most certainly. But it is always possible to find one who will turn a blind eye for a consideration.'

'But he must then move his guns and other arms south and west to the Spanish lines.' I remembered with a shiver my alarming journey in that direction with Berden.

'Aye. He might use pack mules, but I think it more likely he would send his goods by water. This country is criss-crossed with rivers and canals.'

'I remember.' I took a final pull of my ale. 'But why do you think Mark Weber would have left in his company, apparently on friendly terms?'

'He must have convinced Parker that he was an ally, Kit. Do you know much about this man Weber?'

'Not a great deal. Like Parker, he is half English, half Dutch. Phelippes and Sir Francis both believe him to be trustworthy. Not all of the agents are. Some play a double game.' Like Robert Poley, I thought, my personal enemy, who is as trustworthy as a snake.

'So unless he has turned traitor, he must be trying to spy out Parker's activities,' Ettore said, 'to report back to Sir Francis.'

'That would not take him over three weeks.'

'No.' He looked at me soberly. 'Some serious mischance may have overtaken him.'

'That is what I fear,' I said. 'He may be dead.' I had not put it into words before, but now that I did, it somehow seemed more real.

He nodded.

'If you can wait a day or two, I will set some enquiries in motion. They need to be discreet, even casual, but I will find out what I can. Someone may have heard or seen something about the movement of Parker's goods from Amsterdam, which will give you a starting point.'

It was more than I could have expected. I was reluctant to endure even this short delay, but I would need to be content.

Chapter Thirteen

*I*t would be two days before I heard from Ettore. I found it difficult to occupy myself in a strange town where I did not speak the language, despite the fact that almost every person I met had at least a little English. On the first day after visiting Ettore, having kicked my heels at the inn for half the morning, I decided to visit the minister Dirck de Veen at his church, where I learned that no one had ever been brought to trial for the murder of Hans Viederman.

'I fear the town authorities do not take very seriously the death of a beggar,' the minister said sadly. 'They say it was a falling-out amongst thieves, though Hans was no thief. And there would have been nothing in his cottage to steal. It was a tragic loss of a life. A man once so gifted. Such a waste, such a waste.'

'At least his dog survived,' I said hesitantly.

'Ah, the poor creature! It ran off and was never found again.'

I realised, of course, that I had not seen the minister after Berden and I had headed south before Christmas. 'I have the dog, Dominee de Veen,' I said. 'He followed after me. Indeed, he saved me from an attack by an armed man down near the Spanish lines.'

'You have the dog!' His gentle, worried face broke into a smile.

'He is in London with my father. He was injured, helping me, but he is recovered and grown quite hearty now. I have called him Rikki, for I did not know his name.'

'I do not think I ever heard Hans speak his name,' de Veen said. 'But this is good news indeed. One small spark of light in a sad business.'

'So who do you think killed Hans?'

He shook his head. 'I cannot say. Who would do such a thing?'

'I think he was killed because he knew something. Something that was a danger to someone who took violent action to stop his mouth.'

He turned on me a look that was suddenly less unworldly, and I realised that I had perhaps underestimated him.

'That may well be true. I only remembered, after you had gone, that other time. A man came asking where Hans lived, a day or two before you found his body. I was busy with some of my parishioners when he was here and it had slipped my mind.'

'Was it Cornelius Parker?' I asked eagerly.

He shook his head. 'No, I know Mijnheer Parker. No, it was a slightly younger man. Now, what is his name? He used to be a merchant, fallen now on hard times.' He ran his fingers through his bush of grey hair, leaving it standing on end.

'Was it van Leyden?'

'That's the man! How did you guess?'

I shook my head. It did not want to involve the minister too deeply in this dark business. 'It was but a guess,' I said vaguely. 'I had seen him with Parker, and seen Parker with Hans.'

I turned our talk to other things, which, since it was the commonest topic in Amsterdam, concerned the likely arrival of the Spanish fleet. The Hollanders themselves had a very small navy, nothing that could give battle to the Spaniards, but their shallow-draft *vlieboten* – something like our small carracks – could manoeuvre in the shallow waters off Flanders and Zeeland, where Philip's large warships could not go. By forming a blockade they could hamper the embarkation of Parma's soldiers on to the barges which were to take the invading army across the Channel to England. I knew that Admiral Justin was moving a squadron of these Dutch *vlieboten* in position to blockade Dunkerque.

'I have heard,' said Dirck, 'that the Duke of Parma still lacks enough barges to transport his men. Some believe he may make a raid on the Zuiderzee to seize any craft that will serve his purpose.'

'So close to Amsterdam?'

It was alarming news.

He nodded. 'One of my parishioners overheard some of the English soldiers discussing how they were to be deployed guarding the docks outside the town, on the further banks of the Zee.'

'Aye,' I said slowly. 'I do not suppose Parma will want to find himself caught up in a fight by coming too close to Amsterdam itself. Now that the Spanish fleet is on its way he will want no distractions.'

I pondered this news as I left the church. Parma would need both weapons and transport. Access to both would be difficult for him, though by now he must have commandeered every suitable barge in the Spanish Netherlands. Ettore had pointed out how convenient Cornelius Parker's legitimate activities would be as a cover for smuggling arms to Parma. As a merchant with vessels of different sizes at his disposal, he might also be intending to supply barges. Every river and canal in this water-logged country thronged with barges. I had seen for myself the daily activity in the town, with barges being loaded and unloaded beside the merchants' houses standing along the canals. The barges moved up and down the canals all day long, some with sails and oars, some only with oars, both within the town and out into the surrounding countryside. No one ever gave them a second glance.

I found that my feet had taken me around the corner of the church and down the narrow alleyway towards Hans's pitiful cottage. In the snowy winter months the place had seemed no worse than shabby and poor, but now in the height of summer, the alley stank like a sewer. The narrow kennel running along the centre of the cobbled way was intended to carry waste down to a canal that I could see at the far end of the alley, but it was blocked now with nameless rubbish. This had dammed up the flow of the contents of piss-pots which had been emptied into the alley and which had now spread in a stinking pool across the cobbles. I picked my way round it, holding my breath. On my previous visit I had been impressed by the cleanliness of Amsterdam, but this place was as filthy as any back-alley in London.

The last house on the left, Hans's old cottage, looked more derelict than ever. No one could be living in it now, not even a beggar, for there were great holes in the thatched roof. Most of the houses here in the town, even quite modest ones, were roofed in terracotta tiles, but this ruined place must be a relic of some older time. I averted my eyes as I passed it, remembering with a shudder the moment when I had found Hans's body, its throat cut, lying in a pool of frozen blood.

I came out of the alleyway into bright sunlight and there at my feet was yet another of the town's many canals. There were no grand merchants' houses here, though a line of a dozen barges lay moored along the canal bank. Just round the corner from the derelict cottage there was another similar building – single-storied, small and dirty, and with a thatched roof, although this one was intact. The single window was shuttered. Considering its look of poverty, it was strange to see that it had a stout new door. And the stout new door was secured by an elaborate lock, clearly also new and shiny, with a lock plate as long as my hand. Curious.

This remote part of the town seemed almost deserted, though I noticed a group of four men walking toward me along the edge of the canal. There was no reason to suppose them in any way unfriendly, but my scalp prickled at the sight of them, walking so purposefully towards me, or perhaps towards that heavily secured building. I withdrew into the alley again and walked rapidly back to the church, then on to my inn.

The next day, still having heard nothing from Ettore, I decide to investigate that remote canal further. I did not return to the point where I had found it before. Something warned me to stay away from the locked hut. Instead I found the canal easily enough by turning down the other side of the church and walking parallel to Hans's alley, along another street which was wider and cleaner. At this point there were no moored barges and indeed this canal, one of the smaller ones, seemed hardly used at all. For the most part, the buildings along the waterside turned their backs on it. As I followed it in the direction that would lead me out of the town, the canal was on my left hand, while on my right for most of the way there was a blank run of brick walls enclosing gardens of houses which faced in the opposite direction, towards a pleasanter part of the town. Finally I came to a large warehouse where a few men were working. Beyond that the canal wandered off into the countryside, heading roughly west of south and soon disappearing amongst dense reed beds.

I wonder, I thought. *If a man wished to move barges quietly out of the town, would there be any better way than this? But perhaps this canal does not go anywhere. It may simply be one of those that the Hollanders dig to drain their fields.*

The paved path which had accompanied the canal to this point petered out, though it was possible to follow the line of water further, along a strip of beaten earth through the reed beds, running parallel to the canal but about two yards from it. Perhaps it was one of the *jaagpaden*, as Captain Thoms had called them, used by men or horses towing barges. I headed slowly along it for perhaps half an hour, through deserted countryside, encountering no one. There was no sound but the soft incessant whispering of the reeds in the slight breeze and the occasional call of a bird. I disturbed a heron who made off with those long, slow wing beats which look too casual to lift the heavy body and trailing legs, yet somehow manage to propel the bird effortlessly upwards. I sat down on the ground, watching it fly as far as the nearest tree, a pollarded willow. There were few enough trees in this flat country of reeds and water, but from a bundle of twigs perched amongst its branches, I guessed that the heron had its nest there.

The silence and the warmth of the midday sun stole over me, so that I lay down on my back amongst the reeds, watching, through half-closed eyes, a grasshopper clinging, above my head, to a swaying stem. The reeds were alive with the leaping of these small green grasshoppers and the faint chirp of crickets, almost on the edge of hearing. Sleep was stealing over me, when the grasshopper above my head suddenly sprang from the stem and disappeared. At the same moment the heron, who must have made a silent return, clattered up from the edge of the canal. Suddenly I was aware of what they had heard, the sound of oars and men's quiet voices.

I rolled over on my stomach and peered through the reeds. At first I could see nothing, then a barge came into sight, rowed by four men and towing another larger one. The sails were furled, for there was not enough of a breeze to aid their labours. Between the two pairs of oarsmen lay a bundle in canvas, perhaps a yard or more long and about as large around as my arms would reach. The following barge was piled high with more bundles, all the same size and shape. In its stern there were three large barrels.

Giving thanks that the reeds were thick here, I pressed my head down against the ground, my left cheek painfully against a sharp stone. My clothes were dull in hue and unlikely to draw attention amongst the reeds unless one of the men were to turn and look in my direction. With the instinct of a hunted animal seeking sanctuary, I closed my eyes and held my breath, until I could no longer hear the sound of the oars and the heron had returned to his fishing.

Slowly I sat up. The sunlight reflected off the water of the canal danced in stars before my eyes. Those canvas bundles meant only one thing to me. I had seen similar ones in Dover Castle. They contained army muskets, half a dozen in each. The barrels might be anything, but my guess was gunpowder or shot. As for the barges, I recognised the leading one by a careless streak of green paint across the bow. I had last seen it outside the locked hut, no more than a few yards from Hans's door.

When I arrived back at the Prins Willem, a message from Ettore awaited me. He had not discovered much. He had managed to find out nothing of Mark Weber. Cornelius Parker, however, was known to have returned from his latest voyage and unloaded a substantial cargo of his usual goods, mainly rich fabrics from the Near East, and a fresh supply of the more expensive spices which were his most lucrative stock in trade. How easy, I thought, to stow those canvas bundles I had seen in amongst the innocent bales of cloth, which would also be wrapped in canvas for protection. An obliging customs official would take a cursory glance at a few bales of damask and nod the cargo through, for a small consideration. Barrels of more lethal goods could stand amongst the barrels of spices, and that same customs official would check the lading manifests and pass them through without opening them. The valuable spices, after all, must be kept carefully sealed, away from dirt and damp.

Ettore had also learned that van Leyden had been seen in Amsterdam about two weeks ago, but not since, nor did anyone know where he was living. After his flight from Leicester's quarters before Christmas, he was not known to have taken any other lodgings in Amsterdam. Ettore believed he had probably been out of town until recently, possibly even out of the country.

I regret, he wrote, *that I have no more detailed information for you, but I will continue my enquiries. Parker's house is located on Sint Nikolaas Straat, not far from the church of Sint Nikolaas. Van Leyden may be living there.*
Ettore Añez.

At these words, I looked up suddenly, searching my memory. When I had first met Dirck de Veen, he had said he was the minister of . . . aye, the church of Sint Nikolaas. I had forgotten that until now. I had never know the name of the street. If that was Sint Nikolaas Straat, then Cornelius Parker's house could well be one of those whose garden backed on to the canal I had been following, only a few minutes' walk from the locked hut and the moored barges.

If only I could see what was in that hut! It was becoming more and more clear that Hans had seen or heard something and perhaps threatened Parker with his knowledge. Threatened, perhaps, to tell the Dutch authorities or the Earl of Leicester. Had Mark Weber also discovered the same thing? He had seemed to the innkeeper to be on friendly terms with Parker, but he could have been playing the part of an agent for the Spanish. Walsingham's agents often needed to pass themselves off as belonging to the enemy. Sometimes they were indeed double agents, but I knew that both Phelippes and Walsingham believed Weber to be trustworthy. Where was Weber now? If he *had* discovered something about the supply of arms, why had he not sent word to London?

I sat in the inn parlour with Ettore's letter before me, brooding over a mug of thick Dutch beer. One voice in my head argued for going to the hut after dark and breaking in. It was vital for Walsingham to know what Parker was up to. But I also remembered Parker's look of barely suppressed violence behind that falsely jovial façade and I remembered Hans lying with his throat cut from ear to ear. The other voice in my head was pure terror.

Andrew! I thought. Andrew was anxious to return to England as soon as possible with the men he had recruited, but must wait until the ship commandeered for Walsingham's business was ready to take me back. Surely it would be reasonable to ask for his assistance? The sooner I was able to follow the trail Weber had laid and find him, the sooner we could both return home. And if there was an illegal trade in arms passing along that canal, it must be stopped. I shrank from approaching the Dutch authorities myself. I had papers from Walsingham, but I knew my youth would tell against me. As for Lord Willoughby, I had already had a taste of my reception there. But Andrew held an officer's rank in the army. Even without Willoughby or the town officers, he could act.

I fetched paper and ink from my satchel and wrote a brief note to Andrew.

I need your help. I believe I have found what Weber was investigating: an illegal supply of arms and barges to the enemy. Can you come to the Prins Willem about dusk? In case I am mistaken, do not speak of this yet to any other.
Kit

I folded the paper and sealed it, using for the first time the seal Arthur Gregory had made for me all those months ago. It gave the letter a more official appearance than I felt it merited, but if Andrew and I broke into the hut together, we could both bear witness to what we found there. If there was anything to be found, that is. If there was not, well then, I would not have made a fool of myself to anyone but Andrew, who would most certainly laugh it off. He might make fun of me afterwards, but no harm would have been done. At least I hoped not.

Marta, the innkeeper's wife, assured me that one of the servants would ride out to the army camp and deliver my letter.

'It is no trouble, Dokter. I know you are here to help us in these dangerous times.'

I gave her a weak smile. I hoped that what I was doing would help, and not cause a scandal. I begged a candle lantern from her, saying that I would need to go out after dark and was not sure when I would return.

I was in such a state of agitation that I could not eat anything, while I waited for the summer dusk to fall at last. Feeling somewhat foolish, I strapped on my sword, which I had not worn since leaving England. It still felt awkward, slapping against my thigh, and I was far from being confident that I could use it. Standing in my room, I tried drawing it once or twice. It came smoothly out of the leather scabbard, but I was slow, far too slow. Sweat began to form on my back and trickle down my spine. Jesu! I thought, I am no hero. I am not cut from that cloth. My stomach churned with nausea.

My window faced west and I watched the sky grow bright with clouds flushed crimson and gold as the sun sank slowly, interminably slowly, towards the Spanish Netherlands. How near, I wondered, had that vast fleet drawn now? Parma would need to have his troops in readiness to be carried across the Channel. If Andrew and I did not leave soon, we might find ourselves trapped in the Low Countries.

At last, as the sky had faded to lemon yellow, there came a tap on my door.

'Dokter Alvarez?' It was Anneke, the innkeeper's daughter. 'There is an English soldier here, asking for you.'

'I am coming,' I called. I slung my cloak about my shoulders. Even though it was summer, nearly the end of July, it might be cold after dark. I had heard a wind rattling the shutters outside the window. Besides, I still had Simon's cloak, a good, dark colour. It would help me to blend into the shadows. I swallowed. There was an unpleasant, metallic taste in my mouth, the taste of fear. I picked up the candle lantern and opened my door.

Andrew left his horse at the inn and we began to cross the town on foot. As we made our way to Sint Nikolaas Straat, I told Andrew everything I had discovered. First, the murder of Hans Viederman when I had been in Amsterdam before Christmas, the behaviour of Parker, the plot which he and van Leyden had seemed to have contrived to poison Leicester.

'Jesu's bones!' Andrew cried. 'I knew nothing of this!'

'It was kept quiet. No need to cause panic. Van Leyden disappeared. My evidence about Parker seems to have been ignored. But now it appears that Mark Weber may have discovered more evidence of treachery, and I think I know what it is.'

Quickly I recounted all that I had found since arriving in Amsterdam this time, and what I thought it meant.

'So you want us to break into this locked hut?'

It sounded absurd on Andrew's lips.

'I may be quite wrong . . .'

'No, I think you may have stumbled upon something. But we need tools – a crowbar at least.'

I gaped at him. What a fool I was! Certainly I was unfit to be an agent. I spoke airily of breaking in, but I had seen the size of that lock. Of course we would need tools of some sort.

Andrew slid an amused glance at me.

'We'll spy out the building first,' he said, 'then decide what we need. From the way you describe the lock, it will not be easy to pick, and I've little skill in the art, though my sergeant has.'

'Should we fetch him from the camp?'

'He's still in England. Unfortunately.' He jerked his head. 'Down here, is it?'

We had reached the alleyway. 'Aye,' I said. 'Down to the end and round the corner on the left, facing the canal.'

It was impenetrably dark in the alley and we had not yet lit the lantern, so that we could not avoid the noisome liquid which had spread even further than before, but when we emerged at the canal-side, the reflection of the sliver of moon off the water gave us light enough to see the hut and – all too clearly – the massive lock on the door. Andrew shook his head at the sight of it.

'There's no hope of breaking that, Kit, nor the door. It looks to be cross-planked in oak.' He tried to get his fingers round the edge of the shutters which barred the window, but they too were made of thick oak boards.

'I wonder–,' I said.

'Aye?'

'Perhaps we could find our way through the back. The cottage round the corner in the alley, the one where Hans lived, is quite derelict. We could easily get in, but I cannot remember whether there was a way out at the back. If there is, it might be possible to approach this building from behind.'

'Worth trying,' he said, turning back at once.

Standing before the half-open door of the cottage, my nerve nearly failed. My reason tells me that ghosts do not exist, but it took every ounce of courage to enter that cottage in the dark, with the memory of that murdered man lying on the floor as vivid as if it were still there.

'Best light that lamp,' Andrew said.

I nodded, and fumbled with flint and tinder, for my hands were shaking. I had it alight at last, but shielded it from the street with my cloak as we crossed the threshold. It would be as well to avoid being seen.

The place was even more forlorn than I remembered. The few sticks of furniture were gone, looted by other poor cottagers for their own houses or smashed for fuel during last winter's cruel weather. There were a few shards of pottery lying beside the cold ashes on the hearthstone, and the floor spat and crunched under our feet with grit blown in from the street. There was a rustling in the battered thatch from nesting birds or mice, but living creatures did not frighten me. Once we were inside and Andrew had dragged the door as closed as possible on its sagging hinges, I raised the lantern and looked around. In front of me a patch of the beaten earth floor was stained a darker colour.

'That was where he was lying,' I whispered.

Andrew nodded absently, but this place held no horrors for him. He had walked over to a far dark corner where there was another door that I had not noticed before. He struggled to open it, but it would not move, either warped or blocked by something on the outside. He heaved with his shoulder, but still it would not budge. I joined him, holding the lantern out of harm's way and together we threw ourselves against the door. It shivered and cracked apart, sending Andrew sprawling half inside and half outside, while I just managed to grab at the splintered frame before I fell on top of him.

He clambered to his feet, brushing away fragments of rotten wood and rubbing his knee, which had struck a large rock. It had been wedged against the door from the outside, intended to prevent its being opened. He took the lantern from me and held it up beyond the gap where the door had been. The flickering candlelight revealed a small yard enclosed on two sides by this cottage and the adjacent locked shed, and on the remaining two by the blank walls of two other houses. As we had hoped, there was a door into the other building from the yard.

Without speaking, I pointed across the yard, where a row of barrels stood, like those I had seen on the barge. Andrew nodded. He seemed to be searching the ground for something. There was a clutter of rubbish strewn about and he stepped out into the yard to examine it.

'This might serve,' he said softly, holding up a piece of bent metal. 'Near enough to a crowbar.'

It hardly seemed necessary to keep our voices down. The noise we had made breaking down the cottage door must have been heard as far away as the church. I picked my way around the ruins of the door and walked over to the other building. This back door did not bear a vast lock like the front, but it was almost certainly bolted from the inside. I doubted whether Andrew's makeshift crowbar would be sufficient to lever it open.

'There is another window here,' I said, hardly above a breath. 'The shutters are old. I think we might be able to open them.'

He came up beside me.

'Too small.'

'I think I could get through.'

He sized me up with a quick glance. 'Perhaps you could.'

It proved easier than we had hoped. Andrew set the lantern on the ground and inserted his metal bar under the bottom edge of the right-hand shutter. Almost at once it swung out, snapping the hook that had held it shut. Then he reached up and grabbed the second shutter, which swung out unresisting. I took off my bulky cloak and laid it on the ground next to the lantern.

'Give me a leg up, then pass me the lantern.'

When I was sitting on the sill, with a leg on either side, I leaned toward the inside of the building and moved the lantern from side to side. Like Hans's cottage, it consisted of just one room, but this room showed no sign of being lived in. It was stacked high, all along the wall to my right, with more of those long canvas bundles.

'I'm going to take a closer look,' I said, and dropped down inside, tripping over my wretched sword and falling flat on my face in the dirt. The lantern tipped crazily sideways, but I managed to right it. The candle flickered wildly, but did not go out.

The bundle on the top of the nearest stack was just a few feet away. I felt it all over with my left hand, still holding the lantern in my right. The contents seemed to be long tubes of metal, but I could not be sure. In irritation, I put down the lantern and tugged at the end of the canvas. One fold fell open and finally I could see what lay within.

I stumbled over to the window.

'Aye,' I hissed. 'It's muskets. Dozens of them.'

'Do you think you can lift one of the bundles out of the window?' I could not see him, but he must be just below the sill. 'We need evidence.'

'I think so.'

It was heavier than I thought, but I managed to drag one of the bundles to the outside wall. Raising it to the window was more difficult, but as it teetered on the sill I felt Andrew take the weight.

'Better get out of there now,' he whispered. 'I thought I heard someone coming along the canal.'

I realised that this would be more difficult than climbing in, for there was no one to give me a leg-up. I could hear the approaching footsteps myself now. More than one man. I passed the lantern out of the window.

'Douse it!' I said. 'The light may be visible through the cottage.'

One of the barrels, I thought. *I could climb out by one of the barrels.* I grabbed the nearest and started to roll it under the window. My hands were slippery with sweat and I kept losing my hold on it, but at last I had it in place. They might notice that it had been moved, but that was a risk I had to take.

Something troubled me. There had been an unmistakable stench over by the barrels. I realised that I had been half aware of it before, ever since climbing in, but had been too caught up in examining the guns to attend to it. My eyes had grown accustomed to the near dark of the room and while we had been here the quarter moon had climbed a little higher, throwing an oblique shaft of silver light through the window, just catching the edge of something in the corner beside the barrels. Torn between the need to escape and the anxiety to put to rest the fear that stench had awakened, I crossed quickly to the far wall and looked down.

I had not been wrong. A man lay there, huddled into the corner, where he must have been flung some days before. I crouched down and lifted his flaccid arm, although I already had my answer. He wore a simple signet ring on his hand, which his killers had not troubled to remove. I recognised the design, like the ring I wore on a chain round my neck. I slid it off the unresisting finger and dropped it down the neck of my shirt. Then panic seized me and I scuttled toward the window and escape. As I climbed on to the barrel and threw myself on my stomach over the window ledge, I could hear a key scraping in the lock on the other side of the room.

Andrew grabbed me by the back of my doublet and dragged me down on the other side. I fell into the yard, scraping the palms of my hands and jabbing my side with the hilt of my sword. As I scrambled to my feet, I could just make him out in the gloom, pushing the shutters back into place.

Without speaking, we each caught hold of an end of the bundle of muskets and were stepping over the threshold into Hans's cottage when I remembered.

'My cloak!' I whispered.

I darted across to get it, and as I did so a line of light appeared between the shutters. The men had a lantern. Any minute now they might notice that I had moved the barrel.

I was back at the cottage in a moment and picked up my end of the bundle, tucking my cloak under my arm.

'I have the lantern,' Andrew said, barely above a breath. 'Don't want to leave anything to draw attention.'

Then we were out of the cottage and stumbling as fast as we could up the alleyway.

When we reached the church, Andrew stopped suddenly, so that the muskets hit me smartly in the belly.

'Careful!' I said. 'That hurt.'

'I'm sorry. But look, we can't go through the streets of Amsterdam carrying this. I don't want to have to stop and explain to the Watch.'

I sat down suddenly on the church steps. My legs had begun to shake and I realised I was drenched with sweat.

'I found Mark Weber,' I said. 'He's dead.'

Andrew gasped. 'He was in there?'

'Aye. Thrown into a corner like a pile of old rags. Dead at least a week, I'd say. Probably longer.'

He shook his head. 'They must have found him out,' he said soberly. 'So you have done what you came for.'

'Not as I had hoped. What shall we do? Go to Willoughby?'

'From what you've said, he isn't likely to receive us or take any action in the middle of the night, or even tomorrow. Those men are probably planning to ship another load out by barge during the night. Time must be running out for them. No, I think the only thing to do is for me to ride back to the camp and inform my commanding officer. He will listen, I'm sure. We can send out a squadron to round up these men before they get very far, and even if we miss them, we have these as evidence.'

He poked the canvas with his toe.

'But what shall we do with these,' I said, 'if we aren't to carry them through the streets?'

I was happy for him to make the decisions now. I felt weak and my heart was still racing.

'We could push them in behind those pillars.' He indicated the shallow portico between the steps and the door of the church. 'But I think you should stay here and guard them. You have your sword, haven't you?'

I had indeed. All it had done was to hamper me climbing in and out of the window. The thought of standing guard over illegal guns in the dark, in a foreign town, was terrifying, but what could I do? I could hardly reveal my identity to Andrew. I gulped and nodded.

'Very well,' I said. 'But I'm a poor swordsman, if it should come to a fight.'

'Lie hidden and it isn't likely to.'

We thrust the bundle of muskets into the narrow space between the pillars of the portico and the front wall of the church, then Andrew was off, running lightly down the street in the direction of the inn.

I shook out my cloak and wrapped it around me, for, in the stillness after the stealth and fear, I was suddenly cold. There was just room for me behind the pillars next to the guns, if I sat with my back braced against the wall and my knees drawn up. I was cramped and cold, still shivering from the aftermath of our break-in. Mark Weber, a decent man, so I had been told, left to rot in a corner like a dead rat – my fingers still felt the touch of that limp hand, and my nostrils were full of the stench.

If I had not managed to climb on to the barrel, if I had taken a few more moments to throw myself through the window . . . I felt bile rising in my throat and tried to swallow, but suddenly found myself vomiting. I had eaten little all day and I managed to avoid staining the precious evidence, but my throat burned with the acid of my stomach and I longed for water.

I am not sure how long I crouched there, cold and miserable, before I heard the footsteps. One person, a heavy man, was coming up the alleyway toward the church. I curled up like a hunted animal, burying my face in my knees and praying that no part of me or my dangerous charge could be seen in this dark corner. The footsteps stopped. I swear I could hear him breathing, just yards from where I was concealed, holding my own breath. The moment seemed to stretch out for ever.

'Nee.' The man's voice was as clear as if he stood within arm's reach. 'Nee.' Then a string of Dutch I could not understand. But I knew that 'nee' meant 'no'. They must have realised someone had been in their locked building, either because the barrel was moved or one of the bundles of muskets missing. Or because the hook which secured the shutters was broken. If they had investigated further, they would have found the smashed door at the back of Hans's cottage.

259

My lungs were bursting. I would have to breathe soon. Another voice, further away, impatient. The man beside the church called something, then I heard him turn and make his way back down the alleyway. I let my breath out as carefully as if he were still there. Minutes passed. Then I heard the unmistakable sound of oars from the direction of the canal.

I had no idea how far away the English army camp lay, or how long it would take for Andrew to ride there, rouse an officer, rouse a squadron of soldiers, and return, but there was comfort in the fact that it was a windless night. The men on the barge would not be able to sail, they could travel no faster than they could row. Nor could they turn aside. Sooner or later, the mounted soldiers would overtake them.

They caught the men in the early hours less than ten miles from Amsterdam. When the men and barges had been secured, an armed guard posted around their storehouse, the town authorities roused from their beds and Cornelius Parker's house raided, someone remembered me. By then I was so stiff and cramped I could barely stand, but a cheerful young trooper loaned me his horse and walked beside me back to the Prins Willem, where an exultant gathering of English and Dutch soldiers was just sitting down to a huge breakfast prepared by Marta.

'This is Dr Christoval Alvarez,' Andrew said, presenting me to a saturnine man with a long, clever face, 'who discovered the treachery of this group of traitors. Kit, this is Sir John Norreys.'

I bowed deeply, to conceal my surprise. I had not expected Norreys himself to take part in the operation. He bowed in return.

'We are in your debt, Dr Alvarez,' he said. 'Through your actions you have prevented a substantial shipment of arms from reaching the enemy.'

By neither Andrew nor Norreys was Sir Francis's name mentioned, but it hung in the air between us. I was certain that Norreys knew, or had guessed, why I was in Amsterdam and on whose orders.

When Andrew and I had drawn aside, I asked, 'What will happen to Mark's body?'

'They will send it back to England, to his family. A ship is leaving today and will take him, but the Dutch authorities will not give us leave to go until Parker and van Leyden have been questioned and we have given our evidence.'

'You found van Leyden?'

'Aye, he was in Parker's house, both of them sleeping the sleep of the just while their men carried out their traitorous business. I expect they would have left soon for the Spanish Netherlands themselves, had we not caught them in time. A good night's work, Kit.'

'Aye.'

I was glad they had caught the men and saved the arms from reaching Parma, but I could not rid my mind of the tragedy of Mark Weber, a man I had never known. It was not an uncommon fate for one of Walsingham's agents, but that did not make it any easier to bear.

In the event, Andrew and I were kept chafing in Amsterdam for days, while the slow processes of the law ground on. I managed to despatch a coded report to Walsingham, detailing all that had happened, by the good offices of Ettore Añez, who was able to send one last ship across the Channel as the Spanish fleet drew nearer. I also entrusted to Ettore's courier the signet ring I had taken from Mark Weber's hand.

At last we were free to go. All this time the *Good Venture* had waited in the Amsterdam docks and Andrew's recruits had kicked their heels in camp. When we were not being questioned or writing out our accounts of what had happened for the Dutch lawyers, Andrew put in a few hours of training with the men. It was hardly enough to turn them into troopers, but they might prove useful as mounted messengers. I also persuaded him to teach me how to mount by vaulting on to a horse from the rear. It was not difficult with one of the quiet pack ponies and I even tried it once or twice with a larger horse, but I was uncertain how Hector would respond to the shock if I ever attempted it with him. Someday I would need to train him, if I ever had the opportunity to ride him again. It would overcome my need to find a mounting block whenever I rode him.

On the day we left Amsterdam Andrew marched his men down to the *Good Venture*, while I followed some way behind, reading a quickly scribbled letter from Ettore Añez, whose ship had just returned from England.

The two fleets engaged off Plymouth near the Eddystone rocks on the twenty-first, with no great losses on either side. The English ships kept their distance, bombarding the Spanish with their guns and manoeuvring around the larger enemy ships. Medina Sidonia tried and failed to get close enough to grapple and board. Then all was thrown into confusion. Drake, whose ship was meant to be leading the fleet, went off on a raiding expedition for plunder, leaving the English fleet in disarray. There was a further skirmish off Portland two days later. The Armada is now said to be making for Calais, ready to escort the barges of infantry across the Channel. If your ship leaves immediately, you should reach Dover clear of the fighting.

Ettore, however, was to be proved wrong.

Chapter Fourteen

*W*e were somewhat crowded aboard the *Good Venture*, with the addition of Andrew's twenty recruits as well as a full ship's crew, but I cared little for that. I was on my way home to England at last, on the twenty-ninth of July, and that was all that mattered. I smiled to myself at the thought, leaning on the stern rail and watching Amsterdam disappearing as we set off down the waterways that would take us to the German Ocean and the Channel. It was true. I did indeed feel as though I was going home. Although I had lived in England for more than six years now, I had never before thought of it as my home. Amongst my fellow Londoners I was still viewed as one of those they dubbed 'Strangers' – foreign immigrants and refugees who were not full-blooded Englishmen. We had fewer rights than true citizens, were restricted in our businesses and ownership of property. Those with wealth enough could, like Ruy Lopez, compound for a form of limited citizenship by making a substantial payment, but I could not envisage such a thing for my father or myself. Nonetheless, as I turned my back on Amsterdam and watched the sailors plying their oars, my heart lifted at the thought of London and even poor, dirty Duck Lane. Soon I would sleep in my own bed and take up my rightful work in the hospital.

'You are looking very cheerful, Kit.' Andrew leaned on the rail beside me, watching the dip and thrust of the oars. We were making good time, though the wind was not in our favour at the moment.

'It's good to be going home,' I said simply.

'Aye. I've had my fill of Amsterdam.'

'I liked the Hollanders.' I wanted to be fair. 'Apart from van Leyden and Parker. They are not so different from the English.'

'Perhaps. But you cannot say you liked that gaggle of lawyers, picking over the evidence like crows over a dead cow.'

I laughed. 'I suspect lawyers are the same the world over. The longer time they can take over their business, the higher the fees they can charge! At least Norreys outwitted them in the matter of the muskets.'

'Aye.' Andrew grinned. Norreys had firmly taken possession of all the muskets, gunpowder and shot, carrying everything off with him as he returned to England, well ahead of us.

'If we have to row all the way,' Andrew said, with a jerk of his head toward the sailors, 'we won't be home for a week.'

'I expect they'll hoist sail once we reach the sea. It's so narrow here that there's no room to tack. They can move faster under oars.'

'You sound very knowledgeable in the ways of ships.'

'I made a long voyage by sea from Portugal to England. I came to understand a little then.'

'Why do you never speak of Portugal, Kit?'

He asked without any intention of probing unkindly, I was sure, but I stiffened.

'Because I do not choose to. That part of my life is over. I choose to forget it.'

I knew that I sounded rude and ungracious, but what else could I be? It was impossible for me to say to him, truthfully, 'I was the daughter of a distinguished professor, and lived a privileged life amongst the Portuguese aristocracy and intelligentsia. My grandfather is one of the greatest landowners in the country. I did not even dress myself or brush my hair in those days – my every need was met by servants. Despite being a girl, I was taught by some of the great scholars of our country. Until it all ended in blood, fire and horror.'

No, I could say none of these things, but I was sorry that Andrew looked offended, for he had been a good and trustworthy ally on more than one occasion now, and I did not want to lose his friendship. Let him think of me only as a young man like himself, an assistant physician and a code-breaker for Walsingham, and forget my Portuguese past. I began to talk of the *Good Venture*, its sleek lines and manoeuvrability., and the difficult moment passed.

We had been unable to set out from Amsterdam until late afternoon, but Captain Faulconer was confident we would reach the coast in time to catch the tide, though it would mean night sailing in order to reach Dover. Before we left, a message had reached him that the Spanish fleet was now anchored off Gravelines, not far from the French border and the nearest point in the Spanish Netherlands to the English coast. Thanks to Admiral Justin's squadron of *vlieboten*, the fleet could not – for the moment, at least – move further along the coast of Flanders to rendezvous with Parma and his barge-borne troops, for these were the shallow waters where the great warships could not venture, unless the shoals were clearly indicated, and the Dutch sailors (who knew the waters intimately) had removed all the sea marks.

As we drew nearer the coast, the wind began to rise, blowing strongly from the southwest. Clouds were building up and the sky grew dark. It would be a rough crossing to Dover and as we met the first waves offshore, several of the soldiers turned pale and one began to puke. A sailor took him roughly by the shoulders with a curse and thrust his head over the starboard gunwale of the ship, so that the wind carried the vomit away into the sea. The ship began to dance and pitch, but the sails were soon raised and she heeled over and began to cut through the waves like a dagger through silk. I drew a deep breath of the salt-laden air. It was wonderful to be moving swiftly at last, and the *Good Venture* stood out into the open sea with her starboard side low in the water. I saw that Andrew, solidly confident on shore, wore a look of some alarm.

'We shall need to give the shoals off Flanders a wide berth,' Captain Faulconer said in my ear. He had come to stand in the stern beside the helmsman, keeping a sharp eye on the course he was steering. 'The Hollanders may know those waters without marks, but I am not so confident. They shift constantly. They may not be quite as much of a death-trap as our Goodwin Sands, but I should not like to find myself amongst them with the dark coming up as fast as it is.'

It was indeed growing dark. We must have taken longer to navigate the canal than I had realised. We were more than a month past the summer solstice now, and it must be nearly ten of the clock. In our haste to make the crossing before the Spanish fleet moved nearer, we had not taken a meal sitting in the captain's cabin, but had eaten, like the sailors, on the wing, helping ourselves to rough chunks of bread and some sort of meat pasty, brought out on deck in buckets. For a moment, a chill finger of fear touched me, so that I shivered. I should not like to navigate these waters in the dark, between an armed enemy fleet and the dead hand of the Goodwins.

We had been sailing, I suppose, a couple of hours south along Flanders, but standing off from the coast, when I noticed a flickering light ahead of us. Although we seemed to be moving fast, the wind was almost head-on, so that the sails were close hauled. And although we had caught the last of the ebb tide as we left the Low Countries, the tide had turned now and was against us. So that, though we appeared to be moving rapidly through the sea, we were probably not making nearly as much headway relative to the land.

The captain, who had gone forward for a time to see to the close adjusting of the sails, was coming back to the stern, where I had found myself a seat on a water barrel. I had not seen Andrew for some time and wondered whether he too was feeling the effects of sea sickness.

'Captain,' I said, pointing ahead and slightly to port, 'what is that bright glow over there? It looks like the lights of a great city, but I thought there were only small towns along this coast.'

He came to stand beside me and raised his hand above his eyes to cut out the small amount of moonlight breaking through the racing clouds. For a long moment he said nothing.

'Fire. It is fire.'

'Fire? Would the Spanish have set fire to a town? I thought they were well within their own territory.'

'No. I think not. It looks like fireships to me.'

266

Fireships! I knew what that meant. Floating infernos that could wreak terrible destruction. Loaded with gunpowder, they would be set alight, their sails trimmed to carry them down on an enemy fleet, while their emergency crews leapt into boats and escaped. Only a few years before, the Dutch had used fireships in an attempt to break the siege of Antwerp by the Spanish, but they had failed and the city, one of the great cities of Europe, had been lost. Leicester had made an ill-judged attempt to send fireships down on to the Spanish besiegers off Sluys – his one effort to aid the garrison – only to have them turned back against him. Were the Spanish now using fireships against our English fleet?

'Ours or theirs?' I asked.

'No way to tell, from this distance. We must go nearer.'

'Nearer to the Spanish fleet?' My voice shook with alarm.

'We must.' He was brusque. 'If the Spaniards are sending fireships into our fleet, there will be men in the water. We cannot sail past and leave them to drown.'

'They may be English fireships, sent against the Spaniards.'

'They may.'

He turned away, shouting for his second in command.

'This ship was commandeered by Sir Francis Walsingham,' I said, ashamed of my fear even as I spoke. 'Your orders were to sail directly to Dover.'

He barely glanced at me.

'You are the only civilian on board this ship, Dr Alvarez. I have a crew trained in gunnery. Captain Joplyn has a squadron of men who can handle muskets or engage in hand-to-hand fighting, if it should come to that. Our duty now is to investigate and, if necessary, join our fleet to rescue survivors or engage the enemy.'

'Well,' I said with resignation, 'at least I can patch up the wounded.' I tried to appear calm, but the thought of sailing straight into battle made my stomach clench with fear.

'Aye. That you can do.' Faulconer turned away.

The fireships, if that was what they were, must have been farther away than I realised. With the wind and the tide largely against us as we headed even more south-westwards, dawn had broken by the time we came within sight of Gravelines, where the

267

Spanish fleet had been anchored. Even before we could see anything clearly, we could hear the boom of cannon. The pall of black smoke cast by the fireships had been augmented by clouds of paler smoke from the ships' guns. We could see the flashes as the cannon fired, followed by the ear-splitting crack of the explosions, like lightning in a storm, followed moments later by the crack of thunder.

As we had run south, the sailors not occupied in handling the ship prepared our own six cannon, and I found myself playing the part of one of those young boys, such as Captain Thoms had been, carrying gunpowder and shot up from the hold to place in readiness for the gunners on the gundeck. Andrew's men had primed their muskets and stood watching expectantly as we drew nearer the battle. Even those who had been prone with sea sickness were on their feet, alert, looking eagerly ahead.

As I passed Andrew amidships, I said accusingly, 'You and your men look as though you are enjoying this.'

He laughed. There was a gleam of wild delight in his eye. 'This is what we are trained for, Kit.'

'Well, I am not,' I said dourly. 'I am trained to save lives, not to take them.'

When we were at last close enough to make out something of what had happened, we could see the burnt-out hulks of eight ships and even to my untrained eyes it was clear that the fireships had been launched downwind from the English fleet on to the anchored Spanish ships as they lay, apparently securely, at anchor in the night. Now the Armada fleet was scattered across a wide expanse of ocean in disarray.

'Our fireships have caused them to panic,' one of the ship's officers said in satisfaction. 'By the looks of things they have cut loose from their anchors and fled in all directions. Medina Sidonia will have a fine time of it, trying to call them to order now.'

I thought with a shudder how terrifying it must have been to be roused from sleep to see a monster of fire bearing down on you, with nowhere to escape except by a leap into the midnight sea. And I knew that most sailors, superstitiously, refused to learn to swim, for they believed that, if you fell or were cast overboard, it was better to drown quickly than to struggle against death, only to drown in the end.

I saw the captain coming toward me and caught him by the sleeve.

'The fireships were certainly ours, then?'

'Aye.' He grinned mercilessly, rubbing his hands together in glee. I had not seen him so animated before. But I thought of those men, leaping into the Channel, their clothes perhaps on fire, weighed down by their breastplates and helmets.

'Will any still be alive, the men from the ships? You said you would come to try to save them.' I knew it was a poor chance, after the time it had taken us to arrive, but a few might still be struggling to stay alive, or stranded on sandbanks amid the rising tide.

'Save them? I came to save Englishmen.'

'What will happen to them?' I asked.

'Who?' He stared at me blankly.

'The men in the water.'

'They will drown, of course. Do you expect us to rescue them? Spaniards?' He laughed incredulously and I was silenced.

Yes, they were Spaniards. But. . . the stench of burning flesh, the breastplate pressed to the chest like a branding iron, the drag down, down into the green depths of the sea. Fire and water. Lungs struggling for air. No kindly landfall now, only the dark hell of the ocean bed.

'There are English galley slaves on some of those ships,' I protested.

He shrugged. 'If a ship goes down, the galley slaves go with it. They are chained to their rowing benches.'

He turned his back on me and hurried away. English galley slaves or Spanish sailors, he had no mercy for them.

Never caught up in a battle before, on land or sea, I found it difficult to understand what was happening. It was clear that the enemy ships were no longer in the formidable crescent formation which had sailed inexorably up the lower reaches of the Channel. Our fireships, if they had done nothing else, had cut a swathe through Sidonia's careful formation and even I could see that the Spanish ships were randomly scattered across the sea in front of us. Already it was clear that one or two had sailed too near the shoals and were stranded there. Our English navy, bearing down on the Armada with all the strength of a following wind, were keeping their distance, so that the enemy could not execute their favourite tactic of grappling and boarding. Instead, the English ships kept up a regular bombardment from their guns from windward, so that, as the Spanish turned broadside to them, in an attempt to level their own cannon, they heeled over, exposing their lower hulls. The English gunners were taking careful aim, intent on holing them below the waterline, which would inevitably sink them.

Our own *Good Venture* had swept away to starboard, and was now aiming to swing round and join the English fleet. As one of the sailors ran past, I called out to him, 'Why aren't the Spanish ships firing back?'

He paused only for a moment, grasping the rigging he was about to climb.

'Poor gunners, the Spanish,' he said. 'They fire once, then get ready to board and fight hand-to-hand. Can't reload fast enough, see? No match for our lads.'

With that he began to swarm up the mainmast as easily as if it had been a ladder on dry land, though we were heeling over so far that he was half laid over on his back as he climbed. It made me dizzy to watch him. I dragged my eyes away and saw that we were approaching very near one of the outlying Spanish ships, a large carrack at least twice our size, probably one of the merchant ships commandeered for the Spanish fleet. I realised that Captain Faulconer did not mean to sail tamely round to join the fleet. He meant to attack now.

Almost as soon as I grasped what was happening, I heard the gunports on our port side flip open. The gun crews were standing ready and as the captain dropped his hand, holding, absurdly, a red silk handkerchief, another officer, standing at the bottom of the steps leading down to the gundeck, dropped his hand. Below us, the gunners lit the powder in the pans and the three guns fired simultaneously. The ship bucked like a frightened horse and for a moment I thought we had been hit, before I realised it was the recoil of the cannon. Already the men were reloading and they seemed to be cheering, but the sound came muffled to my ears, which were deafened by the noise.

They had scored a hit. I could see timbers falling from the superstructure of the Spanish ship, caught up in a tangle of ropes and canvas. Then, before our crew could let fly a second volley, I watched a single Spanish gun run out, pointing directly at us. So they did not always abandon their guns. Everything seemed to move in slow motion, in a silent world – the Spanish cannon lifting its muzzle like a pointing hound, the captain raising his hand to signal the next firing from our ship, while all around a tangle of ships lumbered though the smoke and flashes of the gun battle.

Then somebody hit me hard on the back so that I fell to my hands and knees on the deck. Even deaf as I was, I sensed something fly over my head and crash into the rigging where moments ago the sailor had been climbing. Dust and fragments of rope fell around me, and there was a heavy thump that I could feel through the planks of the deck. For a few minutes I was dazed and confused, then I managed to get to my feet. Apart from a few bruises I was unhurt.

I looked around, still unsure what had happened. Then I realised an enemy cannon ball must have hit the rigging of the mainmast close to where I had been standing. Whoever had pushed me over had almost certainly saved my life. The thump I had felt on the deck was the sailor falling from the mast. Still weak in the knees, I staggered over to him. There was no blood that I could see, but his eyes were closed and he was not moving. I knelt down beside him and felt for the pulse in his neck.

'Is he dead?' It was one of the other sailors, leaning over me.

I shook my head. 'Stunned. And he may have broken some bones. Did you see how far he fell?'

'About half the height of the mast. Lucky bugger! Any higher and he'd have gone into the sea. Lower and the bastards would have got him with their shot.'

'Was it you pushed me over?'

'Aye.' He grinned, showing a set of broken and missing teeth. 'Near thing, that was. Want to keep your head down when there's shot flying.'

'I'm grateful. You saved my life.'

He shrugged. 'Any time. Watch yourself.' And he went away whistling, as if he was enjoying a day of leisure, instead of leaping along a deck that shuddered as another round blasted out from our cannon.

I spared a glance at the Spanish ship. Somehow we had manoeuvred round to their windward side and had already broken two great holes through the ship's port side, one below the waterline and one above. They could not keep her heeling over like that for long. As soon as she was on an even keel the sea would rush in through that lower hole and the ship would soon founder. Through my muffled ears I could hear faint cries from the bowels of the ship, from the trapped galley slaves or the doomed sailors. There was nothing I could do for them. Our own fallen sailor, however, I could help.

Captain Faulconer soon abandoned the maimed ship to her fate and brought the *Good Venture* round to head toward the rest of the English fleet. The mainsail drooped, for the damage to the rigging meant it could not be properly trimmed, but the strong wind on our port bow bore us along on staysail and foresail. The heavy Spanish ships were wallowing about, scattered across the sea and seemingly unable to make such good use of the wind as our small, nimble English ships could. They were being blown inexorably up the channel towards the German Ocean.

As soon as I could, I persuaded two of Andrew's soldiers to help me carry the injured sailor below decks. Here on the gundeck amongst the smoke and stench of the cannon was no fit place for a man with a possible head injury, who might find it difficult to breathe. Already I could see by the angle of his left leg that it was almost certainly broken; it would need to be set and strapped in splints. Captain Faulconer turned from inspecting his supplies of gunpowder and shot and saw us.

'Take him to my cabin,' he said. 'Away from all this.'

It seemed he cared for his own sailors, if galley slaves and foreign sailors earned none of his sympathy. We had to carry the man back up the companionway, for the door of the captain's cabin was raised part way above the deck, behind the rudder, with two shallow steps leading down into it. We got the man on to the captain's cot and peeled off his breeches. Like the other sailors, he wore the loose slops which allowed for easy movement around the ship and were equally easy to remove over the injured leg. As I had feared, the leg was broken, but it was a single clean break and could have been much worse. I sent one of the soldiers off in search of some light boards I could use for splints, while the other helped me strap the broken limb into place. Although the sailor made some groaning, snorting noises, he did not wake while I was doing this, for which I was grateful, for a conscious patient will flinch as you set a bone, making the process much trickier.

The limited medical supplies I carried in my satchel did not provide enough strapping, so I tore off the long tail of the sailor's shirt and used that instead. I had some poppy syrup, however, so I mixed some of it with wine I found in the captain's cupboard. Once the man woke I would give it to him to ease the pain.

The soldier came back with two thin planks which would provide adequate splints to hold the leg rigid until I could bring the man ashore. With that thought, I turned and asked, 'Could you see where we are? Is the battle still going on?'

I realised that my hearing had recovered and there seemed less noise than before surrounding us.

'We're in amongst the English fleet now, Doctor.' It was the soldier who had fetched the wood. 'The b'yer lady Spaniards are running away downwind like a pack of sheep. We're following and firing from time to time, but they can't get away fast enough, the b'yer lady cowards. Me and the lads, we never even got a musket shot at 'em.' He hawked and would have spat, to show his low opinion of an enemy who would not stay and fight, but realised he was in the captain's cabin and began to cough and choke instead. His fellow grinned and thumped him on the back till he got his breath back.

'Let them go,' I said with a grin. 'You bloodthirsty fellows! The sooner they are gone from English waters, the better.'

At that moment my patient began to stir and I was occupied giving him the poppy juice and reassuring him that no grave damage had been done to him or to the ship. I nodded to the soldiers to go.

'I thank you for your help,' I said. They went off, still grumbling that they had had no chance to use their muskets against the enemy.

Once the sailor was eased and falling asleep, I went out on deck myself. The entire scene had changed. The Spanish fleet, in a ragged cluster, was sailing before the wind in a north-easterly direction, or else they had simply given up and allowed the wind, which was still blowing strongly, to take them where it would. The English fleet was following demurely behind, occasionally letting off a round of shot when the distance between the fleets allowed. Over towards the starboard shore, which must be France, or the Spanish Netherlands, or even free Flanders, a few enemy ships had pitched up, either caught on the shoals or seeking refuge after serious damage.

I found Andrew down near the base of the mainmast, where some of the sailors were fixing up a jury-rig for the mainsail. Andrew, like his men, was disappointed at having had no opportunity to join in the fight.

'You will have opportunity enough,' I said tartly, 'if those ships make landfall in the Thames or along the Essex shore. Every soldier we can muster will be needed then.'

'They are running away with their tails between their legs like beaten curs,' he said. 'They will not dare to attack now. They've not managed their rendezvous with Parma's land army. Without them, what can a parcel of sailors do on land?'

'Perhaps,' I said, 'but I would not be so confident until every Spanish hull is out of English waters. Remember, they are carrying soldiers as well as sailors. Where do you think they will go from here?'

Captain Faulconer must have heard me, for he joined us.

'This wind has been our saving. It has made it possible for us to use our guns as they should be used, keeping them at a distance, and herding them away from their Netherlandish army. If it continues to blow, they will be forced out into the German Ocean and we will block their way back down the Channel. There is only one way they can go. Up the east coast and around the top of Scotland. Good luck to them!'

He grinned, his mouth fierce in the depths of his black beard. 'Those are wild waters, up there in the north, where the

German Ocean and the Atlantic meet, knocking their heads together. The heights of the two can vary by several yards and they tussle against each other like savage boars. Then the ships must find their way through the scattered Scottish islands and down past Ireland, before ever they see the Bay of Biscay and Spain again.'

As the afternoon wore on, the English fleet began to lose interest in chasing the enemy. They had been seen off with very little loss of life on our side. When it seemed that the last dying efforts of the battle were over, I tackled the captain.

'Where are we now?' I asked.

'Nearly back where we started,' he said. 'Off the coast of the free Netherlands.'

'There can be no reason for us to linger any more, Captain,' I said. 'You know that your orders from Sir Francis were to return directly to Dover. I have no criticism of your wish to do your duty and join the battle, but now we must make all speed back to England.'

I realised I sounded somewhat pompous. 'Besides, your ship is in need of repairs and one of your sailors should receive better care than I can give him on board ship.'

It seemed I had no real need to persuade him, now that dusk was creeping over us. There was little attraction in hanging about out in mid Channel or pursuing the Spaniards east and north. He sent a messenger over in a dory to Sir Martin Frobisher's flagship, the *Ayde*, which was lying near to us, hove to, with an explanation of who we were and why we were now leaving for Dover. In half an hour the messenger had returned with Frobisher's agreement and we turned south and west again. At once the waves slapped us hard and the wind fought against us. It was going to be a rough sailing, and once again by night.

Until now we had been running before the wind in pursuit of the scattered Spanish fleet which was limping away into the dark waters of the German Ocean. Even at a distance we could see how many of the ships bore the scars of battle – broken masts and spars, canvas and rigging dragging along decks and over the gunwales, shattered planks where hulls had been stove in by our cannon balls. They would have a journey of many hundreds of miles before they could reach a friendly port. I wondered whether they could hope for a welcome on the Irish coast. Periodically during the Queen's reign attempts had been made to launch attacks on England by rebels in Ireland in alliance with Catholic forces from Spain or France. There was a chance we might see those ships again, sailing toward us from the west. However, unless they could join forces with Parma's land army still stranded in the Low Countries, they could not pose the threat that we had survived by this day's action. Without that strong south-westerly wind, what might have happened?

And it was a fierce wind indeed, for as we turned head into it, the *Good Venture* shuddered like a frightened horse, trying to leap sideways on to the blast, while the sailors struggled to keep her on her new course. Despite the jury rig, our own mainsail was but partially serviceable. We must depend for the most part on the foresail and staysail. To add to our difficulties, the tide, having ebbed during the battle, had turned again and was flowing up the Channel in the same direction as the wind. Against these two implacable forces of nature, the *Good Venture*, fine ship that she was, could make but slow progress.

As it was growing dark, the crew began to light lanterns and hoist them aloft, fore and aft, to make our presence clear to the remainder of the English fleet, which loomed around us in the gloom. Lights were being raised on other ships as well, and soon a constellation of nautical stars was dancing above the waves while the stars overhead appeared and vanished as the clouds continued to roll eastwards on the high winds of heaven. For the most part the English fleet was hove to, but a few, like us, were fighting their way south and west – some, no doubt, also making for Dover, others heading further, for Plymouth or Portsmouth. Either they were damaged or the commanders of the fleet had sent them home bearing despatches or wounded men.

'It's a wild night we'll have of it.'

Andrew was standing beside me, grimly clutching the lee rail with both hands. Each wave that rolled past, as we dipped and rose again, sent a slap of spray over the gunwale that doused us both.

'There's little we can do on deck,' I said. 'I want to see how my sailor with the broken leg is faring. He may have woken now. Where are your men?'

He grinned. 'Lying low on the gundeck and trying to keep out of the way of the sailors' feet. Those who aren't puking over the side.'

'Still? I thought they had found their sea legs during the battle.'

'They had other things on their mind then. A marvellous cure for sea sickness. Besides, we were sailing with the wind then. Not like this.'

Even as he spoke, a larger wave crashed over the gunwale, soaking him from shoulder to hip and calling forth worse language than I had ever heard from his lips. It was cold, too. It might be high summer, but the sea was cold, cold.

'Come,' I said, curbing my laughter at his look of disgust, like a night-prowling cat who has had a bucket of slops poured over it. 'We can surely take refuge in the captain's cabin. He will be too much occupied with sailing the ship . . . in . . . this.'

I had nearly lost my footing as the ship climbed another great wave, then plunged suddenly down the other side. Staggering, and grabbing a handhold of any spar or rope or rail that offered, we made our way to the stern and the sanctuary of the captain's cabin.

Someone had lit a lantern here and hung it from one of the low overhead beams that supported the raised poop deck above us. The injured sailor was stirring as we came in, blinking in the light like a confused owl.

'How are you feeling now?' I asked, perching on the captain's bunk on the side away from the broken leg.

'What happened?' he said. 'By the cross, my head hurts.'

'I've some sympathy with that,' Andrew said..

'A Spanish cannon ball tore our rigging when you were halfway up the mast,' I said. 'You fell and hit your head. And broke your leg.'

He managed to raise his head and shoulders far enough to peer down at his leg splints in bafflement.

'Don't you remember?' I said. 'You woke before and I gave you to drink, something to ease the pain.'

He shook his head, then groaned and clasped it in his two hands.

'Is there more of it? My head feels as though it's being used as a blacksmith's anvil.'

I got up to prepare more of the poppy juice in wine, but I would not make it so strong this time. Battling as we were against those great waves, we might have more casualties. It was difficult to keep on my feet and I must clutch at the edge of the captain's table to stop myself falling over.

'You're the army captain, an't you?' He was squinting at Andrew, as though keeping one eye shut made the pain in his head less.

'Aye, Captain Joplyn, come from Amsterdam.'

'I remember that. Picked you up and rowed down the canal. There was Hell's own wind out on the Channel. By God! The Spanish!' He started half out of the bed, but was held back by the weight of his splints. 'What's become of the bastards?'

'Run away,' Andrew said complacently. 'We shot 'em to pieces. That Hell's wind, as you call it, was Heaven's own wind. Drove the bastards away and gave us the weather gage. Those that didn't founder are hurpling away into the German Ocean.'

The two men grinned at each other. Well, let them glory in the victory. I couldn't but rejoice that the Spanish, my ancient enemies since childhood, had been driven away, but there kept flashing before my eyes a vision of men being dragged down into the cold green waters to where their limbs would tangle in forests of slimy weed and the crabs come scuttling to pick their bones clean.

'Here,' I said briskly, 'drink this. It will help with the pain. Once we are back in Dover we can make a better job of that leg.'

He drank the wine gratefully and I poured a beaker each for Andrew and me, thinking I would have been glad of the addition of some poppy juice to help me sleep through this violent tossing. It felt as though we were being thrown first to starboard and then to port, while making no progress forward. The cabin was above the waterline, for which I was grateful, for below decks you could hear the cruel sea just on the other side of the thin planks of wood which were all that stood between us and death. Yet even in the cabin we could hear the slap when one of the larger waves crashed high against the side of the ship. These seemed to be coming more frequently.

'They'll be baling out,' the sailor said. 'With this sea running, she must be taking water over the side. You're sure we an't holed?'

Andrew shook his head. 'It was only the rigging that was damaged, and a small tear in the mainsail.' He glanced at me. 'I'd better go and make sure my lads are lending a hand with the baling out. No point in them sitting idle.'

After he was gone, the sailor lay back and looked as though he was dozing. I went over to the window let into the rear of the cabin. There was little enough to see. No lights from other ships showed. Black clouds raced past over the face of the moon, which peered out fearfully from time to time. The lantern hoisted over the poop deck cast a semi-circle of light on the water below the stern, illuminating the swirling wake cutting through the black water and the foam-crested waves which rose and fell behind us. The whole ship was speaking, her timbers groaning, her canvas slapping, her ropes whining through pulleys. The *Good Venture* was a stout ship, but she hated this treatment as much as I did.

I was still looking out at the demon-dark night when Andrew returned.

'I've managed to find some food,' he said.

Until that moment I had been ignoring my aching stomach, but now I realised that no one on board ship had eaten for many hours. What Andrew brought was unappetising enough in the normal way of things – rock hard ship's biscuit, some strips of dried meat of unknown origin, and some small wrinkled apples – but at that moment I believe I could have eaten anything. We sat opposite each other at the captain's table, greedily tearing at the food with our teeth. At least we showed enough restraint to set a portion aside for the sailor when he woke. After chewing up the apples, cores and all, we washed it down, recklessly, with the last of the captain's wine. Andrew caught my eye and winked.

'I'm sure he has more, stored away. In any case, we need him to keep a clear head.'

'What is it like, out there on deck?' I said.

'Rough. We're just off the Goodwin sands, one of the sailors told me.'

I shuddered.

'I'm going to see for myself.'

I thought, if we were likely to go aground, I wanted to be out there to see it coming.

The sailor groaned and raised his head.

'Go if you must,' Andrew said. 'I'm staying here. There's rain coming down now. I'll give the man his food. You'll not stay long, I'll warrant you!'

I opened the cabin door, and the wind thrust it against me so that I nearly lost my balance. I had to lower my head like a charging bull to make my way into it, and I struggled to close the door behind me. After the lantern light in the cabin, it took time for my eyes to adjust to the darkness on deck, for the high-riding ship's lamps cast little light down here. A small stinging rain smarted my face like flung sand, so that I screwed up my eyes as I picked my way carefully forward. The ship climbed each oncoming wave as if it were a mountain, balanced on the top, so that it seemed it must slip backwards. Then it tilted and plunged downwards so that the bows were buried in the trough of sea between one wave and the next. For a painful moment it felt as though the ship would plough directly into the next wave, drowning us all, then slowly it tilted and began to climb again. I was thankful that I had been spared the sight of this while I had been in the cabin. For hours now the ship had ploughed on against these great seas and the wind that tore at her canvas, but steadily she was making her way forward. If we were indeed off the Goodwin Sands, we had not much further to go.

Clutching the railing at the side of the short companionway that led down into the cabin, I turned slowly to look behind. The change in position made my head swim for a moment, as the ship pitched forward and at the same time rolled over to starboard then back again. A bout of queasiness stirred in my stomach, and I thought I was going to succumb to the pervasive sea sickness, but I closed my eyes and it passed.

When I opened them again, I tried to make out where the Sands were, but I could see nothing. Astern, however, on the far horizon, there was a lightening in the blackness of sky and sea. A band of paler darkness was forming, dividing the two. Dawn was coming.

I turned back to look along the deck, where I could now make out the figures of sailors, some trimming the sails, some passing buckets up from below decks in a chain of men, baling out the seas as they washed over the gunwales and poured down below decks.

'Well, Dr Alvarez, not long now.'

The captain came to stand beside me. He looked exhausted, but calm. 'See that glow over there?' He raised his arm and pointed over the starboard bow. 'That's the old Roman lighthouse at Dover. They keep a brazier burning there as a signal. We'll be there in an hour. Two at most. And the wind is slackening. It often does at dawn.'

To me the wind seemed to blow as fiercely as ever, and the rain was falling more heavily, but I fixed my eyes on that distant watch-fire. We had come through battle, storm, and sea. We were nearly home.

Chapter Fifteen

J stayed at Dover only long enough to change into dry clothes, eat a hearty soldier's breakfast and bespeak a post horse. Andrew and his men had already received their orders. As soon as they were equipped and mounted, they were to ride to the Essex coast and stand guard in case the Spaniards, moving north, attempted a landing at one of the ports there. I could have waited to have their company on the way to London, but using post horses I would travel faster and I was anxious both to report to Sir Francis and to go home to my father.

Andrew and I parted in the castle stables.

'Next time you plan one of your dangerous ventures,' he said, 'give me fair warning, so that I can ride in the opposite direction.'

I laughed. 'I do not choose them.'

He gave me a wry smile. 'They seem to seek you out.'

'I am going back to the quiet, calm work I am trained for. Mending the bodies of the sick and injured.'

'Aye, I have reason enough to be grateful for that. How is our injured sailor?'

'Well enough. I have left him in the hands of the army physicians. They think no harm has come to the limb, for all the tossing we took on the way home.'

'I hope I never have to make a sea journey like that again.'

He groaned and shook his head. 'I thought the ship would break in half.'

Secretly I'd had much the same thought myself, but I mocked his fears and we parted with laughter.

I stopped about ten miles south of London for the night and reached Seething Lane early the next morning, where I was called immediately into Sir Francis's office together with Phelippes, to give an account of all that had happened in Amsterdam and of my small part in the sea battle off Gravelines. They had already received the report I had sent ahead from Amsterdam, and Sir Francis had spoken to Sir John Norreys about the treason of Parker and van Leyden, but I was able to answer their questions about such details as were unknown to Sir John.

When at last I was free to go, I decided to take a wherry upriver, to save time. There was the usual cluster of boats at the Custom quays, and I picked a wherryman I knew to be a speedy oarsman, who kept his boat upstream of the Bridge. As he rowed, we spoke of the Armada. He was one of those wherrymen who had volunteered to serve in our scratch navy and had been at Gravelines, but his ship had lost its mainmast and returned to Gravesend for repairs.

'I'm not sorry to be back in London,' he said. 'Those sailors live like pigs. If our ship hadn't been damaged, I'd still be sleeping on some gundeck out in the German Ocean, eating pig swill. And never a farthing of pay yet.'

The London wherrymen are known for their gloom and grumbles, but I had some sympathy with this.

'Surely they will pay you soon,' I said, 'once the Spanish ships are finally seen off and the ships stood down.'

He gave a sarcastic snort and made a few pithy comments about fine gentlemen who used their ships to plunder and make their fortunes, while others endured enemy fire – a remark aimed at Drake's latest exploits.

After landing at Blackfriars Stairs, I made my way quickly to Duck Lane. The sun beat down on the nearby shambles in Smithfield, sending the stench of blood and ordure wafting over this whole part of London, even smothering the more delectable odours from Pie Corner of fresh-baked pastry and good beef gravy.

The door of our house stood open to admit a little air, for it could become very close at the height of summer, and I was still some yards away when a tawny shape of fur and solid muscle flew down the steps and hurled itself at me so hard I fell backwards onto the packed dirt of the street. Before I could stop him, Rikki had bathed my face with a loving and very wet tongue.

'Get down, you mad creature!' I said, struggling with some difficulty to my feet.

My father was standing in the doorway, his face alight with laughter.

'He has missed you.'

'As I have missed all of you. Over a month it has been.'

'Aye.' He put his arm around my shoulders and drew me inside, Rikki weaving about our legs and nearly tripping me up again.

I took up once again my divided life between the hospital and Phelippes's office. It was as though I was two completely different people – the quiet physician, going about a worthy calling, and the ambiguous agent in Walsingham's service. Even in the office I could hardly reconcile either persona with a reckless house-breaker and adventurer. The events in the Low Countries began to take on the atmosphere of a dream. At Seething Lane we were the first to receive all the intelligence relating to the Spanish fleet, as the scattered ships hobbled northwards. The Spaniards made no attempt to land in Essex or elsewhere along the east coast.

The reports of their retreat moved even that cool and imperturbable man Walsingham to tears.

'Almighty God sent a great wind from the southwest which broke and scattered that arrogant Armada to the four winds,' he said. 'Victory at last is ours.'

Soon it was on everyone's lips: 'He blew with His winds, and they were scattered.'

God, it seemed, was on our side. The Enterprise of England had become England's victorious enterprise.

I could not quite trust the victory, although Sir Francis seemed convinced of it. For weeks afterwards word came in – and was discussed eagerly in the hospital and on the streets – that limping and broken Spanish ships had been sighted in the German Sea off the Wash, then far to the north rounding the top of Scotland, and finally wrecked in the wild Atlantic waters off Ireland. I do not know how many survived to return home, but the bodies of the Spanish dead and the wreckage of their ships washed up on our shores for months. Stories from Ireland were wildly different. Some said that the Irish had cut down the Spanish sailors as they struggled ashore from their wrecked ships, so that the very breakers of the Atlantic turned crimson with their life blood. Other stories, more worrying to Sir Francis, held that the Irish had welcomed their Catholic brothers with open arms and were mustering an army with them to attack England across the Irish sea. Whatever the truth of it, no invasion seemed imminent, as far as the agents in Ireland reported.

Our ships returned to their ports once the Armada had vanished into the north, but hidden behind the general rejoicing a grim shadow lurked. The men of our fleet had sustained the usual battle injuries, but the gods of war had laid a different curse on the victorious soldiers and sailors. A man would come ashore from his ship, join his friends for a drink at an inn, then collapse in the street and die within hours. There was no warning. No visible symptoms marked out those who were doomed from those who were untouched. Two men might share the same meals, fall asleep in adjacent hammocks. In the morning one would wake, the other lie stiff and cold. Whispers of witchcraft ran darkly through the streets. Others saw the hand of God in this. Had we become too arrogant in our victory? Or – whispered amongst those who still inclined to the old faith – was the Pope's blessing upon the Spanish attack bringing down on us a righteous punishment? Witchcraft, retribution or natural disaster, the outcome was the same. Men were dying, and dying in large numbers.

The morning after a number of the ships were reported to have berthed at Deptford, my father received a message from the authorities at St Bartholomew's.

'You must pack your satchel, Kit,' he said. 'We are sent to Deptford to treat the sickness which is spreading amongst the men. Bring all we have of febrifuge medicines and tincture of poppy for the relief of pain.'

He was packing his own satchel as he spoke.

'What are the symptoms?' I asked, as I secured cork stoppers with wax and then wrapped the glass bottles in rags for safety.

He shook his head.

'From all I have heard, no one can be sure. Only that those afflicted are seized with raging fever as if they would catch on fire, and the pains they suffer are acute, so severe that some have leapt into the river to seek death, as the only way to escape.'

I shuddered. 'I heard that some have simply been found dead and cold in their beds, with no sign of illness at all.'

He nodded. 'Whether these are two different forms of the sickness, or two completely different afflictions, who can tell? It cannot be the plague, for there are no marks of the plague on them.'

That was one hopeful sign, for the plague could sweep through London in days, mowing down all before it.

'And it is only the men from our fleet who are affected?'

'Aye. Sailors and soldiers both.'

'Gentlemen and officers as well?'

'I have not heard so.'

'Could it have come from the common men's food?'

'Perhaps. Yes, that's well thought of, Kit. It might be wise to take vomitories and enemas as well. Though I have not heard that there have been signs of food poisoning.'

I reached down the additional medicines from the cupboard. If it was food poisoning, surely all of the men would have been seized with the illness. Still, best to be prepared.

He took out a handkerchief and mopped his face. 'Are you ready?'

I nodded and shouldered my satchel. We left Joan instructions for the next few days, not knowing when we might return, and I warned that I would expect Rikki to be fed and cared for. If he was not, she should answer for it. We turned our backs on our house and made our way down to the river.

The summer heat had continued stifling in Duck Lane and on the wherry the slight breeze over the river brought welcome relief. My father wiped his face again.

'Are you well, Father?'

He did his best to smile. 'I find the heat more trying as I grow older. I will soon feel better in this cooler air.'

I frowned. I had never known him mind the heat before. Indeed England's weather was far milder than the summer's heat we had left behind in Portugal. He was more apt to complain of the cold in an English winter. Whatever was afflicting the men at Deptford, I hoped it would not be infectious, for my father did not look well.

All too soon the trip down river was over and we found ourselves amongst the ships moored five or six abreast along the quayside. The quays themselves were eerily deserted and at first we could find no officer, but at last an elderly man in clerical dress, disembarking from the nearest ship, directed us to a small building, hardly more than a shed, where we found a harassed-looking junior officer who appeared to be the only person in charge.

'Physicians from St Bartholomew's? The Lord be praised,' he said. He had removed his ruff which lay, grubby and creased, on a table amongst a pile of documents. He has loosened his shirt strings and his hair was unkempt as a neglected birds' nest. He looked as though he had not slept for many nights.

'Not that there is much you can do,' he said. 'They are dying almost before we know they are sick. Even on the few ships still patrolling the coast, in case of further attack, men are dying. Every day we have word of men buried at sea. With these crews berthed here at Deptford I am trying to send as many home as can walk.'

He gestured towards the documents. Discharge papers, I guessed.

'But some of those who are well will not leave until they are paid, and no pay has come for them yet.'

'What? They defeated the Spaniards, but they have not been paid?' My father was incredulous.

The man shrugged. He looked at though it did not surprise him. 'Quarrels amongst those who must find the coin, I suppose,' he said. 'No one gave thought to pay when we were mustering for war.'

'But if you send sick men out into the country,' I objected, 'you may spread this disease even further. It could ravage every village and town in England.'

He shrugged again. 'I cannot help that. We cannot feed them and I've been ordered to dismiss them.'

It sounded as though these men were being treated as mere parcels of inanimate goods. They had served their purpose, and now there was no more need of them.

'Where are they, the sick men?' my father asked.

'Sick and well, they're still on board the ships. We have nowhere else to put them.'

And so began our grim task of treating the heroes of the Armada. The sick men were lodged in hammocks strung between the cannon on the gun decks; those not yet struck down squatted anywhere they could find space, playing cards, dicing or throwing the knucklebones.

It quickly became clear that we were dealing with two illnesses. It addition to the mysterious affliction, there were many obvious cases of the bloody flux.

'The wisest course,' my father said, 'would be to separate the cases.' He looked about him in despair at the men all crowded together, sick hugger-mugger with well. His shoulders sagged defeatedly. We were standing on the gundeck of a large warship, a galleon carrying forty demi-culverins.

'I'll talk to the men who are yet unaffected,' I said.

For years I had followed my father, taking my lead from him, but I realised now that I must act for myself. My father was simply too tired to confront what seemed a task far beyond our capabilities. I had noticed a big man of middle years to whom the others seemed in some ways to defer. He had a broad, sensible countenance and a quiet manner. I asked his name.

'Tom Barley at your service, Doctor.' He gave me the ghost of a smile. 'Not that there is much service I can do you.'

'That is where you are wrong,' I said. 'We need to separate the men. Move those with the flux aside to separate them from those with this other sickness. And I want the men who are well kept away from those who are sick.'

'There's nowhere else for us to go, Master.'

288

'Why not up on deck? It's summer weather. It's cooler up there and you will be in less danger of the sickness. Is there spare canvas? You could rig up a shelter to protect you from the sun.'

He grinned. 'The officers won't allow that. This is where we must stay. Orders.'

'There are no officers,' I said bluntly. 'They have taken themselves off.'

'No wonder. They'll not be wanting the sickness, and no blame to them.'

'Then I will override their orders,' I said. 'Can you and the others here,' I gestured towards the men playing cards, 'help me move the men with the flux? They can probably walk, but they will be weak. And I'll need some to help to clean this place.'

The stench from vomit and diarrhoea was overpowering. I could not understand how they had endured it so long. Why had they not taken some action themselves?

With Tom Barley's help and the eventual, if reluctant, assistance of the others, I managed to move the flux victims to the far end of the gun deck, so that there was at least some space between the two groups. The men fetched buckets and mops to swab the deck and I persuaded them to open the gun ports so that the cleansing breeze could flow through, although some swore they would be punished for acting without orders from their officers. When the gundeck was clean, Tom Barley and another sailor found some spare sails and set the men to erecting a canvas shelter up on deck.

While my father began to treat the flux victims and to give what relief he could to the others, I went with Tom and three other fit men to visit ship after ship, to try to create some order out of the hellish chaos. On some ships the men were willing, on others there was hardly a man left standing, and the sick stared at me with the dull hopeless look of those who can see Death coming, his sickle already glinting in the corner of their eyes.

And so began our long exhausting days at Deptford. It was fruitless and dispiriting, for the illness, whatever it was, sprang up without apparent cause and we could do little except relieve the terrible fevers which affected the patients and comfort their dying moments. One moment a man would be raging at the heat, throwing aside any bedding, begging for water, the next he would be shaking, crying out that his limbs were frozen. Though his teeth chattered, sweat poured off his brow. The ships echoed with their howls of pain and their hacking coughs. Some imagined they saw snakes dropping from the beams above them, others screamed that monstrous spiders were crawling all over them. Those who lived more than a half a day began to develop a rash, though most died within hours. The worst was the pain they suffered. Headaches which seemed to blow their brains apart, agony in all their joints.

On the third day, as we paused briefly to drink some small ale and eat a pasty which had been sent down to us from the hospital, my father said, 'I think it is a form of typhus, though it is far worse than any I have seen before.' He looked resigned.

The diagnosis was not much help to us, for there was no cure. Either the body was strong enough to fight it off or – more often – it succumbed. However, separating the patients may have helped check the spread of the illness. As those with less serious cases of the flux recovered, we sent them to lodge with the fit men up on the open deck. Those who were weaker either died of the flux or contracted the typhus. Tom Barley had appointed himself our lieutenant, helping with some of the treatments, going with us from ship to ship to ensure the men obeyed orders. He also went with me to the shed on the quayside, where I demanded better rations for the men, who were down to maggot-ridden ship's biscuit and rancid water. No help was forthcoming there, but I sent a letter to Walsingham, begging him to use his influence, and gradually some better stores arrived – fresh bread, ale, some cheap cuts of meat, and a couple of barrels of salted herrings.

I had taken to sleeping on deck myself, when I could spare the time to sleep, and one early morning I found myself being shaken awake by my father.

'Kit, wake up! Tom Barley is struck down.'

I had feared it, as I had feared that my father, growing old and weak, would take the illness. But my father was spared and it was Tom who now lay in a corner of the gun deck, sweating and raving and striking out wildly. It was impossible to get him into a hammock in that state, so we made him as comfortable as we could on the boards of the deck. I forced febrifuges down his throat, though he fought me, and I bathed his burning limbs, dosed his pain with poppy juice and fed him sage pounded with honey for the cough that wracked him every few minutes.

I blamed myself for using him as an assistant. If he died, it would be my fault. But his body was strong and struggled against the illness. After five days he was no longer delirious, and at the end of a week it was clear that he would recover.

'I've never known anything like it, Doctor,' he said to me shakily, managing to hold a spoon for the first time himself. 'My head – it was like, I don't know . . .' He moved his head, and touched his temple gently with his finger tips. 'I can't find the words. It was like there was a cannon in there, that kept blowing up. Not one shot after another, see. But all the time.' He took a deep breath. 'I just wanted to die. Just wanted to stop the pain. If I could have got up on deck I'd have throwed myself in the Thames.'

Tom was one of the last cases. The men who had recovered were sent off to their homes, still without pay. Even those who had refused to go earlier had grown so fearful of the illness which had killed so many that they trudged off, to try to beg their way home. I demanded that the harried officer on the quayside write out licences for them to beg, for without a licence a wandering beggar can be confined to the stocks by any parish official who lays hands on him. The final group of men, weak but recovering, were moved to St Thomas's, the hospital south of the river. Tom refused to go with them.

'I'll manage the walk home to Rochester,' he said, 'given I take it slowly. I'll fare better in the clean air of Kent than shut up in St Thomas's.'

My father gave him five shillings. 'It is no more than you deserve in payment for the work you have done for us,' he said, 'caring for the sick.'

'You should buy a place with a carrier,' I said, 'to spare you the walk. You are not yet back to your full strength.'

But he merely laughed and shook his head. 'I've better use for five shillings than to waste it on a carrier. My wife will be glad of it.'

The last we saw of him was his back, sturdy but stooped, as he set off along the road leading southeast.

Our work in Deptford finished, the last morning spent moving the final patients, my father and I took a wherry back up river to St Bartholomew's. We were quiet most of the way and I watched my father nodding in and out of sleep as his chin fell forward on his breast. We stopped at our house for a meal and a change of clothes before reporting back at the hospital. Although my father revived a little with a good meal inside him, I could see he was fighting to stay awake.

I laid my hand on his arm. 'They don't expect us until tomorrow,' I said, 'and it's nearly evening. I will go and see what's to be done in the morning. Do you go and rest on your bed, you'll be the fitter for work tomorrow.'

'You're a good lad, Kit,' he said, mumbling a little.

A slight shock ran through me. We were alone, and when there was no one to hear he usually relaxed his guard and acknowledged me as his daughter. Bitterly, I thought: *Soon even I will forget what I am, who I am.*

He allowed himself to be persuaded to bed and I took myself off to the hospital, where I reported to the deputy superintendent before going to the wards. The first person I met there was Peter Lambert.

'How was it at Deptford?' he asked, without preamble.

'Grim.' I could not bear to say more. 'Are there many new cases here?'

'Plenty. Those navy saw-bones have sent on all their bungled work to us.'

I groaned. The naval surgeons, I had to concede, worked under terrible conditions, sawing off half-severed or crushed limbs while cannon balls crashed overhead, in a welter of blood and screaming men. Usually there was no way to save a man's arm or leg. But the filth amongst which they operated meant that the terrible wounds, even when they had been cauterised with hot iron and coated with tar, almost always became infected and could turn gangrenous. Very few of our men had been killed in the battle itself, but many had died, and were still dying, of the typhus and bloody flux, and of their wounds.

The next morning my father and I were back in the wards, which were full of wounded sailors and soldiers. My father looked better after his rest, more at ease amongst these familiar surroundings. Unlike the cases in Deptford, it was clear what we could do for these men, removing stinking bandages stiff with blackened blood, cleaning and salving open wounds, easing fever and pain. Where gangrene had taken hold, we had perforce to send for a surgeon to cut back more of a damaged limb.

Men died.

Sometimes, I thought that death was a more merciful end than the future which awaited our crippled and broken patients whose lives henceforth would be nothing but misery and destitution.

Three weeks after our return from Deptford, Simon Hetherington arrived on our doorstep one early afternoon, when my father had sent me home to rest from the long hours of caring for the sick. We had not met for months and I noticed that he had grown even taller since I had last seen him. My heart lurched at the sight of him and I admitted to myself how much I had missed him. Andrew was a fine companion in a scrape, but somehow Simon touched something within me that I did not want to analyse too closely. He was dressed today quite grandly, in a costly velvet doublet. I had not thought that actors' earnings would rise to such finery.

'Not sporting with your friend Kit Marlowe?' I said caustically.

He grinned. 'Marlowe is abroad somewhere, on one of his secret missions. I must needs make do with Kit Alvarez instead. Now that he has returned from his own mission abroad.'

'I hope you have not come to fetch me to the Marshalsea again.'

That was more than two years ago now, I thought. Nearly three.

'Not to Master Poley, certainly,' he said. 'I hear that he is still in the Tower, and living like a king.'

I knew it. It was one of the first things I had asked Phelippes when I returned from the Low Countries. As long as Poley was imprisoned I felt my secret identity was safer.

'You keep your friends amongst the prison warders, then?'

He laughed. 'Still a sharp tongue, I see, Kit! You have not come to Durham House of late.'

293

'We have been too much occupied with the men who served in the fleet against the Spanish, first in Deptford and then here with the men who survived the virulent epidemic that wiped out whole ships' crews, but instead have lost limbs.'

I turned aside to the task I had been engaged on when he arrived, tidying the shelves of tinctures and salves, noting down what new supplies we needed.

'While the country rejoices,' I said, keeping my back turned to him that I might not betray my feelings, 'they forget that men of our own were killed and injured. And as well as the sawbones during the battle, our surgeons at the hospital have had more than a few amputations, and we must care for the men after their butchery. It's not a pretty sight,' I said bitterly, 'to see a man first lose his leg and afterwards find the gangrene creeping up the stump of it. And there have been festering wounds from shot. We have brought in four whole barrels of Coventry water to cleanse them. And even in the short time they were at sea, many of them contracted scurvy.'

I turned back and glared at him, as if it were his fault.

He raised his eyebrows enquiringly.

'It makes me so angry!' I said. 'We physicians tell the sea captains what they must do – some fresh fruit for the men, or at least a little lemon juice. Too costly, they complain. Why, all they need, if they will not carry lemon juice, is a little *cochlearia officinalis* – scurvy grass is the common name. It's to be found all round the coast, as if God planted it there for the sake of seamen!'

I spun round and gestured at our medicine cupboard, to make my point with greater force. 'We keep it all the time here and in the hospital for the children of the poor, who are as likely as seamen to suffer from a bad diet. So easily cured, but so painful a disease, with swollen joints and bleeding gums, and the teeth growing loose and falling out!'

'You really care for your profession, do you not, Kit? Such passion!'

'Of course, I do!' Then I smiled apologetically.

'I am sorry for ranting like one of you players, but I hate to see uncalled-for pain. There is pain enough in the world.'

I did not tell him, for I had been sworn by Sir Francis to secrecy, that it was now estimated that, although only a hundred men had died in the battle, eight thousand had since died of sickness and wounds. The horror of it haunted me.

'True indeed, there is too much pain in the world. But can your patients spare you to come and see my profession, my passion?'

'What do you mean?'

'Have you heard of the new piece, *Tamburlaine the Great*?'

'Everyone has heard of it.'

'Kit Marlowe wrote it.'

I made a face. I could not hide my dislike.

'He thinks somewhat well of himself, I know,' Simon conceded, 'but he has good cause. He and Tom Kyd, they are writing a whole new kind of play. Come with me and see! *Tamburlaine* is to be played this afternoon at the Rose, with Ned Alleyn as Tamburlaine again. Come, and you shall see and hear such wonders as you have never seen or heard before.'

'Are you to play in it?'

'No, it is Henslowe's company, but next month I am to play Bel Imperia in Kyd's *Spanish Tragedy*. After that, they are to let me take men's parts.' His eyes gleamed. Ever since I had known him he had longed to make the move from playing women, despite his successes.

Eventually, I allowed him to persuade me. To leave behind all the sickness and death which had surrounded me these last weeks – it was a temptation I could not withstand. Although I did a grown man's work, I was still but a girl of eighteen. And I could scarcely admit to myself how much I liked his company and his way of looking at the world, so different from my own. I would never have admitted it to him. Yet my heart gave a little jerk of pleasure as we set off from Duck Lane, Simon whistling a new street ballad that was on everyone's lips. We walked over the Bridge again, in the same direction we had taken nearly three years before, to the new-built theatre, The Rose, belonging to Master Henslowe, on Bankside, near the bear-gardens. Simon seemed to know all the people in this strange world of playhouses, so, without money changing hands, we found ourselves in threepenny seats with cushions, looking down on the stage. I had never before been seated so grandly in a playhouse.

'Everything looks quite different from here,' I said.

'You will be able to see better how everyone moves about the stage, instead of craning up at the actors' feet from below, like the groundlings, until your neck is stiff. It's important for the actor to use the whole stage.' He made a sweeping gesture, indicating the apron stage and the inner central chamber, and the upper stage on the large balcony behind the main stage.

'Your sometime player,' he said, in a schoolmaster's voice, 'your guildsman or schoolboy, will stand stiff and recite his lines to the audience, like a stuffed peacock. Your true player lives his part. He ignores his audience for the most part, walks about the stage as he would do in life, and talks to the other players. He will only speak directly to the audience when he wants to invite them into the play, or else when he puts his inmost thoughts into words, so we can share them. Then we seem to see inside his very mind. Do you understand?'

'I think so.' It had not occurred to me that the players' trade was so complex. I had thought they simply conned their lines and then spoke them, though I had often listened to Simon talking about the way he imagined himself into a part. I had never thought about the way the players moved about on the stage or where they directed their words.

'And notice how we use the different parts of the stage. The inner stage can be a private room, concealment for a spy, a place to die in – so we can draw the curtain across, you see? The balcony can present the ramparts of a castle, or a city wall, or the lookout of a ship, or the upstairs room of an inn, while the lower stage is the castle court, or the ground outside the city, or the stable yard of an inn. Do you not see these very places when we describe them? Though they are nothing but the parts of a wooden playhouse, open to the sky, like any bear-pit?'

I nodded slowly. It was true. If the play was well written and played with the skill Simon described, I felt myself to be in a palace or on a battlefield or in a crowded street. When an army crossed the stage, I saw an army, though there might be no more than half a dozen players pretending to be many.

'Yes, you are right,' I said. 'And it makes me wonder: How can we know substance from shadow? How know what is real, and what is pretence?'

I thought of Walsingham's projections two years before, and the Babington plotters, who were – or weren't? – puppets whose strings he pulled. Perhaps all that terrible affair was no more real than a play in the theatre, with Walsingham as playwright and Phelippes as his theatre-master. I had stepped on to the stage to play my tiny rôle, then exited into the darkness of the tiring-house.

'A play is another kind of reality,' Simon said seriously. 'We make something new, a New World which is as real to me, at any rate, as the unseen world of Virginia that Raleigh speaks of so much. I do not think that is pretence or deception. It is beautiful. It has fire and passion. It is a world we create as surely as the Creator created this world we walk about in.'

I laid my hand on his arm and glanced about. 'Be careful, Simon, what you say. Your words could be taken for blasphemy.'

He gave me a strange look, then shrugged and smiled, and pointed up at the turret above the upper stage, where the flag was flying, to show that a play was to be performed this afternoon. A man had appeared up there. He raised a trumpet to his lips and played a fanfare. The noise of the audience faded into expectation. The play began.

It was like no play I had ever seen before. At the end of it, through the clapping and cheers and the bowing of the actors, I felt numb. It was terrible and beautiful, frightening and inspiring, and I was trembling as though I had lived the actions of that man, suffered the fate of his victims, been borne along by his triumphs. I said not a word as we descended the long dark staircase and emerged into the fading summer's afternoon, jostled and elbowed by the crowd, wrapped in my own cocoon of silence against their noise.

'Well?' said Simon, as we walked back along the river toward the Bridge.

'Yes.' I said. 'I think I begin to understand.'

Chapter Sixteen

*B*y the beginning of September my life had fallen back into its old familiar pattern. Phelippes hardly needed me now, so that I began to spend much more time with my friends at the playhouse and was even able to join Raleigh's circle at Durham House once again. Marlowe, mercifully, was away on some business of his own or Walsingham's and Poley remained imprisoned in the Tower. After the excitement and terrors of the summer months I was glad to be back enjoying the rich poetry of the new plays which were creating such a sensation in London, while the discussions at Durham House reminded me of nothing so much as those long tranquil evenings at home in Coimbra, when my father's university friends would sit out in the garden in the twilight after dinner, amiably disputing some nice point of philosophy or listening with keen interest to the details of some new scientific discovery made by one of their number. My sister Isabel, my brother Felipe and I would sometimes creep out into the shadows and listen to them, sitting on the steps of the fountain, while bats swooped overhead, feeding amongst the umbrella pines, and the distant music of my mother playing the virginals wound its way between the deep, quiet voices of the men.

This was the life I preferred – my work at the hospital and the occasional evening at Durham House. The longer it continued the more the memories of what had happened in the Low Countries faded away, so that it seemed like a dream. Then early in September news spread rapidly through London that Robert Dudley, Earl of Leicester, had died. It came as a shock to many. On his return from the Low Countries he had shown himself more decisive and vigorous than ever he had been abroad. Perhaps the threat to the very nation of England aroused some strength in him that he had never found before. He had built an army camp at Tilbury as defence against an attack up the Thames, the camp to which Andrew and his men had been sent. And when the danger was past, he had ridden through London in glory, as though single-handed he had defeated the Spanish. I had seen him myself, and although both he and his horse were gloriously caparisoned, there had been a feverish look to his eyes which did not bode well. I had not been surprised when I heard he had travelled north to Derbyshire, to take the healing waters at Buxton. It was on the way there that death had suddenly overtaken him. He was fifty-six, several years younger than my father.

All his life he had been loaded with honours and offices, and I knew that Sir Francis respected him, despite his failings as a leader in war. Above all, however, it was common knowledge that he was something more than another courtier in the eyes of the Queen. In the years before ever I was born, it had been rumoured that Robert Dudley hoped to marry the Queen, and there was much scandalous talk which never quite died away. Whatever the truth of it, I remembered how courteously he had received Berden and me on my first visit to Amsterdam, a courtesy not extended by his successor Lord Willoughby. And if he had laughed at my warning of a plot to poison him, he had made amends later.

Standing in my chamber at home, I took out the medal he had sent me and ran my thumb over the raised image of his head, then turned it over. NON GREGEM SED INGRATOS INVITUS DESERO. Perhaps he did feel with some justice that the Hollanders were ungrateful for his efforts in their country against Parma and his Spanish troops, but nonetheless I could not forget what had happened at Sluys, all the men dead and wounded there.

How would the Queen take his death? How could anyone know the true feelings of a queen, certainly of a queen who – by all accounts – was as inaccessible as a fortress? On one of my occasional visits to Seething Lane about the middle of September, I put this to Phelippes. Having met Leicester, even dined at his table, and now carrying about with me his medal as a kind of talisman, I felt an odd personal interest in this.

'How did Her Majesty take the Earl's death?' Phelippes said. 'You have not heard? I thought it was common knowledge. She locked herself in her chamber, would allow no one to enter, took no food or drink. For days, this was.' He shook his head in wonderment.

'In the end, Lord Burghley ordered the door to her chamber to be broken down. That took some courage! He feared for her safety. Even for her life. No one knows what happened then, but I do not suppose he was kindly received. At the very least she was alive and has resumed her duties.'

I am sure he did not mean it unkindly, but his words chilled me. She had resumed her duties. It was difficult to think of the Queen as a person, she was a symbol, God's anointed, ruler absolute of her country and of her church, England personified – yet she was a woman, too. A woman who had lost the man she had loved all her life.

For some reason these thoughts troubled me in the weeks that followed. Leicester, after all, had seemed no more than common flesh and blood when I had met him. He was grandly dressed, his rooms were elegant, but encased within it all had been a mortal man.

It was the third week in October that I received a strange missive from Sir Francis, brought to me at the hospital one morning by Thomas Cassie, seeking me out where I was in the stillroom with Peter Lambert, assessing what supplies would be needed for the onset of winter. I recognised the seal on the letter and looked enquiringly at Thomas.

'You do not usually come here,' I said. 'Could it not have waited until I was at home? Am I needed at Seething Lane?'

Cassie shrugged. 'I know only that I was to find you out at once and see it directly into your hands. Sir Francis is at Greenwich. The letter was brought to Seething Lane by a court messenger.'

Very strange. I broke the seal with my thumbnail. The contents were brief and startling.

You must present yourself at Greenwich Palace at three of the clock this afternoon. Ask to be directed to me. Wear your best garments. W.

I stared at Cassie. 'I am summoned to be at Greenwich at three this afternoon. There is barely time!' I turned to Peter. 'You must tell my father, Peter. Explain. Make my excuses.'

He nodded and leaving them both staring after me I hurried from the hospital, glad that our house was but a few minutes' walk away. My best garments? Did he mean me to wear my physician's gown? I decided I would do so. I could always shed it, if needed. I had not so many clothes that I took much time to decide what to wear. I had one quite good doublet that I wore when I went to Durham House, and a pair of breeches that would pass muster. I found a pair of stockings whose only mend was in the heel, where it would not show, and I rubbed my shoes clean of dust with a rag, which I thrust into my pocket, so that I could rub them again after I arrived. Over all I donned my gown, and set my square doctor's cap on my head. I squinted at myself in my mirror of wavering glass. My hair was perhaps overly long, but there was no time to visit a barber. Still, at court I believed men wore their hair longer than did the common sort.

The only way to reach Greenwich in time was to hire a two-man wherry – an extravagance I could have done without – and to ensure that they were capable of shooting the Bridge. It is a risky business at the best of times, but I knew I could not stop and leave one wherry on the upstream side, cross by land to the other side of the Bridge, and take another wherry on the downstream side.

'Tide's at the ebb, Master,' the older wherryman said. 'We'll shoot the Bridge, never fear.'

I did fear. I had never done it, and more than one had died under the Bridge, where freak twists in the water could smash a boat against the piers like kindling. All went smoothly enough above the Bridge, but I could see that the force of the river, with the tide behind it, was flowing fast. The wherrymen hardly needed their oars, save for the odd stroke to keep the boat on course. We seemed to be approaching the Bridge much too fast, swept down the river helpless as a leaf, toward its towering pillars. From the level of the river it loomed like the ramparts of a castle. There was a great deal of water coming down the Thames and as it reached the Bridge it was funnelled beneath the arches, where it fought the stones to find a way through. There seemed hardly enough room for even a small boat to squeeze through the narrow space between raging water and damp stone.

There could be no turning back now. I clutched both gunwales of the boat convulsively, my knuckles showing white with the strain. We were being tossed like a hapless cork upon the swirling water. The boatman shouted something, but I could not hear him, for the roar of the water was echoing now like a man's voice crying out in a cave. Instinctively I ducked my head. From the corner of my eye I could see the green slime on the curved roof of the tunnel as we bucketed through, the men fending us off the stones with their oars. The roaring in my ears was like a storm at sea. And then we were through! The river spread itself out like a quilt, like a wild animal released from a cage, suddenly tame.

The men set their oars in the rowlocks again, and we proceeded calmly on our way as if we had never passed through that watery Hell. My heart was fluttering in my chest like a bird trapped in a chimney.

The rest of the way to Greenwich the men rowed steadily, but the flow of the river also carried us along, so that when I disembarked at Greenwich stairs I reckoned I had a good half hour in hand. I shook out my gown, which had been bunched together in the boat to keep it from the wet, and made my way with what dignity I could muster to enquire of a servant in royal livery where I might find Sir Francis Walsingham. My legs were trembling still from shooting the Bridge.

It seemed Walsingham was occupying the same apartments where I had brought messages to him before, two years ago now, at the height of the operation against the Babington plotters. The rooms were located in one of the innermost parts of the palace, close to the royal quarters.

'Come in, Kit.' Sir Francis's face, as so often, showed the strains of illness, but today he also appeared remarkably cheerful. 'Come in and take a seat. We have a few minutes.'

'A few minutes, Sir Francis?' I said, sitting where he had indicated. 'For?'

'For me to explain why you are here.'

I nodded, folding my hands in my lap and waiting.

'It has been noted,' he said with a smile. 'Your good service in the Low Countries. First in foiling an attempt on the Earl's life – may he rest in peace – and then in uncovering a treasonous plot to supply arms and equipment to the enemy. Her Majesty herself has taken note.'

I looked at him in alarm. 'Her Majesty?'

'Aye. She wished to express her thanks to you in person.'

I gaped at him. 'But–'. I could think of nothing to say.

'I will conduct you to her shortly. You will make your obeisance and not speak unless invited to do so by Her Majesty.'

This seemed even more terrifying than shooting the Bridge. To be face-to-face with Elizabeth Tudor. Gloriana. Queen by God's good grace. The greatest Protestant monarch in the world. And now, after the defeat of the Spanish fleet, the monarch of the oceans. I began to shake and thought I might very well be sick.

'Do not be alarmed, Kit,' Sir Francis said kindly. Clearly he could read my appalled expression as easily as a schoolboy's primer. 'She is well disposed towards you. There is nothing to be afraid of.'

That was all very well for a man to say who dealt daily with our great monarch, but it did nothing to steady my knocking knees as he led me toward the innermost of the royal apartments. I was glad I had worn my gown, which concealed much of my trembling.

The double doors were opened by liveried servants. I heard Walsingham presenting me as if his voice came from a long way away. My eyes were cast humbly down. I was aware of rustling gowns, silk upon silk, a heavy scent of many perfumes – too many perfumes – billowing and mingling in a great wave across the room. I bowed deeply, in the courtly fashion I had learned from Simon and the other players. I hoped my hat would not fall off.

'You may stand, Doctor Alvarez.' A voice filled with a certain wry humour spoke from somewhere above my head. 'Let us see you face.'

I straightened and raised my eyes. At first I was aware only of a living tapestry of colour, a flower-garden of velvets and silks and brocades, where rubies and emeralds and pearls nestled instead of bees or butterflies, and dyed plumes of exotic birds nodded instead of fresh green branches. Then this overpowering riot of colour resolved itself into a group of ladies and gentlemen clustered about one central figure, poised as if in some theatrical tableau. And that central figure was far more splendid than the rest, attired in cloth of gold, with a ruff of lace so fragile it seemed impossible that human hands could have wrought it. The hair was the colour of a fox's pelt, piled high and laced with pearls.

Yet for all that splendour, it was the eyes which held you. Her face, no. It was painted and powdered till it became a mask. And I realised now that her whole body was encased, wired and boned and caged within those magnificent garments, until the only parts free to move were the long fine hands gripping the arms of her throne and those remarkable eyes. Suddenly a terrible sense of pity overwhelmed me. This woman had been trapped from childhood into a role she must play or die. And she had played it magnificently. A woman, ruling England better than any monarch before her, yet a woman declared a heretic and a bastard by the ruler of the all-powerful Catholic Church. A woman dressed in gowns and jewels worth a city's ransom, yet a woman playing a man's part. A woman who had loved a man, but could not marry him, and his loss gleamed in those eyes which, despite all the efforts of her tiring-women, bore the unmistakably traces of much weeping.

We were not so different, this great monarch and I.

She was speaking now, thanking me for exposing the treason of Parker and van Leyden.

'And we understand,' the Queen said, and there was a faint tremor in her voice, though she strove valiantly to conceal it, 'we understand that it was you who saved a dear friend from an evil plan to poison him. We shall not forget that you gave him a few more weeks of life.'

'Your Majesty,' I said, bowing again and moving backwards toward the door.

I raised my eyes a final time and something flashed between us, across that jewel casket of a room.

Her eyes widened. And I thought: *She knows.*

The Author

Ann Swinfen spent her childhood partly in England and partly on the east coast of America. She was educated at Somerville College, Oxford, where she read Classics and Mathematics and married a fellow undergraduate, the historian David Swinfen. While bringing up their five children and studying for a postgraduate MSc in Mathematics and a BA and PhD in English Literature, she had a variety of jobs, including university lecturer, translator, freelance journalist and software designer. She served for nine years on the governing council of the Open University and for five years worked as a manager and editor in the technical author division of an international computer company, but gave up her full-time job to concentrate on her writing, while continuing part-time university teaching. In 1995 she founded Dundee Book Events, a voluntary organisation promoting books and authors to the general public.

Her first three novels, *The Anniversary*, *The Travellers*, and *A Running Tide*, all with a contemporary setting but also an historical resonance, were published by Random House, with translations into Dutch and German. *The Testament of Mariam* marks something of a departure. Set in the first century, it recounts, from an unusual perspective, one of the most famous and yet ambiguous stories in human history. At the same time it explores life under a foreign occupying force, in lands still torn by conflict to this day. Her second historical novel, *Flood*, is set in the fenlands of East Anglia during the seventeenth century, where the local people fought desperately to save their land from greedy and unscrupulous speculators.

Currently she is working on a late sixteenth century series, featuring a young Marrano physician who is recruited as a code-breaker and spy in Walsingham's secret service. The first book in the series is *The Secret World of Christoval Alvarez* and the second is *The Enterprise of England*.

She now lives in Broughty Ferry, on the northeast coast of Scotland, with her husband, formerly vice-principal of the University of Dundee, a cocker spaniel, and two Maine coon cats.

http://www.annswinfen.com

Made in the USA
Lexington, KY
21 September 2017